# Red Kingdom

a Little Red Riding Hood retelling

RACHEL L. DEMETER

**RED KINGDOM**
FAIRY TALE RETELLINGS, BOOK TWO
Copyright © 2024 Rachel L. Demeter

Cover Design: GetCovers
Editing and Proofreading: Jenny Sims

All rights reserved. No part of this book may be used or reproduced in any way by any means—except in the case of brief quotations embodied in critical articles and reviews—without written consent of the author.

**Your mental health matters.**

This is not your grandmother's *Little Red Riding Hood*.

*Red Kingdom* is a dark historical romance set in a war-torn kingdom. As such, it contains graphic subject matter and mature themes, including grief, strong violence, and death. Your discretion is advised.

*For my daddy.
I know you're proud.*

# Part One
# Winter

# One

"ONCE upon a time, there lived a little country girl, the prettiest creature who was ever seen. Her mother was excessively fond of her, and her grandmother doted on her still more. This good woman had a little red riding cloak made for her. It suited the girl so well that everybody called her Little Red Riding Hood."

— Charles Perrault

### The Kingdom of Norland, 1455
### Winslowe Castle

The sigil of the Black Wolf rose in the darkness like a waking nightmare.

Princess Blanchette Winslowe, the third of her name, edged away from the castle window and the horror it held. The charge of hundreds of men on foot—a peasant's army—led by a single mounted figure.

The Black Wolf himself.

He'd positioned himself in the vanguard, front and center, just like in the ballads that sang his praise.

She'd often seen him seated in a place of high honor at her father's feasts but never in his element like this.

The fighters emerged from the wood's dense cover beyond the gates. Unified cries funneled up the battlements and shook the walls where she stood. Blanchette's heartbeat echoed the fierce volley.

She felt the castle stir to life below her slippered feet. The volcanic rumble of voices and clanking armor exploded as squires readied men for battle and boys reached for their fathers' swords.

Panic seized Blanchette. Her legs were rooted to the rushes, weighed with awe and terror.

How could they not have been prepared for a siege such as this?

*How could Father let this happen?*

*How?*

"Princess!" Her lady-in-waiting's voice thrust her from the trance. Insistently tugging her arm, Elise, a girl with wide, restless eyes, fidgety hands, and mud-brown hair, said, "We are not safe here, Princess! Come this way. We must find a passage out of the castle. We must—"

"No, Elise, no!" Blanchette resisted the pull with what could only be described as deadweight. Horror, shock, and cold shackled her in place—but most of all, a sense of devotion stilled her. "My brother, my mother... my grandmother... I must go to them. I won't leave them here to die."

"Then you will follow them into the grave, milady. I beg you; your father's men shall aid them well."

She glanced away from Elise's pallid face and into the night again. The number of fighters had thickened, and worse, she recognized a score of the faces under the Black Wolf's banner.

Elise's words were true.

*Many men shall aid him well, but their swords shall not sing for Father tonight.*

Traitors.

Monsters.

Every one of them.

Even though she'd heard whispers of a brewing uprising, she'd never imagined a revolt like this. It'd struck as suddenly and as fiercely as lightning.

It was a nightmare come to life.

*Fitting,* she thought, watching the legendary Black Wolf cut through three of her father's soldiers like a knife through butter. *A turncoat army led by a turncoat knight.*

Elise hastily set a red riding cloak across her shoulders. Smoothing down the wool, Elise's hands fumbled and tripped over each other, absent of their usual grace. Next, she knelt, slid off Blanchette's slippers, and replaced them with tall cattle-skin boots. Blanchette stood motionless, unable to tear her eyes away from the mayhem.

"Please, Princess, hurry and come with me," Elise pleaded while she seized Blanchette's arm and dragged her from the window. Blanchette fought to shake her off, but what her lady lacked in strength, she made up for in fear and the instinct to escape certain death. Her eyes grew impossibly larger, filling her pale face. "They are so close so soon. We must make haste! We—"

"Stop it, Elise. Let me go! Now!" A slap across the girl's face punctuated her words. Elise gaped at her and held her red cheek for a long silence. Blanchette stepped back, fastened her cloak's tie, then whispered in a shaky voice she hardly recognized as her own, "I pray you stay safe, Elise. But no one shall keep me from my family. Not even the Black Wolf himself."

The rebels were making headway into the outer bailey. The Black Wolf raised his longsword, and the men flanking him quickly tempered into an impressive pincer formation. This show of discipline unnerved Blanchette more than the actual bloodshed. Then she noticed a black figure darting through the commotion. An *actual* wolf was leaping at soldiers and tearing out their throats.

*God, have mercy on us all.* She touched the cross hanging from her neck and said a prayer.

Incoherent shouts took shape and became one voice, a fused battle cry that sent chills down her spine. *"Death to the king! Death to King Bartholomew! Death to the king of Norland!"*

Grasping her cross like a lifeline, she absorbed the scene with an unwavering intensity. She'd grown up to the twang of swordplay and quivering arrows and axes ringing against steel, yet she'd never witnessed war firsthand.

It was day and night. A different game entirely. A misstep meant death, and a missed parry cut far deeper than a man's pride. The fight was desperate—castle-forged swords against crude bronze axes, soldiers and knights against townsfolk. Families pledged to the crown flew their banners, as well—House Baldwin's gnarled elm tree, House Rutger's prancing destrier—but those soldiers and lords stood on the wrong side of the battle line, and they'd crudely painted the Black Wolf over their own sigils.

More traitors.

*Everything has changed in one night.*

*Or have I just been sleeping?*

"Princess? Blanchette? I-I'm so frightened."

Forcing her gaze from the swarmed bailey, she stumbled to Elise and held the girl's body. They were both trembling. Hot tears soaked the front of Blanchette's cloak while they silently hugged and cried together.

"Shh... I am too."

The unrest of the battle grew around them and penetrated the stone walls. Blanchette and Elise held and comforted each other for several moments—not as a princess and her lady-in-waiting but as two friends saying goodbye.

---

Our reinforcements shall hold.

*The defenses will shield us and the knights and soldiers who man them.*

*Winslowe Castle shall not fall.*

*Not tonight, and not any other night to come...*

Blanchette reassured herself, once, twice, thrice, as if her thoughts alone might will the sentiment into existence. Every few steps, a soldier raced by, adjusting his blood-soaked weapon, paying her the same care as the suits of armor that stood sentient on either side of her. Even so, she raised the red riding hood to conceal her identity. Most of the men held mere scythes and rusted axes, yet they wielded them with a knight's bravado. She felt the passion of their war cries as they echoed off the castle walls and through her bones.

Her home had been fast asleep not long ago, and only a single wall torch lit the winding hall. Wavering light danced off stone, steel, and silk tapestry.

She continued to hold on to her hope even as the roar of the siege crescendoed, and one of her father's guards bled out seven feet away.

God be good. He'd called for his mother with his last breath.

Nay, this was no siege. It was a sacking.

*Winslowe Castle shall not fall,* she repeatedly prayed as it indeed fell.

---

SHE SLIPPED THROUGH THE CORRIDORS—THE same halls she and her beloved siblings had once fancied as a playground. Familiar ghosts manifested within those shadowed crevices. She saw them more clearly than the battle itself—her dear brother Willem hiding behind a tapestry, her seven-year-old self with her liripipes pulled over her head as she and Isadora raced through the hall playing come-into-my-castle... and her governess's outraged cry at such naughty antics.

Each step took Blanchette farther from the light.

Each step snuffed out her hope and unleashed a cloud of doom.

Clasping the cloak around her body, she leaned against a black stone wall to collect her nerves and breathe. Rain began to fall, mocking the tears she refused to shed. Its rhythmic melody punctured the din of the battle. She held her cross and prayed between shattered breaths.

The castle trembled. War cries resonated. Heated commands and screams blared. The crash of swords and shields and hurtled boulders shook the very marrow of her bones. And that terrible chant was repeatedly yelled with a frightening passion: *"Death to the king! Death to King Bartholomew! Death to the king of Norland!"*

Then she heard the portcullis's ominous clang as its rusted iron teeth rose from the ground. The deafening roar rebounded against the castle walls in a dizzying burst. It went on for what seemed like a lifetime—a robust groaning that came and stopped, a dragon stirring from sleep.

*A song of death and the loss of hope.*

The symphony concluded with the drawbridge's deep moan as it lowered and settled into place. The frantic pounding of boots on wood rose around Blanchette and rolled like thunder.

Tears finally came to her.

The formidable walls of Winslowe Castle might have held off a siege for an entire season, but it fell within an hour without loyalty.

Without devotion, it was nothing more than a peasant's hovel.

Her queen mother had taught her well. *A castle is only as strong as those protecting it.*

Hidden in the shadows, shaking from her grief and terror, the princess both laughed and sobbed at her mother's wisdom.

※

Blanchette finally reached her grandmother's royal privy and, as of late, her sick room.

A musty smell hung in the air. Not even the fresh rushes

underfoot could mask it. It was a scent Blanchette was coming to know well—that heady perfume of death.

Grandmother Sybil Winslowe lay in the four-poster bed, her frail body trembling. The hulking piece of furniture dwarfed her emaciated form. She held a spotted fist against her mouth and prayed between frantic sobs. Her voice sounded weak, barely above an airy whisper. A breath away from death.

Smoke rose from the hearth, which the servants always kept burning for Grandmother no matter the season.

*But where are the servants now? They've abandoned us—every one of them.* Blanchette swatted away the smoke as it made her eyes water.

Then she fell to her knees, grasped Grandmother's brittle hands, and peppered kisses along her swollen knuckles.

"Oh, Blanchette... Blanchette, you are alive," Grandmother said in a parchment-thin voice. "Thank you. Thank you. What a blessing. God is good..."

"Shh," Blanchette consoled, squeezing Grandmother's delicate fingers between her own. "Yes, I am alive, and I am well. And I won't leave your side. I shall never. You know that, don't you, Grandmother?"

Grandmother's sobbing tapered off. The pain appeared to melt from her face, and Blanchette glimpsed the girl she'd once been. She also saw her mother's fire in those intelligent blue eyes. The Winslowe's Parisian blood and upbringing had equipped them both with an edge that went unrivaled in Norland's court. It'd taken them far and, for Grandmother Sybil, had remained an endless source of pride. She'd clung dearly to her French roots and accent throughout the years, a sophisticated lilt that brought charm to every word. Even the dour ones.

*Especially* the dour ones, she sadly reminisced.

"Sweet Blanchette. You... you are too good for this world. Too kind and sweet and far too dear. You don't deserve this, to suffer such brutality and betrayal. You are dear to me, so very dear..." A horde of screaming rebels thundered past the privy. Thank God they lacked the wits to enter. "Such savage animals," Grandmother rasped. Blanchette had to lean in close to hear her words. "A pack of wolves."

*Wolves.*

*The Black Wolf of Norland, stalking and tearing apart my very home.*

The hair on Blanchette's neck prickled.

Winslowe Castle shook beneath and around them. The din of enemy intruders and clashing weapons rocked the walls.

"Please, let me help you," Blanchette said, growing desperate with her panic. "*Please.* There is time yet—"

"For you, there's all the time in the world. For myself... well, I have known a blessed life," Grandmother said, reaching up and cupping Blanchette's tearstained cheek. She rubbed her thumb pad across her skin in a rhythmic, soothing gesture. It was something she'd often done when Blanchette was a baby. "Having you as my granddaughter has been one of the greatest blessings of my life. Now come here, my sweetling, come closer to me."

She did as Grandmother Sybil bid and was rewarded with a kiss on her forehead. Her lips were dry husks, and she heard a rattle in her breath. Blanchette embraced her with all the love and heartache she felt. She savored the warmth of her delicate body and the softness of her skin and inhaled the rosewater that clung to her hair and neck.

"Grandmother," Blanchette whispered, fighting to suppress her sobs. Tears and useless panic would get them nowhere, least of all out of this privy chamber. "I-I can help you. I can get us out of here. I know I can. Please. Just come with me. I beg you. *Please...*" She adjusted her grip on Grandmother's reed-thin back and gently urged her toward the edge of the feather mattress. The castle thrashed and shook like a living thing withering in agony.

"Oh, my sweet girl. You know well I can barely make it to my chamber pot," she said with self-deprecating humor, a toothless grin lighting her features. Then she grabbed Blanchette's arm with surprising strength and held her still, her eyes imploring, pleading, looking deep within. "Escape this place. Through the tunnels. Do it for me, Blanchette, and for your people, if not for yourself."

*My people have betrayed me.* She shook her head stubbornly. "Don't ask that of me. I won't! I can't. I cannot leave you here. I shall die first!"

Grandmother surrendered to a smile, smoothed her fingers over the cloak, and absently meddled with its fabric. "You're wearing the riding cloak I made for you three winters ago." Blanchette weakly returned her smile as a dark, painful silence swelled between them. That silence spoke volumes, impossible truths, and things they dared not say. "You *can*, Blanchette, and you will. You are capable of more than you know. You are good, and you are strong. Much stronger than your father's ever been, God forgive his soul," she emphasized with a squeeze of her arm. "My time has come. But you are my blood, and you shall survive this. You shall grow old and weary like me, with grandchildren at the foot of your bed. Swear to me. Promise me, Blanchette. Promise me, and you shall leave me well."

Blanchette studied every detail of her grandmother, tucking them in a secret and hidden corner of her heart—her white and neatly plaited hair, the back of her hands, swathed with a bluish web of veins, and the deep-set smile wrinkles framing her eyes.

Those blue eyes were fixed on her now.

Staring. Searching. Imploring.

"I promise."

Blanchette stood with a last kiss from her grandmother and a playful pinch to her cheek. With a shaky inhale, she prepared to do the hardest thing she'd ever done.

But a voice stilled her.

"Princess Blanchette?"

*Yes, yes, God is good.*

Blanchette crossed herself in a clumsy movement as hope stirred anew.

She nearly wept at the sight of Thomas, a servant who'd stood by her crib twenty-one years ago while the bells of Winslowe Castle rang from dawn until dusk. He'd helped her collect kingswood from the forest and taught her how to fish from the nearby Rockbluff River that she'd adored so much. His neatly combed auburn hair and freckled face were a welcome sight indeed.

"My mother? My brother, Willem?" she asked, scrambling over to Thomas and grabbing his chainmail jerkin. Blood stained the metal and darkened her fingers and palms. He'd suffered injuries already.

"They are safe, Princess. Away from the jaws of the Black Wolf."

She exhaled a sigh of relief, and then a weary smile formed on her lips. "Oh, thank God for you, Thomas. Are you sure? They are well?"

"Yes, they are safe, Princess," he reaffirmed. He flashed a smile that didn't fit right.

"Help me, then. Help me get her out quickly. Please, my grandmother—"

*Crash.*

Winslowe Castle rumbled and quaked. On the opposite side of the bed, Thomas crept beside Grandmother Sybil, where her head lay upon a throne of feather pillows. She shouted protests at them, begging them to use any spare moments to smuggle Blanchette away. Blanchette merely hushed her grandmother and implored her to remain calm.

Thomas stood over her and locked gazes with Blanchette. She saw something in his eyes that made her shudder.

Something she didn't like.

Something that caused her hair to stand on end.

A sudden and deep hatred.

The sounds and smells of the battle raged on and closed in on the three of them like a shroud. The scent of death had already begun to take hold and waft down the corridors. Thomas's gaze rose to the large viewing window, where the night appeared as black as ink.

Neither the moon nor a star was in sight.

"Thomas? What are you doing? We haven't time for this!"

He stared at that blackness, apparently watching something unfold inside his mind. "I can't recall a winter harsher than our last one," he said slowly, speaking with the voice of a man drunk on grief. "My family... I visited them as often as I could. I tried to help them out as best I could. Watching them waste away, starve, freeze... before my very eyes. Well, that's not something a man soon forgets, Princess. I believe I have your father to thank for that."

It happened in a chaotic blur of movement.

Thomas seized Grandmother's neckline and jerked her up and forward.

Blanchette cried out, but it was too late.

"Thomas! Are you mad? Stop that! I command it!"

Grandmother flayed and cried out, victim to the man's brute force, her eyes wide with sudden horror.

This was *Thomas*, her dear friend, a man she'd trusted with her very life—

He unsheathed a dagger and swung it down in an arc. Blanchette screamed and shot forward, the world barely visible through the surrounding chaos. She yelled. Felt the sounds leave her throat, yet she was deaf to the world. Deaf to everything but that blade whilst it thundered down, down, down and pierced Grandmother again and again.

Blanchette screamed once more, her voice a raw clap of thunder in her throat. She fought to wrestle the dagger from Thomas, that dear old friend, that servant who'd once taught her to fish and played tricks on Governess Agnes...

The dagger flashed down and sliced Blanchette's cheek. She barely felt it.

*This is what Father always boasted about at his feasts.*
*This is battle fever.*

Meanwhile, Thomas laughed and sobbed in a frenzy while he continued to rain half-hearted gouges upon her grandmother's motionless body.

*He's mad.*

*He's mad, and I am lost.*

*We are all lost.*

Blanchette threw herself between them, knowing it was too late even through the hazy chaos.

Grandmother had already taken her last breath.

She was gone from this world.

*I shall kill him for this betrayal. Thomas will pay for this treachery before I leave this privy.*

Something dark and dangerous stirred inside her. Blanchette flew at him like a loosed arrow and battled for the dagger with every fiber of her being. Blood made the hilt slick and slippery—*like a fish,* she thought with mad irony—and she dreamily felt its metal slice through her palm. The battle fever ran high indeed, and she paid no heed to the pain. Instead, she saw red and heard her own blood rushing in her ears. They danced like that for a minute—three minutes, seven minutes?—she could not say. Could not think. Could barely gather a coherent thought apart from *I will kill him.*

Thomas tried to grab her throat, but he seized her necklace instead. He snapped the cross from its silver chain.

It fell from her neck and out of sight.

Into darkness.

Finally, the dagger squirmed out of their hands and clattered onto the stone floor. Blanchette dropped and raced toward it, the red riding cloak dragging behind her.

*You're wearing the riding cloak I made for you three winters ago...*

Thomas made a similar dash. She grunted and kicked the dagger with her foot. It slid part way under Grandmother's bed.

She scrambled backward frantically, her eyes never leaving the monster before her.

Thomas rose from the floor, slow and steady, only three feet away. He advanced on her with deliberate, horrifying ease. Blanchette felt as the cut on her cheek seethed. Warm blood curled around her chin. She swiped at it with her forearm, spreading it across her face like war paint.

"*How?* How could you?" she sobbed, her breaths coming short, shaky, shallow. Inversely, her anger came in powerful waves. She could taste her blood on her lips. "In God's name, *how?* Answer me! You monster!"

"Monster? Your father's the monster. He always has been." He prowled forward, inch by terrible inch. "I shall drag you before the Black Wolf by your hair if I must. But first, we are going to have some fun, Princess."

His words fueled her.

*I promise.*

Hands shaking, red-hot anger piping in her veins, she scooped the dagger from the under the bed and thrust it through Thomas's neck. Metal slid through layers of muscle and tendon. She met Thomas's eyes, watching as whatever lived there faded into darkness.

*Good, let the darkness swallow you.* She lodged the dagger a little deeper, then twisted. She felt the blade work against a wall of muscle before hitting a sweet spot.

Thomas uttered a single word. It might have been *sorry* or *forgive me*, but perhaps that was only her imagination at play.

Blood bubbled from his mouth. She watched with bitter satisfaction as it dripped from his chin and slid down the shaft of his pierced throat. She dislodged the dagger, shuddering deep, then stepped back. He collapsed to the floor, his life's blood pooling around his head in an unholy sea of red.

*Death surrounds me.*

The thought barely registered before a crash resounded, snapping her focus into place. It propelled her into survival mode.

Her coolness surprised her. She hiked up her nightdress and stepped over the fallen corpse. Blanchette glanced at her grandmother. That image would forever be carved into her mind and heart. A day would never pass when she didn't see Grandmother Sybil's limp body and those bloodstained sheets.

Blanchette inhaled a strained breath as the sounds of war and death flooded the castle in an ever-expanding wave. She shuffled over to Grandmother, knelt at her bedside, then clasped her hand. Studying her pale, lifeless complexion, she smoothed her thumbs across the delicate web of bones and raised veins.

She'd been impossibly frail for so long, a gentle light constantly fading into darkness. She felt that darkness now, pressing down on them, windowless and starless and infinite. Was Grandmother resting? Finally at peace? Blanchette increased the pressure of her hold as if the movement might prevent her grandmother from leaving her.

But she was already gone.

Grandmother Sybil's signet ring looked impossibly large on her thin finger. Blanchette studied the crest of a black raven against a sunrise in a field. She felt a fire kindle inside. Gently, she slid the ring off her finger—after giving it a few turns to maneuver it over her arthritic knuckle—and gripped it in her bloodstained palm.

She wiped the blood from her face with her forearm again—cringed at the heat oozing from her wounded cheek—then stole one last look at her beloved grandmother.

"I *will* keep my promise," she said.

Then, with a whip of her red cape, she fled from the privy and returned to the shadows.

---

SLINKING THROUGH THE GREAT HALL, Blanchette fought not to look down at the strewn bodies lest she see a face she knew. She slid against the stone walls and prayed no one would recognize her. They would parade her head on a spike if so.

*Dear God, please let my mother and brother be alive.*

*God, be good...*

Every corner she turned brought that terrible prospect and a new horror. She would round a corner, and there they'd be, as clear as Norland's blue sky on a summer day—her parents and brother torn from limb to limb, bleeding out like slaughtered lambs.

*Devoured by the Black Wolf.*

She clasped the dagger in her sweaty palms. The steel felt heavy in her hand, yet it armed her with courage.

*My promise.*

That also gave her courage.

Her gaze darted about the room—at the well-armored knights and the soldiers gripping oaken shields. What she'd give for a bit of armor instead of the red cloak. Hastily, she wiped the dagger on the said cloak, unable to bear the sight of her grandmother's blood. The slash on her cheek throbbed. Burned. Tears tracked Blanchette's face as she felt herself beginning to black out... to fall into dangerous darkness, a beckoning void from which there'd be no return.

If she fell into that darkness, she'd be lost.

*My promise.*

She inhaled a long, steadying breath, then blew the air out. So very slowly. All around her, steel clashed against steel, and the prospect of life and death balanced on every strike. The great hall was hazy with smoke and heavy with the scents of musk, sweat, and the tang of blood. Banners and tapestries draped the gray stone walls, and at the far end, the ever-stoked hearth roared on through the chaos.

*Devil's flames.*

A blond man dressed in a ragged tunic, mismatched armor, and a tapestry of facial scars caught her stare from across the room. She saw the realization in his eyes... watched as he crossed the hall with fast, determined strides, wiped sweat and blood from his brow, then lifted his rusted sword out in front of him. Blanchette jackknifed in the opposite direction and adjusted her grip on the dagger. It wasn't easy with her sweaty palm. The man thundered toward her—struck down a soldier in the middle of his charge—his sword raised and ready, poised to strike death.

*No.*

Blanchette inhaled deeply and summoned all her focus. Although he was much larger than she, reckless impulsiveness got the best of him. He shot forward with no discipline or thought.

Blanchette thrust the dagger through the air with a war cry. Steel squelched through fat, muscle, and the ragged fabric as she killed her second man of the night.

Blanchette pulled the dagger out with an agonized sound, her hands stained with fresh blood, her heart beating a tattoo against her ribs. She watched in silent horror as red seeped from the blond's mouth in a glossy ribbon. He blinked, then collapsed at her feet.

*Blood.*

*So much blood.*

*So much red.*

She was drowning in it.

She glanced out a slanted window and saw her brother, Willem, below. A pair of laughing soldiers paraded his body. Three arrows were embedded in Willem's chest. He was also missing an arm and a leg.

*Murdered.*

*Mutilated.*

She felt as she tried to scream, to cry out at the horror, but the sound died inside her throat.

Death at her feet. Death in her home. Death in the air.

Death screamed in every corner of her mind.

Then she saw him.

Rowan Dietrich, the fabled Black Wolf of Norland, strode through her castle like a waking nightmare. His armor was crudely made, black as the surrounding night, the helm's dark metal twisted into the shape of a wolf's snarling head. But the most striking thing about him was his height. He towered above the other fighters and battled with a chilling methodicalness. How he moved and fought frightened Blanchette the greatest.

He looked collected. Even mildly amused. As if this were nothing more than a game. Blood soaked his sword as the blade whirled, whipped, slashed, and claimed lives in a macabre dance of death. And that wolf clung to his heels, its muzzle wet with blood, snarling and leaping at any man who dared come close to its master.

*Monster. Demons.*

The Black Wolf of Norland had always had a mist of legend around him. She remembered the stories her mother and governess had often whispered after the feasts and in the dark of the night.

"To me," the Black Wolf called to a soldier a few yards away, his deep voice effortlessly carrying above the tumult. He didn't need to yell, not even over the mayhem. The force of his tone was enough.

One of her father's guards raised his blade, but too slowly. Rowan Dietrich's longsword cut his head off, then came flashing back in a terrible two-handed slash that took another soldier in the leg.

With quivering anger, she realized that this man—this wolf, this *beast*—was the reason the sky was falling on her family. She clutched the dagger, wishing she could stand a chance against him. How good and *right* it would feel to plunge the blade deep into his heart and avenge what would likely be the end of her family's dynasty.

Of course, she'd never survive him or his demon wolf. And if she was ever to avenge her family, if she was to keep her promise, survival meant everything.

Without her survival, her family's legacy—her promise—would turn to dust.

Blanchette slipped forward. She stuck close to the walls and kept her head low. To any of the fighters, she was just another helpless servant trying to escape the bloodbath.

Then a familiar shape caught her. It was under the great table that spanned the length of the hall.

*Elise.*

Except now, her lady-in-waiting's garb was hiked up around her midsection; her pale thighs, smeared with her own blood, lay outstretched and bent at awkward angles. Blanchette knelt and cupped Elise's cheek only to find her neck had been slit open. She reeled back with a scream that died in her throat again.

"Oh God. Oh, no, no, no. Elise... God, I'm so sorry... my sweet Elise." Yes, her friend was dead and defiled, yet her staring eyes still *lived*. They seemed to look at Blanchette with a silent plea, asking her... for what? Blanchette was trapped in her home, in a waking nightmare, where she felt her sanity wearing thin.

She closed her eyes and saw what had unfolded, her imagination filling in the blanks. In her mind's eye, she watched as poor, sweet Elise's body was torn open, then her neck.

Blanchette gazed down at the bloody dagger in her hand, and the desire to push it through her own chest overwhelmed her. She held it up under the wavering torchlight and brought it to the front of her breast.

One movement.

One little push and it'd all be over.

*Just one.*

She glanced down at her red riding cloak, where the blade's bloody, sharp edge glistened. Torchlight set the metal aglow as it hovered above her breast.

*No. I must escape... for my family, my legacy, and Elise.*

*I must live. I must avenge them.*

*I must keep my promise.*

She lowered the dagger, fled the great hall, and turned down a long, dank corridor, which spiraled down to the kitchens, pantries, and buttery. The secret passageway to the underground tunnels, if she had the focus to find it.

The stairwell was mercilessly steep and narrow. Thomas once told her it was designed so enemy soldiers running up it would have their sword hands against the wall; the tight and curving stairwell would make it near impossible for them to reach for their weapons.

*Thomas.*

Blanchette turned her body slightly to fit the slim opening better. Her boots thrummed against the stones and echoed her heartbeat.

*Elise.*

She tumbled down three stairs, then righted herself with a pained groan.

Her brother's mutilated body.

Those three arrows sticking out of him.

She saw Willem clearly in her mind, loosing arrows at a bundle of hay.

Horror.

Horror.

Horror.

Blinding terror bubbled inside her. She went still, suddenly unable to stir a limb. Her legs failed her then, and her strength abandoned her. Sagging against the coarse wall, shock and terror and heartache assaulted her as the brutal image of her dead grandmother raced through her mind.

*Elise's mutilated and broken body.*

*Her staring eyes... eyes that still lived and spoke and pleaded.*

*The Black Wolf cutting through my father's men.*

And those cheers.

They were the worst of all.

She sucked in breaths through a raw throat. A lifetime seemed to pass before she heaved herself over, her muscles quaking, and she emptied her stomach onto the floor.

Purging her stomach allowed room for sound.

The scream that ripped out of her body dwarfed every sound she'd ever made or heard. It came from a dark place and entered an ever-darker world. Tottering, almost falling over her own stupid feet, she scrambled brokenly down the remaining stairs, her breaths emerging in panicked huffs that made her head spin.

*I'm going to die here.*
*We're all going to die here.*
*They're all dead, my whole family is gone, everyone I love.*
*It's written on the walls...*

The scream came again, this time with manic desperation. Her screams echoed and racketed shrilly through Winslowe Castle, her family's house, where death now reigned high. She screamed and screamed some more. The sounds came from her swollen throat and reverberated like the bells of hell. She *felt* her screams more than heard them; she felt as the walls of her throat tore and bled against those screams.

Then she fell silent. She stared dumbly forward while her mind slipped into a state of unreality.

"Princess!"

Five minutes later? An hour? An entire fortnight? Blanchette had no way of knowing how much time had passed when she felt herself pulled off the floor and into a pair of muscular arms. She gazed up into a face she recognized well, one of her father's most loyal knights.

*Loyal,* she thought with a shudder. *What does that even mean?*

Did he mean to kill her? To bring her to the Black Wolf?

*I'd rather be dead.*

She tried to speak, but the words dried on her tongue. She was as limp as a rag doll, her throat a raw wound. Absently, she watched as the dark walls slid by her, and he carried her down, down, down into the bowels of the castle. The knight spoke, his voice steady and comforting.

"Thank the Lord I heard your screams. Don't know how I knew they were yours, but I knew. Thank God, I somehow knew." Blanchette felt herself recovering. She squirmed and tried to break free of the knight's hold, not trusting, needing to feel her own feet touch the floor... her home's soil. She needed some form of grounding, no matter how trivial. "Nay, it'll be fastest this way, Princess. Just keep still, and let me carry you out."

"My family," she asked, her voice a thin and painful whisper. "My mother and father... God, help *them*! My brother and-and my-my grandmother..." He gave no sign he'd heard her. Blanchette squeezed her eyes shut as she felt the tears return. He carried her through her home in this way—through that battleground of horror and death.

Torchlight flashed against the walls as two young soldiers raced down the winding stairwell.

"He has her—he has the princess!" one boy called to the other, his high voice echoing in the corridor. "Get her, damn you! Don't let them escape!"

Blanchette felt her feet touch down and saw as Sir Lionel made quick work of the offending soldiers. They died at her heels, their stabbed bodies smashed against the wall. They slid to the ground in a puddle of blood and piss. Blanchette's heart pinched at those young, sightless eyes staring at her. Unlike Elise's, they did not live. They did not plead or speak. They had faded into darkness, where they would remain forever.

"The secret passageway—the hidden tunnel—"

"Sealed off, Your Grace. The surest way out now is through and forward."

*Through and forward.*

*Through a graveyard and forward on to what?*

Blanchette shivered. The hope she held in her heart faded with every breath.

"Those were naught but farm boys," she whispered, the words grating against her sore throat. "I've seen them playing in the fields from the castle windows."

Sir Lionel nodded, then took hold of Blanchette's forearm. "It's a sad song, for certain, Princess. Many more boys shall fall before this night ends," he said. "Now, come with me while there's still time."

Blanchette reached for her cross but found it gone.

The inner bailey was a coliseum of death. The rhythmic crash of steel against steel, the guttural sobs of dying men, and the musky scents of blood, sweat, and rain all melded together.

Blanchette had never seen an actual battle before. More than half the fighters wore peasant garb and held flaming torches. Light glinted off the mail and plate armor of her father's men, all slick from the rain and bloodshed. The ground had turned to slush and mud, and her house's royal standards burned, wilting to ash.

Perhaps the most unsettling was the lack of disparity between friend and foe. Walking beside Sir Lionel, Blanchette watched soldiers and servants she'd known since she was a babe cut each other down.

Each step had to be measured, exact, without falter—or it would mean certain death. Disbelief overcame her. She became detached as if witnessing the scene through a third person's eyes or wading through a nightmare.

Blanchette felt helpless and loathed herself for it. The soggy ground slushed beneath her feet, and she fought to keep her balance. Sir Lionel carved their way through the commotion, his longsword easily hacking down peasants and traitor soldiers and servants. Careful to circle her, he kept her well-guarded from the occasional straggler who recognized Norland's princess.

What the rebel peasants lacked in formal training, they appeared to make up with in passionate bloodthirst. She kept the dagger at a point in front of her, ready to spill blood again if needed.

*I promise...*

Her heart thudded against her ribs. She surveyed the tangle of bodies and clashing steel, looking toward the castle gatehouse.

That was where the real battle raged on. Guards loosed rocks, arrows, and hot pitch through the murder holes and machicolations. Blanchette watched in horror as the steaming black liquid drenched a peasant below. Guttural sobs burst from his mouth before he collapsed.

Then he was silent.

*Mother.*

That thought anchored her again. Her mother and father could still be alive. They might have escaped through the tunnels before being sealed off. It was a slight chance, a fragile hope, but she clung to it all the same.

*I must survive. For them. For all of us.*

"It's the princess! STOP HER! Don't let her escape! STOP HER, you fools!" A peasant—a boy, by the look of him—screamed over the commotion. He and three others heeded his cry and raced over, their swords and axes drawn. Sir Lionel made quick work of them, thrusting his longsword through their neck, gut, and chest with a beautiful and terrifying swiftness.

They gained ground that way, Sir Lionel cutting through attackers with his knight's grace, Blanchette clasping the dagger in her trembling hands and inwardly chanting her prayers. Her tactics proved useful thrice more times, as she mortally wounded two peasants and slid the steel through a third man's throat.

Spilled blood and bowels scented the air. She fought not to see more than she needed to or hear things she knew would forever haunt her.

She'd never sleep peacefully again.

"This way," she said to Sir Lionel as loudly as her damaged throat allowed. "I know a postern gate. Along the castle wall, I can take us—"

Molten pain seared through her. She would have screamed in agony had she any voice left. She felt herself buckling at her knees, then glanced down through hooded eyes and found a cut blooming on her left leg. She never saw the blade or the fighter who'd wounded her. Gasping for breath, she sucked in the cold, precious air and felt the rain pelting her body.

Sir Lionel cradled her in his left arm and fought with his right. By God, they were both going to die. She helped direct him in a thin voice, despairing as the onslaught of attacks grew increasingly dangerous. The howls of the kennel dogs rode the shrieking wind—a mournful song that sent chills down her backbone.

A mail-armored soldier hacked through two of her father's men and stood toe-to-toe with Sir Lionel. Steel rang against steel as their swords clashed and cut through the air, the rain and blood glittering on the metal. The ground came rushing up as Sir Lionel dropped her to combat a counterstrike. Shaking in pain and dread, Blanchette flipped over and watched through a curtain of tangled curls as the knight and the soldier battled in a small clearing.

*The dance of death.*

The soldier was a poor match for him—a second of hesitation left his side open, and Blanchette felt a wave of relief as Sir Lionel buried his longsword deep in the man's hip.

He freed the weapon with a grunt, swiped blood off the slippery hilt, and then turned back to Blanchette. "Princess, we—"

An axe was embedded in Sir Lionel's neck. He stared into her eyes, red spurting from his lips. His mouth moved, but the gurgle of blood drowned all words. The killer dislodged the axe along with pieces of his spine, and his glare fixed on Blanchette. A dark promise shone in his colorless eyes.

She fumbled onto her feet, clasping her leg, pain screaming through every limb, every muscle, every sinew.

*He means to kill me, and not with a quick death.*
*I will die slowly.*
*I must escape.*
*I must.*
*I must.*
*I must...*

The soldier snaked through the clamor of steel and screams and death with Sir Lionel's blood on his raised axe. Fear and pain paralyzed her while she commanded her wretched body to move.

*At least try, damn you!*

She stumbled away as fast as her wounded leg would allow. She glanced over her shoulder, the soldier closing in on her.

*God, help me.*

An arrow through the brain sealed his fate. Its wooden shaft pierced one side of his head and came out the other. She'd never know whether an enemy, friend, or God was to thank for that.

She limped on, sticking to the walls and shadows again, terror rising inside her.

"Follow the curve—the curve—of the castle," she murmured simply to keep herself conscious. "Down those well-hidden stairs... down to the left... next... next to the buttery..."

The Lord was on her side for once that evening. She remained below the notice of the rebels and traitors as she painfully clambered to the secret stairwell. The buttery was empty except for the rows of barrels lining the walls. A brazier had been lit, and she thanked the Lord for that small mercy too.

Shadows crawled up and down the walls. Her trembling hands ran along the uneven stones, feeling for the hidden crevice... the one which would give way to the spiral stairwell... if only she didn't lose consciousness... if only...

*I'm not mortally wounded. The pain is dire, but it also means I'm still alive, still drawing breaths. Still able to stand and fight and journey on.*

*Please don't be sealed off.*

She slipped through the stairwell... through the tunnel... through and forward.

*I shall not allow the darkness to seize me. Not while my mother and father may still breathe. Not while my brother's death and the attack on my kingdom remain unavenged.*

She reminded herself of that every time she sensed her strength flagging and the darkness fighting for her. She felt it reaching, reaching, reaching. It clawed within the night, waiting around every corner, hiding in every crevice, and glaring down from each murder hole. A lifetime seemed to pass before moonlight shone at the mouth of the tunnel and the blessed rush of the river washed over her.

Horror and relief swept through her by turns. Dead bodies were strewn about the forest floor—servants, peasants, soldiers. On the bank of the river sat a rickety rowing boat. Her mother and father waited inside it, three guards flanking its front. Light shimmered off their gold cloaks and helms, and Blanchette felt an equally vibrant spark of hope burst inside her. *Strange,* her mind absently registered, seeing her king father dressed in mere bedclothes and not some fancy doublet. *Have I ever seen Father out of embellishment and finery?*

*Do I even know this man?*

The river itself was a wild torrent. Rain fell from a black iron sky, pelting at the tumultuous water. Trees poked out from the river, their naked limbs reaching out like the arms of drowned men. The rain swelled the river, and it flooded the bank. Traveling it would be perilous, perhaps mortal, but escaping on foot would mean certain death.

Blanchette limped toward her parents, sobbing. Her tears mixed with the rainwater as her mother clambered out of the boat. Exhaustion was visible in every line of the queen's beautiful face. Blood matted her blond hair, and her bedclothes were torn and tattered. She stumbled over a rock and into the rushing river. A guardsman helped her up.

Blanchette embraced her queen mother, tears of horror and gratitude and love spilling down both of their cheeks. After a moment, Queen Joanna held her at arm's length and gently stroked her daughter's face.

"Grandmother. Willem. They are—"

"Yes. They are gone, which is why we must fight. This is why you must fight, no matter what... no matter how fleeting hope may seem. Do you understand me, Blanchette? We never stop fighting. *Never.*" Her mother smiled sadly, her hands cupping either side of Blanchette's head. She ran her thumb across her wounded cheek, making Blanchette wince.

"Your cheek. Oh, my sweet girl. You're covered in blood!" She glanced down. "And your leg. You—"

"It's okay. I'm fine, Mother. Really, I am."

The din of the raging battle rode the thin, whistling wind and filled the woods.

"We must go," the queen commanded, and her guards rushed into action.

One guard aided Blanchette to her feet and into the rowing boat. But nothing was to come quickly or without a fight. The woods itself seemed to roar to life. She heard the peasant soldiers before she saw them. She listened to their yells and erratic commands. Those sounds mated with the wind and the mournful bay of far-off kennel hounds.

Then the woods seemed to split, to part like the Red Sea in the pages of Exodus. A score of peasants rushed toward the bank, their excited voices a rough thunder that thickened the mayhem. Blanchette scanned the faces—more farm boys, a steward, a cook —finding so many she knew. The number of traitors alarmed her.

Her heart grew as cold and hard as ice.

The king of Norland drew his longsword and proudly stood inside the rowing boat. "Kill them, guards! Kill them all! I want them dead. I want this river to run red with their blood!"

*He's a fool,* she realized for the first time in her life. *A fool whose cruelty has killed us all.*

Steel kissed steel while the song of battle rang out. The guards easily cut down the peasants, but they were vastly outnumbered. A few swarmed the boat as Blanchette, her mother, and a guard rowed it downstream. Her father thrust his longsword down and pierced one of the farm boys through the eye. He withdrew the blood-soaked weapon and kicked the body into the river. Blanchette watched as the current turned red and swallowed the boy up.

Blanchette and her mother held each other. She watched through the wind and rain and her tears as the last of their guards was taken down with arrows. Watched as her king father cut away two more peasants, and the face of the castle grew farther and farther away. The trees seemed to come together, a great dark curtain closing at the end of some farce.

The water ran red, just like King Bartholomew had promised.
*Yes. This is all just pretend... a farce.*
*A tragedy.*
The boat rode the current, battling the turbulent water with every stroke. They took a sharp bend, and the boat jumped. Water rushed over the side, soaking them and stealing her last breath of hope.

Blanchette muttered a silent prayer. The dark and pelting rain made the river nearly impossible to maneuver. The water itself was a muddy color mixed with red.

Their lives were in the hands of a higher power now.

It went on that way for nearly a mile—water sloshing over the sides, the veil of darkness making every deadly turn unpredictable. Blanchette shivered from fear and cold. That chill had numbed the pain in her leg and across her wounded cheek.

She continued to hold her mother, feeling very much like a child.

*She's all I have left.* Her father had always been a stranger, now more than ever.

Blanchette heard the enormous splintering crash before she felt it, like a sword splitting an oaken shield in two. The boat reared up, tossing the three of them from its mouth. The cold rush of water hit her with the force of a thousand daggers. She struggled against the rapid current, the river foiling her every stroke and breath.

*Norland wants me to die,* she thought in despair. *It's trying to smite my family from its soil.*

*Am I paying the price for my father's sins?*

She glanced at fragmented images of her mother and father. She watched as the king flew against a riverbed rock with a force that must have split his head open. The current pulled Blanchette under.

She emerged again.

Her father was nowhere to be seen now... but what might have been blood and guts *were*...

Her mother's body floated a yard away and was thrown about like a rag doll.

Thrown and torn and tattered.

*No.*

*No, no, no.*

Only a gnawing emptiness remained where hope had been moments ago.

*I will not surrender. Not without a fight.*

Blanchette's determination to survive flared in her mind and body. She struggled to stay afloat as her skirts threatened to drag her down again into the murky depths. But fight she did. The current snatched her cloak and garment, whirling her about and dragging her back and forth. The cold, dark waters closed over her head, and the struggle to rise above the surface became too great of a burden. She sank into the stygian void.

Her arms slowly ceased their labor.

Darkness finally came upon her and swallowed her up.

# Two

"WHOEVER FIGHTS monsters should see to it that in the process he does not become a monster. And if you gaze long enough into an abyss, the abyss will gaze back into you."

— Friedrich Nietzsche

Blanchette was lying face down, her body sprawled on the bank and half-submerged in the Rockbluff River. The dirty taste of mud and muck filled her mouth, and her wounded cheek burned like hell. She ground her teeth against the filth, against that grainy texture and slush. Nausea hit her hard. She lifted her head with a violent cough, spat out the water, and then emptied her stomach onto the ground. Her body protested, convulsing in dry heaves.

Pain and coldness shackled her in place. And not the chill in the air. It was a misery, a profound sense of hopelessness, unlike she'd ever known.

A mounting wind moaned and whistled, snapping off branches and rattling the trees. Thunder and the mournful howl of wolves rumbled in the distance. Blanchette shuddered, then felt herself growing sick again.

Reality crashed down and capsized her thoughts as efficiently as the river had capsized the boat only hours ago.

*Has it been hours? Minutes? Days?*

*Or was it all a horrific nightmare?*

The traitors. The attack on the castle, the violent assault on her home. All of those faces she had recognized. Grandmother's blood staining her hands.

She remembered that most of all.

Darkness came again to the Rockbluff River. And this time, she welcomed it like an old friend.

---

SHE AWOKE.

"Mother?" Her voice was a whisper, drowned out by the thundering river and her exhaustion. The rain had momentarily stopped. Pain spiked through her cheek and leg as she squinted against the blanket of the night. The darkness pressed down as hard as the cold. Moonlight battled to shine through the trees—just enough filtered through to illuminate the limp figure lying next to her.

Blanchette crawled over to the body. Fear mounted inside her, the horror of everything sucking breaths from her burning lungs.

*I should just close my eyes and fall asleep.*

Perhaps she'd wake from this nightmare when she opened them again, safe and warm and inside her solar with her governess.

*I shall not die like this—alone and cold and frightened of the dark.*

Vomit running down her throat, she shifted and fought to pull herself out of the river's bank, grasping, grasping for purchase, grasping for anything. Her fingers curled into the wet earth, and mud sloshed below her cut and bleeding leg. Despite the numbing coldness of the river, pain jackknifed through her with each movement. God, that ice cold paralyzed her body and soul.

She strained forward and fought to climb out of the shallow bank. That simple exertion purged the breath from her lungs. She moved a few inches, then slid backward in vain as the current wrestled for her. Her county, her very soil, betrayed her. The river itself wanted to spirit her away, and those protruding tree limbs reached for her like arms.

She laid her head on its side and fixed her gaze on her mother's drowned body. She'd smashed against the rocks several times. The impact had burst open her arms and chest. Her blood ran thick and black in the grim darkness.

"Oh, Mother..."

Blanchette wished for death at that moment.

Darkness swept her away again, but she never woke from the nightmare.

***

SOME MEN CALLED HIM A CONQUEROR, others a liberator. Some whispered murderer.

But most men were sheep, and he was a wolf.

Rowan Dietrich, the Black Wolf of Norland, removed his helm and set it on the chair's massive curved armrest. He was neither a lord nor a nobleman by any stretch of the imagination, yet he sat on a throne fit for a king all the same.

He even sat on it with grace.

He'd been born into a great house, he supposed, but that house was long gone—only dust in the pages of history.

And now the dust had finally settled.

Rowan adjusted his body with a tired groan, the sound emerging from his bones. Gnarled tree limbs snaked together to form the chair's arms, and a slab of rough-hewn stone served as the backrest. It was an imposing seat to look upon and a pain in the arse to sit.

*No king or man should sit on a throne comfortably. Not while the burden of the realm lays upon his shoulders.*

Rowan reflected that King Bartholomew had hardly sat on the throne at all. He watched as light from a torch caught in his helm's crude metal.

His wolf, Smoke, sat beside the chair—an extension of himself. His flinty dark coat resembled his namesake, and his yellow eyes shone like lanterns. Rowan kneaded the scruff of his neck. Silent and still, Rowan and Smoke studied the legendary throne room of Winslowe Castle.

It was a vast, shadowy space, lit only by the hearth and flickering torch set in a sconce along the wall. The stone floor was cold and hard underfoot, and the ceiling loomed forty feet above, lost in darkness. Tapestries adorned the walls and depicted scenes of battles and hunts. Their rich colors were muted in the dim light.

The throne itself was draped in a velvet cloak and adorned with gold filigree, and its high back was carved with the kingdom's crest.

Ravens in flight.

In front was a long carpet leading up to the raised dais.

In the hall's corners, looming gargoyles watched over all proceedings, their stone eyes gleaming in the torchlight. A hearth sat in a far junction. The fire was large enough to roast an entire ox, and the sound of the crackling flames added to the eerie atmosphere of the room. The air was thick with the smell of smoke.

Despite the warmth, a sense of foreboding hung over Rowan. The shadows seemed to move and twist as if alive, and the flickering torch cast eerie patterns on the walls. It was as if the very stones of the castle watched and waited.

Biding their time.

The throne room of the castle was a place of power and intrigue, where the fate of kingdoms could be decided with a single stroke of a sword.

He'd seen it happen firsthand and in this very room.

He'd been here before, of course... more times than he could count. For the feasts and hunts and to pay court courtesies to a man he'd considered a friend.

Rowan traced the chair's woodwork with his index finger while gazing at the royal crown. It sat beside him in the heart of a wood-and-stone footrest—a medley of solid gold, rubies, sapphires, amethysts, and intertwined gilt tree branches.

He'd yet to try it on. He'd come close shortly after he'd taken the castle—but his hands had hesitated in midair before the thing ever touched his brow.

*Why? Why such hesitation?*
*It is mine. I need only take it.*
*But do I want it?*
*Nay, I never have...*

He affirmed that it wasn't a crown he'd lust for; it was blood, he thought, his gaze tracking over the gleaming rubies.

It seemed he'd planned for this moment since he was a boy just out of his swaddling clothes and off his wet nurse's breast. Yet the victory lacked sweetness.

It tasted bitter.

It was the child's savage death. Prince Willem, the fourth of his name, Norland's future protector and king, had been murdered and mutilated by his men.

Rowan's hand slid away from Smoke's slick coat. He clasped the armrest with an iron grip, and his nails dug into the wooden limbs while fury built inside him. He clenched his fingers, forcing his anger to simmer down and bow to reason.

*I shall rectify this crime. I didn't liberate Norland only to trade one atrocity for another.*

Yet that was precisely what'd happened. Disobedience and a lack of honor were things Rowan Dietrich couldn't tolerate. Not as a commander. And not as a knight of the realm.

"Sir Rowan?" his guard asked from his position before the throne. Rowan had forgotten he was there. The man bore an unfortunate, long, flat face, a blunt beak of a nose, and eyes so dark they appeared black. The torches set his chain-link armor aglow. It was the only thing on him that didn't lack vibrance.

Tracing the intricate metalwork of his wolf's helm, Rowan absently signaled to the guard. "I'm ready now. Bring them to me."

"As you command," the man said, eyeing Smoke and exiting the throne room with purposeful steps. That rapping sound echoed Rowan's errant heartbeat. He sat up a little straighter and set his eyes into a hard line.

He waited.

And waited.

*I shall not balk, no matter how desperately they beg.*
*I am hewn from stone, much like this very chair.*

Minutes later, Sir Edrick, Rowan's chief captain and lifelong friend, escorted three soldiers into the throne room. Smoke bristled his coat and bellowed a guttural growl through bared teeth. "Hush," Rowan commanded, and he did. But somehow, Smoke's silent golden stare was far more unnerving than the growl.

Rowan rose from the chair, and for the first time, he felt like an ascending king.

He came forward in a swift movement and neatly folded his hands behind his back. Then he descended the seven stone steps that heightened the throne from the rest of the chamber. The soldiers saw something in his eyes. Their expressions visibly tightened as if pulled taut by a string.

"You three were quite busy last night," Rowan said slowly.

The soldiers shared a glance, then a small chortle. "I believe we all were, Your Grace."

Rowan stepped forward again. The soldiers didn't stir, though he saw it took great effort for them not to shift away. Their discomfort rewarded him with a perverse satisfaction. "I am no king. And you three are no longer men of mine." They said nothing and just shared another glance with furrowed brows. "I see you are confused," Rowan pressed on. "It's rather simple, so let me enlighten you. I had given a specific order regarding how the Winslowe children would be handled. And that order was *gently.*"

Realization flashed in the soldiers' eyes. One dared step forward: scruffy-haired, wary, his skin wrinkled like old, tanned leather. He removed his cap, then ran an unsteady hand through his thin hairline. His voice quivered once he found the pluck to speak. "We d-did. We handled him g-gently. The Lord as my witness. We were only trying to do right by you, Rowan." His eyes shifted to Smoke.

"Do not call me Rowan."

His cheeks flushed, and he twisted the cap between shaky fingers. He tried to smile, but the gesture fit poorly.

"Then... how shall I address you?"

"As Sir Rowan Dietrich, the Black Wolf of Norland."

"You are the Black Wolf of Norland, now more than ever," Edrick suddenly cut in, his voice a sharp whip. As timid as the soldier was, Edrick sounded equally rigid and coarse. He was half a foot shorter than Rowan but hewn from the same stone. His eyes were shallow pale depths that were hard to look in for too long. A thinning hairline hovered above narrow gray brows.

"But this conquest was a hero's errand," Edrick said. "You know this. You were right to take the city. But a clean slate is a *clean* one—one that surviving heirs cannot taint. You've won this day. You've won the soil and the stones in which we stand... the citizens' hearts as well. These three men performed the dirty work, so you might keep your hands and name clean. As your friend and adviser, Rowan, as someone who's been with you since the very start, take the credit and allow these damn soldiers to carry the blame. Let the people see you as a liberator and this lot as the murderers. A commander who kills men loyal to him won't have followers for long. Keep them alive."

*He dares to lecture me? Especially having been there from the start?*

Rowan said nothing. And said nothing. And said nothing.

Finally, he stepped forward, past Edrick, until he stood eye to eye with the scruffy-haired soldier. Smoke hunched his back, his fur bristled and eyes shining. A deep snarl came forth, rolling out of the beast's throat like thunder. Rowan lay his hand on his longsword's wolf pommel, then addressed Edrick. "I've heard your words. And I reject your counsel. Now, have your men located the princess?"

Edrick exhaled a breath, then matched Rowan's stance and hit him with an ice-cold stare. "They have not."

"See that they do," Rowan finished, turning back to the soldier. Smoke padded to his feet and stood beside Rowan. His lips peeled back to reveal a toothy snarl that gave way to another low growl.

"Now. I gave you a command. One you disobeyed. There is a reason I give orders, and you follow them. Men like you *are* the very reason I took this city. I mean to purge it, and the purge shall begin with you three on accounts of treason and insubordination."

The scruffy-haired soldier dropped to his knees and shoved his palms together. Smoke lunged forward and nipped at his face. He wheeled back, and Rowan reassured his wolf with a firm touch. "I beg you! I harmed no child, no woman. I-I only watched. Made sure the king's guards wouldn't... interrupt. I never touched the prince. Never would, never would violate one of your commands, sir. I live to serve you."

"I appreciate your loyalty. You shall die serving me as well."

"I know you are a reasonable and just man. I harmed no child. I harmed no one, I swear it. I only stood by and watched for Winslowe's guards."

Rowan considered that for a moment. He thought of another time, another place, another set of guards. How many soldiers had stood by that night, *watching*, guarding the door?

"I see," he finally said, his voice sinking into a rumble that sounded like Smoke's growl. "It's decided, then. You shall die last after you *watch* their executions. Sir Edrick, bring the other forward and leave this one behind."

Edrick did as ordered. The men struggled and cried out in overlapping pleas. Rowan unsheathed his longsword from its scabbard; the scrape of metal sounded deafening inside the throne room. The blade seemed to shriek as it came free. He lowered the sword to a point as if he was creating knights of the two men instead of headless corpses. "Kneel. I command it. Serve me loyally and kneel."

When they refused him again, Edrick kicked them hard in the back of their legs. The two soldiers collapsed to their hands and feet. Rowan allowed them a moment to regain their dignity and sit in kneeling positions.

All the while, the watcher watched.

"Please, sir, please. Show us mercy, as you have for so many."

A whisper of sympathy passed through Rowan, but then he thought of the prince's mutilated body. They hadn't just executed him with a swift blow, as Rowan intended to do now. They'd tortured him—holes and burns and cuts had riddled his lean body.

*He was just a boy.* Anger quivered through Rowan, though his expression gave nothing away. He stood straighter, his hazel eyes beating into the kneeling soldiers.

*The wolf neither bows nor breaks before the sheep.*

"Please, sir... I beg you."

"Remind me of your names," Rowan said, calm but firm as steel.

"Mercy, sir."

"Mercy?" Rowan echoed. "That's quite an unusual name. Can't say I've heard it before," he said in a dry tone that lacked humor. "You slaughtered the prince of Norland like a lamb. After the city had surrendered. A quick death *is* a mercy. If God were good, you'd suffer the same as the prince, cut for cut."

Silence held.

They offered no names to him. *Very well.* Rowan closed his eyes and muttered a prayer. After he was done, he whispered to the first soldier, who was now moments away from his death. "If you have any last words, I ask that you speak them now."

Naked panic appeared in his eyes. He squeezed his hands together again as if in prayer. That stoked Rowan's anger.

"Quit your pleas. I am no god. I'm just a soldier and now the lord of this castle."

"Indeed, sir... and as such, you can let me live. I've fought for you and would have gladly died in your name. You can choose to answer injustice with mercy."

Rowan inhaled, taking in a lungful of the castle's drafty air. Idly, he looked past the cowering man to Edrick, who had a flat expression on his face and ire in his eyes. "I thank you for your loyalty. But I didn't take this castle on a whim or tyrant's errand. I mean to bleed out the corruption, and I will. Starting now."

And so it began.

The silence that followed was complete. Rowan dug the point of his longsword into the rushes and said the old words with solemn duty, words he'd heard a hundred times before and would likely recite a hundred times more.

"Through this holy anointing, may the Lord, in his love and mercy, help you with the grace of the Holy Spirit. May the Lord who frees you from sin save you and raise you. I, Rowan of the House Dietrich, by the will of the Lord and all that is righteous, do sentence you to die."

The longsword hammered down with a fist of justice, and the watcher cried out.

*Three,* Rowan Dietrich dejectedly affirmed. *Three guards had stood outside the door.*

---

IT WAS A FIRST BREATH.

But what had she been born into?

Blanchette woke with violent coughs as water spewed from her mouth. Gentle hands flipped her over and patted her back like one might a babe. Her fingertips dug into the moist earth. Blanchette felt as her stomach muscles contracted and voided her gut of more water. It spilled from her body in a painful torrent. Dawn's first light glinted through the trees and illuminated the muddy floor.

"There we are. Get it all out, milady. Purge yourself despite the pain," a man's voice urged, his tone gentler than his hands.

Then another voice cut through the haze—a child's voice. It was light. Airy. Almost angelic. "Is she going to live, Pa?"

"I believe so, if God wills it to be. And with our help, of course." Blanchette felt herself being lifted from the muddy ground. The man groaned from the exertion.

"What if they come back? I'm frightened."

"I'm certain they will. But we won't be here when they return."

Pain spread through Blanchette. Her body felt like a rag doll. She remembered her mother's limp body and expelled a drawn-out sob. The man groaned again, then spoke to the boy. "Help me, Petyr. Your old pa's back isn't as strong as it once was. There we are now. Careful, but quickly..."

# Three

Sunlight shone across the river. Princess Blanchette Winslowe, little more than a girl, ran at a breakneck speed and stripped off her wimple and habit. She rejoiced at the feeling of the sun on her skin, the wind in her curls, and the dirt under her heels.

It was her kingdom's soil. A very part of herself.

"Oh, Princess! Princess, no! No, no, no, oh Lord, be good!" Governess Agnes called after her, carrying her heavy black skirts and fighting to keep pace. The sharp angles of her face pinched together in horror and dismay. It was rather endearing. "Princess, that is most unseemly! You mustn't—oh, you naughty girl! No, no, no! Get back here, you bad thing, or the king shall have my head!"

Blanchette's boots and socks came off next. She glanced over her shoulder at her governess, who was huffing and puffing like some beached walrus.

"Lord, have mercy!" she lamented whilst Blanchette donned nothing more than her smallclothes and strangers looked on.

The material ballooned around Blanchette's body as she submerged herself waist-deep in the calm Rockbluff River. Wading forward, her blond ringlets dragging behind like a queen's train, she felt at one with her home's soil. Rock and mud slid underfoot.

*She squeezed her toes and sank them deeply, savoring the feel of the earth and pebbles. The feel of her home.*

*All the while, her governess stood at the bank's edge, her hands planted on her hips, her pale cheeks puffy and reddening with every breath.*

*"Join me, Governess. It shall do you well, I promise!"*

---

*I promise...*

Blanchette slid out of the darkness and into a new world.

She woke with tears falling down her cheeks. Sunlight broke through a set of rough-spun curtains and pierced her eyes.

*Where am I?*

Groaning, she rolled away from the stab of light. The room was small, adorned with only the bare necessities of a chamber pot, an oaken table, and a rickety wooden chair. A cup of water sat on her table, two heels of bread, a burned-out candlestick, and a small pile of fresh bandage dressings.

The slightest movement sent her head spinning like a toy top. Her body screamed in pain as she jolted into a sitting position and shoved a tangle of matted curls from her eyes.

Then it came to her.

*The siege...*

*Was it only a nightmare?*

*Have I slept?*

*Am I still asleep?*

Disorientation hit her hard. Her temples throbbed against her skull as she fought to recall everything.

The night came to her in bits and pieces, like a half-remembered dream from her childhood. And every memory, every moment, was soaked in blood.

Aye, her thoughts ran red. As red as her riding cloak—the one her grandmother had made three winters ago.

*How did I end up here?*

And how, in God's name, did she survive?

"Help me," she whispered, not knowing who she spoke to or implored. "Please, help me. Please..."

Her breaths grew shallow and rapid. Choked tears came to her, and the pain they caused sent her reeling onto the bed again. Her throat burned.

Pure *misery*.

There was no other word for it.

Lying on her side, her face against the hard plank, she examined the room numbly. She took in shapes and colors yet felt disconnected all the same. Nothing seemed to exist outside of her terror and that feeling of hopelessness.

"No, no, no, no. This isn't real. This isn't happening, none of this is happening... not truly." She whispered between knife-like convulsions. Her breaths came fast and panicky, and she felt like she was on the verge of passing out.

*I'm still sleeping. When I awake, I shall be back in my chamber with the walls of Winslowe Castle all around me.*

*Snug and safe and well-guarded...*

She blinked away her tears.

*Wake up, Blanchette.* She smacked her cheek with her palm. A bandage covered one of them. She hit herself again and again with a bunched fist.

*Wake from this nightmare, you stupid girl. Wake up!*

She beat her face with balled fingers, the tears falling silently, willing herself awake, willing the nightmare to fade into shadow.

But the room remained before her. She stilled her fists in midair.

Then she traced the bandage on her cheek, and Blanchette Winslowe knew she hadn't slept.

---

THE DIN of approaching footsteps roused her from the depths of a nightmare. They clanked lightly against the floorboards, yet the mere presence of sound made her head throb. Every bit of her body pulled taut like an arrow preparing to be loosed.

She couldn't remember any details of the siege, couldn't recall those moments that would forever scar her, yet one memory remained loud and solid and sure.

*My promise.*

Now, someone was coming.

She had to escape this place... wherever she was. Fight or flight instinct kicked in. She could barely move, let alone run, so she looked around the room for something to protect herself with. The memories continued to return, slowly at first, like water pressing against a dam.

*The dagger.*

Blanchette fumbled at her clothing. She noticed the dress was two sizes too large and made from threadbare wool. She searched the room again, the reality of the situation coming into focus with each movement, each breath, and each thought. Someone had draped her red riding cloak over a chair that she didn't notice at first. It hung next to her bed and up against the wall.

*My red cloak.*

*My grandmother.*

Tears pricked the corners of her eyes as she winced, remembering it all with a sudden clarity.

*God, help me...*

*Help us all.*

Footsteps again.

Blanchette sucked in a shaky breath, her gaze on the closed door. *I must be safe. I have been cared for... but for how long and by whom?*

The footsteps halted outside the chamber. Blanchette nearly collapsed as she fumbled from the bed. Her leg ached terribly. She snatched the dagger from her riding cloak and filled her hand with the cool metal. Her palm was bandaged too.

The door pushed open. A bright-eyed, redheaded child poked

his face inside. Blanchette relaxed and felt some of the tension leave her body.

He was a little boy, his hair a mass of unruly crimson locks that framed a dirty, freckled face. The child, who looked eight or nine, raised an equally dirty and freckled hand to his cheek and rubbed his eyes.

"Hello," he greeted with a very point-blank tone and stare.

Blanchette studied his inquisitive features. "Where... where am I? Who else is here?" Each word grated. Her throat was a raw wound, and her voice a strained whisper.

His slim, reed-like shoulders dropped, and his chin lowered several inches. "Just me and my pa. The soldiers should be here soon with food from the big castle."

*Plunder and loot stolen from my home.*

The tension returned at full force. Blanchette braced against her grip, her hand unconsciously tightening around the dagger's hilt.

He eyed the dagger and shuffled back a step. "Are you going to hurt me?"

Blanchette felt her hand shaking in midair. She slowly lowered the dagger and set it out of sight. "No-no, of course not. I'm sorry. I'm just confused. Confused and lost. I..." She glanced around, her head spinning, her fitful thoughts crashing into one another.

She watched as the boy wandered farther inside the room, curiosity outweighing his fear. "Pa fished you out of the river. Like a trout or something, I suppose. I didn't know that's where ladies come from."

Blanchette felt a laugh on her lips. But the thought of the river and her horror stole it away.

And laughter? How could she possibly laugh?

*Does happiness still exist in the world?* She felt tears prick her eyes again and vigorously blinked them back. "Where... where is your mother?"

"She died. It was one of the king's soldiers, Pa said. He broke her into pieces. Pa says the Black Wolf pulled the soldier off her, but Momma was already gone. It was years ago."

"Oh, I'm... I'm so very sorry." The words sounded and felt empty.

The realization hit Blanchette like ice water to the face. She was *their* enemy, while the man who ordered the siege and destruction of her family, the beast who'd doomed all she'd ever cared about, was their *hero*.

Did these peasants know who she was?

And if they didn't, what would happen to her when the truth emerged?

Suddenly, the home began to quake; the rough-spun curtains twitched, and the glass of water on the end table rattled like creaking bones. The little redheaded boy gasped. A smile spread across his face. Naive hope shone there. "It's the Black Wolf, the Black Wolf! Pa said he'd be coming to us, and he's here, just like he promised!"

*I promise.*

Blanchette swept the curtain aside, her heartbeat thundering. Men on both horses and foot marched through the clearing. Bannermen flew the Black Wolf; it swept through the wintry landscape, a predator hunting its prey... yet she watched as the townspeople greeted it with reverence, like a symbol of hope. They rushed out of their timber-and-thatch houses, crossing themselves, yelling prayers as if welcoming the second coming of Christ. A small blond girl danced on the dirt road, and for a moment, Blanchette saw herself as a child. The girl's mother, a tall, willowy figure wearing a sunny smile, grabbed the child's hand and drew her near her flowing skirt.

A breeze lifted the silk banner on the lance, and it fluttered outward, making the embroidered black wolf at its center appear to stretch and prowl. "I know you're excited, sweetling, but we mustn't get in their way. Come now, stand back," the mother mildly reprimanded, pulling her daughter out of the way of the marching soldiers.

One foot soldier halted in front of them and reached for the mother's hand. He kissed her knuckles, then lowered to a knee and playfully ruffled the girl's blond hair. Blanchette felt something twist inside her chest... remorse mixed with bittersweet longing.

"Petyr?" a man called out, his voice muffled by the partially shut door. The scuffle of boots followed. The little redheaded boy, *Petyr*, stood in the doorway as the man appeared behind him. His hair was just as red, and his pale skin equally freckled, though he held muscle and bulk where his son was slender. She guessed he was in his mid-forties. Slightly balding. Leathery wrinkles disrupted an otherwise handsome face, and his body was hewn from years of laboring.

"Ah, well, your fever has broken," the man said to her. "Is the pain awful today?"

Pain? Yes, it was unimaginable. The worst she'd ever known. Her heart was a raw wound, and numbness and disbelief were the only tethers keeping her attached to this world.

"I feel fine," she finally answered. Speaking those words was a battle. They grated against her sore throat, where she was sure the skin was scabbing.

"Ah, good to hear," he said. His voice sounded vaguely familiar—an echo from a distant dream.

*I heard him on the riverbank. After...*

She stopped her thought there, not wanting to recall the horror from that night again.

Blanchette tracked a fingertip over her face, where she felt a healing wound that started at the corner of her lip and stretched to her ear. She was afraid to see herself in a looking glass but inwardly scolded herself for having such a petty concern when her family had lost their *lives*.

"Where am I exactly?"

The man frantically shut the curtains and turned back to Blanchette with a poorly worn smile. "This is my home, sad as it is," he said with a wave and a crooked grin. He draped his palm on

Petyr's head and mussed his bright red hair. "And this—well, this is my son, as you might have gathered. My name's Jonathan, milady."

He hesitantly strode through the chamber with long steps, then sat on the edge of the hard mattress. Silence filled the room, broken by chattering voices beyond the home. "Do you remember anything of these past three days?" His boy came up beside him and leaned against the bed. He studied her with large, expressive eyes that seemed to fill his face.

"The past... *three* days?" The revelation startled and terrified her. She vaguely recalled flights of nightmares and dreams, each woven into the other in an unsettling patchwork of feverish imaginings.

Fever dreams. She thought hard, trying to untie reality from fiction, but everything was muddled and drenched in blood.

*So much red,* she mused, looking at her cloak.

"My family... they're all dead, aren't they?"

"Yes. Yes, they're dead." He hesitated, giving Petyr a strange, sad look. The boy leaned against him, and Blanchette felt something dark and ugly tug at her heartstrings. "I'm so sorry, milady. I... I can only imagine your pain. My wife died a few winters ago. She was the prettiest lady you'd ever seen... and the best mother to little Petyr here. A seamstress," he continued with a proud smile as he waved to the blanket and Blanchette's dress.

Blanchette swallowed, then inhaled a shaky breath. Absently, she meddled with her signet ring. Images spun through her mind, blurring into each other, distorting and cracking her poor grip on reality. "Your son mentioned her death before you came in. I hope the man paid with his life."

"He did," Jonathan agreed, smoothing Petyr's unruly hair. "The Black Wolf saw to that."

*The Black Wolf.*

The mere mention of him made her skin tighten and crawl. Jonathan's features softened at her distress. He gently laid a hand on her shoulder and shook his downcast head. "I know what he took from you. I can't imagine your pain, milady, but—"

"Yes, you can." She shook his hand off her shoulder. She locked onto Jonathan's eyes with a steady gaze, her insides clenching against the force of her anger. "No matter, the Black Wolf is still a monster. He ravaged my family and home like the beast he is."

*He knows everything, yet he's protecting me. He will surely sell me to the Black Wolf.* Blanchette searched his weathered, kindly face, looking for the truth.

All she found was that lopsided grin.

Jonathan forced another smile to his face that fit all wrong. "Yes. Well, let me find you something to eat. A nice stew should be manageable, I think?"

Blanchette nodded, then released a breath she hadn't known she was holding.

Jonathan nudged his son toward the door. They both paused beneath the archway as the din of the soldiers resounded beyond the house. Jonathan looked at Blanchette apologetically. But before either of them could speak, a sudden knock blasted through the home. Blanchette jumped at the sound, her heart hammering along with the pounding.

Jonathan nudged his son from the room. "It would be best if you remained here, milady. And stay perfectly quiet and still. You, too, Petyr, just like I'd told you."

She nodded. No more words were needed. She was sealed inside the room a moment later as she listened to the Black Wolf's soldiers parcel out food and goods from her home.

She sat on the rigid bed, her knees pulled to her face. She squeezed her eyes closed and fought to calm her breathing. Her throat felt raw, her heart more so...

*Surely, he shall sell me as a hostage... that's why I'm here, why he saved me.*

Yet the door never opened again.

Muffled voices seeped through her wall. Petyr's excited cry. Jonathan's gracious words and incoherent mumblings.

It was all a jumble.

*My world is a jumble. A shattered dream.*

But one voice she heard with perfect clarity. "We believe the princess escaped the castle, likely with an escort. Maybe you've seen her or know someone who has?"

Blanchette breathed a vain prayer and reached for her cross, already knowing it was gone. She heard Jonathan's muffled voice, but she couldn't make out the words over the pounding of her own heart.

She lay back on the bed and stared at the cracked and peeling ceiling. She heard the excited commotion in the village, felt hot tears streaking her cheeks, and below all that, the whisper of her own hoarse voice, "I promise. I promise. I promise..."

# Four

Wet earth and pine needles sloshed under Blanchette's bare feet as she raced through the woods. Light snow fell and numbed her body. Her heels were cut and bleeding, yet the pain didn't hold her back; it propelled her forward and lit a fire inside her soul.

The chase was on, and all she could bring to mind was her promise to her grandmother.

A wolf's melancholy howl rose around her and trembled through the trees. The cry held a note of despair and a tone of human suffering. A flock of ravens burst from the grasses and thickets. She felt lightheaded and winded. Her red riding cloak streamed behind her, whipping in the musty air like a queen's trail.

*But I am no longer a queen, am I? Not even a princess. Just a lost and frightened girl, running through the woods and trying to find my way home with a bloodthirsty predator on my heels.*

The wolf cried out again, closer this time, calling for her, *hunting* her. The sound came from everywhere at once—the wood's sloping ridges and mossy crests, the deep ravines, the half-nude tree branches, the moist soil and divots of mud, the tangled roots beneath her toes, and the huge moon that shone through the branches and shed its illumination as best it could. Even the wind caught the sound and exhaled it in a long, cool breath.

She paused, paralyzed by that haunting melody, and pulled the red hood up and into place.

*He shall hear the beat of my heart*, she despaired. *He shall hear my heartbeat and find my hiding spot. Then he shall devour me like he devoured my home and family.*

Suddenly, the woods grew quiet and still; even the wind held its breath. The one sound that penetrated the din was Blanchette's own heavy exhales. She pushed her spine against the trunk of a tree and stifled the sound with her palm. Salt from her sweaty skin seeped between her lips and flavored her tongue.

She felt it before she heard it. That tightness on the back of your neck and across your heart... an ominous breath on the back of your neck...

A guttural growl emerged from just ahead, low to the ground and between entwined trees with gnarled limbs.

The muzzle emerged first, snarling, flashing a mouth full of dagger-like teeth. Its mottled fur was heavy and wet with red. The monster licked its chops, sending blood sprays down his neck and into the soil. Its eyes glowed, a piercing gold—no, no, a *hazel*— two orbs made all the brighter by its black fur.

He slinked forward, his fur standing on end, his head low and predatory... and between his blood-soaked teeth, he grasped a severed arm. It appeared ghostly pale, whiter than the snow gliding around them. The fingers lifelessly flopped as the wolf came forward and into the clearing. Blanchette's insides curdled as the wolf dropped the thing before her feet as if he were making a gift of it. Its eyes looked human and seemed to implore her.

*What do you want from me? You've already taken everything from me!*

*I have nothing left to give!*

She gazed down at the slender, pale arm that blended into the snowy ground. The fingers were heavy with gold and jewels—and one bore the signet ring of House Winslowe.

"Willem, no..." she said, but the wind and snow and her own breaths whisked her voice away and carried her words into the dust. The wolf caught notice of her voice. It craned its dark head back, those familiar eyes staring into her own. They dug deep... but for what?

Whatever he found in her gaze, he didn't like. His lips curled into a vicious snarl, flashing stark-white teeth that dripped blood.

*My brother's blood.*

Blanchette clasped the riding cloak more firmly about her body and eased back, her eyes never leaving the beast lest he finally attack and rip out her throat. Dead leaves crunched below her feet, though the soft, fresh-fallen snow muffled the sound of her steps. The growl that issued from the wolf's belly was horrifying to behold.

It was a warning. A herald of death.

The wolf advanced. Blanchette turned and fled without another thought. She zigzagged through the trees, branches snaring her hair and face, the soles of her feet growing wetter, slippery with blood, pierced by thorns and rock. The wolf's thrashing followed her, and the wood came to life with his growls and bloodthirsty snarls. She could even hear the click of his jaws as he snapped and tore at the empty air between them.

She needed to catch her breath, just for a moment, or she'd faint away. Could she spare the second? She was tired of the chase. So very tired. She glanced over her shoulder as she continued to jackknife through the tangle of roots and branches, every inch of her body on fire despite the cold.

It was her undoing. The hem of her riding cloak caught under her foot and sent her crashing to the wet ground.

Then the Black Wolf was on her, the pressure of his heavy body at her back, his sharp teeth around her neck like a hangman's noose...

He bit down, and her blood ran red.

Darkness gave way to light. Blanchette woke violently, sweat and tears flowing down her face. Trembling hands shot to her neck, feeling for gashes and blood. There was dampness beneath her fingertips, but it was only night sweat. Terror crept inside her while the realization set in. If she didn't escape soon, she'd never honor the promise she'd made to her grandmother on her deathbed.

Blanchette felt like she was suffocating. She stumbled from the bed and wrapped the threadbare blanket around her. She struggled onto her feet and limped a bit, groaning at the pain in her leg.

She crossed the chamber's doorjamb and entered the sitting room. It appeared Jonathan and his boy were gone at the moment. She breathed deeply, relishing the solitude, her gaze darting about the humble room.

A patchwork of colorful tapestries danced before her eyes and took her breath away. The otherwise barren room was filled with decades—perhaps a lifetime—of fine needlework. She lowered her gaze to the rug beneath her feet, where she stood in the heart of Norland. It was an embroidered map; she knelt and ran her fingertips over the intricate needlework, caressing a deep blue patch that resembled the Rockbluff River.

*Where my parents took their last breaths.*

She scanned just beyond that river to the dark gray fortress that loomed beside patches of vivid greens.

Winslowe Castle. Her home.

Suddenly breathless, she crawled forward until she was positioned beside the knitted castle. A bone-deep exhaustion and misery swept over her. She lay in the fetal position, her aching body wrapped around the castle. Inhaling slowly, she welcomed the air into her lungs and wished it could carry away her pain. She stared forward and forced her breathing into a steady rhythm. Her heart was like a drum, all of her wracked with its beat. She drew her legs in tight against her body and stared forward.

And stared.

And stared.

Her eyes didn't take in detail, only shapes and colors. She forced the dark thoughts away and made herself just *be*.

If only for this moment.

In front of her, the hearth burned low. A huge iron pot hung over the simmering flames. Ladles swung from the mantel, and two chipped rocking chairs sat in front. A medley of scents flooded her—tender meat, the crisp citruses of Norland's native herbs, and the rustic aroma of simmering ale.

*All the sensations of my home.*

Her strength was robbed by grief. If she hadn't been lying on the floor, she would have collapsed. Curled up there, wrapped around the map of her kingdom, she sobbed. Her body shook with its force.

Then her eyes grew heavy. Soon, she cried herself to sleep, like children do when they're unhappy.

*Please,* she thought, *don't let me dream again.* And she began to dream.

---

Torchlight shimmered off the dank walls as Rowan and Edrick traveled down the winding stairwell in Winslowe Castle. The halls were so slim they were forced to walk single file.

"If the rumors are true, secret passages exist that may never be traversed again. Henry Winslowe IV had them built during his reign in case the royal family ever needed them. He killed the servants who carved out those tunnels... and the knowledge of them died with him. It's a shame the queen and king didn't use them a few nights ago," he finished with a smile.

"The secret passages matter not," Rowan said, picking up his pace. He took the steps by threes. "The one thing that concerns me resides in these walls."

"Yes, the food stores," Edrick said. Rowan nodded grimly.

Rowan and Edrick passed through the bustling kitchens. The

scent of broiling meat filled the air as cooks and servants lowered their heads and hastened their work as they moved through. Rowan pushed open a wooden door, sprinting down the narrow staircase and into the larder.

"Tyrant glutton," Edrick cursed as he and Rowan examined the bounty before them.

He wasn't wrong.

Row upon row of neatly stacked jars and caskets covered the large basement, each filled with enough provisions to feed several families for seasons. The air was thick with the salty tang of preserved meats and the sweet, musty aroma of grains and legumes.

Rowan gazed upon the rows of cured fish, their flesh glistening in the dim light. They were salted and dried to perfection. Beetroot, cabbage, and onions swam in a vinegar brine.

Cheese blocks, wrapped in cloth, were stacked on the shelves, each one a different age and variety. Young cheeses, tangy with the taste of fresh milk, sat alongside mature cheeses, their flavors deep and complex.

Grains filled large sacks in one corner of the larder. Barley, wheat, and oats.

And honey, the sweetest of all the larder's treasures, was stored in pottery jars.

Finally, the casks of wine and ale were lined at the back of the larder. He smelled the rich, fruity aroma of the wine and the hoppy scent of the ale.

Rowan clenched his jaw tight and felt his teeth grind together. He tightened his fingers into a ball.

He imagined the people outside the walls struggling to survive on such meager rations. Such a stark contrast between the abundance within the castle and the poverty outside.

"It shan't go to waste," he whispered, his gaze tracking across the overstocked shelves. "Every man, woman, and child will have full bellies come morning."

Edrick silently nodded.

"The princess has not been found," Rowan finally said in a flat voice, turning to Edrick. It wasn't a question.

Edrick looked at him stiffly. "One of the villagers took pity on her, I'm sure. But she shan't stay hidden for long. I'll lead the search myself."

"As long as she's out there, everything we've fought for is threatened. We need to find her and keep her under lock and key."

"Under lock and key?" Edrick scoffed. "No one with the name of Winslowe can live. You know this." His eyes remained flat and unchanging.

"She's more valuable to us alive."

"Not if she brings an army to the castle gates. And not if the people rally behind her. All will be lost. Everything we've fought for."

"What do you know of loss?"

Edrick's eyes finally shifted. Rowan watched as they darkened, and something ugly reared in their depths. "More than you know."

Rowan returned his stare for several moments of silence. "I'm sorry. I spoke out of turn."

He heard muffled talking and laughter up the stairs in one of the halls. And beyond the walls, the clang of steel reverberated.

"She shall be dealt with appropriately," Rowan whispered. "Your only job is to find her. Now see it done."

---

STALE HEELS OF BREAD, a simmering stew above the fire, and a grief that seemed to deepen rather than heal filled the passing days. Petyr's oblivious laughter was difficult for Blanchette to endure. It seemed impossible that there could be people who still laughed and played and hardly cared about the downfall of a great house.

*Nay, I am still alive, keeping my grandmother's vow.*

Blanchette watched the banner of the Black Wolf fly through

the village each of those days. Her heart remained a raw and aching wound.

Her actual wounds hurt monstrously as well. Jonathan had applied a salve on her cut cheek, hand, and leg—one of her own making and from herbs he'd collected at her request.

Her hatred for the Black Wolf had become an obsession. She'd grown to blame every little misery on him, and the one thing that kept her going was that very hatred.

*I shall fulfill my promise.*

Blanchette stared into the hearth, where the cast-iron pot dangled over the fire. The aroma of stewed rabbit, carrots, onion, and barley infused the small space, yet Blanchette's stomach roiled. Outside, the sky was black and slick as ink. Moonlight streamed through the rough-spun curtains, casting a glow across the oak floorboards. The shadows lengthened and danced, moving like living things.

Beyond the home, wind and rain pelted the thatched roof.

*The rain sounds like tears.*

*Like my family weeping.*

Little Petyr sat cross-legged on Norland's rug, his ruddy cheeks flushed with warmth and excitement. He held a wooden toy in his small hands, carefully carved to resemble a gallant knight atop a steed. The knight's hand-painted shield bore a faded emblem, and Jonathan had shaped the wooden horse to mimic the graceful curves of a destrier.

Wrapped in a homespun blanket, Blanchette watched the boy play out a grand battle between his knight and an imaginary dragon. Absently, she ran her fingers over the blanket's threadbare material. Once, the blanket had been beautiful and vibrant, but now it was sun faded and worse for the wear. She enjoyed its warmth all the same.

Petyr's laughter rang out like a bell as he made the knight swing his sword.

"Look, Blanchette, look! Look, or you'll miss it! Sir Aldric is about to face the fearsome dragon of the Dark Woods." The wooden knight charged forward, the horse's hooves clattering on the rug.

Blanchette leaned in closer, her eyes following the imaginary duel. "Oh, I see him," she whispered. "Sir Aldric is a brave and noble knight indeed."

Petyr nodded vigorously. "The dragon breathes fire, but Sir Aldric is too fast. He dodges the flames and strikes the dragon's belly with his sword!" Petyr moved the knight and mimicked all the necessary sounds.

Blanchette felt herself being drawn into Petyr's world of make-believe. "Well, don't stop there. What happens next?"

Petyr's eyes gleamed as he continued. "The dragon roars in pain—*ROARRR!*—and runs into his cave. Sir Aldric is victorious!" He raised the wooden knight in triumph, his face beaming.

Blanchette managed a small smile. "Well done, Sir Aldric," she whispered. "You are a hero of great valor." She saw her brother, Willem, kneeling on the rug for a moment, his blond curls shimmering in the firelight. She blinked, and the vision disappeared, leaving behind Petyr and his unruly red hair again.

"Do you think he should rescue the princess from the dragon's cave?"

Blanchette's gaze fixed on the hearth's dancing flames. "That would be a noble quest, wouldn't it?" she said, her voice tinged with sadness. "To save a princess in distress."

Petyr nodded and flashed a gap-toothed smile, then went back to playing knights and dragons without a care.

Since the siege, Blanchette's emotions had ranged from sorrow to rage to a grim acceptance. And every dream had been flooded with shades of red and black—blood and the Black Wolf of Norland.

The monsters found her whenever she slept. She'd journey down into the earth, where her dead kin rested in her family's crypts. She would take shelter behind the stone statues and sometimes even inside the tombs.

But the Black Wolf would always find her. His eyes would

glow in the darkness as he stalked through her family's turf, his head held low, slobber and blood dripping from his powerful jaws. She'd wake as he pounced on her and went for her throat, crying out, her face wet with tears, night sweat everywhere—

"Ah, Petyr, it's time for bed," Jonathan said as he entered the home and shut the door behind him. The rain had drenched his shaggy-looking cloak. He peeled it off and flung it next to the hearth to dry. "Off with you now," he said, ruffling Petyr's curls. "Or you'll wear poor Blanchette's ears off with your chatter."

"Aw, alright. Good night, Pa. Good night, Blanchette."

Blanchette smiled at the small boy as he vanished into the back chamber with Sir Aldric in tow.

Jonathan set down a wooden basket and chuckled, shaking his head. "His enthusiasm is never-ending, and I'm afraid he's grown quite fond of you."

"And I of him," Blanchette said. "He reminds me of my little brother."

Sadly, he looked at her, then sank into a parallel rocking chair. This shared time together had become a ritual. Most nights, Jonathan would sit at her side, murmuring soft words and happy tales.

He'd rapidly become a friend and a blessing.

"The days are getting shorter." Jonathan's lighthearted voice shattered her thoughts. Her foot found purchase on the floor, and the chair stopped rocking. "You're looking better tonight, Blanchette," he continued when she said nothing.

She sucked in a long breath. "Well. I'm not feeling much better."

"I admire you. I do. I admire your strength."

She turned her gaze back to the fire. The flames leaped and cracked, bathing her body in warmth.

"Strength," she echoed, her voice distant to her own ears. "Strength, you say... yet I sit here, pitying myself while my family rots in the ground. I couldn't save them; I couldn't even save myself. I would have died if you had not fished me from the river. Strong is the very last thing I feel."

Rhythmic creaking filled the walls as Jonathan rocked in the chair. Blanchette wrapped her arms around her midsection—gave a slight wince at her sore muscles—then allowed herself to be lulled into a semi-relaxed state.

"May I tell you a story? If it pleases you?"

Blanchette nodded. She urged her chair into a calming sway that she kept in sync with Jonathan's voice. He had a charming accent she couldn't quite place. "Yes... I've always loved stories."

Jonathan nodded, his thin, weathered lips lifting into a smile. He rose from the chair and checked on the stew, stirring it with a satisfied grunt. "My wife and our daughter often attended the king's tourneys."

"You had a daughter?"

"Her name was Martha," he began, dropping some dried herbs into the stew and giving it another stir. "She was a talented seamstress." He waved nonchalantly at the rug with his free hand. "Colette died three winters back. Colette was our daughter." He stared blankly at the stew, and Blanchette watched as the steam curled his thinning hair. "Wasn't enough food to go around then, you see, and it was monstrously cold."

*His daughter had starved and froze to death.*

"Oh... I'm so sorry."

He cleared his throat and returned his attention to the stew. "As I said, we used to venture to the king's tourneys. Martha and I didn't care for them much, but Colette adored them. She loved the magic, the chivalry, the romance. Her favorite part wasn't the joust—no, Petyr fancied that most—but when the knights gave their favor."

Blanchette let her eyes slip shut as her mind reeled back to those thrilling days and nights. She could smell the dirt upheaved from the horses' hooves. She heard the clash and ring of armor, the crowd's cry, and the applause of a hundred hands coming together—a *realm* coming together, if only for one day.

She recalled riding to the tourneys with her queen mother, enclosed in a litter with curtains of crimson silk so delicate she could see right through them. They turned the world red. And when those draperies swayed, the world became altogether incoherent. The truth of Norland, the humanity of their capital, remained out of focus and hidden away.

The townsfolk would gather in the thousands to watch the games. The splendor of it always left her in awe—the shining armor, the shouts of the crowd, the banners snapping in the wind... and the knights themselves, the knights most of all.

What a simple time that had been.

"Colette was quite sad that day. See, she had a hound she loved dearly. The poor mutt drowned in the river that morning. She watched the joust through her tears... completely unmoved as the knights cantered out and clashed lances. Then the king mounted his horse and rode onto the field—a vision of shining armor, dust, and crimson silks. He pulled a handkerchief from under his gold gauntlet and tossed Queen Joanna his favor."

Blanchette nodded. She relaxed as the memories washed over her in a gentle tide. She remembered that day with absolute clarity. The colorful banners waving, the smell of dirt and grass and fine foods, the sound of merry chatter and beating hooves as lances came together in a rush of pleasure...

Yes, life had been so simple then. So simple and pretty and... *false.*

*Make-believe,* she thought as Petyr's wooden knight galloped through her mind.

"Queen Joanna stood in the pavilion, dressed all in white and looking like an angel. She waved the handkerchief for the crowd's pleasure. Her eyes came to Collette's from across the rows of seats that separated us. She smiled and weaved through the throng until she stood before my little girl. Colette just sat there, red-eyed and silent." A forlorn smile came to Jonathan's face. Blanchette felt herself holding her breath as he went on.

"The queen, bless her, curtsied before my daughter and

handed her the handkerchief." Blanchette watched as Jonathan smiled again, the lines around his eyes creasing. Then he went to his feet and opened a clay canister in the makeshift kitchen.

He pulled out the red handkerchief. "We've risked our lives keeping you here, true," he said, snaking the faded material between his fingers. "But the daughter of a lady like that—a lady like Queen Joanna... well, she's damn worth saving. And so are you, Your Grace."

# Five

"AS LITTLE RED RIDING HOOD was going through the wood, she met with a wolf, who had a very great mind to eat her up, but he dared not, because of some woodcutters working nearby in the forest. He asked her where she was going. The poor child did not know that it was dangerous to stay and talk to a wolf."

— Charles Perrault

It happened on the seventh day.

A knock blasted through the home that could've woken the dead. Each strike was laid with intent and strength. The sound pulled Blanchette from the depths of yet another nightmare.

She rose from the rock-hard bed, her body slick with sweat. She limped over to the door and eased it slightly open. The erratic pitter-patter of drumming feet and an excited voice echoed behind the door. Jonathan reprimanded Petyr and commanded him to settle down. The walls muffled his voice.

Petyr must have obeyed, because Jonathan opened the front

door a moment later. If he'd spoken a greeting, Blanchette didn't hear it.

"Pardon me. I hope I haven't disturbed you and your family." A deep, husky baritone resounded; the same force that laced the knock minutes before shivered through each of his words. Blanchette, too, found herself shivering... *but from what?*

"Not at all," Jonathan replied. "It's an honor to receive you, sir."

There was an exchange she couldn't hear. A shuffling of activity she couldn't see.

"My men have brought provisions. Food and goods," the man replied in that deep timbre. Excited chatter again from Petyr, followed by the clamor of heavy footsteps and overlapping voices. "Don't be afraid. He won't harm you or your child."

The soldiers had returned to ration out loot from her home. Her heartache darkened into anger.

She listened as Petyr hooted with delight.

Blanchette sucked in a breath and edged closer to the door. She nudged it open just slightly, looking into the home's heart. What she saw sucked another breath from her lungs; kneeling on the floor was a mountain of a man—one she recognized immediately... one who'd come to haunt her nightmares and terrorize her waking thoughts.

Her obsession.

The source of all her misery.

His wolf's helm, constructed from crude black metals, was pulled up, exposing his face to her. His eyes struck her the most, a light hazel drank in the sun that filtered through the window. They exerted kindness as he watched Petyr play with a wooden horse and pulley. His full lips even turned up into the semblance of a smile.

The child dragged the toy across the rickety floorboards, his laughter in the air. That black wolf was in the room, too, sitting quaintly beside its master and watching the child with a slight tilt. The scene might have been adorable in any other circumstance.

Jonathan smiled down at Petyr. Tears glittered in his eyes. "It's a pleasant sound to hear again, sir, my child's laughter. You couldn't have brought a more precious gift."

The Black Wolf nodded. A queer expression darkened those sharp, austere features. Shadows deepened his hazel eyes. Blanchette felt her breath quicken and the anger build. He was the reason for the doom of her family... the destruction of her home, and the loss of everything that had mattered.

It was all because of that monster.

She forced herself back inside the chamber and silently shut the door. Tears stung her eyes. She blinked them away and pressed her back against the wall, her heartbeat erratic. She curled her knuckles into her palms, feeling the signet ring cut into her skin.

"Do you have other children?" the Black Wolf asked in his deep, husky baritone. She felt his voice in her bones.

"No, no, sir."

The heavy pitter-patter of paws. Blanchette's stomach clenched as she heard a deep sniffing from underneath the doorjamb.

That demon wolf.

She edged away from the door, stumbling back. She slapped her palm over her mouth to seal off her erratic breathing.

Nails scratched at the wooden door.

The men's voices grew silent, then the wolf's howl filled that silence.

Feral. Haunting. Wild. Not of this world.

It was an eerie, human sound that caused her stomach to drop.

Then heavy footsteps headed straight for the door.

*The Black Wolf's coming for me.*

She curled her fingers into fists and raised them against her cheeks in a silent grimace. She choked back her scream. Bit her lip until the metallic flavor of blood filled her mouth.

Blanchette burst toward the window—but the Black Wolf

snatched the trail of her cloak. He reeled her to him, like a trout caught on a line, and dragged her bodily into the room.

Trembling from her anger, she glared straight into the Black Wolf's eyes.

His stare locked on her own. The wolf's lips curled, exposing its razor-sharp teeth. The creature was huge, well over two hundred pounds. Rowan silently set a hand on its back. The wolf quieted and sat beside him, its lantern-like eyes burning into Blanchette.

Absently, she heard Jonathan speaking. His words were a clumsy mess. "One of my daughters, sir. She hasn't been well. She's been resting in the chamber, see."

"You said you had the one child."

*You murdered my family—murdered everything I've ever loved.* A scream churned inside her. It rolled up into her throat like bile, but she choked it down.

The Black Wolf said nothing for what felt like minutes. The very air seemed to thicken with the tension. Blanchette struggled with the desire to take two steps back, but she stood tall and still, refusing to show fear in the face of her family's killer.

"You..." Her voice sounded hoarse and somewhat delusional.

The Black Wolf attempted a smile. "Come forward," he commanded in a voice she dared not deny. He reached out a hand gloved in kidskin and ran his fingers through her blond hair. Then his shrewd eyes—eyes that missed nothing—probed Jonathan's child.

"Even a blind man could see she lacks any resemblance to your son."

"No, I wouldn't suppose so. She's not of mine own blood, sir. A foster girl—"

"Yet she bears a striking resemblance to the late royal family. Why were you hiding from me, girl?" She said nothing. She bit her lip until blood filled her mouth again. "Now lower your red hood." Blanchette froze, unable to stir a limb. "That was not a request," the Black Wolf pressed on. The words shivered through her. He stood perfectly still as if made from stone. The wolf sat just as still, its attention riveted on her every breath, every movement. Its body was wound tight, like a coil ready to spring at the slightest provocation.

Blanchette inhaled a sharp breath and brought her fingers to the edge of the hood. She felt the hate seething in her stare. She flipped back the hood with a silent prayer.

"Just as I thought." The Black Wolf turned back to Jonathan. "Perhaps you know something I do not, my friend." No one dared to speak, so he went on. He walked around her—nay, he *prowled* around her—his fierce hazel eyes taking her in from head to foot, then back up again.

"My men have lined and fished that river since the boat capsized. Maybe half a dozen times. Her mother, fair Queen Joanna, had washed up ashore. No sign of Princess Winslowe has been discovered, however. Yet I see a blond beauty standing before me, who'd be just about the princess's age and aesthetic."

*He doesn't recognize me from all those feasts...*

Jonathan feigned a look of surprise that his innocent and honest nature hid poorly. "Princess? I... I don't believe so. It is quite news to me if she is. Look at her, sir. She is dressed in rags like a common peasant."

"Of course she is," the Black Wolf said dryly. "She's in disguise, as any lady with half a mind would do."

"Do you take the Black Wolf for a fool?" one of the soldiers said while the two others slowly drew swords from their scabbards.

The Black Wolf knelt beside Petyr, who clung to his father's trousers and hid his face there. "What's your sister's name, little one?"

Petyr said nothing, bless him.

"Drawing swords on an unarmed man and his children," Blanchette spat. "You call that justice?"

The Black Wolf rose to his full six-foot-five height. He swooped forward in a rush of movement and grabbed

Blanchette's trembling hand, which was half-buried under the red cloak. He held it up in midair as if he meant to kiss it before a first dance... but turned it slightly instead, so the signet ring twinkled traitorously in the morning light.

Blanchette felt her throat fall into her stomach. He started to slip the ring off her finger, but she jumped out of his wretched reach. She felt his eyes burning down at her, *into* her, and she returned his glare with equal hatred.

"You really are the princess."

He knew. They all knew.

And she felt liberated by that fact. "You stole everything from me, everything that I loved! You are worse than the stories say. No, you aren't a wolf. You are a monster."

The Black Wolf stared down at her for a long silence.

And he did not speak.

Everyone in the room seemed to hold their breaths; even the wind beyond the home ceased its rattling. After what felt like a lifetime, he said simply and with quiet authority, "I am neither wolf nor monster. I am Rowan Dietrich, and you are my prisoner."

She darted toward the door, her injured leg screaming from the pain.

Rowan said in a low, stern voice, "Seize her."

It happened in a flash of movement. One of his soldiers grabbed her arms and clasped them behind her back. The wolf went wild, snarling and snapping at her ankles in a frenzy. Its growl was thunder, volcanic and deep and black as the night.

She squirmed as they tied restraints around her wrists. When all her efforts failed, she contented herself with spitting in the Black Wolf's looming face.

She thought he might strike her. Instead, he gave a dark, rumbling laugh void of humor or mirth. Chills raced down her spine. He wiped away the spit with a gloved finger, his gaze staring her down like daggers. Tears pricked her eyes, but she blinked them back, refusing to shed them in the face of her enemy.

His voice was calm and steady, though an undercurrent of hatred spilled through his words. "You'll live to regret that, Princess." He turned his eyes on his men as she struggled against their iron hold. "Load her up," he said, speaking like she was another piece of cargo or plunder.

"Kill me and be done with it!" she screamed at him from the chamber of her raw throat and heart. "Kill me and be cursed!" She kicked at the soldiers, watching through a curtain of tears that blurred the towering monster in front of her. One soldier groaned and yelled a curse as her knee slammed into his groin.

"Feral bitch!"

The Black Wolf merely gave another rolling laugh.

"Kill me! Do it!" Blanchette's cry almost sounded like a plea. The self-loathing that filled her brought bile to her throat. She felt it bubble up and spill over her lips. Her breaths shortened, and a trembling rage shook her to the marrow of her bones.

Even worse, she felt her grandmother's disappointment from beyond her grave.

"Black Wolf! Kill me as you murdered my brother!"

That provoked a reaction from him. His eyes hardened into two ice chips. Blanchette shivered from their coolness. "I didn't lay a finger on your brother. Of that, my hands are clean. I am no murderer. I am a liberator."

"Liberator? Clean?" Her anger mounted to a boil, and she shook from the force of it. "There is nothing clean about you. You have lived as a monster and shall die as one, maybe by my hand. The only thing you inspire in others is treachery. That's the name of your legacy since you left my father's army!"

"Maybe I shall die at your hand. But not today." He turned to Jonathan; his mouth set into a wolfish grin. "Gag her and arrest this traitor. Bring his child to the orphanage but see that no harm comes to him. He's a ward of Norland now," he commanded his men in a growl that rang true to his name. A soldier forced a musty, damp cloth between her teeth and vomit-covered lips, silencing her. She supposed it should have angered her, but a queer sense of relief washed over her.

Finally, she could rest.

She watched as the Black Wolf's soldiers collected the child she'd come to care about, watched as Jonathan slid her a heartfelt goodbye and was restrained, watched as the wolf trailed after its master, understanding the hunt was over.

She fought her body's desire to faint dead away. Her house's words echoed inside her like a war cry. They sheathed her in sentimental armor.

*This can't be.*
*This isn't how it's supposed to end.*
*I had promised... I promised.*

Blanchette glanced at Petyr, who looked utterly confused and lost—*how could his hero do this?*—and then she looked forward and to her fate.

*I promise.*

---

BLANCHETTE RETURNED to a home she no longer knew or recognized, surrounded by walls that no longer barred an enemy but housed one.

Banners hung from the walls bearing the sigil of the Black Wolf.

A brazier burned off to the side, its flames licking the image of a snarling wolf. Blanchette trembled at the sight and lurched upright. She was in one of the extra chambers serving as her cell.

*Foreign,* she thought, as her boots touched the stones. *No longer my soil,* her mind reaffirmed with each step, her gaze warily taking in the changes. They were both big and small. Some could be seen at a glance; others would only be noticed by someone who'd lived here all their lives.

She'd expected the door to be locked. Her heart thumped in alarm as the handle answered to her hand and turned.

She nearly walked straight into the guardsman posted outside the room. His eyes reminded her of two dirty patches of ice; his skin had a leathery way about it and was spotted with brown freckles, his thin hair a dirtier brown. That stare was hostile. Even the Black Wolf's gaze hadn't matched it.

*He hates me.*

He grabbed her shoulder with a mailed hand. She winced from the grip, which felt like an iron manacle. "About time. Come."

"Get your hands off me."

"Sir Rowan demands your attendance. You've kept him waiting long enough."

Blanchette bit back her curse, not wanting to tempt how that mailed fist would feel against her cheek. "You must beg his forgiveness for me," she spat, even as his eyes sharpened at her defiance. "I've no desire to look upon the face of my family's killer."

He snapped then. "I'm no killer. I'm Sir Edrick, Rowan Dietrich's right-hand man and captain." She felt that mailed hand as it latched onto her arm in a painful, viselike grip. She gave a shallow scream, sure her bone would snap in two from the pressure.

"And you are fortunate I'm so obedient to Rowan's commands," he said, his voice a whip. "Were it up to me, I'd have you drawn and quartered before the kingdom."

Her stomach roiled at his words, and her skin broke out in goose pimples as he drew nearer. The heat of his breath fell upon her, its scent tinted with ale. "I took the innocence of one of your ladies the night your home fell, you know," he said, whispering as if the words were an endearment. "She cried out for you. Does that make your heart weep, Princess?"

*Oh God... Elise.*

*I am lost.*

"You disgust me. You are no knight, not even a man. You are nothing but a cold-blooded murderer. And *I* shall have you drawn and quartered the first day I come into my throne."

He laughed at that, a harsh, joyless sound. Her blood ran cold as his grip tightened, and he pushed her against the closed chamber door. The hot sting of his breath scorched her neck, and the door's coarse wood dug into her flesh. A little cry escaped her.

"Your family were the murderers, Princess. An entire kingdom starved and bled beneath their negligence and iron heels. But the Black Wolf has changed all of that. You're in a new world now. Our world. So you best wake up. You are a princess of nothing, the third and last of your name, a prisoner in your own home, and another disgrace to your family's legacy. Now come."

---

SIR EDRICK BROUGHT Blanchette to her father's solar. The fabled Black Wolf of Norland lurked behind the massive oaken writing desk, sifting through her family's ledgers and personal letters.

The actual black wolf she'd seen during the battle and inside Jonathan's home sat beside the man. It was beautiful. Deadly looking. And very protective of its master. The creature lowered its head, its lantern-like eyes fixed on her. She carefully treaded inside, the wolf measuring her every movement. It rose to its feet and emitted a low warning growl that pricked the hair on her arms.

*Demons. The two of them.*

"Stand down," Rowan whispered, and the wolf quieted its growling and glanced up at its master expectantly.

Sunlight shimmered through the window, illuminating the hard lines of Rowan's face. She observed him without his knowing—taking in the tension that furrowed his dark brows and how he'd absently curse and scratch at the dark stubble on his chin. He'd lower his hand every few moments and stroke the wolf's dark fur.

She would have fled the room had the captain not hovered directly behind her—a flesh-and-blood shield.

A heavy, four-poster bed dominated the room, surrounded by linen hangings. Her father's oak chests sat in front of the bed, and a flock of carved ravens adorned the wooden stakes. *A bed fit for a king.* Rushes were strewn underfoot: an exotic blend of basil, balm, chamomile, costmary, daisies, lavender, marjoram, and mint.

There was also a bench and a table bearing a silver flagon and cups. The Black Wolf's hauberk gleamed on a stand of crossed ash-poles with his snarling helm secured at the top. The furniture was heavy and ornately carved, its colossal size balancing the room's dimensions. Beneath it all lay a brightly patterned octagonal rug. Winslowe Castle was a seat that represented domain and power. Blanchette reluctantly admitted that Rowan Dietrich sat it well.

That queasy feeling rose inside her again.

"My Lord, I've brought the girl as you requested."

*The queen,* she amended. She had to bite her tongue from screaming it.

The Black Wolf's attention snapped from whatever he was reading.

Sitting in her father's solar among her family's possessions and most private correspondences, he made a jarring sight. Anger simmered inside her, and holding her tongue took every ounce of restraint.

He stood and wheeled around the writing desk, his broad body blocking the sunlight through the window. For a moment, the light transformed him into a formidable silhouette—a dark cloud shielding the sun. The wolf tracked his steps. Its wise, yellow eyes missed nothing. "Wait outside the solar, Edrick. We shall discuss our plans after."

The captain gave a curt nod, then threw Blanchette a pointed look and obeyed the command.

She gave a mocking, delicate curtsy, moving with a sophistication she knew Rowan could never equal. She wanted him to feel unclean. Like a true invader. "Shall I address you as sir? The Black

Wolf? My Lord? Your Grace? Your identity seems to change quicker than I change my smallclothes."

He gave a small, crass smile that she didn't like at all. "The Black Wolf has a nice ring to it."

Blanchette stood a little straighter and forced herself to meet Rowan's piercing hazel eyes. She tried not to pay attention to the wolf at all, lest she lose her nerve. "I see. Well, you *are* a lord now by right of conquest. I'm sure that brings you great satisfaction."

He crossed his arms over his wide chest and measured her with his gaze. Those eyes were like hands, and she could feel them on her body. "I am a lord and was always a lord and not the first lord of my house. And by right of conquest, I am king of Norland, should I choose it."

Blanchette swallowed against the lump rising in her throat. "I shall never kneel for you."

"And I shall never bow to you," he parried. The wolf wheeled around his body. Rowan absently placed a hand on its back, like a soldier placing a hand on his sword's pommel. "Though you did just curtsy for me," he murmured, that cruel smile making another appearance.

Her body vibrated with disgust. She wanted to yell a thousand obscenities, to tear this monster apart with her words, if not her hands. Instead, she felt tears wash up and into her eyes.

Her voice shook as she spoke. Raw emotion broke up her sentences. "You sit there at my father's study, your hands still wet with his blood. You were supposed to be his friend! Now, you stand before me," she said as he looked down at her. "H-how can you? How could you do this? Why did you even call me here? Why am I still alive?"

He came forward, his long legs eating up the distance between them in a few swift strides. The wolf kept pace beside him, its massive paws barely making a sound. *Like a ghost,* she thought with a shiver. "I wanted to see how you're faring. You were limping."

"*What?* You are mad."

He reached out and lightly rested his hand on her leg. She winced backward.

"Perhaps I am mad," he said with a shrug. "Your injury. Let me see it."

"Wh-what?"

"Your leg. Let me have a look at it. My patience is limited, unlike my authority."

She withdrew from his touch, her hands trembling from the force of her emotions.

"So be it. If it's infected, let it rot off."

She studied him with a level gaze, her eyes never leaving his own, as her right hand slowly lifted the hem of her dress. His eyes moved away from hers. He dropped to a knee and examined her leg, gently running his fingertips over the healing skin. She'd expected pain and harshness yet was met with tenderness. The deftness of his touch shocked her. "Slightly red," he murmured to himself. "Looks to be healing." The Black Wolf sighed, and she felt his hot breath fan against her thigh. She tensed, and her cheeks flushed.

Good God, she felt lightheaded.

Rowan came to his feet and rubbed at the stubble on his chin. Blanchette slowly dropped the material of her dress, her heartbeat pounding.

"You loathe me. I understand that," he said in a slow, careful voice. "You desire to avenge your family. I respect that. And I understand that too. It's not my desire to see you suffer any more than you already have. Your father did not die from my greed but from his own."

She burned to scream at him, to rush to the desk, where she knew her father stored gilded daggers and dirks... to thrust a blade through his eye or throat, then give a little twist for good measure.

She knew all that was a foolish fantasy. It would get her nowhere. She had to play the complacent and dejected captor while plotting her revenge and escape.

*It's the only way... the one way I can keep my promise.*

His boots thundered as he strode over to the studded door. A metallic groan sounded as he raised the crossbar and swung it open, then addressed his captain, who stood guard just outside. "We'll be wanting a hot meal and some refreshments. Call the healer as well to check on her wounds. And hurry."

"You keep great company. How long has he been your captain?" she spat, not even wanting to speak the vile man's name.

"Edrick has been with me since the beginning," he replied.

"The beginning? Beginning of what?"

He paused, his eyes climbing up and down her body in a lazy perusal. "What do you know of the Black Wolf? What do you know of me?"

Blanchette hesitated, her ignorance hitting her at full force.

*Play the game.*

*But how can I play a game when I don't even know the rules?*

That terrified her beyond comprehension.

She swallowed, then absently toyed with her signet ring. The sigil seemed to drink in the hearth's fire, setting the stones and gold ablaze. Her thoughts darkened uncontrollably; an image of her grandmother's stabbed chest... Elise's neck slit like a slaughtered deer... of her brother's mutilated body and her drowned mother.

"I know you have bled my home," she said in a low whisper. She didn't even reach his shoulders. The Black Wolf had the widest chest she'd ever seen, with hard, dark features that took on an almost boyish quality in some moments. He held himself with pride, yet an unmistakable weight lurked in those hazel eyes. "Your captain defiled and murdered my lady-in-waiting. She was only a girl and a dear friend to me."

Something flickered in his gaze, but it vanished as quickly as it had appeared. He waved her off with a deep sigh and turned to the hearth. "You shall have another lady-in-waiting. Two, three, four, if it pleases you. It makes no matter to me."

"It mattered to me!" she shot, her voice choked. "Have you so little regard for human life? Of course you don't. Look at the blood you've shed over one evening. Many of my father's men still rot in gibbets, while others melt away in the black cellars. You have taken everything from me."

She watched with silent anger and awe as the hearth's flames licked over his granite features. A lifetime of war and battles, of loss and labor had hewn them, she knew, yet her heart held no room for pity.

He gave a curt nod as if completing some inward conversation, then jolted toward her. "This is the way of war. Your father knew this better than anyone. And now he has borne the consequences of his hunger—his desire for power. Blood for blood. Is that not what the wise men say?"

She shook her head. "The wisest men say turn the other cheek. Words you clearly have never followed."

He released a dark chuckle that sent a shiver down her spine. She shuddered uncontrollably but refused to stand down.

"My father—"

"Look around you, girl; look beyond the capital's walls and your bedchamber. Look further than you have ever before, you poor blind chit. Your kingdom was *already* bleeding because of your father, not I. Beyond these walls live women and children and boys and babes. You may not know their names or have ever seen their faces, but they were at your father's mercy, nonetheless. And just because they are strangers doesn't make their suffering less real."

Abruptly, he strode to the window. She watched him with a quickening resentment as he examined his newly gained castle, its landscape kissed with the pink glow of a new day. He looked at it all as if it belonged to him.

*Mine.*

*My birthright.*

Blanchette forged her expression into one of hard iron. "You shall pay for this. We have powerful alliances. *You* are the blind one. My sister is the Queen of Demrov—"

The Black Wolf's great barking laugh made Blanchette's skin

ripple. He smiled, showing a flash of straight white teeth. "Has your governess taught you nothing? You've been living under a rock, Princess. Demrov just suffered another invasion. They are also bleeding from the gut and grappling with France. And, as I understand it, you haven't seen your sister in years, since shortly before her coronation. You have been living beneath a cairn built of privilege and oblivion. You are a little girl, living a small life built from lies and fantasy."

"I'm living as your captive!" Blanchette retorted, the heat rising in her cheeks. "And how dare you call my father a tyrant when you've taken our home by force—by murder! When you've lain conquests across all of Norland since you were little more than a boy!"

Any good humor she'd seen in his face moments ago faded like a setting sun. He put a smile on again, but it didn't fit. His eyes grew cold. He closed the distance between them again in a few determined strides.

"You are so very young and ignorant," he said matter-of-factly. "I pity you. Truly." He whispered the words as if awakening her to a deep, dark secret. One she'd been in denial about. His voice sounded flat and emotionless, yet something cold moved in his eyes. It gave her a sudden chill, and she staggered back a foot despite herself.

"Maybe so. But you are old and bitter." In truth, he didn't look a day past his mid-thirties, but she flung the words at him all the same. He received them well, with a wolfish smirk that befitted his name. When he grinned, it was slightly crooked and wholly mischievous.

"So here we stand—a young, stupid princess and an old and bitter knight. What a delightful pair we make."

A long silence. The wolf stirred at Rowan's side.

"I ask again. Why am I still standing here at all? Why haven't you executed me? You've torn out my whole family. What's the blood of one more *stupid* princess on your hands to you?"

*EVERYTHING,* Rowan thought, his eyes fixed on her with a fascination that alarmed him. She had grown uneasy under his perusal, but the fire he'd quickly come to know never faded from her gaze. Those eyes were an ocean-like blue with tiny flecks of gold visible only from an intimate nearness.

He stood that close to her now. Too close, yet she refused to back down. He felt Smoke slide against his leg. Rowan passed a calming stroke over the wolf's long, lean back. The beast bristled under his palm.

He tried to recall seeing her at Bartholomew's feasts and tourneys. *She'd been a girl then.* A beautiful woman stood before him now. Blanchette Winslowe had a smattering of freckles across the bridge of her nose as if some fairy had placed them there on a whim. Large, expressive eyes, with lashes as golden as her hair, filled her face. She'd been raised behind the walls of her father's castle since birth, under the strict instruction of her governesses; the glow of untapped and untouched innocence stirred something dark in him... a hunger for something he didn't know he craved.

As a commander and a lifelong soldier, Rowan had a way of recognizing strength and perseverance at a glance. There was a fineness in her, a loyalty and courage that commanded his instant respect and attention. She'd not be disregarded or controlled as easily as he'd believed.

And he enjoyed a challenge.

"What do you plan to do with Jonathan and his child?" she suddenly asked, her voice cutting off his focus. Her tone sounded accusatory, and her eyes echoed the sentiment. He saw that fire stir there, simmering, simmering, simmering, melting away the frosty blue of her eyes. The warrior in him marveled at its heat.

"What would you have me do? He's committed treason."

"Will he get a traitor's death, then?"

Rowan hesitated, understanding that his following words

would shape their dynamic indefinitely. He'd need her as an ally, however impossible that might be. Executing a man who'd risked his life and his family's for her wouldn't likely win any affection.

"Tell me... what would your father have done?"

He saw she had a retort ready but bit it back. Her gaze lowered, and she inhaled a long breath. The exhale steamed in the cold air. Meddling idly with the sleeves of her dress, she finally admitted, "He would have executed him and made a show of it. He'd be drawn and quartered, pieces of him rotting in gibbets outside the castle as we speak."

Rowan rubbed his chin thoughtfully, calculating his following words, his next move, his best forward strategy. He paced to the desk and filled a glass to the brim. He drank deeply from his goblet, perhaps to drown his shame.

"You ought to drink with me, Princess. It can bring you some peace," he said, drinking from his goblet with a shrug. "For a little while, anyway."

Reluctantly, she reached for her goblet. Slender fingers wrapped around the silver cup, her signet ring flashing in the hearth's glow. She drank deep as her eyes never parted from his. Impressively, she drained half of the goblet. Rowan felt a smile crawl across his lips.

Her eyes flashed, unamused. "There is only one thing that could bring me peace."

Rowan felt a shudder move through his body. Her gaze held firm on his, full of dark loathing and bitter heartache.

He knew those feelings all too well.

He'd seen that look every time he glanced in a looking glass.

"And what is that?"

Blanchette looked away and closed her eyes. Rowan took the chance to admire her without restraint. The way her long fan of lashes rested against her porcelain skin and the dusting of freckles that covered her high cheekbones—one which was scarred quite badly.

Her pert features drew tight, and she visibly cringed at the pull of the scar on her cheek. Her eyes snapped open again, and that anger returned in full force. "You owe me more debts than I care to name. But let's start with Jonathan, shall we?"

"He will stay my prisoner for the time being. And he shall remain unharmed. You have my word."

*The word of a traitor*, her eyes said. But she nodded, the gesture not reaching her gaze. "And... and what about me? Shall I be kept as your prisoner in my own home?"

He'd never be the lord of Winslowe Castle as long as she lived. Not truly.

He gazed down at her, transfixed by the forwardness of her stare, watching the rise and fall of her breasts as she awaited his reply. The longer that silence stretched, the more her resolve appeared to weaken. Something visibly snapped in her. Her chin lowered, and her long, honey-dipped lashes veiled her eyes. Rowan set two fingers under her chin and tilted her head back. Her eyes slowly opened again, and tears glittered there. His heart churned at the sight.

But his anger also awakened.

"You are too valuable," he said, the tips of his fingers lingering on her chin. That small patch of flesh felt as warm and smooth as fresh-spun silk. "And I'm no murderer. You shall remain under my protection if you don't give me or my men reason to subdue you."

"Your captain," she said. "The man who brought me here. He is a monster. I told you what he did to my lady. Why do you have him at your side?"

*She lies.* Rowan stared at her for a long silence. "He's been with me since the beginning... nay, before that. He is hard, cold steel. This is true... but I've seen the good in him. The loyalty."

"Loyalty?" She spat the word like it was an obscenity.

"Yes, loyalty. I've always fought to see the light in others, to see the good. It's why he's by my side and why I was by your father's for so many years. But as the seasons turn... well, seeing that good is getting more difficult as the world grows darker."

"That's one thing we can agree on."

An image from moments before came to mind: Rowan kneeling beside her, his breaths fanning on her milk-white thigh.

Then the door burst open. Rowan jumped away from the girl as if he'd been committing some cardinal sin.

Two guards entered, carrying an injured soldier between their bodies, who looked like Christ being dragged from his cross. The wounded man's arms were spread wide, wrapped around either side of the guards' necks. His head lolled as blood streamed down his pale face.

Rowan crossed the solar in three great strides and instinctively stood before the men in a battle-ready stance. His palm wrapped his sword's wolf pommel.

"Sir Harrison," Rowan said, his teeth gritted. "How did this happen?"

"Just outside the castle," one man replied. "A Winslowe soldier."

"That will kill him. I've no doubt." The voice came from behind Rowan, solid and confident in its airy tone. "The wound shall fester, and he will die before the week's end." Blanchette held her head high and her gaze steady. The only giveaway of her nerves was her trembling hands, which grasped the back of the chair and fiddled with the ornate wood. "He needs a salve made from kingswood. It grows in the forest, along the riverbank—"

"I bet it does." The guards exchanged angry looks. "Do you take us for a couple of idiots?"

"Kingswood, you say?" Rowan asked, waving at his men to be quiet. She nodded with urgency.

"Sir, it's clearly a trick to rid you of one of your most valuable captains."

"Maybe so." Rowan turned back to the girl, admiring how her golden hair shimmered in the afternoon's light and the quiet fire in her eyes. "And maybe not."

"I speak truly," she reaffirmed. "Is it unfathomable that I'd want to ease a man's suffering? You are welcome to disregard my words and let him die. It's no matter to me," she snapped, mocking his earlier words. "It'd serve you well."

He stared into her eyes, unsure of what he was searching for. He expected her to squirm and back down, but instead, she held his gaze. "Fine. I'll permit you to check the stores," Rowan answered. "Under guard, of course."

He saw plainly that she didn't like that, and it took every ounce of her willpower not to object.

She exhaled audibly, then stepped past Rowan and near to the soldier. He felt the breeze of her body whisper by and the subtle scent it carried. She waved her hand toward him, her eyes blazing with a heat Rowan could feel. "Get a poultice on that wound, or your captain shall bleed to death on my father's floor."

---

Torchlight shimmered off the walls as Rowan and Edrick traveled down the winding stairs to the training yard. Smoke padded off into the shadows.

"Did you harm her lady-in-waiting?" When Edrick said nothing, Rowan grabbed his collar and slammed him into the wall. "Tell me the truth of it."

Edrick studied Rowan with a steady gaze, his expression unreadable. As it always was. Rowan often valued that skill when they bargained with the enemy, yet he despised it now.

Edrick vibrated with a quiet, barely restrained tension. His eyes were always a little too probing, his brows drawn too tight, and his lips sealed against harsh counsel. The only restlessness he ever showed was his right hand. It constantly felt for the pommel of his sword and seemed most at ease when resting there. Rowan had known Edrick since they were boys. Sometimes he hardly recognized the man his captain had become. "Of course not. I did as you commanded. Many died that night."

Rowan loosened his hold on Edrick's collar and stepped back.

He continued moving through the castle halls and signaled his captain to follow. "Death is the way of war, and blood is oft the price of liberation. But that's not what I'm asking. Did you defile and murder Princess Blanchette's lady-in-waiting?"

Edrick met his gaze, and his words came easily. He laid a hand on Rowan's sleeve and said, "Nay, Rowan. My focus was on killing your foes, not whetting my lust."

Rowan considered him for a moment, his thoughts traveling back several decades.

"Forgive me, my lord," Edrick interrupted as if reading his thoughts. "Forgive my audacity, but I was there all those years ago. I stood by your side. I know what *they* did to your wife. Even worse, I saw what it did to you." Edrick moved his hand away from Rowan's sleeve. "I would never betray you like that. Not your family's memory. Not in an entire lifetime. The girl is angry and clearly sowing the seeds of discord."

Rowan nodded, abashed with a sudden shame. He placed his hand on Edrick's shoulder and squeezed, returning the sentiment. "I know. Forgive me."

Edrick stepped away. A solemn look crept to his weathered face. "There are important matters for us to discuss."

"The girl." Rowan shrugged and continued walking. "She may prove useful to us. She knows the castle better than anyone."

*Better than anyone who's still alive.*

"Maybe so... but to the people of Norland, she is still their princess—their heir. Especially if you refuse a coronation. They favor her. God help them, but they do. I've talked to men and women. She's a stronger symbol than the Black Wolf."

They crossed a stone bridge and stopped in the middle. Rowan sighed and glanced at the soldiers sparring in the bailey and the lush wood beyond the castle. He locked gazes with a guardsman manning the watchtower. Rowan nodded, then looked back out at the dense trees.

*Smoke is probably in there now, hunting for prey.*

Suddenly, Rowan felt the weight of the castle above and around him. He felt each stone pressing down, smothering his heart and mind beneath the burden. How he wished he could vanish into the wood as easily as Smoke. To lose his way, run from all this horror, and live away from the bloodshed...

He glanced up at the battlements and dark turrets of the castle, knowing the ghosts of Winslowe Castle would follow him anywhere he went.

*There is no escape.*

"What am I supposed to do with the rest of my days?" he whispered to Edrick. "Sit on a throne and listen to the misgivings and schemes of a thousand men? I thought this... this victory might bring me solace."

"Both of us have lived as soldiers, and we shall die as soldiers. Arrange a war council. Let them sit in your stead. Your destiny, Rowan, is not to be king, not to waste away the hours scheming and hearing trifle misgivings. You are a conqueror. We've captured Norland—"

"*Liberated Norland*, you mean."

"Yes, we've liberated Norland and made her ours. We shall garrison here," Edrick said, waving to the horizon. "It's a superior spot for our councils and scouting the coastal villages and ports."

"And what of the girl?"

Edrick shook his head. "We have two options as I understand it," he said calmly. "We can either execute her, or you can wed and bed her. You either claim your place through fear or through an alliance. Keeping her alive is dangerous, Rowan." A warning sharpened his voice.

Rowan shook his head, his gaze riveted on the nearby village. Black smoke spewed from a chimney, and the church steeple jutted into an overcast sky. He could make out the townsfolk as they went about their business.

"No, Edrick. I shall not execute her. I will not bring more brutality to a kingdom that's only known winter and bloodshed."

*There must be another way.*

# Six

Blanchette lay on the feather mattress and stared at the ceiling. She examined the cracks and crevices interweaving in the ancient stonework. A spider scurried across the ceiling's length, disappearing into an indentation. How she wished she could vanish with such ease... but hiding from this horror would get her nowhere. It'd be a betrayal to her family.

Groaning, she adjusted her sore leg. She lifted two fingers to her face and tracked the raised scar. It'd already healed quite cleanly.

Would her heart ever do the same?

She sat up and averted her gaze to the pinkening horizon. The rain and wind sounded thin and wild, gasping with a sharp northern winter on its breath. She glanced at her hands, which were gripping her bedsheet, and noticed they were trembling. She studied her palms and the fine lines spanning them. She hardly recognized her own hands. And that terrified her.

She was a prisoner in every sense of the word and felt stupidly afraid. The drugging effects of battle fever had now worn off, and the ashes had settled, leaving a stark reality in their wake.

And an acute loneliness.

She felt that most of all.

*I am all alone now...*

A hard knock disrupted her thoughts. She turned to the door, her heart racing from the sudden bang. The knock came again, followed by Sir Edrick's slick and booming voice. "I have need of you." She cringed and cursed as she swept on her cloak.

She clasped the garment, needing to shield herself from Edrick in any capacity she could. Then she yanked open the door, her skin already prickling from the prospect of speaking to him. He stood in his customary stance—feet planted wider than his hips, one hand preemptively on his sword's pommel. His eyes glinted with a dislike that rivaled her own.

"What do you want?" she asked in a clipped tone while she stood a little straighter and matched his stance. In her mind's eye, she heard Elise's cries and pleas.

*My dear friend.*

She felt the weight of her arms as they shared that last goodbye.

Edrick remained in stony silence. At last, he stepped aside.

Tears sprang to Blanchette's eyes—but, for once, they were tears of joy.

Her governess was dressed like she always had dressed and looked as Blanchette had always remembered her—a high-necked black dress, matching wimple, her face as sharp as an axe, and an ornate silver cross hanging from her neck. Blanchette charged forward, bursting past Edrick, and threw her arms around Governess Agnes's slight body.

"Oh, my dear girl," her governess said as she frantically smoothed down Blanchette's curls. "My dear, dear girl... sweet, sweet, Blanchette..." Blanchette returned the affection. Tears spilled from her eyes, and she gripped Agnes Belfort tighter as if the gesture might prevent her from being stolen again. "Good Lord, thank you... thank you... I had hoped and prayed... I had prayed for you, for this, Blanchette... that you still lived..."

"I survived. Whether I'm living... well, that's questionable.

How-how did *you* make it through everything? I was so sure you were dead," Blanchette said.

"I was sure I was going to *be* dead," she replied in her regal French accent. "I hid in the chapel during the battle. God be good, no one thought to look there."

"The Black Wolf's men wouldn't think of the chapel," she murmured, looking hard at Edrick. He was trying to eclipse the moment—to steal the breath of happiness from this reunion. She saw it in every sinew of his body and how he'd partially drawn his sword.

He couldn't steal this from her, though. And Blanchette took pleasure in that fact. She turned back to Governess Agnes. She studied her governess—her gaunt skin and the heavy shadows under her eyes. A new fragility seemed to press down upon her. A terrible thought took hold. "Agnes... have—have you been in the chapel this whole time? Since the siege?"

Governess Agnes pursed her lips and gave a sharp nod. "God proved sustenance enough for me. The Black Wolf himself found me just this morning."

Rowan's visit to the chapel struck her as strange.

Blanchette glanced about the long, dim hallway, then up at Edrick. She grasped Governess Agnes's thin forearm and guided her inside the bedchamber. Quickly, she shut the door and heard the muffled roar of Edrick's heavy footsteps as he stormed off.

*Good,* she thought. *Take your anger with you and ride off a cliff.*

Governess Agnes lowered onto the edge of the mattress, and they both seated themselves.

She traced the scar on Blanchette's cheek with the whisper of a touch. "Who did this to you, Blanchette?"

Bile rose in her throat. Once again, she found herself back in her grandmother's privy, Thomas chasing her... his dagger ruthlessly raining down again and again.

"Thomas. I've known since I was a babe. He—God, he—"

"Yes, I remember him well." Governess Agnes seized Blanchette's hands and squeezed them affectionately.

Blanchette studied her governess's pale hands. Paper-thin flesh stretched over her skin like butter spread too thin over bread. She imagined her hands withering away... the flesh shriveled like rotten peel, leaving behind frail bones that would soon turn to dust.

She couldn't bear losing Governess Agnes.

Not after everything she'd endured.

"He got what he deserved. I made sure of it."

Blanchette felt Governess Agnes's stare as if she was digging for something hidden behind her faint smile. "If you want to talk about it... discuss that night, I am here, Princess. You can unburden yourself."

Blanchette scoffed, the bitterness rising within. "*Princess*... am I, truly?"

"No," Governess Agnes replied, her thin lips set into a line. "You are the queen."

Blanchette bit back a sudden laugh, then swatted at her tears. "I suppose I should be. Did he harm you in any way?"

"Edrick was rough and unkind, but no, he didn't harm me."

"No, I mean Ro—the Black Wolf."

Governess Agnes hesitated. "He was cordial. Even gentle." She pursed her lips again as if the words had left a foul aftertaste.

Blanchette gazed out the window. The world continued to unravel before her, a ball of yarn loosening, loosening, loosening. She heard the faint din of sparring swords clinking and Rowan's spirited commands. The sunset was in full effect now, blazing across Norland's sky in tones of pink and blood orange.

"I could barely stand," Governess Agnes said, "when he came to the chapel. I shrank against the wall and prayed to God with my face hidden in my hands. I couldn't bear to look at the man who'd destroyed your home." Her voice sounded feeble; its spirit was stolen not from physical deprivation but spiritual. Blanchette studied Governess Agnes's tightly drawn features and swallowed against the knot in her throat.

"What happened?"

"He carried me from the chapel and brought me to his solar." *You mean my father's solar,* she thought, that familiar rage bubbling inside her. "He urged me to drink water and had food brought from the kitchens. Then he sat and observed me. He watched me like he'd never seen my like before. And perhaps he hadn't."

"Did... did he speak to you at all?" she asked, recalling his somber and withdrawn disposition. He seemed to be a man of few words.

"Yes, as I cleared the plates of the food before me," Governess Agnes replied, the slightest hint of a smile tugging at her lips, "he asked about you. Well, about you and me. How long I'd been in your family's employ and what our relationship was like. Things of that nature."

"I see," Blanchette said, the lump rising in her throat again. She gazed out the window as her pulse raced. As far as she knew, Governess Agnes had never told her a lie; she was a woman of God, loyal and honest and stern but right in all things. She closed her eyes and inhaled a breath that rattled inside her chest. "Agnes... you've known—*you knew*—my family longer than I had. You lived here before I was born, stood at my crib, and guided me when I took my first steps."

"And I wouldn't have had it any other way."

"Did he deserve it?"

"Who, my dear?"

"My-my father. Us. What the Black Wolf did... was it *just*? Was it right? They call him 'the people's champion.'"

Governess Agnes exhaled a long, weary breath. She raised one of her thin brows and silently shook her head. "You, your siblings, your mother, blessed be their souls, are nothing like King Bartholomew. It's unfortunate such loving people had to live within his walls." She hesitated, visibly searching for the proper words.

"Please. Just tell me."

"I've known many royal ladies and men during my life. Never had I seen his like. He was cruel and self-righteous, my sweetling, and a great coward. We all reap what we sow. We are all subject to God's judgment. His judgment day had come, my child, and my heart breaks that you and your family had to suffer for it."

"The people—they seem to love him. Here, I am powerless. I am lost." Blanchette shook her head. "I must go. I must find a way to Demrov. The queen and king shall rally to my side. I know it. Queen Isadora is my sister, and Demrov is our ally. They can set things right again."

*But were things ever right?* Blanchette shoved the question from her mind.

"My dear child, you are the last of your family! That would be a treacherous journey—perhaps impossible. I'd go mad with worry. Please, do nothing so rash."

"What *would* you have me do, then?" Anger crept up on her like a storm cloud sliding across a summer sun. She heard the fear and love in Governess Agnes's voice. They were quite evident. But she heard something else, too, something that muffled all else. *Stop fighting, Blanchette. Stay captive in your own home and accept your fate.*

Governess Agnes must have read the hurt in her expression because she said, "You've always had a mind of your own. You were never one to sit idle. How many times I chased you through the bailey and courtyards and wood while your sister complacently worked at her embroidery with the other noble girls." She smiled a nostalgic smile, then softly touched Blanchette's cheek where her scar lay. Blanchette raised her own hand and placed her palm over Governess Agnes's. "Your mother was intelligent and fierce. And you are very much your mother."

Two pike-wielding guards flanked Blanchette as she strode through the drafty corridors of Winslowe Castle. Light snow dusted the hexagonal-shaped windows and threw slanted prisms across the floor. Everywhere she looked, Black Wolf standards prowled where Winslowe's ravens once flew.

In her mind's eye, the great hall transformed into a glittering court again—a promising and promiscuous realm of flirtation and intrigue. The scent of honeysuckle and nightshade still lingered in the air; airy laughter filled the walls, and once again, she was home. She saw her mother and sister whispering to each other, her brother, Willem, racing through the crowd of people, much to Governess Agnes's distress. And she saw herself hiding behind a tapestry, watching court life unfold from her own little corner of the world. But when she looked about herself, the castle resembled a limbo. Rowan's men had stripped it of its tapestries and royal standards. Now, it lay before her—naked, vulnerable, and without an identity.

Where was she? At court in Winslowe Castle? Or in the Black Wolf's prison?

*His den, more like.* She shivered.

Then she turned a corner and saw the Black Wolf's banner hanging from a mantel, covering her family's royal crest.

More importantly, who was *she*?

*A princess, a queen... or a wolf's prey?*

※

Later that day, Blanchette knelt before a wounded soldier as the weight of the great hall pressed down on her. Her nerves were a mess while she poked the needle through a soldier's skin and then pulled it through. Ghosts from a lifetime ago rose around her—the lively din of a thousand feasts, the music of drunken laughter, and the clattering of goblets and fists pounding on the oaken tables.

She glanced up into the gallery and saw musicians holding

vielles and lutes. Their sweet melodies echoed in the cavernous room.

She heard her mother's laughter most of all. She listened to the melodic ring of her voice as she and her brother catapulted sweet cakes at one another. Her queen mother would halfheartedly scold them, an ever-present smile lurking beneath that frown.

"May I ask you," she said to the soldier while she continued her needlework. "Why do you follow him? You lay before me, gravely wounded. You were prepared to give your life for the Black Wolf. You were ready to sacrifice everything. Why? You were part of my father's guard since I was a child. Why make such a sacrifice?"

The soldier groaned and sat up as if something prideful in him insisted he take charge of his body. He studied the Black Wolf's banner that hung before them. "That sigil," he said, his voice fraught with pain as Blanchette continued tending to his wound. "Before Rowan Dietrich, that sigil was a gray wolf. The Black Wolf came into being about a decade ago. He's the very reason my children are alive. And that's a debt I'll spend the rest of my life paying."

An hour later, Blanchette collected a candle from the table, lit its wick, and left the great hall with determined steps. A wicker basket hung from her shoulder.

The flame bathed her face and danced across her taut features. She should have taken the stone staircase and returned to her chamber. Instead, Blanchette veered off into a dark hallway, where she was instantly grateful she'd brought the candle.

As she rushed by various rooms—the kitchens, the scullery, the larder, the buttery—voices clapped through the otherwise still castle like thunder. Every time she turned a corner, Blanchette held her breath, expecting to run into one of the Black Wolf's pike-wielding soldiers. Luck seemed to be on her side for once.

The candleholder trembled in her grip as she grew closer to her destination. Her eyes studied the ancient stone walls, searching, searching...

A slight indentation—an irregularity only visible to someone who knew where to find it—caught the corner of her vision. She glanced over her shoulder—then over the other one—and looked down the long corridor. She switched the candleholder to her left hand and steadied her grip. With her right hand, she reached for the jutting wall slab—a secret door—and pried it open.

She wedged inside the passage.

Her candle illuminated what would have been pitch darkness. Blanchette ventured down the black tunnel. She'd only been down here once while playing as a child. She'd never forget the terror she'd felt, the sensation of being swallowed by a black beast. The air was damp and heavy with the scent of age-old secrets, each step echoing in the abyss. The tunnel's walls were impenetrable, designed to be completely soundproof.

The tunnel's walls were not merely solid but formidable. They'd muffle any prisoners' screams.

She felt those walls pressing down on her now, a palpable darkness that choked all sight and sound. After about a hundred feet, she reached a fork. She took the left path and felt the ground slope beneath her feet, leading her deeper into the bowels of the castle. She imagined she was inside a colossal sleeping dragon, rushing through his long, spindly neck, seeing only the flicker of light through clenched, needle-like teeth.

Muffled talking—barely audible over the beat of her own heart—jarred Blanchette from her thoughts. She rounded a sharp corner and finally reached her destination. Three sconces flashed brightly within the dark chamber of cells, casting a glow in the otherwise black belly.

Blanchette rushed to the first cell, her heartbeat pounding in her ears. Jonathan was crouched in the far corner, his arms wrapped around upright knees.

"Jonathan." He stirred from his sleep at the sound of her voice, then rose onto wobbly legs.

He looked disoriented. His eyes resembled two open wounds, and his characteristic smile was buried beneath sallow skin.

Anger, rage, resentment—the full force of it all—roiled inside her gut. He stumbled to the front of the cell and grabbed the iron bars.

"Blanchette? Good God, you are a welcomed sight."

She forced a smile, then passed a flask of water and a heel of bread through the bars. "As are you, my friend. Here."

He took them and immediately downed the flask.

"Slow down. Please, not all of it at once. I'm not sure when I can return."

Wiping his cracked lips on his sleeve, Jonathan said, "Aye... where is he?"

Blanchette hesitated. "Your child is well. I promise you."

"Where is he?" he asked again. Blanchette noticed his hands trembled as they held the bars. The question sounded like a plea.

"He's at the orphanage, waiting for your release. I shall see that he's well cared for."

Jonathan breathed a long sigh, then returned the flask to his lips. He drank slowly and deeply while the darkness pulsed around them.

"I wish I could believe you. I can imagine how lost and miserable he feels," he said, speaking more to himself. Or to the darkness.

Blanchette stepped closer to him until she pressed against the bars that separated them. "I want you to trust me as I trusted you." She stared into his eyes and found a world of pain—one she knew all too well. Her heart twisted in knots. The Black Wolf rose in her mind's eye—a waking nightmare—that crudely made armor, his swift and deadly arrogance, the glint of his sword as it cut down her father's men. "I am in your debt, Jonathan. And I fully intend to pay it. You saved me. You risked your life and your child's life for me. In this short time, you've become a dear friend. My mother always said being a queen was quite like being a parent. All the people are your children, and you must see they're well cared for. Well, my father failed in this duty. But I shall not."

She held the candle close to her face and watched as the light played across his taut features.

Jonathan finally smiled, then nodded as if affirming some inward thought. "Stay safe and stay strong, my queen. God knows this world needs you."

And with a last backward glance, Blanchette left Jonathan to his shadows and returned to her own.

---

Rowan's warhorse surged with power as his hooves kicked up mud, grass, and rock. Fifty mounted soldiers followed in his wake; Winslowe Castle fell behind them in a wash of gray stone. The green of the wood and the town's buildings and steeples drew closer, puncturing the horizon.

Rowan urged Sunbeam forward with slight pressure from his thighs. The beast responded with regal elegance as the drumming of his hooves became a rolling thunder. Smoke darted beside them like a dark shadow.

The landscape of Norland rushed by in a ribbon of greenery and a churning overcast sky. Edrick kicked his courser with fierce grunts until he fell in beside Rowan. Sir Royce and a handful of soldiers followed them.

*Another pirate raid,* Rowan thought with a curse. He'd received word thirty minutes before while reviewing the day's training plan. A group of pirates had landed seven longships along the coast and taken to raid and pillage the nearby villages. They usually remained at sea, attacking ships that dared to cross into their territory. Among the waves and sea storms and drowned legends, they reigned high and inspired dread. It struck Rowan as unusual that they'd targeted the coastal villages.

*The royal family's fall has made Norland vulnerable and open to threats.*

It was an open door he meant to close. Blanchette's delicate features entered his mind. Rowan felt the stirrings of battle fever leap into his veins as he and his men rode past the town and toward a village.

The carefully paved roads and stone walkways gave way to indistinguishable dirt paths that crisscrossed each other and seemed to lead nowhere. The town's taverns, businesses, and bustling shops soon fell behind Rowan and his escort. Norland's coastal villages' poorly tended wilds and all-important trade ports lay ahead.

Three miles later, the breeze carried the salty scent of the sea.

Five miles later, smoke and ash choked the air.

Seven miles later, the scent of death mingled with that smoke. As Rowan approached the village, the stench of death grew stronger and overwhelmed him. The thick smoke in the air burned his eyes and made them water. He could hear the distant caws of carrion crows as they paid court to the bodies that littered the ground.

His heart sank as he reached the top of the precipice and looked down at the village. The once bustling town was nothing more than a smoldering ruin. Skeletal frames, blackened by the fire ravaging the village, were all that remained where the homes and shops once stood tall and proud.

Rowan felt a knot form in his stomach as he dismounted from Sunbeam. Heat emanated from the ashes as he went down to the village. *Merciful Christ. I'm going to cook in my armor.* Debris and the remains of what had once been people's lives littered the ground. He felt the weight of the tragedy pressing down on him at the unbearable sight.

As he wandered through the village, he heard the faint cries of the survivors, mourning the loss of loved ones. The sound was haunting. The villagers huddled together, their faces etched with fear and pain and despair. Rowan watched as Smoke lowered his head to the dirt and tracked the dead and dying.

He felt a deep anger and sadness as he surveyed the destruction. He glanced over his shoulder, where his black wolf banners flapped in the breeze. Sir Royce bore his flag; his eyes were a winter's chill. Unreadable. Jonas, who Rowan had recently taken on as his squire, was beside him on a courser that was rearing from the scent of death.

*I shall have to help Jonas train that beast,* Rowan absently thought.

The smell of death was all-pervading. He mounted again and rode through the terror.

He saw mothers cradling their dead children, their faces twisted in grief and pain.

Rowan pulled Sunbeam to a stop, then dismounted in a single movement. He felt himself swell with anger and heartbreak all at once. The child lying before him was only three. Eyes as gray as Norland's sky stared up and saw nothing. Rowan felt a shaky breath hitch in his throat. He swept matted dark brown hair from the boy's face, then ran his palm over his eyelids and shut them. His gaze traveled over the child's body. He silently shook his head at the arrow shaft embedded in his abdomen.

*Probably not a quick death,* he thought, his fury building.

"I'm sorry, lad," he whispered, then rose to his feet. "I wish I could have been here sooner." He examined the carnage and bloodshed once again. "Much sooner."

He couldn't change the past but could ensure a different future.

*I shall do everything in my power to make it so.*

Smoke lowered his muzzle and licked the boy's cheek, and without another backward glance, the wolf strode into the wood and lost himself in the thicket of trees to hunt.

<hr />

Blanchette hardly crossed the great hall and audience chamber before two guards stopped her.

*I truly am a prisoner in my own home.*

She sighed wearily and eyed the gleaming weapons. Dawn's first light caught and rippled along their smooth metal. Then she averted her eyes to the portly guard before her. She didn't recognize these men. They hadn't belonged to her father's guard. Through the slits in the man's helm, his eyes shone like dagger points, and in a startling realization, she saw he *hated* her.

He hated her without knowing her at all.

And she hated him. She locked that hatred in a corner of her soul, where she now kept all her grief and loss.

"Pardon me, sirs, but I should like to pass."

The fat guard's eyes narrowed at her demand. He stood a little straighter. "That's fine, my lady, but my lord requires you. And you're in no place to make such requests."

A shiver snaked down her back, though she set her features into a hard line and refused to show fear or anguish. She'd never get used to hearing him be called lord of *her* castle.

"Well," she said, smoothing down the front of her dress, "we shan't keep Lord Dietrich waiting then, shall we?"

He sat before the hearth, which had appeared to have burned out hours ago. Ashes and dust filled the dirty mouth of the fireplace. Her eyes drifted to the tiled stone mantel and its carvings of her family's sigil. Years of smoke blackened the crests and distorted their shapes. Yet there they hung all the same, just as they had across the generations, greeting her like old friends.

A heavy fur-lined cloak draped Rowan's body, fastened around his neck with a snarling wolf clasp. His dark hair fell above his collar in thick ink-black waves. Beard stubble covered his chin and accented the strong cleft. His hazel eyes, usually so attentive and sharp, looked exhausted. Empty. Dark circles rimmed them like two open wounds.

Before she could speak, Rowan shot to his feet and crossed the room in swift and deliberate strides. He had a nervous energy about him—an uncharacteristic restlessness that went against his usual composure. But as always, he moved like a man at war, a man with purpose. Vengeance and ambition powered his steps.

*He stalks about like the black wolf he's taken for his sigil.*

Finally, he came before her, and as he did, her head darted

higher and higher until she could feel the thick knot of her hair pressing into her neck. A dizzy feeling swelled in her. Her heart beat a little faster.

He was impossibly tall and standing far too close. Yet she refused to surrender and step back. She meant to win if this was a game he wanted to play.

Blanchette's eyes flickered from his face and back to the mantel and her family's crest.

"You look awful," she said as they stood within a foot of each other.

Rowan surprised her with a bark of laughter. He raked his fingers through his hairline, then idly sat his palm on his sword's pommel. "And you look lovely, *ma princesse*." His deep voice was soft and thick. His eyes tracked down her dress as if to press his point, and she felt her cheeks warm at the blatant gaze. She loathed herself for it. Hated that she'd found any compliment from his attention or the heat from his warm eyes. She reached for the cross around her neck, only to remember it was no longer there.

Brimming with her own nervous energy, she ran her hands along the sleeves of her dress, absently toying with the material. It was one of her own garments that Governess Agnes had fetched from Blanchette's bedchamber. It slid between her clumsy fingertips—the one tangible thing anchoring her.

"You sat up all night," she accused rather than asked.

His features hardened again. He dared to step nearer, and the wafts of his breath sweltered across her face. He smelled of ale and smoke and the earthy scents of her homeland. That very thought caused her to grow queasy. Angry. And resentful.

*My homeland.*

*Mine.*

"And I'm surprised you sleep so well, Princess."

He kept calling her *princess*—in both English and French. Did he intend to mock her? She wouldn't have it. Her integrity was her own to keep, and no wall he breached would spirit that away.

She craned her neck back again to meet his gaze straight on. His eyes were deep and probing, indecent in their forwardness and quiet confidence.

"What do you know of how well I sleep? You know nothing. I've seen things... horrors carried out on your orders that shall forever haunt me, whether I sleep or dream or am rotting in the ground."

He paused as if digesting her words. When he spoke, his voice was low and intense. His words were like a physical touch. They sent shivers down her spine. She could see the shame and pain etched on his face. He was a man who'd seen and done terrible things, but she could sense that he was also a man of honor.

*I can use that to my advantage.*

He placed his hand on the hilt of his sword, and she couldn't help but notice how his fingers curled around the ivory wolf pommel. *The Black Wolf of Norland,* she thought to herself. A powerful and dangerous man.

*A predator in my home.*

"Maybe so. Yet people have starved by the thousands while your father and his court feasted each night. I've done terrible things at your father's orders. Things I shall never rectify. Within this very city, I've seen children drop dead in the streets, and I could only stand there and helplessly watch. I was a sworn knight, yet powerless. There was nothing I could do, no way I could end their suffering... but that's all changed now. I've heard the people's cries, and I intend to answer every one of them."

"How dare you? You're living a lie. You've bloodied the soil of Norland. You and the traitors who follow you have brought death and devastation! I—"

"*You* are living a lie, girl," he insisted, coming close enough so the heat of his body radiated.

Blanchette held her ground.

"Call me girl again."

Despite herself, a dark thrill ran through her as she drank in the sight of him. At over six feet of uncompromising male, he was imposing and as dark as a shadow. Hazel eyes stared down at her through a fan of thick lashes.

She watched as he shook his head and gave her a hard, measured stare. What was he measuring? And why, in God's name, did she suddenly feel so small? She shivered and stepped back, only in part from the wintery cold.

Swiftly, he removed his cloak. He set it over her shoulders and fastened the interlinked, snarling wolf heads. Heat engulfed her, and the soft, firm weight of the garment seemed to press her through the stones below her feet.

"What are you—"

"You are clearly cold. Now come with me," he snapped, though a new placidness in his voice rivaled the warmth of his fur cloak. He looked her up and down, a sad smile tugging at the corner of his lips. Sunlight danced in his raven-black hair and brought out the shadows in his eyes. His gaze descended on her again. It nearly knocked the breath from her lungs. She settled deeper into his black cloak and searched for warmth.

A coldness surrounded Rowan Dietrich. A winter with no end in sight. She shivered again and unconsciously stepped away from him.

"Keep your eyes open." His voice was a strained whisper. *And so, so very cold.* "There's something you must see."

# Seven

They traveled by horse, a great black beast as formidable and unforgiving as its master. Behind them rolled a large wagon, which Rowan had piled high with goods. Blanchette would have resisted the transport altogether, but Rowan was more than twice her size, so it would've been a wasted effort.

She needed every bit of her strength.

The horse was a destrier. One of impeccable breeding. She knew from the animal's resolute demeanor. Spanish blood showed in the muscular profile of its head, neat ears, elegantly curved neck, deep chest, and powerful rump. Rowan called the monster Sunbeam. A ridiculous name. He'd scolded him like a governess chastens a child when it'd attempted to kick and bite her. Then he'd persuaded the creature to be amicable in muted tones, as one might soothe a lover.

Blanchette would have laughed had any humor still existed in her.

"Sunbeam was a gift from your father," Rowan murmured in her ear conversationally, his hard body pressed against her back. They rode under the raised portcullis and across the drawbridge.

Sunbeam's hooves thundered against the wood and echoed the fierce volley of her heart.

That black demon wolf, Smoke, darted off into the tangled wilderness of the woods.

*Off to spill more blood,* she thought, her mind on the wolf behind her.

The horse's powerful body moved beneath her. She swayed and gripped the reins a little tighter, lest she fall and break her neck. Rowan chuckled in her ear. "After he knighted me, I had the pick of any horse from his stables."

"And you've used his gift to march on his very castle." She could neither hide her disgust nor subdue the anger that welled in her chest. Rage pulled taut across her heart like a strung arrow waiting to be loosed. "It's good to know you have taken your knight's vows with such devotion."

Rowan exhaled a long sigh. The heat of his breath stirred her curls and tickled her nape. She felt him tense against her, his body thrumming with a palpable, barely restrained fury.

"If there was ever a more heartless man than King Bartholomew, I've yet to meet him. And besides," he dared to press on, his baritone voice sinking deeper still, "I gave the vow to my kingdom and the people. I have never wavered from it, and I never shall."

Blanchette resorted to a sullen silence. The carefully knit world she'd known all her life quickly unraveled. Her father... heartless? Was it so? Of course, she'd witnessed his cruelty firsthand... but it was his duty as a king to keep order. Surely, that entailed a harsh hand at times?

It was a narrative she'd told herself often and loudly while tossing and turning at night.

They rode past the great gatehouse. Two round towers, each over fifty feet high, stood on either side of a pointed arch, with a painted statue of King Bartholomew in a niche above its grand entrance. When King Bartholomew sat on the throne, it wasn't uncommon to find the bodies of traitors swinging from the gatehouse and decapitated heads black with tar ornamenting the gates. Now, the only bodies there belonged to Rowan's pacing guards and gatekeepers.

Emptiness filled her, a gaping hole fringed by sorrow, grief, and utter exhaustion. Tragedy had snuffed out her light, and the world slid by her as she observed her kingdom with a strange detachment. As they rode on, she made out the nearby port over the moors; smoke furled from the burned ruins that were once a trading village.

Inwardly, she cringed as a flash of an axe and her father's laughter infested her thoughts. That axe rained down again and again. *It took seven blows to kill that poor man, hadn't it?*

The formidable walls of Winslowe Castle soon gave way to the woods and roads. Rowan tugged on Sunbeam's reins and set down a dirt path bearing to the left and away from the greenery. Clusters of timber houses and the jutting church steeple punctured the horizon. Blanchette felt a knot tighten in her chest as they approached the town center.

Curious faces appeared in the windows. The streets came to life with the townsfolk. Merchants stopped rolling their carts in mid-street and fell silent at the sight of Rowan's arrival. The sight of the Black Wolf's banner was most disconcerting. Where the royal standard once hung from the storefronts flew Rowan's sigil.

Behind them loomed the Winslowe Castle, with its seven shining towers. Ahead of them lay a somber flock of humanity, brown and ragged and unwashed.

The town showed all the features of a bloated glutton; it felt like the caricature of the human body—smelly, dirty, unkempt.

Yet something poked through that sorrow: a tangible hope.

Flanked by two bare-chested children, a reedy-looking woman ran over to Rowan and reached for him. Blanchette felt his strong body shift behind her as he outstretched his hand and touched their tiny fingers.

"Bless you," the woman said, crossing herself with her free hand. "Bless you and all you have given us."

Coins jangled as Rowan passed her a fistful of silver. The woman stepped back cautiously as Sunbeam tossed his muzzle, snorted, and pawed at the ground. The warmth in the woman's gaze froze over; she stared up at Blanchette, her eyes turning cold and hard.

Blanchette swayed uneasily in the saddle as she observed the two children. Thin collarbones protruded, and their ribs showed beneath filthy, tanned skin. They appeared emaciated and a few breaths away from death. Blanchette felt her heart tighten as the world she'd once known crumbled around her. It was falling in an avalanche, and the weight was crushing.

Rowan urged Sunbeam on with a gentle word in French. Townspeople continued to file out of their homes and the shops in an excited rush void of color and the extravagance she'd always known.

"She *hated* me," Blanchette heard herself thinly whisper. "I saw it in her eyes."

Rowan stiffened behind her. When he spoke, the warmth of his breath fanned against her curls. "She hated your father. His kennel hounds likely ate better than those two children. The world they've known has been cruel and unforgiving."

*And so are you.*

Rowan tugged on the reins and brought Sunbeam to a halt. He slid from the horse's back, his movement smooth as silk, and held his arms out to Blanchette. She hesitated. Glanced about at the townspeople encircling them. Then she dismounted from Sunbeam and glided into his embrace. He set her down gently while his gaze locked on hers.

"It's the princess!"

"It can't be. She died in the siege."

"You are wrong. I saw her at a tourney once. It's *her*."

"Yes, she looks just like the queen."

Overlapping chatter pulled Blanchette from her trance. Rowan must have read the fear in her eyes because he set a large hand on her shoulder, leaned forward, and said in a soothing voice, "I won't let anything happen to you. Now come." He urged her to move with a hand on her arm, directing her to the back of the wagon.

She flinched out of his grip. "I can walk, thank you very much," she spat with no gratitude in her voice. She wheeled around him, her heart banging like a war drum.

He'd loaded the wagon's open back with barrels, boxes, and piles of assorted goods. Blanchette's heart sank as one of her father's fine silk tunics caught her eye. She stood back while Rowan quickly worked, unfastening a giant, stringy-looking rope that'd held two of the barrels in place.

Just behind him gathered a cluster of merchants, workers, women and children, soldiers and schoolboys, the young and old. Rowan turned the two enormous barrels upright, checked the etchings on their lids, then hefted one up and set it onto the ground with a *bang*. "These grains shall last you through most of the season, I should think," he said to a man wearing a stained apron and pleased grin.

"Ah, bless you," the baker returned with a gracious bow, signaling to a man behind him. Together, they carried the barrels away from the wagon and into a small shop just off the main road. Rowan caught Blanchette's gaze for a moment and held it. Then he looked down as filthy and fearless little hands tugged at his jerkin.

Two more children flanked his sides. Rowan gripped their small shoulders, directing them back a few steps. "Careful now, mind where you stand. Sunbeam is a beauty for sure, but a temperamental beast," he murmured as he sealed gazes with Blanchette again. The children were a mousy-haired pair—likely twins—with crystal-blue eyes, trusting and unscathed by the world and wars.

"Sir, sir!" one girl said, her voice as high and light as Rowan's was dark. "Have you brought anything for us? Have you?" Rowan's lip quirked at the corner. He placed a gloved hand on her head and ruffled her stringy curls.

"We have," he replied, gesturing at Blanchette with his other hand.

All eyes were on her, but she only felt Rowan's gaze. He stared at her for a long silence, his face's hard, rugged lines softening. She eased forward until she stood beside him and before the girl.

Blanchette forced a smile and felt the scar on her cheek pull tight. "Hello. What are your names?"

"Brienne," the girl answered, then pointed at her sister. "This is Cassandra."

"I see," Blanchette carefully said, "and where are your parents?"

Brienne dropped her chin, her blue eyes filling with a darkness she recognized all too well. "My mama died when we were born. And Papa died during the battle."

By battle, Blanchette knew she meant the sacking of Winslowe Castle. Blanchette shut her eyes, looking deep inside herself. Then she opened them again and placed a hand on Brienne's bony shoulder. "Mine, too, sweetling. I'm so sorry. I... I know your pain." She felt Rowan's stare all the while.

The tension loosened as he strode back to the wagon and ruffled through the goods and provisions again. He pulled a small wooden box forward and carried it to the twins. He opened the lid, revealing a swarm of fine silks and linens—garments Blanchette knew to be her own.

Rowan hesitated and caught her gaze in an unspoken question. Blanchette ran her fingers over the materials, then withdrew a deep-green woolen cloak. Forcing her smile back into place, she knelt before Brienne and swept the garment over her slim shoulders.

"Ah, a bit too long, but you'll grow into it quickly. It brings out your lovely eyes."

"Oh, thank you, thank you!" The girl gaped at the cloak and rubbed the material in visible disbelief.

Blanchette tried to summon feelings of hate; she fought to recall all the destruction and horror Rowan had caused. She glanced down at Rowan's cloak, fastened around her neck with the wolf heads.

She should have been seething with hatred, yet on that crisp morning in late winter, watching the twins gush over garments that had been gathering dust in her own wardrobe, she felt an odd sense of contentment. She cursed herself more for it, but it persisted, much like the first rays of light bursting through a blanket of clouds.

And it seemed to come from everywhere. Norland was alive with it. That feeling—that fragile burst of hope. The children's elated smiles were part of it. The glances and chatter of the townspeople, which had turned from disdain to curiosity to outright acceptance, were a part of it. The way they smiled at her as she moved through the throng and handed out blankets and garments and toys was a part of it. The silky timbre of Rowan's voice as he passed out provisions was a part of it. The way men and women reached for him and touched his fingertips was a part of it.

Rowan's protective and persistent touches were also a part of it.

They spent much of the morning in that way until a crush of appetizing scents rolled from a nearby tavern called The Chatty Horse. Rowan paid the innkeeper a handsome sum of silvers, then stored Sunbeam in the stable, where a bright-eyed boy had enthusiastically fed, watered, and brushed him until his mane shone. Blanchette had asked if he were worried he'd be stolen. Rowan assured her that the only thing a thief would leave with was one less hand. She almost laughed at that but caught herself in time and felt any good humor sour into darkness. The pervasive magic of the morning was quickly fading away. Blanchette felt bitterness rise in its place.

The Black Wolf introduced her to a new world; drunken laughter and lively conversations filled The Chatty Horse in a warm flurry. Townsfolk congregated at a dozen tables, passing around stories, songs, flagons of ale, trenchers of freshly baked bread, and platters of sweet cakes. The thrum overwhelmed Blanchette as she and Rowan seated themselves. Boisterous conversations hushed to low murmurs. She felt the townsfolk turn their attention to her and the Black Wolf of Norland. Blanchette glanced at the faces of knights, children, and laborers. She took a deep breath to slow the frantic beating of her heart. The innkeeper, a large woman with restless eyes and hands that moved with a bustling efficiency, rushed over to them.

"The Black Wolf of Norland in my own hall! Gracious Lord!" she tittered. "And Princess Blanchette," she said. She bent into a clumsy curtsy, not accustomed to the movement, her ruddy cheeks brightening. "Such an honor to host you both, milord and milady. Anything you like, anything at all, 'tis all on my house," she said, peering down at Blanchette. She grabbed a tray of fresh cakes from the next table and plopped it down. The two laborers sitting at the table didn't look happy about that. "Milady, you're even lovelier than all the talk."

Blanchette felt the color rising in her cheeks—not from the compliment but Rowan's attentive stare.

He reached for a cake and popped it in his mouth. He waved apologetically at the two laborers. Then he ate two more cakes. She watched his strong jaw and chin work. "She certainly is. And these are even sweeter than the praise I've heard among my men. As are you, Madame Bouvier."

The innkeeper tittered again at the compliment. "I'm going to have a special meal cooked up for you two! Oh, you just wait and see. Never will your tongues have touched something so sweet..." And with that, she bustled into the kitchens, leaving Blanchette and Rowan alone at the table.

Blanchette fidgeted with her wooden cup. Rowan pushed the plate of sweet cakes toward her, but she shook her head. Nausea rose in her stomach.

"How old is he? Sunbeam?"

She watched as he sliced off a sizable chunk of bread with

precise, strong motions. Rowan took a deep swallow of ale, set the cup down, then studied her intently.

"When did King Bartholomew knight me. That's what you're *really* asking." Blanchette said nothing. "Well, I'm not sure of Sunbeam's age. I know he's far from a spring foal... but your father knighted me about fifteen years ago come winter, after the Battle of Shadowmoor... when I still fought and commanded men beneath my father's Gray Wolf banner." He laughed a full, robust sound, then took another swig of ale. Beads of liquid clung to his lips, and Blanchette caught herself staring. "You were likely practicing your needlework and royal curtseys while I was kneeling as a boy and rising as a knight."

"Once more, you are mistaken. The only needlework I'd have been practicing was tending to wounded men, and the only stitches I made were those I pushed through their skin. In fact, I tended many of the men from the Battle of Shadowmoor. That naval uprising nearly devastated the Northlands. Or at least my father had claimed."

"Is that so?" he asked, a strange and not altogether unsettling twinkle in his eyes. "I may have use of you yet."

Blanchette felt a fission of anger. "Now you go too far. I am Lady Winslowe, and I've helped tend the ledgers and accounts since I could talk. My mother made certain of it."

"Beautiful and resourceful," he said as if speaking to himself.

"Norland is my *home*—it always has been my home and always shall be. It's my duty to care for it. And that's a bond I shall never break. Never will I abandon my home or people."

Rowan sat back and idly rubbed his thumb and forefinger together. The inn's hive of activity seemed to fade away for a moment, leaving only him. Then he spoke, breaking the odd spell his gaze had woven over her. "Aye, these are your people," he said, glancing toward the cheery innkeeper, who was making her rounds with great bravado. "Then don't abandon them. Serve them. Help me. Help me with the ledgers, the accounts, the running of the castle—"

"Serve *you*, you mean."

She watched as his mouth ticked at the corner. He fought off that smile, then folded one arm on the table and leaned forward. She could see the muscles straining against his tunic.

"I have no interest in wearing a crown or sitting on a throne. My duty is here," he said, waving his hand at the buzzing room. "I serve the kingdom and those who cannot serve themselves. That's it. You may hate me and even wish me dead with every breath, but don't punish your people."

---

*So her education wasn't lacking*, Rowan thought. But it stretched only as far as her governess's lessons and this "needle play" she claimed to be skilled at.

Indeed, Blanchette looked like a stranger in her own town, among her own people. He pitied her for that. He saw the rage building on her face, in her eyes, and in how she held herself. And he felt a mirrored restlessness rise inside himself. He fought to restrain it like one might restrain a wild horse.

Rowan gestured the room and its tenants with a vague wave. "This is the real Norland, Blanchette." She visibly stiffened at the sound of her name, her great blue eyes widening with a sudden vulnerability. He leaned forward ever so slightly, his fingertips coming together in a steeple. "These are your people; you don't have to feel like a stranger here. Like an outsider."

Her gaze sharpened, and her brow furrowed. "'Tis easy enough for you to say. You're their champion. I... I represent their suffering." That vulnerability appeared again. She tried to hide it and did so quite well, but Rowan Dietrich was a hard man to fool.

"Not so," he replied. "Well, for some... yes. But for many, you remain a symbol of hope." He tapped his fingers against the table and held her wary stare. He recalled Sir Edrick's words from days ago. *She's a stronger symbol.*

His gaze slid across her delicate features, then locked on her scar. Delicate, yet as strong as any soldier he'd ever commanded. Her poise and strength came together in a breathtaking tapestry of day and night. Rowan felt every muscle in his body tighten at the prospect of holding her in his arm, feeling those lush curls strewn across his chest, damp from their lovemaking.

Those thoughts alarmed him. She looked at him, her blue eyes dark with an emotion that might have been anger or lust.

*Nay. She loathes me—and for a good reason.*

Her bravery and softness drew him in with equal enthusiasm, fueling his admiration for her.

The silence stretched on as he examined Blanchette, and she studied him. Her eyes narrowed, and suddenly, he felt like she was seeing *into* him.

"Tell me something, Sir Rowan. Something real. Something that isn't fable or legend. I want to know about Rowan Dietrich, not the Black Wolf."

Absently, she reached for her neck—for a necklace that was no longer there. When he gave no reply, she stared straight into his eyes, unblinking, her thumb and index fingers rotating the signet ring in circles.

Rowan leaned back in his seat and felt his pulse quicken. He glanced inwardly—into his past, into his losses, into his victories and heartaches. Through all those memories and secrets, it was a crisp blue gaze that called out to him.

Those eyes stared back at him... eyes that were wide and gentle yet held an intensity too great for their years. Eyes not so different from the ones looking at him now.

Blanchette stared at him from across the table while those *other* blue eyes stared at him from within. Both pairs seemed to implore and plead with him. He felt cornered, like a wolf backed against a wall.

So he did what he did best, the very thing that had kept him strong and in command all these years. He hardened his mind and heart, feeling a set of immaterial armor settle into place.

Securely. Resolutely. Completely.

"Rowan?" Blanchette said. Her soft voice swept over him like a summer breeze, and he felt it pulling at that armor. Rowan resisted it, guilt swarming him from the inside out.

*Has she said my name before in that tone? Not one of hate—but of wonder and the slightest hint of compassion?*

He couldn't bear it.

"Why? Why must you know? Why should I waste my breath?" he snapped through a clenched jaw. His rising indignation fueled itself. He wasn't accustomed to losing his composure, yet here he sat, undone by a slip of a girl. He clenched his hand, balling his fingers into a fist. "I brought you here to see the truth, and you're still blind to it. There's resilience, and then there's plain stupidity. What would my mere words prove?"

She opened her mouth to speak, then quickly shut it. Those bright eyes danced across his face, examining every feature like he often studied battle plans. Finally, she spoke again. "Then answer me this. Why did you visit the chapel? And why did you help my governess with such... compassion?"

The simplicity of her question stunned him. He glanced about the tavern, observing the cheerful faces and the ebb and flow of the conversations.

Rowan had led more vanguards than he could recall. He'd stared death in the face just as many times. He'd endured wounds that tested his mortality, yet on this strange morning, he'd never felt so... small. So mortal. A shiver of fear ran through him.

He'd felt this depth of terror—yes, *terror*—only once before.

And now he felt again. While eating sweet cakes. In the middle of The Chatty Horse. Whilst lounging in a shaft of broad daylight.

Rowan folded his hands together, then leaned forward. He softened his voice to a whisper, allowing it to fill the space between them. "We don't have to be enemies, Blanchette."

*She could be a powerful ally,* Rowan thought, Edrick's words racing through his mind. "We can be very close allies. Even friends."

She grabbed her cup of ale and raised it to him before drinking. Whether it was in mockery, he could not say...

# Eight

Edrick silently led Blanchette through the halls of the castle. Everywhere she looked, she found a hostile glance, an unfamiliar sigil, a tapestry depicting a world she'd never seen. Winslowe Castle had once been as familiar to her as the back of her hand; now, it resembled a prison, and its ancient stones were crushing her beneath their bulk.

A light rain fell outside and pitter-pattered all around her. Although it was a chilly night, the stone walls were warm to the touch. Hot water rushed through them like blood churning through a man's veins. She laid her palms on the stones to better feel the pulse of her home.

"Keep up," Edrick snapped, his drawn features made even more hostile. A few moments later, he stopped outside Rowan's solar. "Not a move from you." His heavy fist banged at the door. "My lord, Blanchette waits without."

He never referred to her as a princess, she noticed. But was she even a princess any longer? She was the first and last of her name, a hostage in her own home.

The door flew open. The Black Wolf stood beneath the archway, his massive frame dominating the space. Smoke lurked just behind him. She heard the heavy fall of his paws as he crowded beside his master, those lantern-like eyes glowing. Rowan's gaze flickered to her own, then found Edrick.

Blanchette stepped forward. Her heartbeat fluttered against her ribs, though she kept her voice steady. At least she hoped she did. "Sir... I am sorry to disturb you. I was hoping you might permit me to visit the chapel." She gestured to Edrick. "He insisted I speak with you first."

"The chapel?"

Blanchette swallowed and toyed with her signet ring. "Yes. I should like to pray tonight." She glanced at Edrick. "Alone, if I may."

*All I need is a few moments alone.*

"Sir? Show some respect. You are addressing the rightful king of Norland, girl. You—"

"I am not a king, *sir*," Rowan snapped, cutting his captain off. Smoke loosed a low, rolling growl and raised one of his paws. "And as long as we're observing court courtesies, she is still your princess. I command you to address her as such."

Edrick scoffed. His eyes raked down Blanchette's body, a look of revulsion swimming in their depths. "Have you forgotten who she is? I have not. Your men have not. Your sisters and mother, bless their memories, have not. She is the enemy, with the traitor's blood running through her veins." She shivered as Edrick glared at her. "Blue eyes. Like an ocean." He turned back to the Black Wolf. "You'll drown in them before all this is over."

Rowan stepped out from the doorframe and toward Edrick. They were both tall and well-muscled men, their bodies hewn from years of sword fighting and soldiering, yet Rowan loomed over him. His hazel eyes blazed in the torchlight, and his baritone voice sent another shiver through her body. "If I'm the king you believe me to be, you're guilty of insubordination. I have hanged men for less."

"Aye," Edrick replied with a shake of his head, "you have hanged men for less. But they were lesser men." And without another word or backward glance, he vanished down the long corridor, his clanking armor still audible as he walked out of sight.

*Spirits walk these halls now. Souls of the damned.*

Rowan exhaled a sharp breath. "This is still your home. You may pray as much as you'd like, but not alone. I shall escort you to the chapel myself."

Side by side, they walked through the dimly lit halls of Winslowe Castle. The wolf padded beside them, as silent as a shadow.

*Just like smoke,* she thought with a shudder.

Rowan carried a torch. Blanchette looked up at him, into his set, granite expression, watching as the firelight illuminated his grim profile.

She found sadness in his hazel eyes, a sorrow that nearly stole her breath away.

"Why did you defend me?"

"I don't completely lack courtesy or decency. And besides, you aren't to blame for... for what happened."

"And neither was my mother or brother, yet your men murdered them all the same."

Rowan came to a dead standstill. He shot toward Blanchette, the torch setting his features ablaze. His eyes sharpened and filled with an absolute loathing that unleashed another shudder through her. "Those were *not* my orders. Unlike your father, I do not condone the murder of women and children. I *condemn* it."

Stubbornly, Blanchette shook her head and matched his stare. "Your captain is right. You are a fool and a hypocrite as well. You brought death to my door," she said, her voice rising, her breaths fanning the torchlight and causing it to waver. She heard the wolf stirring beside them and imagined how it'd feel to have those powerful jaws clamped around her throat. "My family would be alive if it weren't for you, yet they rot while you still stand here and breathe the air. What kind of justice is that?"

She should have held her tongue, she knew. She should have continued to play the game, as Governess Agnes instructed... yet she trembled with the desire to unleash her fury and heartache. She couldn't contain it. A hundred images knifed through her thoughts in a cutting wound. And that wound was bleeding.

The words rushed out of her in a great landslide of emotion. "And not your order, you say? You're truly a great and noble soldier—even your men defy your word. You come here, to *my* land, my home, expecting to hold a kingdom. You have condemned yourself."

"Those men have paid for their folly with their lives," he whispered, his voice laced with venom and something else. Something she couldn't quite place. That tentative note of emotion twisted in her belly. Smoke growled again, softly at first, the rising sound filling the hall like a thunderclap. "I'm a far better soldier than your father ever was. As you said yourself, I'm still breathing the air. I'm still standing. Now, come and pray your prayers. You better hope God is listening tonight."

The Winslowe's private chapel was still and quiet. It was intricately built into one of the buttresses, and unlike the larger one on-site, which welcomed the soldiers and houseguests, only the Winslowes prayed here. It was a sacred space. The heart of her home. At least it had been, once upon a time.

The chapel used to bring her warmth and hope. Now, it felt bleak and cold. Blanchette tightened her cloak about her body and eased inside. Rowan and his torchlight followed her. She peered up at the tall, curved wall and watched as his shadow moved against the stones.

She felt him standing behind her, huge and imposing, intimately close.

*This is the monster her governess had once warned her about. The villain of the stories she'd whispered to me and Isadora and Willem by candlelight.* She thought about how young and naive they'd been, remembering how those tales had made her and her siblings giddy with fright.

"*Please tell us more, Governess Agnes. We want to hear more about the Black Wolf!*"

*The monsters have come for us all, not as myth or legend, but as flesh-and-blood...*

A curdling sense of doom rushed through her and heightened the dark chill of the chapel. She yearned to raise her red hood and flee into the night, yet wherever she'd go, those monsters would follow.

Blanchette moved to the center of the circular chamber, her boots rapping against the stones. The curved walls tapered together at the highest point in a slender steeple. Teardrop-shaped slits served as the windows, and intricate, detailed carvings decorated the pillars. Blanchette gazed up at the angels and celestial realm overhead, which were illuminated by Rowan's torch. She exhaled and felt a calm wash over her. Faint beams of moonlight trickled through the teardrop windows and danced along the walls.

Rowan stood just behind her; she felt the heat of his body. The stones amplified the sound of his heavy breaths.

"I spent little time in the one we had," he whispered. "When I was a boy, I mean. It was large, right next to the armory, always filled with soldiers trying to make peace with God. This chapel... it's nicer. Small, but intimate... as if the Lord may truly stop and listen to any words passed within its walls."

Blanchette turned and gazed up at Rowan. The movement sent the hood tumbling from her head. "I never took you for a pious man."

"Lord, no," he said with irony and a great bark of laughter. "I've seen far too much. I've had too many prayers go unanswered."

"So you don't believe in God?" she asked.

"If there's something up there, someone just and loving and

kind... well, then why is there so much hatred and injustice in the world?"

"Because of men like you," she answered before she could catch herself.

A flash of rage, then an injured look. Tense silence crept into the chapel, and for a passing moment, Blanchette felt an apology form on her lips. Within the quiet din, the rain picked up. Its rhythmic melody puttered against the stone walls. Thunder roared, low and ominous, like the growl of a great beast waking from its slumber.

"Rowan, I—"

"I shall take that as my leave, Princess. I'll be waiting without. Do your duty. Pray your prayers." He was mocking her, she knew. He hung the torch in a mounted sconce, then departed from the chamber with those swift, confident strides, Smoke trailing him.

Emptiness rose around her. Blanchette released tears she hadn't realized she'd been holding back. She collapsed to her knees and let them wash down her cheeks and neck. Bittersweet relief filled her. And within the solitude of her family's chapel, she found she could not pray.

Perhaps she and the Black Wolf were more alike than she dared admit.

*Good*, she thought, as the tears dried on her cheeks and grew cold. *I can also be a wolf.*

⁂

BECAUSE OF MEN LIKE YOU.

Rowan allowed Blanchette her solitude and listened from outside the chapel while she sobbed. He sank to his knees, a strange knot tightening around his gut. In that queer moment, their despair became one. Sitting in the dark hallway, he leaned against the door's iron-studded panel while a thousand haunting sounds and sights rose in his mind.

The ghosts of his past returned with a vengeance.

How would it feel to not suffer alone? How would it feel to hold someone, to whisper his darkest fears to another, and fall asleep in each other's arms? He'd never had that. Not with his wife for the better part of their marriage. Nor with Kathryn years later.

"You're here for me, eh?" he murmured to Smoke. Rowan wrapped his arms around the beast's thick, dark neck and nuzzled his fur. He could smell the ash and maple wood and dirt and the musty Rockbluff River. He hugged him tightly and felt the wolf's rough tongue on his cheek.

Minutes crept by. Blanchette's sobs abated into soft cries and then silence. Rowan eased the door open to check on her. She was fast asleep on the stone floor, her pale cheeks stained with tears. Torchlight washed over the gentle curves of her body. The red riding cloak had fallen open to reveal a cream-colored dress. Beautiful and classic, much like Blanchette herself. The swell of her breasts blended into the material.

He knelt beside her as his heart rapidly drummed against his ribs. He bit at the fingers of his gloves and unsheathed his hand. It trembled in midair as he reached out. He held his breath as his palm lowered to her curls. They felt like silk against his skin. He couldn't recall ever touching something so soft. She was beautiful and warm yet as strong as steel.

Rowan never cared about what others thought of him, yet as sudden as a storm, he couldn't bear the fact that she detested him.

He watched her sleep. Whatever remained of his heart did strange flips. He felt foolish. Conflicted. Guilt-ridden. Yet he also felt at peace. Her lips moved as she slept on, murmuring incoherent words... pleas? Prayers? Curses? He lowered his head close to her own.

The warm rush of air from her breaths stirred his hair. A lush fan of lashes clashed against the whiteness of her skin; they were slightly darker than her hair, the tips a gilded bronze. She trembled in her sleep... from the nightmares or cold, he could not say.

A primitive longing triggered in him. One he hadn't felt for years. One he damn well imagined he'd never know again.

He reached down and laid his hand across her chest. His palm tingled at the feel of her heartbeat. The desire to give her the warmth and protection of his own body frightened him more than he dared to admit.

Rowan stood and unfastened his cloak's ties with fingers that shook. He swished off the garment, then knelt again, draping the cloak over her. He backed against the wall and stood in the shadows, watching her for several minutes without moving. A serenity came to him as she stopped trembling and relaxed into his cloak.

Then he watched as Smoke padded close to her. He lowered his muzzle and sniffed her hair and the cloak, taking in her scent, determining whether she was a friend or still a foe. Dizzyingly, he walked round in circles three times—then lay down next to her, fitting his body in the curve of Blanchette's. He gave a human-like sigh and lowered his muzzle to the ground. Almost triumphantly, the wolf eyed him from the chapel floor before drifting off to sleep.

※

BLANCHETTE STIRRED at the sensation of falling. She gave a thin gasp, then took in the chapel's dimness. Groaning, she scrambled into a sitting position. Her wounded leg felt sore from lying on it. She tried to rub the burn out—and was met with the heavy fabric of Rowan's cloak and that *wolf.*

She jumped up with a gasp. Smoke's head jerked in alarm. He sat on his haunches, looking at her expectantly. His golden eyes shined in the dark chapel. The wall sconce had sputtered out.

Recalling her conversation with Rowan, she skimmed her fingertips along the fur-lined collar and wolf heads. Her dream came tumbling into her forethoughts. Her mother had stroked her hair, her fingers deft and compassionate and filling her with comfort...

*How real it'd felt,* she thought, her eyes connecting with the wolf's steady gaze. The beast refused to break their melded stares.

Those golden eyes unnerved her but also provided a strange comfort.

*Like Rowan Dietrich.*

Blanchette blinked once, twice, three times.

*What am I doing? I'm a Winslowe. I'm a raven, not a wolf. I'm a fighter.*

Her father might not have been a saint, but he'd been a fighter. She owed it to him, to her mother, her grandmother, her brother, Willem, and even her sister in Demrov to keep her promise.

To keep fighting.

That was the fire she'd needed.

Blanchette stepped over Rowan's cloak, then raced out of the chapel and up the winding stairwell, her heart pounding in her throat. A musky sweat tingled on her skin. Rowan wasn't outside the chapel. She thanked God for that small mercy.

Smoke watched her vanish into the shadows before he scurried off—probably to find prey and rip out its throat.

The wind whistled through the castle's ancient stones, filling her home with an ominous breeze. Blanchette grasped a torch, watching its light crawl up and down those walls, furthering the illusion that the castle was a living entity.

*Can it hear me? And would it even listen?*

*Protect me,* she prayed. *Guard me and keep me safe.*

She exhaled a breath as her foot touched down on the last step. She hurried through the long, dark hall and felt snowy air whip her cheeks as she crossed the courtyard bridge. The clatter of swords rose in the night.

She looked down and saw Rowan's men sparring and loosing arrows on a line of straw men. The sound of the arrows reminded Blanchette of a flock of ravens taking to the sky. *I am a raven.* Standing off to the side, Rowan stood in a wide stance and crossed his muscular arms. Her thoughts danced back to the morning in the village... to the warmth in his eyes, the compassion in his voice, and the solid feel of his body as they rode Sunbeam.

She paused without thinking in the middle of the bridge, her gaze chasing restlessly across the scene. He made an awe-inspiring sight—snowflakes dusted his broad shoulders, his eyes set into a hard, scrutinizing gaze, and his ink-black hair fluttered in the wind's icy breath.

*When did it start snowing?*

She frowned, realizing the extent of her confinement and solitude.

Every few moments, Rowan would call out a simple change: *don't strike so early, keep your body at an angle, keep your expression straight, or you'll give away the game.* The men would implement the corrections and perform the move again. Their desire to please Rowan was tangible. She felt it even from the top of the bridge.

Rowan's husky voice funneled up the battlements and came alive on the bridge, seeming to join her right where she stood. Then his gaze followed. Her heart skipped a beat as Rowan's stare fixed on her. She thought he'd yell and draw his sword. Maybe run after her or send a score of his guards or Smoke on her like wolves hunting a deer. Instead, he simply smiled.

It was a ghost of a smile—more of a grin, really—but in that second, his stern demeanor altogether shattered. It struck her as an involuntary gesture... as if Rowan himself didn't realize he smiled up at her.

She'd known of the Black Wolf for nearly half her life.

*Who is this man?*

He wasn't breaking their melded gazes, just like Smoke hadn't in the chapel...

Blanchette winced as the torch's flame nipped at her cheek, so distracted was she. That gaze pinned her. She swallowed and edged away from the balustrade, her heart racing, her emotions a wild tumult. They regarded each other a moment longer. Finally, he cut off their stare with a sharp nod.

*What does that nod mean?*

*And why do I even care?*

Then his deep baritone swelled the courtyard as he resumed directing corrections at his men. He never yelled or shouted; his voice's steady, confident inflection was commanding enough. He appeared to do everything with calculated control. Blanchette scandalized herself and wondered how he'd handle himself if a woman ever took power.

A young boy sparred against a man almost twice his age and size. The wooden swords clapped together, and the redheaded boy stumbled over his own feet. He slipped on a patch of ice and fell hard, smacking against the ground with a jarring *thump*. Rowan approached him and knelt on one large, well-muscled leg.

*Why isn't he sending his men after me?*
*Doesn't he know he's playing a dangerous game?*
He trusted her, at least a little.
Just enough to fill her with an irrational guilt.
And just enough to leave her an opening.

Blanchette sped to the end of the bridge, the wind thrashing at her cheeks and fluttering her red hood.

The tower of the rookery came into sight; she picked up her stride and lifted a torch from a sconce to illuminate the frosty darkness better.

"Slow down there, milady," a masculine voice commanded. Blanchette's breath hitched as she met the speaker's face, then she felt the blood drain from her cheeks. Sir Jamie Oswald had been a soldier of her father's. He'd fought beside him on the battlefields, had jousted against him at tourneys—and he'd turned his cloak to side with the rebels.

With the Black Wolf of Norland.

"Sir Jamie," she said, her voice slow and careful but not without a bite.

He had the decency to look down. He bent into a shallow bow, his eyes still averted. "Princess, it's unsafe for you to wander alone. Come—"

Blanchette shoved at his hand and took three steps backward.

"You are correct that it's not safe," she said, her voice sharpening. "And this is still my home, sir. I shall wander wherever it pleases me."

Something darkened in his gaze. He closed the space between them and reached for her arm again, a bit too forcefully. "This is no fairy tale. Rowan Dietrich took this castle, and to him alone it belongs."

Blanchette whipped the torch at his grasping hand. He wheeled back with a curse, allowing her enough time to speed toward the rookery. Rage bubbled inside her and pumped her veins with battle fever. She felt for her dagger, buried inside her red cloak, and filled her hand with it. She prayed she wouldn't have to use it, but seeing Sir Jamie had sparked an inferno inside her soul.

She'd stop at nothing to see this carried out.

No more soldiers or guards rushed at her or stopped her as she continued onward. Not when she crossed the bailey and watchtower, then headed to the dark and jutting rookery tower. Urgency fired her steps. She smoothed the red riding hood over her head and nervously meddled with the lace. Her steps doubled their pace... and the frantic beat of her heart as well.

She glanced over her shoulder, paranoid she was being followed. She was convinced she'd turn and find Sir Edrick just behind her, his eyes victorious, or Smoke readying to pounce.

She raced up the winding stairwell and found herself in a circular tower with stacked cages. The pigeons cooed and flapped their gray wings at her appearance. Their mad fluttering echoed the rhythm of her heart.

She had only minutes before she'd be found.

Blanchette dug the parchment from her cloak and took one last glance at her handwriting.

*My dearest Isadora,*

*Come quickly. I shall try to escape from the Black Wolf's jaws myself but come, regardless.*

*Take back what is ours.*

*We are at your and King Adam's mercy.*

*Your loving sister*

With a deep breath, she opened the cage belonging to the capital of Demrov, grabbed a pigeon, and carefully tied the parchment to its leg with unsteady hands. It bobbed its dark head and cooed.

"Fly," she commanded, and the pigeon flew.

## Fifteen years earlier

THE CLANG of swords and the cries of men filled the air as Rowan Dietrich knelt before the king on the grisly battlefield. The smell of smoke and the metallic scent of blood hung heavy in the air, and the sound of wounded men groaning in pain rose around him.

Rowan felt the weight of Bartholomew's sword on his shoulder as the king knighted him. The cold metal sent frissons down his spine. He looked up to see the king's stern face, etched with the lines of battle and determination. Bartholomew's eyes met his, and for a moment, Rowan felt as if he could see the weight of the kingdom's troubles in them.

King Bartholomew laid his sword on Rowan's shoulder and spoke, his voice strong and masterful. "By the power vested in me, I knight thee, Rowan Dietrich. Rise, Sir Rowan, and serve your king and kingdom with honor and courage."

As Rowan stood, the king placed his hand on Rowan's shoulder and said, "Repeat after me. I, Rowan Dietrich, solemnly do swear to serve my king and kingdom, crush the enemies of the crown, and uphold the honor of knighthood. I shall be loyal to my word, king, and country until death parts us."

Rowan repeated the oath, his voice filled with conviction. King Bartholomew smiled tightly and finally said, "Welcome to the Order of the Knights, Sir Rowan. May your sword always be sharp and your heart be filled with courage to serve the realm."

The king moved on to the next soldier, his sword already touching the man's bloodied shoulder. He had no time for sentimentality or ceremony, his mind only focusing on the next step in his plan.

*He has no time or no room for love.*
*Only for blood and victory.*

Coursers whinnied and stomped, their armor and trappings bloodied from the fight. Men tended to the wounded, binding the injuries and administering what little medicine they had. Rowan could see the defeated enemy soldiers guarded by the king's men. Hatred and fear filled their dirty faces.

They had good reason to be afraid. King Bartholomew rarely left survivors.

Rowan peered at the king, who gave him a backward glance—a *warning* glance—before moving on to the next soldier. He should have been filled with pride, yet a dark foreboding twisted in him. He glanced at the battlefield, staring at his banner whipping against a red-and-gold horizon: the gray wolf of House Dietrich.

*Why,* Rowan despaired, *does this feel so much like the beginning of the end?*

# Nine

The following evening, Blanchette stood before her chamber's looking glass as Governess Agnes fastened the ties of her dress. The silk shimmered, a deep sapphire with a lattice of gold threads and embroidered vines. Delicate lace and small woven roses decorated the bodice.

*Who is that girl?* she wondered, assessing herself as if meeting a stranger. She looked like an impostor of her former self. All the lines and angles appeared correct, but on deeper inspection, they rang false. She still held herself with a proud and regal posture—her shoulders elegantly rolled back, her back straight as an arrow, her chin tipped upward—yet her skin had lost its lively flush, and her eyes were absent of their usual brightness. They looked tired too. And why not? She still cried herself to sleep most nights.

*Who am I?*

She lifted a hand to the scar on her cheek and traced the ridge. In her gaze she saw the horrors from which she'd never recover. A dark truth lurked in their depths, a new awareness and knowledge that filtered her every glance.

She'd told Governess Agnes all about the chapel and rookery —about the letter she'd sent to her sister, Isadora, and the irrational guilt that filled her afterward.

"The world isn't so black and white as the Good Book might have us believe," Governess Agnes had said while she helped Blanchette step into her dress. "And perhaps the Black Wolf isn't as well... black... as he seems."

*A Gray Wolf,* Blanchette had thought, *like the banner his father had flown.*

That brought her thoughts full circle. "My father's eyes," Blanchette spoke to her reflection in the looking glass. Governess Agnes's hands paused in midair. She stepped beside Blanchette and wrapped her arm around her. Standing together, side by side, they studied their reflections as if looking for some epiphany. Or a secret that could set things right again.

"Yes, my dear," Governess Agnes said through a smile that flashed her gapped teeth. "Your father was regally handsome if nothing else, and you do have his eyes."

"Is... is that all I have?"

Governess Agnes ran her fingers through Blanchette's long curls. The movements gently pulled at her scalp in a rhythmic, soothing way. They reminded Blanchette of her dream in the chapel... of fingers running through her hair in a sweet caress.

*Had it been a dream?*

It was a strange thing—feeling so homesick *while* at her home. *Home isn't a place or a castle or even a kingdom,* she mused. *Home was my family.*

"You have your father's eyes. Perhaps his fair skin too," she continued in a slow, careful voice. "You have your mother's enchanting hair and smile, certainly. But most important, you inherited this from her." She placed her palm against the beat of Blanchette's heart.

Blanchette smoothed down the front of her dress, her blue gaze darting from her own to Governess Agnes's. Finally, Governess Agnes set the wimple over Blanchette's gold curls and artfully adjusted the flowing silk. Delicate woven roses adorned the fabric, which was inlaid with small pears and gold silk.

"Why would he want to sup with him?"

Men like Rowan Dietrich rarely did anything without measured incentive. Usually one of personal gain. Edrick had delivered the summons that morning. Blanchette's thoughts traveled to when Rowan had taken her into the heart of her city. She'd never felt so connected to Norland than when she knelt before those two children and beheld the suffering in their eyes.

She recalled the letter she'd sent, too, and the help that may or may not be coming.

Governess Agnes cleared her throat and glanced over her shoulder even though the chamber door was firmly shut. She met Blanchette's reflection in the looking glass with solemn eyes. They were full of wisdom and love. Blanchette's heart ached from the affection she found there. She smiled at Governess Agnes and held her hand.

Governess Agnes's voice lowered, sounding very much like a conspiratorial whisper. "Listen to me, dear, and listen closely. If you share another thing with your father—and there's only one other—it's your temper and... well, your rather impulsive nature. I've seen how stubborn you can be, God save us." Governess Agnes squeezed her hand.

"That's *three* things."

Governess Agnes cracked a smile. Then she stepped in front of Blanchette, effectively blocking their reflections, and placed her small, gloved hands on Blanchette's shoulders. An edge came into her voice that demanded Blanchette's full attention and prickled her skin. "The lesson you must learn quickly, my dear, is *patience*. You must be clever with this man... this Black Wolf, this Rowan Dietrich. If you truly wish to escape"—an uncharacteristically sly smile shaped her lips—"perhaps even *win* him over... let him underestimate you. You are a raven. Remember that. So be clever and fly when it's time. But only when it's time. Isadora will send help. I know it in my heart... but be patient, my dear, and I promise you'll be rewarded tenfold." She continued to smooth out Blanchette's wimple and the fine material of her dress. Blanchette gave a small yelp as Governess Agnes pinched her cheeks, bringing color to her fair skin. "Ah. There we are. The Black Wolf shan't stand a chance." Governess Agnes stepped back with a nod of approval. Then, in a regal voice that sent more needles across Blanchette's skin, she recited, *"Patience is better than pride. Don't be quick-tempered, for anger is the friend of fools."*

Blanchette thought again of the bird she sent from the rookery.

She nodded at Governess Agnes.

This was naught but a waiting game.

She could be patient. She could play for a little while.

*Meanwhile, let the Black Wolf play at swords.*

⁂

SHE ENTERED the chamber in her red riding cloak, looking every bit like a queen. Rowan came to his feet instantly because her very presence demanded it.

Her posture alone told Rowan precisely what she thought of him summoning her, and he admired her even more for it. He admired how she held her shoulders up and back as if whatever burden he'd lain there couldn't bring her down. He admired the unrelenting tilt to her chin, how loose curls spiraled out from her wimple in defiance.

He admired the fight she had in her, even in the presence of a wolf.

But her eyes fascinated him most of all.

She came right up to him—his heart leaped without warning at her intimate nearness—then she placed a delicate hand on the back of the chair he'd risen from. *His* chair.

"Pardon me," she said, that steady gaze locked on his. Pushing past his body, she sat in the gilded chair at the table's place of high honor. Then she untied her cloak with trembling hands.

It was the one giveaway to an otherwise relaxed and self-assured demeanor.

She glanced around the room, her eyes narrowed with a poorly masked anger. Rowan bit his cheek, knowing his mirth would only fuel her ire.

"Where is your beast?"

"Smoke? He's hunting in the woods."

Rowan couldn't take his gaze off her. Twin candelabras flanked the table, casting a delicate glow over her face. The wound on her cheek had transformed into a thin, raised ridge. It added fierceness to her beauty, a contrast to those fine, regal features. It reminded Rowan of what she'd endured, what she'd survived and could survive, and that even one as gentle as Princess Blanchette could be his undoing if he didn't tread carefully.

She exuded confidence she'd lacked in the tavern, which showed Rowan just how well-crafted she was for castles and throne chairs.

*Hell of a lot better than me, that's for certain.*

*She's trained her whole life for such a seat.*

She stared at him coolly, her eyes never wavering, her red lips tilted at the corners.

Or was that just his imagination? The open ties of her gown revealed a patch of creamy white skin that rose voluptuously from the bodice.

She looked good enough to eat.

A servant placed a decanter of ale and two goblets before them. Rowan poured one, then handed it to Blanchette, allowing a tense silence to linger between them.

Finally, she spoke, her voice firm and smooth as silk. "A pity our steward died in the attack. It would have made your invasion much easier had he lived."

Rowan's gaze dragged into hers. "Many good people died that night, Blanchette."

"Yes... I would like an active role in all matters related to Norland. As you haven't seen fit to chop off my head, I should like to use it. The ledgers, coffers, stores—I shall oversee all of it."

Rowan tossed back a hearty swallow of ale. Then he

drummed his fingertips on the oak table as he watched Princess Blanchette watch *him*.

"Done. I'll have the ledgers delivered to your chamber. And so long as you follow my orders, I'd be honored to hear your counsel."

"You'd be honored to hear it," she echoed with a scoff. "But will you be honored to heed it?" She fidgeted with her signet ring, her cool armor beginning to crack and show vulnerability. "Very well. As it happens, I have a request I'd like you to meet here and now."

Rowan sliced into his mutton, then stabbed the meat with his fork more aggressively than needed. "I would allow you to ask it of me."

She tensed, her lips pressed into a hard line, her eyes harder still. Then she gracefully cut into the mutton and took small, delicate bites. She flashed a smile that didn't fit correctly, yet she looked beautiful doing so. "I'd like to discuss your prisoner and my dear friend again. Jonathan. I'd like an update on his child, Petyr, as well. I'd developed a great fondness for him."

"You want Jonathan released."

"I *demand* Jonathan's release."

Rowan sat back against the chair and casually folded his hands into each other. He surrendered to a smile. Just a small lift at the corner of his lip. "I don't think you're in a position to demand anything of me, *Princesse*."

She said nothing; merely laid a fair hand on the seat's armrest and stroked the wood. Rowan watched the way her slender fingers moved and felt his manhood stir.

*How would they feel wrapped around my skin? And those lips. Lips as red as her cloak...*

"Oh, I think I am, sir." Her eyes said *I'm in the position of high honor.*

Rowan leaned forward and spoke directly to her blazing stare. "I understand you owe this man a great debt, but let me explain something to you. A lord who allows a criminal to walk freely is no lord to be feared."

Blanchette dropped her gaze and scoffed into her barely touched mutton. "I thought it was the people's love you desired. My father already had their fear. So you've effectively changed nothing." She glared up at him, her voice cracking with emotion. "Look how far their loyalty extended in the end. Men who'd stood by my crib the day I was born tore down my family's walls. You want true loyalty, respect, and order? Then *earn it,* damn you!" She punctuated the words by slamming her fist against the table. The goblets and plates chattered from the strike. "Otherwise... otherwise, it's just more of the same."

Her words hit him hard. His hand tightened on his goblet as he wrestled with what to do, what to say, calculating the best move forward.

Inexorably, he felt his admiration for her growing.

"You... you are right. That is wise of you to say. I shall do that," Rowan said at length, his tone careful yet confident, "and you will help me. As my bride. I'll pardon your friend and release him on the morrow. His boy too, of course. And you and I will enter a formal alliance before the kingdom before winter ends."

The color visibly drained from her skin again. Her fingers gripped the chair's armrest, and her nails dug into the fine wood. He was sure they'd leave marks. "Pardon me? As-as your *bride*?"

Rowan spread his hands wide in a philosophical gesture. "A marriage alliance between the Black Wolf and the Raven."

Rowan watched as she swallowed hard, then exhaled a tense breath. She released the air slowly, and Rowan could hear it pass through her full red lips. "You are mad. You think I'd marry the man responsible for the death of my family?"

Rowan sliced into the mutton and took a big bite. "I'd think you'd want to unify the people and take your place as queen."

Her lip rose into a sardonic smile, which caused the scar to pull taut across her cheek. "And I suppose this is a gift you mean to give me. A role I was born into. One you've stolen from me.

Being Queen of Norland is now my birthright. You're in no position to give me my crown; it is already mine."

"Maybe so. But the kingdom you were born into is not the kingdom you live in now."

She pushed away the plate of food, then locked his gaze. "I have you to thank for that."

"Your father—"

"The Winslowes have sat on the throne for generations. The kingdom has cycled through seasons. This is true, and perhaps my father brought a winter. But even the heaviest snows thaw. And Willem..." Her voice broke off, and tears flooded her blue eyes. She gallantly fought off those tears and pinched her small hands against her mouth. "Oh God, he would have been *good*."

Rowan cursed. Then he closed his eyes, unable to bear the sight of her misery. In his mind, he heard her sobs in the chapel... saw her frail body curled up on the floor, shivering and lost, with Smoke beside her.

*What can I do?*

*How can I ease her pain when she hates me so?*

He reached across their seats with a lowered head and tentatively rested his palm on her hand. She tensed under his touch. He thought she'd scream and pull away, yet she did none of the kind. Instead, she dropped her hand from her face, and he felt her taut fingers loosen under his palm one by one. She released an audible breath that blew between them and caressed his face.

"You will be good, too, Blanchette. You will be wise and just, and you will be *good*. You and I... we could change the course of history forever. These are your people. Now help me put an end to this winter."

She stared at his much larger hand resting on hers; his palm covered her hand completely. Rowan savored the warmth of her smooth skin. The urge to bend forward and kiss her knuckles startled him.

Rowan pulled his hand from her own and returned it to his utensil.

Blanchette stared at him long and hard. "Even if I said yes—even if I... I wanted to... well, I am already spoken for," she added haughtily.

A strange sensation pricked at his backbone. She was betrothed, probably since she was a babe. *Of course she is. She's a prize, with ancient royal blood running through her veins and the face of an angel.*

"Indeed? You're promised to whom?"

She visibly hesitated, then stalled the time by absently fiddling with her goblet. Rowan reached for her hand and wrapped his palm over her fidgeting fingers, effectively stilling them.

"Answer me, Blanchette. You already let it slip. You can't squirt the milk back up the cow's udder if you take my meaning."

She shot a look at him and freed her hand from his. Then she surprised them both and laughed. She pressed her palm to her lips to smother the cheerful burst of sound. He couldn't recall hearing something more beautiful. "In a moment, sir. I'm deciding whether it's in *my* people's interest for you to be privy to such sensitive information."

Rowan tensed against the chair. "Need I remind you that I am Lord of Winslowe Castle now, and you are my subject. So long as I hold this fortress, any information regarding its affairs is mine to know and mine to do with as I please."

She dropped her hand from her mouth and coiled her fingers into a fist. The signet shined defiantly, drinking in the candlelight.

"You've seized and held it. For now. The word shall spread quickly of your conquest. By mouth, by the wings of birds, by ship, and by horse... while many people and houses consider you their champion, I'm not sure my betrothed will share the sentiment."

*A threat, and a poorly veiled one at that.* Admiration and anger wrestled inside him. However, he remained composed and confidently quiet on the outside.

"In fact, sir," she dared press on, "my future husband may not like the idea of you warming his seat at all. And especially not his bed."

*Maybe she's playing me.*
*Perhaps she's simply buying time.*

"So I shall be warming your bed? Is that an invitation?" He laughed outright at the blush on her cheeks.

Her bright eyes churned at his reaction. They were deep and mesmerizing and as blue as Norland's sea.

*I shall fall into those eyes and drown if I'm not careful.* Edrick's ominous warning flashed through his mind. He shook it away and pinned Blanchette with a sharp stare.

"Who is he? Your betrothed?" Nothing. "Come now, Blanchette. Don't be coy with me."

Blanchette brought the goblet's rim to her lips, taking her sweet time, her eyes never leaving him. She took a small, calculated sip. Then she returned the goblet to the table with a loud *bang*. She moved with slow, drawn-out intention, and Rowan knew she was baiting him.

"I desire to have Jonathan released and returned to his child and home, where they shall want for nothing. My father's soldiers —the ones who have remained loyal to *me*, to the crown—I want them released and pardoned, so long as they vow to remain peaceful in their *queen's* name. I shall ask it of them myself if it pleases you."

"They'll say the words to you and walk free… and I'll pay with a knife in my back. I'm not an idiot. And besides, I have already offered them freedom for their allegiance to me."

"It pleases me to hear they aren't bought so cheaply."

"Some of them were. And pray tell, what man can afford *not* to buy his freedom?"

"Men who value their integrity and a sense of justice. The Black Wolf of Norland should understand such a thing."

"Justice," Rowan echoed, a growl churning in his throat. He leaned in close while blood-drenched memories soaked his mind. "Trust me, I understand it well, *Princesse*. I was your father's man once. I know firsthand what he asks of his soldiers... and of the needless blood he spilled. Some nights, my hands still feel wet from it all."

※

Blanchette felt cold inside. Only the supreme force of her willpower kept the goblet from trembling in her hands; only the sound of her grandmother's voice stopped the panic from showing on her face.

*Marry the Black Wolf of Norland?* The very man who'd lead a revolution against her home? The man who'd torn down a dynasty that might have lasted a thousand years?

*He is the people's champion,* a part of her whispered. *You mustn't forget that. The seeds of distress he's sown may be the flowers of spring.*

She looked at him closely. Searched for a trace of softness beneath the rugged facade he wore so well. Images from the village came to mind as she recalled the gentleness and empathy he'd shown those children. She remembered the words the soldier had spoken to her. They weren't empty, bought, or borne of duty. They'd been a declaration of gratitude and love.

*Could I ever love the Black Wolf of Norland? And does it even matter?*

Blanchette had met her betrothed only once, years ago. She held little affection or sentiment from what she could recall of Lord Huntley.

The air seemed to thicken and thrum as Rowan leaned closer to her. Her gaze lost itself in his own. His stare was as commanding as every other bit of him, and she found herself surrendering to its power.

She shook her head, willing away the spell he wove over her. "My father's soldiers—these men you speak of—are simply men like you and me. Like anyone else. They have lives. Families. Daughters. Hasn't there been enough bloodshed? Where does it all end, Rowan? If not here, if not now, then when? You free them—and yes, there's a chance they could betray you. But if you murder them, there's a greater chance their kin will come for you. Maybe not today or tomorrow, but one day. After all, is that not the same fate my family paid at your hands? I could walk the dungeons right now and tell you many of the soldiers' and their children's names. And I could recite which children won't sleep so easily after you've killed their fathers." He began to speak, but Blanchette raised her hand and exacted his silence with that single gesture. Her voice softened to a whisper. "I may be a young girl who knows little of the ways of war or the world... but I know enough. Firsthand. I know the bloodlust that such events can inspire. Would you not agree?"

The silence that followed was complete. Then Rowan rose from his chair and slowly approached Blanchette until he stood behind her. She felt the heat of his body. Her breath caught at how indecently close he was—mere inches away. "So you are saying, Your Grace, one day someone might come up behind me like this..." He rested his hands on either side of her body, enclosing her with muscled arms. He leaned forward as he spoke. The heat from his words fanned the back of her neck. "Without warning, they may *place* their hands upon me," he whispered as he did just that. His palms slipped down the table and rested on her shoulders. Blanchette fought to maintain a regal and queenly posture but felt herself melt into the chair. "Someone will come for me... as sudden as a lightning strike..." Blanchette felt the blood rushing through her veins. She could hear it, too, and her heartbeat as well. His large, callused hands—hands so unlike her father's, unmarred by labor and life—slid down her shoulders. Slowly. Sensually. By God, they felt good. He moved with that practiced ease and quiet confidence. "Is that what you're telling me, Your Grace?" His voice was deep and dark and dipped in honey.

She shut her eyes and imagined the proposal he'd made her.

How would it feel? What would it be like to lie with such a man?

She shivered at the thought, but not entirely from terror.

Rowan stepped back, and his voice sank to a tremor when he spoke. It resonated through her, flooding her veins like the water in the Rockbluff River. Beautiful but deadly, she reminded herself as an image of her mother's torn body surfaced.

"Aye. You may be young, Blanchette, young and beautiful..." The very air seemed to crinkle and vibrate. She swallowed, willing away the war of emotions inside her. His voice was all she could hear, and his transient touch was all she could feel. Within that moment, nothing else existed outside of Rowan Dietrich. "But you don't know so little of the world. Not anymore." She could hear a note of remorse in his voice. She yearned to glance over her shoulder and into his eyes—to read whatever emotion might be there, but she felt frozen. "I shall do as you command, Your Grace. But only with you by my side." Then he shot away from the table. Blanchette's breath caught and held tight in her chest. He glanced back at her. "Accept my proposal, or your father's men shall die as my prisoners."

He reached out and thoughtfully fingered the edge of her red riding cloak. "You always wear this. Why?"

Blanchette finally found her voice. "His name is Huntley. Lord Peter Huntley. And you want a queen by your side?" she snapped, breaking his hold on her. "Then you can earn me too."

---

DARKNESS SURROUNDED HER. Blanchette couldn't move her body.

Trees towered around her like silent guardsmen. Twigs and branches dug into her naked back. She lay in the middle of the woods, each of her limbs tied to a tree trunk with thick ropes. A light breeze stirred across her nude skin like a lover's caress. She shivered and tried to pull at the binds but couldn't stir a limb.

A low growl cut through the woods. She glanced down and straight ahead. Hovering over her lower body was a massive black wolf. Saliva dripped from his bared, stark-white teeth and splattered onto her skin. Moonlight shimmered off his long, beautiful coat and set his eyes aglow. Intelligence brewed in their depths.

Those eyes penetrated her.

He stood above her, each front leg planted on either side of her body as if guarding his prey. Blanchette tried to stir, to cry out—but she found herself very much alone and at the wolf's mercy. He bared his teeth again and slowly leaned down until his head aligned with hers. She shut her eyes tight and whispered a prayer. She felt the beast's hot breath fan against her exposed neck. She waited for the feel of his teeth sinking into her flesh. She waited for her throat to be torn out... but nothing happened.

And then her hands were free. With her eyes still shut, she attempted to push away the wolf's shaggy head. But her fingertips met warm skin.

Human skin.

Her hands trembled as they made their way into a dense thicket of hair. She wound her fingertips in those soft tresses. The earthy aromas of the wood—the damp dirt, the crisp tree leaves, the musty river—melded with the distinct scent of *man*.

Then his voice came—a sultry growl that prickled her skin and made her toes curl.

"Sweet little Blanchette, dressed in her grandmother's red riding cloak and all alone in the deep, dark woods..." She fought to push him away. But suddenly, her hands were pinned to her sides, and Rowan's face hovered above her own. If he leaned forward any farther, their lips would touch.

His hazel eyes bore into hers. They implored her. Shackled her in place.

She felt the heat of his words. Her heart hammered inside her chest, and her blood turned to lava.

"These woods never belonged to you or your family. It's the wolves they answer to... and mine is the voice they obey."

## Red Kingdom

*Out,* she thought as she woke from her dream. *I need out.*

# Ten

"MY CROWN is in my heart, not on my head."

— SHAKESPEARE

The following day dawned clear and crisp; not a cloud could be seen, and the sky rolled overhead in a brilliant carpet of baby blue.

It was a few hours from nightfall but unusually warm. Blanchette felt beads of sweat gather in the heel of her palm as she clutched a straw basket. Sir Royce, a man freshly knighted in the siege's wake, strolled beside her in a jerkin and trousers. One hand grasped his horse's lead; the other rested absently on the sword's pommel. They'd been walking in relative silence for nearly thirty minutes. She'd asked permission to gather herbs from the wood after supper the evening before. Rowan had allowed it, with the exception she'd be under guard, of course. He'd have escorted her, but he and Edrick had busied themselves with their plans.

The wheels in Blanchette's head had turned, and she'd constructed her escape.

True to his word, Rowan released Jonathan that morning and returned Petyr to him, along with heavy chests of silver and provisions. Rowan had reimbursed him well for those miserable days in the dungeon.

Now, a shimmering sun set the wood afire; that light seemed to caress everything. The ancient trees, which were nearly stripped of their leaves, glowed brilliantly. The mossy hills and rises also looked regal.

Norland was alive, and Blanchette felt its pulse.

The clamor and yells of Rowan's men faded away as Blanchette and Sir Royce wandered deeper into the wilderness. The greenery thickened. He stayed close behind her, tailing her at each step. Everywhere Blanchette glanced, she saw opportunity— a tree trunk fat enough to hide her body behind or foliage that could conceal her completely...

The wicker basket shook in her grip as her mind chased how she would outwit this kindly knight.

"How much farther in, my lady?"

"Kingswood grows bountifully along the river," she explained as they stepped under a canopy of trees and followed the chatter of moving water. "It really shouldn't be much farther now."

And it wasn't. Within moments, the Rockbluff River broke into sight. Blanchette's heart constricted, and her thoughts slid to three weeks earlier. She saw herself in the third person, blood dripping from her wounded cheek and tears streaming from her eyes. She saw her father's guards waiting at the little dock, her mother's beautiful features pulled tight into a mask of horror.

The sun shone through the trees, casting dappled patterns on the water. The clear river flowed over rocks and pebbles, imbuing the wood with a soothing sound.

Tall trees lined the river's bank, their leaves rustling in the gentle wind. The music of chirping birds and the occasional splash of a fish breaking through the water imbued the wood. The air was fresh and clean, with a hint of earthy and vegetal scents from the surrounding greenery.

As she walked along the river, its water sparkled in the sunlight, and she saw schools of fish darting through the shallow pools. The sounds of the woods were all around her; the river's gentle flow was a constant companion. It was a peaceful scene. The beauty echoed of happier times, and the serenity of the river was a bittersweet reminder of what she'd lost.

Today and that night were complete opposites.

*Why couldn't the river have run gently, as it was right now?* Why couldn't it have led her family to salvation rather than doom? The night of the siege, the rain had lashed the water and turned it a murky brown in the lantern's light. The water ran clear today, yet her family's blood tainted it all the same.

The frustration made her quiver with anger and heartache. Her breaths shortened, and the viselike grip on her basket caused the wicker sticks to snag her skin. She glanced down at her finger and watched with detachment as a ring of blood circled it.

"Princess?" Sir Royce said, his deep voice cutting through her thoughts. "Are you well? Perhaps we should rest here a while."

*Am I well?* she thought. *The babble of this river is the same song that spirited away my mother. I may not see it, but this water still runs red with her blood. I have lost my family, my home, my very happiness.*

*Your liege lord is the crowning jewel on a crown that never belonged to him.*

"I am, sir, just a bit warm," she said instead, walking toward the bank where flowers bloomed in artful red and paisley blue patches. Sir Royce nodded, then followed her to the edge of the river. Absently, he knelt beside her and ran his fingers across the overlong grass and weeds.

"This is it, my lady? What you came here searching for?"

*You've not the slightest idea about what I came here for.* "Yes, this is the kingswood," she simply said, cupping one of the plant's bright, bell-shaped flowers. Then she put her hands to work, deftly plucking the stems from the sodden earth and placing them in the basket. She covered the vial inside her basket with the flowers, hiding it from the knight.

Sir Royce sensed and saw nothing.

He stood and strolled with his horse along the bank, allowing the courser to graze at leisure and drink from the stream. Her heart raced behind her ribs. Her courage sparked. She felt her chance encroaching. A gentle breeze stirred the river's glassy surface, sending the leafy trees into a noisy chatter.

*Norland is cheering for me,* she mused.

"Where'd you learn about kingswood, my lady?" he asked conversationally.

Blanchette paused and smiled at him, then moved to another nearby patch and continued collecting the paisley flowers. "My brother, Willem, trained with sword and arrow and lance shortly after he began walking. My sister took to embroidery since she was old enough to hold needles. All three of us were taught to sit a horse and proper courtesies... but my talent lies between the pages of books. And so, I read, learned, and helped in all the ways I could. But kingswood specifically? An old friend taught me about it," she finished with a whisper, thinking of Thomas and his betrayal.

Sir Royce patted his horse's side, then knelt beside her. Blanchette tugged kingswood from the forest floor and handed it to him. Her eyes shifted over his shoulder, between the dense trees, as she mentally scouted for the paths least overgrown and the most open.

"How long have you fought for Rowan?" she asked, rising to her feet and brushing off her cloak's red fabric. Sir Royce's mount lowered its head and grazed again, trimming the tall, deep-green foliage.

He hesitated, his eyes pooling with an emotion that hit her hard. "Almost a decade now. I fought under your father's banner before him."

Blanchette felt her breath catch, but she forced that bubbling rage back into her innermost shadows. When he offered no more explanation, she said, "What Rowan has told me about my father... some of the... atrocities he'd committed. They're all true?"

Sir Royce grabbed his courser's lead and guided him next to the stream. "No one knows the pain of grief and loss better than you," he said, his voice slow and words careful. "You and Rowan are more alike than you'd care to wager." He paused, patted the side of his horse's muzzle, then pinned Blanchette with a pointed stare. A smile lifted the corner of his lip. "You remind me of her. Lady Dietrich was quite beautiful. Fierce and intelligent. There is something in your eyes, in the way you carry yourself... I know Rowan sees it too." Blanchette scanned the woods... the ancient trees that stood like quiet sentinels. Images from her dream surfaced. She saw herself lying between them, her limbs tied with ropes, a black, sleek figure hovering above her. She heard the low growl reverberate through the woods, a voice in the wind. Blanchette shook it away and clutched the basket to her chest.

"We should return soon, my lady," Sir Royce said, his gaze rising to a darkening horizon. Blanchette smiled, then motioned toward his flask of water, which he'd retrieved from his satchel. "Might I have some, sir?"

He returned her smile and passed the flask.

She sipped, then studied Sir Royce's kind and weathered features. "His men—even those who were my father's men—they all seem to like Rowan."

"Nay, they don't like him. They love him."

She took another sip. "But why? Why him? Why the Black Wolf of Norland?"

Sir Royce paused, then came to his feet and patted his horse on the side of his regal neck. He gazed into the horizon at the looming castle that shot like an angry fist into the sky.

Blanchette's hands shook as she fumbled with the vial and emptied its contents into the flask.

"Well, because he's one of us," Sir Royce finished after a thoughtful silence.

"Rowan was also my father's man once. One of his closest advisers. My father knighted him—made him who he is today."

She could feel the heat rising in her voice. She fought it down, needing to keep the peace between her and this knight.

"That he did, my lady. His cruelty—his commands—shaped Rowan Dietrich into the Black Wolf. But knighthood isn't a simple path. So many oaths we swear: protect the innocent, protect your king, and remain true. What is one to do, pray tell, when the king slaughters the innocent?" Now, the anger rose in his own voice. "Sir Rowan upheld his vow to *us*—to the people of Norland. That's why we follow him. That's why we love him."

"And he betrayed his king." *I must act fast,* she thought, *or this shall spin out of control, and my chance will be lost.* Fortunately, Sir Royce was petting the courser's slender muzzle, his eyes distant as he gazed into the trees as if he'd see ghosts emerge at any moment.

"He did, Princess. And I pray he'd do it all again."

She sighed and came to her feet, brushing off her skirts again. She stood next to Sir Royce and handed him the flask. "Us Winslowes have always been stubborn. It's hard to stomach the words... but I can see it now. I see why you all love him so."

Blanchette watched him drink from the flask and realized her words were true.

Sir Royce wiped his mouth with the back of his hand. His eyes took on a whimsical look as if he were watching something unfold inside his mind. "I met your father once before, you know. I came with Rowan to the capital on a campaign. To put a stop to some uprising. They were always shooting up, much like weeds. That time, your father ordered us to burn the village before the pirates could pillage it. Rowan asked about the villagers... the women and children who depended on us to protect them. 'Kill them all,' King Bartholomew ordered. 'Burn them to the ground. Let the pirates forage their ashes.' I..."

Suddenly, his eyes grew hazy, and his words became fragmented and slow. "Rowan... we left the castle... I... I don't feel well, my lady." Sir Royce's grip failed him; the flask fell from his hand and tumbled into the stream.

His body heaved over as her concoction worked its magic.

Blanchette watched as he battled to keep his consciousness. Hurriedly, she fetched the flask from the stream and filled it with clean water before tossing it into her basket.

"I am so sorry," she whispered to Sir Royce as she climbed onto the courser's back. Then she dug her heels into the horse's flanks and rode away from everything she'd ever known.

---

"What do you mean she got away?" Rowan tried to maintain the stoic demeanor he was so well-known for, but the anger in his voice betrayed him. Edrick was next to him, bent over the table and surveying a stack of maps of the sea. His head snapped up at the sound of Sir Royce's voice.

The madness inside Rowan pushed through like water through a dam. He stepped closer to Sir Royce, his right hand subconsciously going to his sword's pommel; the other hand found its way into the material of his comrade's tunic.

Sir Royce looked like hell.

"She... I was a fool. She tricked me. Drugged me. I could barely see, sir. She got away with my horse! I—"

"I knew we couldn't trust her! Damn you, Rowan! Damn you!"

Rowan held up his hand and signaled Edrick's silence. "Did you see which way she went?" When Sir Royce didn't reply, Rowan wound his fingers in the tunic and nearly pulled him onto his toes. He shook him like a wolf shaking its kill between its jaws. The terror in Sir Royce's cloudy eyes was palpable. "Answer me, or I'll have your head for this!"

"North, my lord, north! Through the woods. I-I believe she'll follow the river to the port. Likely board a ship there and head for Demrov. Her sister is there."

Rowan nodded, then let him go in a harsh gesture. Sir Royce nearly fell to the floor from the force of it. "Nay. She won't. You stay here, Edrick, and watch the castle. I'll fetch her."

He crossed the solar in long strides, the beginning of battle fever stirring inside him. All the while, Smoke stuck to him like a shadow.

---

He didn't need a team of soldiers or Sir Edrick. They'd only slow him down. He didn't need Sunbeam, the fastest and most devoted destrier he'd ever ridden. He didn't need the kennel hounds to catch her scent or his loyal wolf. His rage was sufficient. He'd chase that godforsaken princess through all seven rings of hell if needed.

Anger roiled inside him—a storm of emotion that thundered in his ears.

Rowan pressed his boots into Sunbeam's flanks as the horse masterfully dodged trees and jumped over fallen logs. Smoke darted beside them, a deft shadow sliding through the trees. The wolf was at home in the wood—at one with the soil and trees and the moon shining above.

Blanchette would set off for the port... or possibly for the castle of her betrothed... and likely under cover of darkness. She'd steer clear of the open roads for certain. She was impulsive, fierce, temperamental... but far from downright stupid.

*Damn fool, trusting a Winslowe.*

Sir Edrick was right.

*He's always been right.*

Slowly, steadily, mournfully, the cry of a wolf filled the forest. The sound carried through the rustling trees and the babble of the streams. There was a pain in its voice—a grief that spoke to his soul's darkest corners.

*Kill them all. Let the pirates forage their ashes.*

Rowan heard the eerie creak and sigh of bodies hanging from trees... swaying, swaying, swaying...

*Let every rebel know what happens when they betray their king.*

He lowered his head as a pair of dangling feet materialized

from the darkness and swayed toward him. He hooked his heels into Sunbeam's haunches and pressed on. He dodged another hanged body. Then another and another. He tugged on Sunbeam's reins and looked about in a panic. *Hundreds* of rotting corpses swung from the trees... an entire forest built from death. Dizzyingly, his mount wheeled in circles as Rowan's gaze scanned the forest of swaying bodies—looking, searching...

*Kill them all.*

He kicked Sunbeam's flanks, sending him jetting forward. But then he reared and released a whinny as if the smell of death sent him into a panic.

*No, the bodies aren't here.*
*It's in my mind.*

But was it?

*I will turn and see her hanging from a tree, her throat red and bleeding, and it will have been my fault.*

*Again.*

He blinked. All the bodies were gone. They'd vanished as if they'd never been.

*Again and again.*

"I'm going mad," he whispered, his heartbeat roaring. "Or am I already mad?" As if in answer, Smoke threw back his head and howled.

⁂

Dusk came with a vengeance.

A chilled wind brought the wood to life; every tree and stream stirred awake and deepened the darkness. Branches rattled like bones, and the river made a constant murmur.

Blanchette dismounted at the edge of the forest. Her thighs and backside were sore and aching. Hunger gnawed at her stomach like a dull knife. The air was cold in her throat, and her mouth felt as dry as dust. Her tongue was a plank of poorly carved wood. The sinking sun cast a glow on the world, drenching the trees and greenery in liquid gold.

She should have traveled farther, she knew... but moving during the day would have been risky. She couldn't chance being recognized and returned to Rowan.

*I will rest, then ride like the devil is on my heels.*

*Or a wolf.*

She'd head for the port... perhaps cut off her hair before then to help conceal her identity.

Soon, complete darkness fell. The courser's ears whipped toward the sound of a snapping branch. Within the canopy of night, it reminded Blanchette of the crunch a breaking bone might make.

More crunching. Rustling.

The hiss of a large body whipping through trees and brush and brambles.

She drew closer to the horse and inhaled a sharp breath. His hooves stomped uneasily, and she felt the tension rising off his warm body like steam off ice.

It came from the deepest shadows—a solemn, drawn-out howl that made her skin crawl. It sounded human in its grief. That howl swelled the wood like a fierce rising wind. The horse whinnied and stomped his hooves, its head nervously shifting toward the sound, which seemed to come from all directions.

It was everywhere.

Hanging from the trees.

Seeping out of the soil.

Whispering along with the Rockbluff River.

That sound filled every crevice of her being. Within her mind's eye, she saw him standing there—the Black Wolf of Norland, donned in that crude armor and snarling helm, cutting through her father's men with a vengeful deliberation...

His longsword would be hanging at his side, wet and dripping blood.

*I need to follow the road. I cannot have him find me.*

The road would pave her path to the port. Without it, the wood would swallow her whole and spit out nothing but bone and ash.

Quickly, she mounted, then wheeled the horse around and away from the rushing stream. She rode alongside the twisting, muddy road.

She ducked beneath canopies of leaves and branches, following the full moon's glow.

Another drawn-out howl shivered through the trees.

A rush of movement again.

Snapping branches.

*Is that the sound of breathing?*

Blanchette kicked the horse's flank. He lurched forward with an anxious whinny and galloped out of the trees and into a clearing.

She turned a corner, pointing her mount north, north to the port... north to freedom, north to a ship which would bring her to her sister in Demrov...

North, away from the wolves, the heartache, and the shadow of her loss.

She yanked on the reins a mile later and commanded the horse to a stop. He pawed at the ground and tossed his head, shrinking at the sound of movement.

*I am surrounded.*

Seven men emerged from the trees. They were mounted on half-starved ponies that looked like they were suffering from some skin disease. Even within the darkness, she could make out the hard lines of the men's faces and the even harder gleams in their eyes. They carried rusted axes; one man slung a bow over his shoulder.

*Brigands.*

"Well met, my lady," said a man with an eye patch and a filthy, tangled beard. "What's a beauty like yourself doing in the woods all alone?"

Blanchette straightened up on her mount and held her chin

high with feigned confidence. "You are mistaken. I am not alone. My brothers took their horses to the streams. They shall return shortly."

The first brigand glanced at the rider closest to him—a gruff-looking man dressed in rags and battle scars. Deep pockmarks covered his face. They tightened as he flashed a nasty grin full of rotten teeth. "Is that so? I think you are lying. I think you are all alone... far from home, an' wearing too many clothes."

Blanchette pulled back on the courser's reins, directing him away from the encroaching men and back into the woods. He tossed his head and stomped at the muddy ground. Blanchette pulled hard on the reins, signaling him right. Instead, he surged forward and broke into a trot.

Then the chase was on. Pounding hooves rolled through the gathering darkness.

It was thunder.

It was mayhem.

It was death coming for her in a black chariot.

Blanchette's breath and heartbeat caught. She grabbed the horse's loose and flowing mane and entwined her fingers in it. With a cry built from desperation, she kicked her heels into his muscular flanks. She flew through the tangle of branches, leaves, and brambles.

Clinging on for dear life, she leaned forward and wrapped her arms around the horse's neck.

Everything happened in a blur. The horse reeled onto his hind legs and released a frantic whinny; the ground came up to hit her hard. Blanchette felt like the air had been knocked from her lungs. She rolled out of striking distance from the horse's pounding hooves. An inch closer and her skull would have been mush.

She lay for a moment, the breath smacked out of her lungs, her eyes fringed with black specks. She exhaled, flipped onto her palms and knees, and began to rise—

—only to be kicked in the stomach. Hard and many more times. She cried out and clutched her belly, then spat blood.

Two of the men dismounted. The first brigand released a huge, ugly laugh that filled the darkness. The other men surrounded her, blocking any paths for escape. Night had fallen, and the man himself resembled just another shadow. Dark, dangerous, and dirty.

*I am going to die here... oh God...*

"Aw, don't be such a poor sport, sweetling. Come closer and give Geoffrey a kiss." The beast who called himself Geoffrey kicked his mount and yanked hard on the reins. The animal spooked and threw his hooves into the air, rearing and almost hitting Blanchette in the face.

Then all seven men were on the ground.

Two of them latched onto her arms and pulled her upright. Her stomach and head burning, they forced her to stand before the first rider. He sneered at her. The movement seemed to deepen those pockmarks and highlight the cruelty in his gray eyes. The three other brigands circled her like vultures zoning in on a kill.

*Or a pack of wolves.*

"Want to try again?" He brought his fingers to her cheeks and idly traced the scar. "My, you are a troublemaker, ain't you?"

Blanchette returned his sneer and saw red behind her eyes. She shot her right leg forward and straight into his groin. Hard. Then three more times. He keeled over at the impact and spouted curses between his gritted teeth. "You'll die for that! I'll kill you."

The other men laughed.

They dragged her backward, trading japes with every step. She screamed and flailed in their grasp, fighting to break free.

*I didn't survive the siege, only to die in the woods.*

Her legs and ankles dragged along the muddy forest floor until they brought her against the back of a tree. One man freed her arm. The other went behind the tree, twisted her arms back and around the trunk, and held her there with an iron grip.

Geoffrey hiked up her skirts, his dirty nails tracking painfully through her undergarments. She squirmed and kicked and fought in vain. Cruel, mocking laughter rang in her ears.

"No! Don't! Please, please leave me alone! Get your hands off me! Oh God, please..."

He struck her hard across the face. The force of the blow sent her head back and into the tree trunk. Black fringed the edges of her vision as the taste of blood filled her mouth again.

"You're in no place to be making demands. And God isn't listening to your whining."

They bunched her skirts up high, causing them to tangle around her waist. She heard laughter swirling around her... cruel, mocking laughter... the sound of her skirt tearing...

*Don't rip my red riding cloak,* she absently thought. *Grandmother made it for me... three winters ago....*

Dirty, rough hands stroked her thighs. And not kindly. *Not like Rowan would touch me.* She struggled against the touch... squirmed and cried out and prayed again and again.

*No one is here to listen.*

"You don't understand! You're making a mistake! I'm the queen. I'm Blanchette of House Winslowe!"

Silence took hold. Then booming laughter erupted once more.

"The Black Wolf killed all of the Winslowes, stupid whore."

She forced her eyes to focus. Stared into Geoffrey's pockmarked face. She smelled his foul breath as it wafted toward her. "You are wrong! I'll see you beheaded for this, I swear it!"

"You take our fucking like the queen you say you are, and mayhap we'll ransom you for gold. Mayhap—"

Geoffrey's words died in his throat as a sword pushed through the back of his head and out of his mouth.

⁂

ROWAN DIETRICH, the Black Wolf of Norland, withdrew his sword from the back of the man's head. The six other brigands slunk backward and fumbled for their weapons. The horses were going crazy at the sight and scent of Smoke—stomping their hooves, rearing up on powerful hind legs. Except for Sunbeam. He remained silent and still, blending into the dark canopy of trees.

From the corner of his eye, Rowan glanced at Blanchette; her dress was torn and dirty, and she fumbled in the dirt, struggling to rise to her feet.

Anger twisted inside him, red and hot.

*I shall kill them all for this.*

One brigand, greasy-haired and pockmarked, dashed at him from the left. Rowan swept his sword in an arc and felt the satisfying squelch of steel sliding through flesh, muscle, and tendon.

Movement from his peripheral vision. Blanchette rushed forward and retrieved the fallen axe. Rowan ran toward another brigand. The man staggered back, nocked an arrow, and let it fly.

It took Rowan in the forearm. Several moments passed before the pain struck him. Then he strode forward, a growl in his throat, as the bowman withdrew a second arrow from his quiver and nocked it again.

He raised to shoot—but Blanchette was there, bless the brave little idiot, both of her hands wielding the axe. She gave a war cry and swiped at the man's midsection. The metal sank in deep, and then she pulled it free with another gut-wrenching sound.

The man crumpled and fell. Blanchette locked Rowan's gaze. Dirt and blood speckled her face.

There were five more brigands. Smoke leaped at one of them, his snarl a thunderclap, his dagger-like teeth tearing into the man's throat. Blood pumped from the gash and soaked Smoke's muzzle. Then the wolf squared himself in front of Rowan and Blanchette, his fierce growl rising in the darkness.

The last three men backed away slowly, their eyes riveted on the wolf and his gore-stained snout. They turned and ran like bats escaping hell. Smoke pounced and wrapped his jaws around one of the men's necks. He dug his fingers into the dirt and leaves, yelling for his mother, blood and flesh coming loose as Smoke worked at his neck until he was silent.

Rowan and Blanchette finished off the last two men.

Then she wandered into the clearing like a woman wading through a dream. The red riding cloak streamed behind her.

She stood like that for a long stretch of silence. Tears and blood and dirt covered her face.

She looked fierce. Primal. Breathtaking.

That tragic vision stole his breath away.

Smoke threw back his blood-soaked muzzle and howled at the full moon. The eerie sound shivered through the night.

"I wouldn't linger long, Your Grace," Rowan spat as he glanced at the arrow sticking out of his forearm and the seven dead bodies. "There are wolves in these woods, and worse."

# Eleven

"LOVE IS PATIENT, love is kind. It does not envy, it does not boast, it is not proud. It is not rude, it is not self-seeking, it is not easily angered, and it keeps no record of wrongs. Love does not delight in evil but rejoices with the truth. It always protects, always trusts, always hopes, always perseveres. Love never fails."

— 1 Corinthians 13:4

"I must find a healer for you right away," Blanchette stuttered once they'd returned to the empty great hall. Smoke lay beside Rowan, his golden eyes glittering. Blood had dried on his muzzle and crusted in the fur around his jaws.

Blanchette turned from him, her stomach aching from the blows. But Rowan's hand shot out and grabbed the fabric of her red riding cloak. She eyed his fingers as they curled into the muddy material. "Stay. Your skills are good enough for my men. They're good enough for me."

She hesitated, glancing down at her hands, which were still trembling from the bloody turn of events. Then she nodded. "Alright. Give me a moment to wash up and gather supplies."

The world was quiet as she walked through the castle halls

and hastened for the well. She breathed in the cold, crisp air and let out a calming breath.

A sense of unreality settled over her. She fought to anchor herself and concentrate on the task at hand. A symphony of creaks broke the silence as the pulley system churned water from the dark depths below. A wooden bucket slowly ascended, dripping with water. Blanchette lowered the pewter flask into the bucket and filled it to the brim. The cold water brushed her knuckles and helped wake her from the trance. She splashed her face, watching the moon shimmering in the bucket. The unsteady water distorted her reflection.

*My God. Who am I?*

*What's happening to me?*

She glanced down at her palms before washing them. They were red with blood.

Blanchette returned to Rowan with the bucket and a basket full of supplies. She swallowed against the knot in her throat and retrieved her dagger from her cloak.

Rowan surprised her and gave a wolfish grin. She held his hot gaze for a moment.

Exhaling a long breath, she dug the dagger's tip into his doublet. Then she slid the blade along the fabric and carefully pulled it back from the jutting arrow.

He winced.

"You must trust me," she heard herself say. Rowan grimaced and then laughed as she applied a salve around the wound's entry point. "Hardly, my lady. After what I've seen and endured tonight, I trust you with my life. I just don't trust you with *your* life."

"That's a dangerous assumption, sir, that could cost your life."

He chuckled darkly again, then hissed through clenched teeth. "I've been called bold before by many of my men. It's a fair assessment."

"Bold, clever, bloodthirsty," she added.

"Dangerous, vengeful, honorable—and let's not forget—a fantastic lover."

A blush crept across her cheeks. She lifted her gaze from her handiwork and studied him.

*He saved me. He and his beast.*
*And I saved him.*
*What's happening to me?* she asked herself again.

※

ROWAN DIETRICH HAD ENDURED a myriad of battle wounds over the decades, yet he couldn't recall a pain more excruciating than that damn arrow. He bit down hard until the metallic flavor of blood filled his mouth. If the task disturbed Blanchette, his impulsive little nurse, she hid it well. Her head was bent, her curls tumbling around her beautiful face. Mud, leaves, and dirt stained her clothing. Her hair was damp from when she'd washed up. She worked meticulously, with a clear focus in her eyes that he could not help but admire and even envy.

She might be hasty and untrustworthy, but she was also brave and as strong as any soldier he'd ever led.

Impulsive and stubborn too. He couldn't forget those.

He'd watched her kill a man right before his eyes.

*She killed that man to save my life.* It was a strange turn of events, to say the least.

He acknowledged she was achingly lovely, too, as he watched the hearth's firelight play off her gold hair and brilliant eyes. An image of her wading through the wood surfaced; how fierce and beautiful and primal she'd looked.

"This will hurt. There will be pain."

"I'm sure."

"A great deal of pain, Rowan."

He savored the sound of his name on her lips. She'd said it in a low, husky whisper that impregnated the quiet between them. "Fortunately, I am no stranger to pain."

He cringed as she pushed the shaft. Wood slid through his flesh. *Pain* was an understatement. His eyes watered, but he fought back the tears. She eyed him warily, her gaze wide... *like a girl in the presence of a very dangerous wolf,* he thought sardonically.

More pushing.

More pain.

The worst pain he'd ever felt.

*I'm going to pass out...*

He bit back a curse and slammed his fist onto the armrest. "*Merde.*"

"My uncle, Sir Andrew, was one of the strongest men I've ever known. Brave and just to a fault. He once told me," she said, eyeing him carefully as she worked, "that bravery is not the absence of feeling but the devotion to do what's required in the face of fear and discomfort."

Rowan clenched his jaw as the damn princess pushed the shaft all the way through his forearm. A scream ripped out of him. Another curse, this one very much in English. He realized he was panting and sweating. Smoke rose from the floor and sat beside his chair; he whined, gently nudging Rowan's hand with his bloodied muzzle. He felt the wolf's rough tongue on his hand and knuckles.

"I'm so sorry," Blanchette whispered. "That was the worst of it."

*If only that were true.* Then she eyed the wolf, her eyes guarded. "He's... he will not rip my throat out? For hurting you?"

Rowan bit back a laugh. "Nay, not unless I order it. He knows we're friends."

She raised a delicate brow and cocked her head. "Friends? Are we now?"

She dabbed the sweat from his brow, and their eyes locked. Her mouth was inches from his. He reflected on her words—the wisdom of Sir Andrew. The king's brother.

"I remember your uncle," he finally said through gritted teeth as she continued. "I fought alongside him many times."

She paused and nodded, catching something in his gaze. "He told me that shortly before he died. They were the last words he ever said to me."

Rowan closed his eyes and went back to that day. He thought of the battle, of fighting side by side with Sir Andrew, Edrick, and the king. They'd made quick work of the invading force and had toasted each other long into the night. The king had found a camp follower to warm his pavilion while Sir Andrew, Edrick, and Rowan had lain under the stars and passed a bottle of ale back and forth until dawn broke.

*That was before everything else. Everything else that led me here.*

*And where is that, exactly?*

Rowan opened his eyes and watched in fascination as Blanchette began sewing his wound. She narrowed her gaze in concentration. He felt the warm caress of her breath. An image surfaced in his mind—Blanchette embedding the axe in the brigand's stomach, blood spattering her face like war paint.

"Blanchette... was that the first time you killed a man?"

She paused her handiwork, then shook her downcast head.

Rowan swallowed, feeling a well of emotions rise inside him. *Of course it wasn't. She wouldn't have survived the sacking without sending a few men to their graves.*

"You may try to run again, but you shall be abandoning me and your people. You call this kingdom your birthright... then stay and help me serve it. Help me bring justice to this world. Do not run again. Stay and fight."

She hesitated but said nothing. Her eyes were fixated on the work before her. She continued weaving the needle and silk in and out of his wound.

He winced at the pain. Cursed again, this time in English. Then in French again. Blanchette muttered some soft words. She glanced at Smoke and said, "So, tell me, sir. How exactly did a wolf come to be in your service?"

### Eight years earlier

Rowan watched as the rabbit roasted on the spit, its skin crackling and grease dripping from the flesh and into the fire. The quiet of the woods—its sheer solitude and immense scope—pressed down on him. Rowan reached for his scabbard and withdrew his longsword. The sound of scraping steel filled the night.

He'd see them hanging if he looked at the trees too long.

All those dead bodies.

That poor young boy he'd cut down and laid to rest.

He felt Edrick's gentle touch and heard his friend's plea. *"Are you willing to pay with your life? That of your family's? Please, Rowan, as your friend, I beg you to consider the consequences... I care for you far too much."*

Rowan brought the whetstone down along the blade, again and again, sharpening it, preparing himself for a battle he'd never win. The sound of stone scraping steel swelled the emptiness unnaturally. And beneath that sound, he heard the thud of his own heart.

A light snow had fallen an hour earlier. Rowan moved closer to the fire, admiring how the flames danced, soaking in the warmth. He watched the snowflakes glide toward him and melt above the flames, disappearing into a black oblivion.

Absently, he brought the stone down the sword's sleek length as his wife's face took shape in his mind.

Again, the whetstone slid down the sleek metal.

The blade seemed to scream as the stone came down. The steel was alive with the fire's glow.

*Blood. So much blood.*

He remembered the words his wife had said to him before he'd left for his campaign. *"You are a pretender. When Bartholomew knighted you, he made a mockery of all of Norland."* She'd always called him Bartholomew—not the king and not King Bartholomew.

Her fond and familiar note hadn't been lost on Rowan.

He watched the snow fall and carpet the dirt floor. A thick silence hit him hard. He stared at his left hand, suspended in midair, and realized he'd paused while sharpening his blade.

He felt eyes on him. He dropped the whetstone and stared into the impenetrable darkness of the woods. All he could make out were the skeletal lines of the trees. The scent of the woods intoxicated him—a complex bouquet of earthiness and pine mingled with a hint of frost. The trees, cloaked in their winter coats, stood sentinel, their branches glistening like crystal chandeliers.

The distant hoot of an owl echoed, adding a haunting quality to the night.

The wood was alive with hidden creatures. Their presence was felt more than seen.

A wind rattled the tree branches.

Rowan held his breath and sat up a little straighter.

More black came out of the black. It was a giant wolf, its yellow eyes shining like lanterns. The firelight danced across its sleek, dark coat, making parts of it look almost blue-black. The wolf angled its large head toward the crackling meat and sniffed at the air. Saliva ran from its jaws and splattered on the snowy ground.

The beast was beautiful in its dark stillness.

Rowan should have wielded his sword and threatened the intruder back into the darkness from whence it came. Instead, he felt himself rising to his feet slowly; his hand reached for the rabbit, moving like an alien thing independent of the rest of him. He tore off a dripping limb. He felt it dampen his fingers and slide down his palm as he lifted the morsel in midair. The wolf lowered its head again and cautiously stepped forward, those glowing eyes never parting from his.

Another sniff. Drool fell from its jaws. Its teeth were long and dagger-like.

The wolf emitted a low, rich growl that reminded Rowan of rolling thunder. That sound rose from the darkness, then dropped away as if fading into the very night. The wolf stalked forward with slow and measured steps, the hunger in its eyes a tangible force. Snow dusted its dark coat, clashing against the fur, melting within moments from the wolf's body heat. It raised a paw and growled again.

"Here, *mon ami*," he whispered, outstretching his hand to offer the rabbit leg. "No need to be afraid," he said more to himself.

With a few cautious steps, he closed the distance between them. Rowan dropped the meat and released his breath. The beast devoured it as he knew it would. He licked his mouth, those sharp teeth flashing. Long tendrils of slaver dripped to the ground.

Rowan glanced at the pommel of his sword—at the snarling wolf's head. He held out his hand and waited. The wolf took another step forward, his teeth bared, then lowered his muzzle to his knuckles. He sniffed at his flesh, then stared up at him. Slowly, Rowan tore another limb from the rabbit and fed it to him from his hand.

He took it quickly.

*The wolf was starving and all alone.*

Rowan lowered onto the ground again, his back resting against a tall oak tree. He unskewered the rabbit with his sword and broke off chunks for him and the wolf. As the night deepened, he heard his voice filling the silence.

"Where's your pack?" he asked, his voice slurred. He realized the ale had gone to his head. The world around him felt unsteady. "My pack's also gone," he said, pointing his flask toward the gray wolf embroidered on his tunic.

He plucked another leg from the rabbit and felt the grease slide down his fingers. The wolf sat up, attentive, his eerie eyes glowing. Rowan carefully leaned forward and fed him the morsel from his hand. He licked his fingers clean, those intelligent, piercing eyes never leaving his own.

"I suppose the pack shall grow soon enough," he said, taking a piece of meat for himself. "She's heavy with child."

He raised his flask in a silent toast, then drank.

He offered the wolf another fat morsel. He ate it straight from his hand again, then nibbled his palm. He rubbed the wolf's ears with his other hand, shocked into silence by how quickly he'd trusted him.

*A black wolf has come to me in my blackest of nights.*

Hesitantly, Rowan tracked his hand over the wolf's smooth, dark coat. The fur seemed to drink in the firelight; he watched, mesmerized, as the flames danced across it.

"I see them... I see them every night and every day," he said, whispering to no one. "I see them even now." Rowan cocked his head back and looked up into a dark ash tree. A body, its face swollen and purple, hung from the end of a noose. It swayed eerily in the breeze, and the smoke from the fire obscured its features. Rowan blinked. It was gone as quickly as it'd appeared.

"What should I do? Go back to the king? What kind of knight—what kind of man, what kind of father—would that make me?"

The wolf said nothing. Of course. Just stared at him with those glowing eyes.

Then the wolf lay down and made himself at home beside Rowan's boots. His eyes darted back to the sigil on his banner: a gray wolf howling against a white field.

Rowan exhaled a breath, then watched as the wolf's eyelids grew heavy and closed. He rested his massive head on his front paws. Rowan watched the steady rise and fall of his back... watched through the flames as they waved in the darkness.

Black smoke distorted the wolf lying beside him.

"Smoke," he said aloud, talking to no one.

And the Black Wolf of Norland was born.

---

ROWAN IDLY RAN his fingers over his bandaged forearm, though his focus was on the sleeping princess beside him. The oversized armchair dwarfed her body. She'd curled up in the satin upholstery like a little kitten, her hands pressed together and stacked under her chin. Firelight washed over her from the hearth, and her striking blond curls appeared to come to life.

His storytelling had lulled her to sleep.

Rowan took her in his arms and brought her to her guest chamber. She felt so fragile in his grasp. A protective instinct thrummed through him.

*No one shall ever harm you again.*

*Least of all me.*

Her scarred cheek was upturned, a rough ridge that started at her delicate ear and spanned to the corner of her mouth.

*A battle scar indeed.*

Rowan reached over with his right hand and pushed back the material of his jerkin. A web of red scarring covered the upper part of his chest. Their scars were connected in a twisted sort of way, as were their fates.

He sat in one of the high-back chairs and planted his hands on his thigh. He watched her, transfixed, as the gentle rise and fall of her chest moved in a soothing rhythm.

*Such a sweet young girl,* he thought, remembering someone else. *A lovely young girl who's known so much horror.*

*How is she now?*

*And does she miss me as I miss her?*

He tried not to bring her to mind—that other girl who he seemed to know a lifetime ago.

*So close yet so far away,* he thought, looking at Blanchette.

Rowan glanced at the partially open door, where he saw the

lantern-like glow of Smoke's eyes. The wolf raised his head, his fur blending into the black corridor.

*More black within the black.*

Rowan felt the hairs prickle on the back of his neck. He came to his feet, quitting the chamber only after pulling the blanket over Blanchette.

---

THE GANGPLANK HIT the ship's deck with a satisfying *boom* that shook the boards beneath Lord Peter Huntley's boots. They'd moved in under the cover of darkness, silent and steady like a predator stalking its prey. He wore his house's sigil on the left side of his jerkin, directly over his heart: a prancing half man, half goat with cloven feet.

The Greek god Pan.

Huntley withdrew his shortsword with a battle cry that his crew passionately echoed. They stormed down the gangplank in a unified charge of steel, shield, and boiled leather.

He'd taken Captain Walsh's crew by surprise. The earth-shattering thud of the gangplank had stirred them from below the deck, putting an end to their fucking or feasting or whatever they'd been occupied with.

Now, the world turned into a fantastic blur of clashing swords and war cries. Huntley pushed himself into the thick of it—the only place he liked to be during a battle. His blood ran hot, the sea air brushing his sweat-slick skin like a lover's kiss, and his shortsword danced in the moonlight, thundering down, down, down.

First into the side of a young man's neck. Huntley screamed from the thrill of it and turned the blade so it sliced through the front of his throat.

*Like a dog,* he thought, tearing out his rival's throat. Another small voice echoed *wolf,* but Huntley ignored that.

He shoved the man to the ground and raised his blade again. An axe came at him from his flank. He dodged it with ease, then ducked under its sweeping arc. He countered with a biting undercut that sent the edge of his shortsword into the man's chest. He'd embedded the metal so deeply it was a struggle to dislodge it from his rib cage. Huntley grunted as he withdrew the shortsword. Then, without a moment's rest, he brought it crashing down and into someone's skull.

Buried deep. It was a struggle to extricate.

Then Huntley resumed his dance.

He noticed one of his soldiers holding an oiled torch and setting fire to a black flag from the corner of his eye.

Huntley moved swiftly. He hacked the burning flag with his shortsword, grabbed the crew member by the back of his collar, and thrust him against the railing.

"Huntley?" he said with a confused expression.

"My order was to lay no damage to the ship. Only to its crew." And without another word, Huntley heaved the man and the flaming flag overboard. He watched the ocean swallow them whole. Huntley slapped the railing with a battle-fever-induced laugh, then turned just in time to slide his blood-soaked sword into a man's fat gut.

The man died with a curse and the name of some poor wench on his lips. Huntley spared a moment to swipe his blade on the side of his shirtsleeves. It was slick, polished with the blood of his enemies.

He surveyed the scene before him, watching his crew cutting down pirates left and right, most of whom had gorged on rum and women minutes before and were ill-ready for battle.

*Father, you'd be proud.*

Huntley stormed through the ship—took one more life to his left, another to his right—and burst through the wooden door that led below decks and to the cabins.

Loud moaning echoed from below. He followed the sound as the wild battle crashed above him like waves on a beach. Soon, he reached Captain Walsh's private cabin. One of his men had mounted some poor girl against the wall and was ramming her from behind.

*Like a fucking wolf,* he thought again. Huntley stalked behind him. He pulled him off and out of the girl. With one swipe, he sliced the man's throat to the bone. He crumpled in a heap of blood and semen. Huntley turned back to the girl, who was cowering against the wall, her entire body shaking.

"Run, run away fast," he said to her.

※

AN HOUR LATER, the sun sat low on the horizon where the sea met the sky. Huntley turned away from the glimmering water and faced the pirate and his crew. Corpses of dead men littered the wooden floor; blood leaked from their knife wounds and spilled in red puddles. They mainly were Captain Walsh's crew, he acknowledged with a satisfactory nod.

Seven of his crew stood around Thomas Walsh, the captain of the *Woodcutter*—their longswords and daggers drawn. They'd gagged him, and his muffled voice fought to wriggle through the sodden bind.

Huntley placed his palm over the pommel of his shortsword, which was tucked away in its sheath. He crossed the deck with determined strides. He walked through this valley of death and blood, tracking his red footprints across the boards.

The captain tried to speak again. He wrestled the ropes that bound his body together.

Huntley gave one of his men a look. That's all it ever took.

His man kicked the captain in his back, causing him to crumple onto the deck face-first. Blood burst from his broken nose and ran into the material. Huntley sighed, then came to his knees. He withdrew a dagger, watched it drink in dawn's light, thrust it under the binding, and tore the material away. Thanks to his men, most of the captain's teeth were missing.

"You know why I did this, old man?" he asked. The pirate

struggled to his knees to better look at Huntley. Or so he guessed. Pirate pride was hard to shake off—even when you stared death in the face.

"You're a pirate killer. A murderer, just like me."

Huntley laughed at that, then stroked the blond stubble on his chin. "Nay, I did this because you are poison, my friend, and you've tainted Norland's water far too long. I shall rid our kingdom of your kind, the land and the sea alike."

"You haven't got a chance against the Black Wolf," the pirate captain replied, spitting blood and a tooth into Huntley's face. Huntley merely wiped it away, his eyes never parting from the captain's. "He shall kill you, and not gently. Aye, mate, he will rip you apart limb from limb like a lamb for slaughter."

Huntley laughed again. "You are mistaken. I am no lamb. I am a god. And Rowan Dietrich is merely one more wolf I mean to slay."

# TWELVE

"Were this a real battle, a real sword, you'd be dead. Several times now, in fact." Rowan stepped forward, cutting through his line of men, and offered his hand to his squire Jonas.

Rowan kept a lean and reserved hall, but the outside of the castle was another matter entirely. The bailey was alive with the sounds of horses, hounds, arrows, and blacksmiths.

*The music of a tentative peace.*

Smoke sat on the sidelines, watching the sparring with a human-like intensity.

Aside from the occasional pirate raid, a fragile serenity had settled over Norland. But Demrov lay to the north, and until he sent an envoy to meet with the king, they were a dangerous threat. Blanchette had made that plain enough, time and again. And to the south loomed her betrothed Lord Huntley and his admiral father.

*Perhaps I can broker a peace with them,* Rowan mused, thinking of the power they held over the sea. Even pirates feared the Huntley fleet. *Sir Royce would be well received.* Certainly not Edrick, who'd grown more and more like a stranger these past weeks. The thought filled Rowan with sorrow. Once, they'd been impossibly close—like brothers. They'd weathered storms together, and now it seemed a storm kept them apart. One Rowan couldn't quite name.

"Sir?" Jonas said, snapping him from his thoughts. He stared up at Rowan from beneath a dirty mop of flaming-red hair. His blue eyes looked as large as dinner plates. Shame lined his bright gaze as Rowan pulled him up to his feet. Rowan held his hand a moment longer. Jonas felt vulnerable under his touch, like he'd break with the slightest use of force or breath of wind.

Rowan didn't like that at all.

He saw himself in the boy's eyes. A boy who wanted to simply be a boy, but the world had other plans for him. The reluctant beginnings of a soldier. *There is no room for sentiment in war,* he heard his father's ghost whisper. *Remember, a soft heart is easier to cut through.* He shook his head, batting away the thoughts.

"I-I am sorry, sir," Jonas said, his head and eyes lowering as he brushed off his jerkin. "I'm no good, am I?" His cheeks turned deep red as he avoided eye contact with Rowan. A light breeze stirred his hair and caused his cheeks to pinken further. Winter still held strong, but the days were growing warmer.

"I don't want you to be sorry," Rowan said. The boy nervously rocked on his heels, his eyes shifting from soldier to soldier. Rowan stepped forward and took hold of the boy's shoulders, stilling his movements with slight pressure from his hands. "I want you to focus. I want you to be ready for whatever this mad world throws at us."

The boy smiled a little, then fetched his blunted sword from the dirt and held it at an angle. In his other hand, he clasped a shield. Foes had beaten away chips of wood, and the Winslowe's raven sigil was half-peeled off.

"Come now. Keep your shield up, Jonas. Like I've taught you. You're a smart boy. You know all this."

Jonas stared down at the shield with a frown. He lifted his sword arm and rubbed away the sweat from his forehead with his forearm.

"It's... it's hard to keep up, sir."

"It's as heavy as it needs to be to stop a sword. Do you understand?" Rowan shook his head and withdrew his longsword from its scabbard. The sweet sound of scraping metal filled the yard. "Now, watch first and learn. Sir Edrick, come forward."

Edrick did as commanded. He slid from the shadows, taking his time, his features drawn into a tight and unreadable expression. But the emotion he lacked in his face showed in his eyes.

*Is that... hatred?*

*Where has it come from?*

*What is happening?*

Then the steel dance began.

Edrick swung his sword at Rowan, only to be met with a swift parry that sent sparks flying from their blades. Edrick retaliated with a quick jab, but Rowan was quick to dodge and counterattack, forcing him to step back and regroup.

Rowan didn't allow it. He glanced at Jonas, who observed from the sidelines with a score of other men and women. Rowan pushed the attack.

Their swords came together in a sweet ring, sending more sparks flying in the early morning air. The clash of metal and the sharp hiss of blades filled the yard as they cut through the mist. Steel met steel with a sweet, harmonious ring that echoed through the training grounds. Each movement was a dance of precision and power as they exchanged uppercuts, slashes, and parries in a breathtaking display of skill.

Edrick swung his sword hard and fast. Rowan easily swept under the blade, then sent his sword flying up to meet the metal. They held their swords together like that, their faces half a foot apart, teeth gritted, Edrick's eyes flashing with something dangerous.

That took Rowan by surprise. His injured forearm began to ache. The pain blazed through him. Hiding his agony, he stepped back and lowered his sword.

"Jonas, do you see—"

Edrick lunged forward and swung his sword at Rowan's midsection, nearly missing his gut by an inch. Rowan was only in boiled leather; that would have spilled his guts if not for his quick reflex.

Rowan threw his sword to the dirt, advanced in three swift strides, and backhanded Edrick across the face.

Hard.

The force of the blow sent his captain to the earth, where he spat blood and a broken tooth. Smoke burst forward, his spine curved, a long, rolling growl filling the yard. His jaws were inches from Edrick, drool spewing from his bared, razor-like teeth.

Rowan clenched his fists. Breathing hard, he fetched his longsword from the ground and strode back to the castle with Smoke at his side.

All along, Blanchette watched from her window.

NIGHTTIME CLOAKED the castle and filled the world with a moonless sky.

Rowan entered the stable. It was divided into neat rows of wooden stalls, each large enough to hold two horses. Wooden bars separated the stalls, and their occupants stood quietly within them, their eyes reflecting the torch's soft, wavering light.

The aromas of fresh hay and straw dominated the air. The unmistakable musk of the horses also held—a blend of sweat and leather that reminded Rowan of home.

The destriers were fierce beasts, bred for battle and loved for their strength and courage. But they were also wild and unpredictable, so taming them was no easy task.

And Rowan had always enjoyed a challenge.

He nodded a curt greeting to the horse tamer, Harwin. The man looked a bit like a horse, with a long face, shifting, black eyes, and teeth too large for his mouth. His clothes were dirty and full of holes, yet he held himself with a king's dignity.

Rowan approached one of the horses—an auburn beauty with a slender head. The horse snorted and stomped her white feet, wary of the stranger. Dust rose into Harwin's face. He coughed madly, a look of defiance on his weathered features, and fanned away the debris.

"That's a hard nut to break," Harwin said to Rowan. "I'd be careful if I were you, sir. She's a mean bastard."

Rowan nodded. "Fortunately, I know a thing or two about mean bastards." Slowly, he reached for the horse's muzzle, brought her face close, and murmured. He felt the horse respond to his touch, and she stopped stomping her hooves a moment later. Rowan eyed Harwin and tried not to smile. It made an appearance anyway, and Harwin frowned and spat into the hay.

"You were saying?"

The horse tamer muttered under his breath and shook his head. Then he exited the stable without another glance.

Rowan exhaled a long sigh, then turned his attention back to the horse.

"What's your name, beauty?" he asked, stroking the horse's muzzle with long, soothing caresses. A white blaze flamed between her brown eyes, contrasting against the darkness of her hair. "How about Shadow? That's as good a name as any?" The horse tossed her muzzle and gave Rowan a gentle nip.

Rowan chuckled to himself. Shadow's ears turned toward the sound, and she responded with an amicable knicker. Then Rowan fetched a cube of sugar from inside his cloak and fed the treat to her.

Rowan had come here to distract himself, but he kept seeing Edrick's angry gaze in his mind. The way his friend's sword had swiped at his midsection. How he'd slammed the back of his hand against Edrick's face and sent him flying to the ground.

*What's happening?*

*I need out. I need to feel the wind on my face and Norland's sun on my back.*

Rowan was riding down the coast on Shadow's back hours

later. The castle towered behind him, the wind swept through his hair like fingers, and his blood came to life as he found a sliver of peace.

※

THAT EVENING, Rowan eased into Blanchette's privy. It was one of the few rooms his men had left untouched. Thoughtfully, he ran his fingers over his longsword's pommel, his breath tight in his chest, the beat of his heart rushing through his ears. Her bedclothes hung from the feather mattress and halfway onto the stone ground where she'd left them.

He imagined her waking the night of the attack. He saw her standing before the window that overlooked the inner bailey and watchtower—staring out into the dense wood where he and his men emerged from the shadows and cover of trees.

Rowan eased inside, his breaths white against the darkness. He inhaled deeply, then ran his gloved hand over the wolfskin blanket. He glanced over his shoulder—saw that he was alone inside her chamber—then removed his left-hand glove. Carefully, ever so slowly, he lowered onto the blanket and smoothed his fingertips over the warm fur. He released a sigh.

*My God, what have I done to her?*

Inhaling a shaky breath, he came to his feet and crossed the privy with determined strides. He ran his hand over the smooth, dusty surface of her bureau. Then he raised his head, and his eyes caught his reflection in a looking glass hanging in front of him.

He looked like a stranger. *A wolf in sheep's clothing,* he thought with bitter irony.

He stepped before the window, where he could still make out his reflection. Raindrops slid down the glass and, by extension, his own face.

In his mind's eye, he saw himself bowing before King Bartholomew.

"*I promise on my faith that I will be faithful to the lord, never cause him harm, and will observe my homage to him completely against all persons in good faith and without deceit. I promise to wield my sword to defend the innocent and to uphold the king's peace. I promise..."*

He felt the kiss of the blade on his armored shoulder, then saw himself rise to his feet as a knight of the realm.

*I promised...*

---

"W HATEVER HAPPENED TO PRACTICING *PATIENCE*?" Governess Agnes asked Blanchette for the third time, her thin eyebrows propped into arches. A well-earned look of judgment lined her sharp face. But her gaze showed a flash of amusement.

"I waited weeks before I attempted an escape. For me, that *is* patient."

Governess Agnes chuckled, then continued darning a pair of woolen socks for the coming winter. "Well, everything worked out, so I shan't scold you anymore. I should have known better, anyhow. You never were one to listen to me."

Blanchette smiled, her mind flashing back to her childhood. She saw Governess Agnes chasing her as she waded into the river and lost herself in Norland's wilderness.

Rowan appeared in the archway with Smoke and cut her thoughts short.

"Governess," he greeted. "Blanchette, come with me."

She bid Governess Agnes goodbye, then followed Rowan down the dark corridor. Smoke padded beside them, moving like a ghost. Sconce lanterns lit the corridors and cast eerie shadows along the walls. They crawled up to the ceiling and across the stone floor. Rowan loomed above her, his features drawn into a hard line.

But his eyes showed something else entirely. She felt an anguish there—a sense of guilt, longing, and, perhaps strongest of all, a *need*. She understood the void he felt, one that he seemed to have drowned in, perhaps years ago.

*Shall I suffer the same fate?* she wondered with a quiver of fear. Already, she could not breathe. How long before the darkness consumed her completely?

"How is your arm?"

He glanced at her and shrugged, a hint of a smile on his lips. "Time shall tell, I suppose."

They walked in silence for another few minutes. The quiet was only broken when two guards passed and greeted Rowan with a bow. Finally, they stopped outside her privy chamber. The one she'd grown up in. The one the Black Wolf had taken away from her so recently.

He turned to her, the sconce light casting his features in a soft, golden glow. Smoke sat beside him, his eyes shining in the dark corridor like stars.

"My chamber. Why did you bring me here?" She loathed how pitiful and feeble her voice sounded. Not like a queen's at all.

His mouth ticked at the corner as if he was battling another smile. "Shall I return you to the guest quarters?"

She stood a little taller and met his hazel eyes. "This is my home. I am no guest."

"Good. Then we are in agreement." When she gave him a confused look, he added, "There has been enough battling, Blanchette. I am not here to fight you. We are on the same side now. I want us to be allies. We're friends now, remember?" He reached out and lightly touched her shoulder. "And I wanted to thank you... for helping me." He gestured to his forearm, his fingers lightly grazing the fabric of her dress.

Silence passed. It was an intimate quiet, tingling with unspoken tension. Blanchette glanced away from his stare and felt a tiny shiver crawl up her spine.

No one had ever looked at her with such... feeling and vulnerability.

*Who is this man, this Black Wolf?*

She recalled his sparring with Edrick and how Rowan had backhanded his captain after he'd nearly spilled his entrails.

*There is a story there. There's more to this man than meets the eye.*

*So much more...*

Her thoughts fell apart as his large hand came to her shoulder. Gently, he turned her body from the door, leaving a trail of desire everywhere he touched. Then he glanced down at her and flashed a full-on smile. She noticed the subtle details in that smile for the first time. How little wrinkles formed next to his eyes. A small dimple appeared on his left cheek. A crooked tooth that added a touch of wolfish charm.

Lifting the crossbar, he opened the iron-and-studded door to her privy chamber. She swallowed hard against the tension and felt tears prick her eyes. Rowan backed into the room, moving gracefully, then held his hand to her. Sunlight poured into her privy and dappled his pitch-black hair with its glow.

"This is your home. Reclaim it."

Blanchette exhaled a long breath. Taking his hand, she watched as his large fingers swallowed hers up. Then she finally stepped into the room and felt an internal landslide of joy and sorrow at the sight of her chamber.

She let go of his hand. Her palms fell to her sides, and she nervously ran them up and down the material of her cloak.

*My red riding cloak.*

She'd seen her chamber thousands of times, of course. Yet experiencing it now, in this light, with the man who'd brought the sky down on her family, was almost too much to bear. The urge to scream, to cry, and to panic hit her all at once. She wordlessly walked the room's perimeter, her hand tracking over her belongings, her heart filled with nostalgia and a dull twinge. She recognized that ache as bone-deep grief. She stood before her bureau and examined the various trinkets on top of its surface. Jewels and brooches. Perfumes. A leather book splitting at the seams. Letters from Isadora, tied together with a red ribbon.

She swallowed hard, refusing to show defeat or weakness in the face of her enemy.

*But is he truly my enemy?*

His men hadn't touched any of these belongings. Not even the jewels.

She glanced out the window at the outer bailey. There, she saw it happen all over again—the charge of soldiers, the Black Wolf of Norland front and center. She also saw Elise's battered body splayed across the stone floor. Her heart burned, and she blinked the image away.

Her mind was a haunted dungeon, swarming with ghosts and the skeletons of a past life. When she met Rowan's gaze again, her sorrow mutated into that familiar anger, that rage, a resentment whose force tore her apart. She stepped past him and crossed her chamber to stand before her four-poster bed. She reached out tentatively—her hand frozen in midair—then stroked the furs with a dull ache churning in her heart.

Wolf pelts.

Rowan stepped beside her, his vast body filling the space between her and the oak poster. When he spoke, the lull of his voice occupied the rest of that emptiness. "I know how it feels to lose someone you loved. Someone you believed yourself inseparable from."

"And what great loss have you suffered?"

Rowan stood so close that she felt the heat of his breaths on her cheeks. She became astutely aware of her own body: her rapid heartbeat, the hotness in her cheeks, a tingling yet not altogether unpleasant sensation running across her skin.

The corner of Rowan's mouth lifted into a smile, but only sadness was in his eyes. "Someone who I once loved."

His gaze met her eyes, and Blanchette's heart jerked at the longing there.

*Longing... for what?*

He released a long-suffering sigh. A heartbeat later, she felt his strong fingers cupping her cheek. They tracked over the scar in a barely-there touch, then carefully followed the curve of her chin. Finally, she released a breath. She shuddered—though not from displeasure or fear—and stepped back and out of his reach.

Blanchette traced the taut ridge of her scar. It'd healed well but would always be a grim reminder of that night.

"You should be proud of that scar," he whispered. "It makes you even more beautiful. It echoes your strength."

She stared up at him, at the warmth in his eyes, for what might have been a full minute.

Then he stepped back and ran an unsteady hand through the waves of his hair.

*Smoke isn't here*, she thought, observing his sudden vulnerability. *And neither is the Black Wolf of Norland.*

Just Rowan Dietrich stood before her. And she saw him plainly.

Blanchette wandered over to the window again. Daylight glimmered across Norland.

It very much held the appearance of a tapestry—the deep green of the wood, the glimmering blue ocean with ships that looked like mere toys at this distance, the town center, and the cluster of peasant homes and farms. Her gaze tracked back to her castle. She made out the elevated scaffold and its vibrant greenery in the corner of her view.

Blanchette brought her palms together as if in prayer.

*I had seen the darkness. I'd seen the horrific reality poke and tear through the tapestry of my life—that carefully woven, intricate threading of court feasts and tourneys. Indeed, that horror had peeped through the threads.*

She'd simply been blind to it.

She glanced at the scaffold and its finely kept green.

"Blanchette?" Rowan's voice cut through the memories, jarring her like ice water to the face.

She exhaled, concentrating on the sensation of the chilly air leaving her lungs. "My father was generous to his allies and equally merciless to his enemies. I shall never forget... it was his most trusted adviser," she said, her heart thundering like a caged bird. "He executed him for treason seven years ago now. He was one of many. I stood here, right in this very spot. Governess Agnes was beside me, clutching her cross to her heart. We watched as the traitor pleaded for mercy. He spoke eloquently, and even my father looked moved. Agnes and I held our breaths as my father signaled over the executioner with a movement of his ring finger. He whispered something in his ear." Blanchette felt the tears sting her eyes. She gazed up at Rowan. "It took seven strikes to separate his head from his body. The first three came down on his back and shoulders. He was alive during all of it. I don't think I slept through a night for years after. And I can still see it. I still hear those screams. And my father's laughter. My father... God, he'd paid the executioner to make a botch of it." She sank into her high-back chair.

Her gaze left Rowan's handsome face as she searched out the window.

*But for what?*

"*That* was my father. Noble King Bartholomew. What does that make me?" Whether she was speaking to herself, Rowan, or some ghost, she could not say. The words had spilled out, unabated, like bile she could no longer keep down.

Rowan knelt before her as a subject might kneel before their queen. She watched him, her breath coming fast, while he removed his leather gloves with his teeth. He took both of her hands in one of his. She exhaled, then moved her fingers against his palm, familiarizing herself with the texture. Calluses and scars —hands that had saved lives and taken lives. She felt the strength surging through him, and she drew on it.

Rowan's other hand lightly rested on her chin. He tilted her head back just an inch, and his eyes never left hers when he spoke. His irises were a warm hazel. There was a sadness in them too. One that echoed her own.

"I've known more kings and commanders than I could ever count. I have seen rulers rise and fall. I've seen what power can do to a man... to those who cannot handle such a burden and break beneath its weight. You, Blanchette Winslowe, are stronger than all of them. And what's more, you have a good heart. A gentle heart. You were born to rule."

He shifted closer until their bodies almost touched. His eyes tracked over her face as if committing every detail to memory. And perhaps he was.

And for a passing moment, Blanchette thought he was going to kiss her.

*Am I relieved? Or disappointed?*

# Thirteen

Rowan sat at the head of the table—a long, ugly plank made of timber and marked with the sigil of House Winslowe. A map of Norland was also engraved in the wood.

It was a seat where kingdoms had been built and destroyed. How many kings had sat before this table? How many schemes were hatched and wars started here in this room?

He recalled his endless campaigns. Campaigns he'd run for a man he'd thought he'd believed in. For a man he thought he'd loved. Campaigns for a man who'd shattered his faith and rebuilt Rowan from the ashes.

*I believe in Blanchette,* he acknowledged.

*Will she crush my faith once again?*

*Look at where such soft emotions have gotten you.*

*Look at the sorrow they've brought into your life and what they've stolen from you.*

*A soft heart is easier to cut...*

Edrick, who always sat to Rowan's right, banged his hand on the table's surface. His other adviser—Sir Royce—sat up a little straighter. Jonas was there, too, looking entirely out of his element. But he was learning fast and was much cleverer than he let on. Rowan would make a general or lieutenant out of him one day.

Rowan kept a lean council. He'd known too much betrayal to do otherwise.

"Blood and battle," Edrick said. "The country is drowning in it again, Rowan. Pirates have been raiding along the coast like we haven't seen in years."

"And we have another problem. Perhaps a larger one." Rowan withdrew a scroll of parchment from inside his cloak. He'd broken the seal an hour earlier when the bird first arrived. He stared at the goat-head wax sigil. His advisers fell quiet and seemed to hold their breath while he unrolled the parchment and flattened it on the table. He covered the engraved map and etchings of Winslowe's ravens.

"His name is Peter Huntley. He's the son of the renowned admiral. His fleet commands the sea and coasts and has for hundreds of years. And Huntley just so happens to be betrothed to Blanchette. The Huntleys were kings once upon a time. I'd helped King Bartholomew crush their rebellion. In fact, I'd led the campaign against them and killed King Lothar myself." Rowan held up the parchment, his gaze slinking across the neat red writing. *It looks like blood.* "Huntley means to take back what's his and not by asking nicely. I reckon he's to blame for some of the pillaging. He's trying to cause unrest."

Edrick's eyes were like ice. He gestured to the letter. "Are you planning to share his demands?"

Rowan gave him a cutting look. "It was addressed to me and me alone. But since *you* asked nicely, yes, I shall." His gaze ran across his advisers' anxious faces, and then he read from the parchment:

"*My dear Black Wolf:*
*You have ravaged Norland for far too long.*
*You've fashioned yourself as the people's champion,*

*but my lord father and I see you for what you are. Just more of the same. A different shade of tyranny.*

*Now, you sit in the capital on a throne meant to be mine. You may not be a king in name, but a king you are all the same, Your Grace. You might remember my grandfather, Lothar Huntley. And you might remember how easily kings fall.*

*As it so happens, it's not a crown I seek from you but the key to Norland. Her name is Blanchette Winslowe, and she was promised to me three years ago. Give her back to me, Black Wolf. Give her back, or I shall take everything from you and more.*

*Yours sincerely, P. Huntley"*

---

"You might have shown me that letter when the bird first arrived," Edrick said to Rowan once the chamber was empty. Only the fire in the hearth broke the silence as the logs crackled and split. It reminded Rowan of crunching bones. He leaned against the mantel and stared into those wavering flames. Smoke had returned from his hunt and lay at Rowan's feet. His eyes, however, were fixed on Edrick.

Rowan observed Smoke's unwavering stare. "Aye, I might have."

Edrick swung before him, and his eyes burned as hot as the fire. "This is not a game," he seethed. "You're making mistakes again. Dire mistakes. Remember what they cost you last time?

They had cost me, too, and I don't intend to suffer again on your behalf, Rowan. Please. I am trying to help you."

Rowan calmly lifted his gaze from the hearth and searched Edrick's face. Madness. Anger. He saw it all there, plain as day. It seemed to build every time they spoke as of late. And something else, too, just below the surface.

Grief.

"No, it's not a game," he agreed. Rowan pushed away from the mantel and stepped toward his comrade, bringing them face-to-face. "But our swordplay in the yard was. Yet you tried to kill me. And I want to know why."

Edrick shook his head. He returned Smoke's penetrating stare. The wolf gave a low warning growl and rose to his feet. He lifted a front paw, his eyes fixed on Edrick. Gently, Rowan placed a hand on the black scruff of his neck to calm him. The wolf settled down and sniffed the air, his teeth still half-bared and paw raised.

"One day you shall," Edrick scoffed. "But not today, Black Wolf." Without another word, he stormed from the room.

But he halted just as he was about to leave. "Are you going to meet Huntley's demand? About the girl? It's an easy way to get him off our backs. Even on our side."

Rowan stared at him for a long silence. The hearth continued to crackle and split. His eyes rose to the sigil that was carved into the wood. He traced it with his finger, outlining the fine details of the raven's wings. "She's not mine to give away."

*She's not mine at all...*

---

BACK IN MY CHAMBER. *Seated next to my dear governess. It's almost like nothing has changed.*

*Except everything has.*

It felt bittersweet to Blanchette—like she was home again for the first time in months.

She and Governess Agnes had spent the better part of the dawn pouring over the ledgers and approximating spring's upcoming harvest. It'd shocked them both, learning just how much food her father had kept under guard. He'd starved half the country. And for what? For his feasts and tourneys and private pleasure?

"All of this... this horror," Governess Agnes had said, her brow furrowed. "I can't help but feel it's a godsend. How many lives shall be saved now? Where death once lay shall be hope." She crossed herself after that, then picked up her needles and began darning some woolen socks.

Afterward, they'd summed the harvest, and Blanchette ordered Rowan's soldiers to deliver enough wheat and barley to last the village an entire year. She'd sent wagons of blankets and woolen coats too. "So long as I live, no man, woman, or child in Norland shall ever starve or freeze to death again." The soldiers had surprised her with genuine smiles and gratitude.

*Queen Blanchette Winslowe. I may not be so in name yet, but I'm the Queen of Norland all the same. And my people are starting to feel it too.*

Now Blanchette relaxed by the hearth. She held a book open across her lap. Her eyes ran over the words, though they hardly made it into her mind.

*"Begin by choosing the appropriate time to gather herbs, typically when they are in full bloom or have reached their peak potency. Use a sharp knife to cut or pluck the parts of the plant you require, such as leaves, roots, or flowers. Offer a silent prayer for guidance and protection as you harvest..."*

Her gaze fell away from the jumble of letters and focused on her barred window. Just outside the walls of the castle, the encampment fires glowed like embers. Rowan's army seemed to grow daily—every time she glanced out the window. She could no longer say whether that was a blessing or a curse.

In her mind's eye, she saw her father riding up on one of his fine horses, a column of men behind him, kennel hounds baying and rushing toward the castle grounds. Even Willem surged forward on his white pony as he chattered with the other noble children. They were returning from a hunt.

And a slaughtered black wolf hung off the back of a wagon, fledged with arrows.

*You were born to rule.*

Except that wasn't true.

Willem had been born to rule.

"Your Grace?" Rowan's smooth, deep voice pulled her back into the moment. My God, he moved with an impressive grace for a man his size. Smoke was at his side, of course, his golden eyes shining like stars.

"My Lord," she returned as she clumsily popped up from the chair and onto her feet. For a moment, his presence seemed to fill the space. Her gaze slowly traveled across his broad shoulders, his leather jerkin, and the long length of his well-muscled legs. Governess Agnes had set down the needles and rose from the chair at his entry.

But Rowan only had eyes for Blanchette. He stared at her intently, and she felt her skin prickle at his forwardness. "Rowan. What brings you here at this early hour?"

He stepped into the chamber and placed his large hands on his hips. His right fingers grazed his sword's wolf pommel and caressed the metal. He'd polished it to a shine, the wolf's mouth snarling beneath his long fingertips. "I hope you're feeling more comfortable in your own chambers."

Blanchette met his gaze with the same intensity. "Yes, well. This is my home. Now and always."

"Now and always," he confirmed with a nod.

Governess Agnes moved past the Black Wolf and gave a curtsy. Before she left the chamber, she tossed Blanchette a rather sly grin over her shoulder.

Once she was gone, Rowan's head fell forward, and his voice softened to an intimate whisper. "It was your brother's home, as well, Blanchette, and it still is."

Blanchette felt tears sting the corners of her eyes.

"Come with me. I have something for you."

Without another word, Blanchette threw on her red riding cloak and followed Rowan from her chamber and into her halls.

---

Rowan, Blanchette, and Smoke came to a dead halt in front of a rusted iron gate next to the postern entry. Somewhere in the wood beyond, a wolf's cry echoed. She met Rowan's eyes and saw that somber note reflected in their depths.

"My family's crypt."

*He truly knows this castle well. Unsettlingly so.*

*Strangely, that made her feel safer.*

Rowan switched the lantern into his other hand, then gently held her arm. She allowed him to lead her forward, though she scarcely felt her feet move. He lifted the wooden latch, and the gate screeched as Rowan pulled it away from the castle's stones.

A deep darkness lay ahead.

The lantern's light chased away that darkness as they walked down the narrow, winding tunnel. She felt Smoke's sleek body as he slid past her, his eyes glowing in the black. His dark fur blended into the surroundings and swallowed him whole. A chill rushed up the stone stairs and engulfed Blanchette. She grasped the cloak tighter around her body while Rowan led the way with his lantern. It swayed in midair, causing shadows to pace up and down the stone walls and ceiling. It was a comforting dance of light and shadow. A delicate ballet of hope against despair. As they traversed the winding tunnel, Blanchette's fingertips brushed against Smoke's sleek fur, a touch as velvety as the night itself. She found solace in the fiery embers that flickered within his eyes, like two beacons in an obsidian sea.

As they wandered deeper, silence took hold. Any clamor of swordplay faded away. That quiet seemed to mute the world entirely.

*As silent as the grave,* she mused with a touch of irony.

That stillness was no mere absence of sound. It was a palpable presence, an ancient force that held dominion over the catacombs and settled like a weight upon her shoulders.

Soon, the tapered stone walls widened, and that empty darkness gave way to tombs and ancient stone statues. Many of those statues were as old as Winslowe Castle itself. They lurked far back in the crypt, the silent guardians of her family's legacy. The recently deceased Winslowes and their esteemed household members stood by the opening.

Blanchette paused as the eyes of her kin seemed to track her every move.

*I have betrayed them all,* she thought as she glanced up at Rowan Dietrich. *What am I doing? I had promised...*

"The crypt goes back almost a mile," She waved her hand, gesturing at the line of stone statues.

"A mile?"

"Well, it felt like that when I was a girl. A thousand years of my family's dynasty lies here, written in eternal stone." She hesitated, then ran her fingers over a statue. She savored the feel of it, the coarse stone plucked straight from Norland's soil. "And now we have returned to the dust... as if we had never lived at all."

Rowan stepped in front of her and blocked her view of King Bartholomew II's statue and tomb. "No. You still stand, Blanchette Winslowe." He grazed a curl that'd come loose from beneath her hood. "You are here to carry out the best of your family. Do you understand me?"

The power of words escaped her. Dumbly, she nodded, watching as the firelight played off Rowan's expression. He looked regal. Beautiful. And darkly imposing.

He walked forward, then stepped to the side, urging the lantern to illuminate a dark crevice along the wall. Gradually, the light revealed everything. Two large chests sat before her, their dark wood oiled to a sleek shine. Their hinges of gold glinted like stars within the crypt. A smaller one of the same design sat beside it. Behind the three gilded chests stood her brother's, mother's, and grandmother's likenesses. Smoke sat beside the chests, as still as the statues themselves.

"I made them myself," he said, gesturing to the chests. "Your brother, mother, and grandmother belong here with the rest of their family." Rowan paused, the lantern's light brightening his gaze. "I'm sorry I didn't bring you here sooner, Blanchette. And I'm sorry I must bring you here at all. Finding a stonemason who knew your brother's likeness took a while. He deserved to be carved by someone who cared for him and knew his face."

*Indeed. Willem was supposed to have much more time.*

Blanchette's chest tightened as she stepped before her mother's statue. "God. Willem, Mother..." she said, her voice choked with emotion. She fell to her knees and wrapped her arms around her stomach. Her cries came softly. Deeply. Smoke leaned forward and sniffed her hair. He licked away her tears with his rough tongue.

She tilted her head back to stare up at Rowan. He stood before her, over six feet of uncompromising male, the hard lines of his face accented in the light. He moved toward the parallel wall and slipped the lantern onto a mounted peg. Then he reached down to Blanchette and offered his large hand. "Thank you, Rowan. Thank you... I..."

"Shh."

She placed her hand on his and came to her feet. Blanchette inhaled, then ran her fingers over the chest's beautiful engraving. Her house's sigil was etched in wood so dark that it was almost black, along with her family's words in elegant script.

She traced her brother's name, feeling connected to her family in a way she hadn't experienced since the siege. Her trembling fingers joggled the latch as she opened the small chest. Inside lay her brother's ashes. She realized it'd been a kindness to her, remembering how Willem had looked that terrible night.

"What they did to him... it was an evil too great for me to

fathom," he murmured as if reading her mind. "It was never my intention."

Blanchette nodded and swiped away tears with the back of her hand. "I know. I know it wasn't."

*Yet if you hadn't come, if you hadn't stormed my home, he'd still be here.*

Her tears turned cold. They dried on her cheeks as a much darker emotion flew through her. Smoke bristled past them and toward the crypt's entrance, the shadows swallowing him up.

"I was never a good child," Rowan murmured, his gaze fixed on where the lantern blazed. "I killed my mother coming into this world. I respected my father, honored him even... yet never forgave him for leaving me year after year, season after season, battle after battle." He ran his fingers across the dusty stone floor, idly fidgeting with loose rocks and coarse stones. "The number of days and nights... the number of hours I sat at my window, waiting for my father to return... incalculable. Those days and hours are nothing but dust in the wind now," he said, brushing dust from his hands. He picked up a stone and turned it absently between his thumb and forefinger. Blanchette watched his large, powerful hands move with fascination. "And when my heart's desire came true—when he returned home—I felt only resentment. Even hatred. Whatever love I'd felt had been extinguished within that darkness. My father... well, he hated me too. He never could forgive me for taking away the one person he'd ever loved."

"Your mother?" She looked up at him, watching as he wistfully stared forward.

"My mother," he repeated. "And I hated her. Because she'd died. I knew that's what had driven him away. After that, I was never a son again. Just another soldier under his command... under his Gray Wolf banner."

Blanchette stared at the stone statue. "It's no easy thing, feeling their absence when their ghosts always linger in the shadows. Nor is it easy to feel that anger. Their passing leaves an emptiness... and sometimes it's less painful to fill that emptiness, even if it's with something ugly." She felt his stare riveted on her. The tears came back to her eyes. She furiously blinked them away. "How do you sleep, Rowan?" She rose and brushed the dirt from her skirts and cloak. "After all you have seen? How?"

Rowan's firm hand was on her shoulder. He placed two fingertips underneath her chin and carefully tilted her head back. His eyes shone in the lantern's light, touching something deep inside her.

"I sleep because there's still beauty in the world, Blanchette. And when I close my eyes, I see that."

⁂

ROWAN GAZED across the desolate moors of Norland, where only shadows walked. He had a toy wolf in his restless hands. It was made of dark wood and had movable limbs, a tail, and a snarling mouth.

Rowan sat until darkness covered Norland, and then he watched nothing at all.

Time warped and wavered. Rowan glanced down at his hands—where a toy wolf once prowled now lay a sword. His eyes fixed on the horizon, he ran an oiled cloth down the cool metal until it shimmered. His hands were large, callused—no longer the soft hands of a boy but those of a man grown.

Behind him, a soft voice fluttered. "Rowan, my wolf..." Gentle fingers came to his shoulders and rubbed the tension away. His hands stilled, and his head rolled back in pleasure. He closed his eyes as his wife kissed his brow. Her long fingers entwined in his hair and tugged softly downward. Then she leaned forward until her lips lay against the rim of his ear and whispered, "If the child is a girl... well, I should like to name her Mary, after your mother."

Then she lay beneath him, her dark hair smattered across the fine sheets, her breasts moving with each thrust. Her hands wrapped around his back, forcing him deeper, her slender hips meeting his movements in that dance as old as time.

*His head lolled forward and nestled her breasts. The heat of her body merged with his own and stoked his inner fire. She moaned his name softly, huskily...*

*He raised his head to meet her gaze—but eyes of blue stared up at him and Blanchette Winslowe's delicate, heart-shaped face.*

ROWAN WOKE with a quivering breath in the solemn quiet of his chamber.

*The royal chamber,* he amended. The hearth burned low. Rowan threw back his bearskin blanket, gravitating to the warmth. He knelt and crossed his arms over his bare chest, remembering his dream, *reliving it...*

His head fell forward in a mixture of despair and desire. Smoke stirred from sleep in front of the hearth and watched him with eyes that glowed like embers.

*My wolf.*

Guilt. Rowan felt that, too, just as strongly. He closed his eyes. Felt the dying heat bathe his sweat-slick skin. He tried to bring his late wife's face into his mind or even Kathryn's... but he only saw Blanchette.

Blanchette Winslowe.

His doom and his salvation.

He was falling for her dangerously fast. As of late, his contentment centered around seeing her happy. He was losing sight of all else.

*This distraction is deadly in more ways than one.*

Rowan exhaled a breath. A wind whistled through the cracks and crevices in the stones of the castle. He stood, his stomach reeling. The Winslowe crown sat on the hearth's mantel.

*Who am I? Who do I want to be?*

*And, most importantly, who am I becoming?*

He paced to the window, then sat upon the ledge and gazed out into the darkness, into those shadowy moors and beyond...

into the woods, then out to the sea. He thought of the dangers beyond the walls—the threats and enemies that stirred within those trees and along the sandy coast.

But from this vantage point, only a stark emptiness lay ahead.

Emptiness lay within too.

*Sometimes it's less painful to fill that emptiness, even if it's with something ugly.*

Rowan sat at the window as the minutes turned into hours. He watched as the rising sun chased away the shadows, and Norland came to life.

He felt that sunrise within—and something stirred his shadows. He rustled through his bureau and fished out a miniature portrait. His heart did a little flip as those painted blue eyes stared back at him.

His mind made up, he swiftly crossed the chamber and gathered parchment and a quill from the writing desk.

He thought of Blanchette. Of the crown sitting feet away from him. Of the miserable father he'd had and the mother he'd never known. Of the Winslowe crypt and of its dark secrets and eternal legacy.

*It was time.*

He was more than just the Black Wolf.

Rowan Dietrich was rising from the ashes now.

# Part Two
# Spring

# Fourteen

"THE WINTER is past; the rains are over and gone. Flowers appear on the earth; the season of singing has come, the cooing of doves is heard in our land."

— Song of Songs 2:11-12 NIV

Weeks passed, and winter bowed down to spring. Flowers bloomed where ice and snow once lay, and the warmth chased away the cold.

Standing on her balcony, Blanchette felt the warmth penetrate her as the sun's golden fingers reached across the horizon. She surveyed her kingdom and inhaled the morning dew. Farmlands stretched out beneath her, a quilt of emerald and gold, where diligent hands worked the soil and coaxed life from the earth. The wood, once veiled in frosty stillness, now rustled with the awakening of spring.

Some peasants had gathered outside the guardhouse gate. She waved and smiled down at them. Moments later, she ordered the portcullis drawn, and she and Governess Agnes brought baskets overflowing with provisions and clothes—bread, fresh fruit, wheat, barley, and cloaks. They excitedly rummaged through the goods and blessed Blanchette.

And for once, she truly *felt* blessed.

She and Governess Agnes returned to her chamber, all smiles and nostalgic chatter. For the first time, Norland felt like a true kingdom, a united realm where brother protected brother and babies were born into the world without the fear of no warmth or food or shelter.

Blanchette sent bountiful wagons down to the village and port daily. The happiness she received from the soldier's reports—particularly the ones about Jonathan and Petyr—was far more than a fleeting pleasure. That happiness brought a sense of fulfillment that went bone deep. This was her calling. Blanchette knew she could be no one or nowhere else. Whether you wished to call her princess, queen, or Lady Winslowe, her place was here, caring for her people.

Governess Agnes sat in the chair by the fire, humming under her breath while mending a soldier's coat. On the table sat crushed herbs and half a dozen vials of medicine they'd just made that morning.

Blanchette thought of Jonathan again—kind, gracious, brave Jonathan and his poor family. Her spirits dampened. She turned to the window and shivered despite the warm air. She wondered how many nights his wife and their children had gone to sleep with empty stomachs. How many nights had they lain awake in silent agony, cursing Blanchette's family... staring down the dirt road and to the jutting buttresses and interwoven towers with hatred in their hearts?

Blanchette visited the infirmary as she so often did, with the basket of vials in tow. Governess Agnes came with her, checking on the wounded men and applying salves to their injuries. She was glad to see the wounds were trivial. The pirate raids had halted, and Norland enjoyed a tentative peace for the first time in years.

Blanchette sat beside Governess Agnes and absently mixed a poultice of fresh herbs and wine as her thoughts wandered. She'd lost count of the stories the soldiers had told her about Rowan. They all seemed to love him dearly—to *respect* him—to feel safe and well guarded beneath his protection.

That morning, she treated a nasty cut on a boy's knee. He'd toppled into the river while playing, earning him a deep and bright red laceration. As she cleaned the oozing blood and applied pressure, she listened to the child babble about his hero, the Black Wolf of Norland.

"There seems to be no end to the praise," Governess Agnes had said to her.

The training yard was alive with the clashing swords and the buzz of arrows cutting through the crisp air. Blanchette stopped mid-stride as Rowan caught her gaze. He stood to the side while a young boy held his own against two men. Jonas, she remembered. He was vastly improving, and she spotted a new confidence in his eyes and movements.

"That's enough for today. Well done, lad. You're getting sharper—thinking like a true soldier now." The young boy nodded with barely restrained pride on his face. Blanchette studied how Rowan's voice gentled when he spoke to him and how his eyes softened when he delivered words that might otherwise wound. The boy looked at him with naked admiration on his bright face.

*Rowan would make a good father.*
*A loving father.*

That thought came without invitation and stunned her. She recalled the boy she'd treated just that morning—the admiration that shone from his young voice and eyes. She shook her head as if shaking his words away, then gathered the material of her skirts and hastened toward the stable.

She felt him beside her before she saw or heard him. *He moves so quietly. Stalking about like a wolf,* she imagined.

"Blanchette." When his voice came, it hit her like a storm. Rowan tenderly clasped her arm. She stopped and realized she'd been holding her breath. She let it out all at once; her skin tingled where his hand was touching her. There was a layer of material between their skin—but she felt him all the same. Strong fingers—long and skilled—held her arm in place. They sent little tremors running through her.

*Fingers that have taken lives and saved lives.*

What would those fingers do to her in the privacy of her chamber?

"I've needed to speak with you." He still grasped her arm. She should pull away—he should know to let go—but they both stood, immobile, connected by that simple touch.

And something else.

Something she dared not think into existence. Something growing by the day.

"Well, you found me, sir." *You hunted me,* she'd almost said. She gazed at Jonas. He was back at it with his sparring sword, doing his best to follow Rowan's instruction. Blanchette scanned the bailey. She found Edrick outside the stable, instructing a group of soldiers. Their eyes briefly met, and Blanchette felt her anger and disgust simmer. Those feelings always sat just beneath the surface, ready to appear at the slightest provocation.

"Jonas is doing well," she said, needing to distract herself from Edrick's stare. *Why must Rowan keep him so close? Why?* "You should be proud." And he was. She saw it in his hazel eyes as they softened at the sight of the redheaded boy advancing toward his opponent.

"He's progressing."

"Where is Smoke?"

"Hunting," he murmured, feeling the words fan against her cheek.

He turned back to her, then led her by her arm.

Moments later, she found herself inside the stables with him. She was brushing out a mare's long mane; it flowed beautifully like a silken banner. Rowan wore shirtsleeves, his tanned throat visible where the laces were loosely done. He murmured something in Sunbeam's ear—a French endearment—then set down his brush. He watched her from the next stall, amusement warming his eyes.

"Weeks ago, you would have never recognized her," he said, gesturing to the mare she was attending. "She was a wild thing. Wary and flighty."

Blanchette gazed at him over the mare's back. "And now?"

"Why, she's as docile as a lamb." His eyes flickered with amusement again. The mare nickered as if in agreement.

*He means me.*

"Her name's Shadow."

"Shadow and Sunbeam," Blanchette murmured, a hint of a smile on her mouth.

Rowan leaped over the wooden wall that divided the stalls with supple grace. The horse whinnied at his approach. He gave Shadow a gentle caress, though his ardent gaze never parted from Blanchette. Then he reached overhead and grabbed a beam. The muscles in his chest and forearms strained as he studied her intently and rocked toward her body. She watched as his biceps bulged against the taut fabric of his shirt. His aroma engulfed her —sandalwood and musk and Norland's soil. Blanchette's eardrums thundered, slamming against her skull in a roar. Impatiently, the mare nudged him with her nose.

But Rowan only had eyes for Blanchette.

"I should like your answer about my proposal. You remember that? Winter has come and gone now."

"How could I forget? It was so very romantic," she said dryly, though her heart continued to roar.

He let go of the beam and stepped toward her. She scooted back, but her bottom bumped against the wall. Battle-hewn muscle and a wooden panel encased her. He stared down at her through his heavy raven-black lashes, a wolfish grin on his lips. She felt the heat radiating from his body and smelled the heady aroma of ale on his breath. She unconsciously drew closer to him, her knees weakening, her body acting on its own accord. Sweat dappled his exposed chest. Her eyes planted on his collarbone. His strong throat. The dark stubble on his chin. Finally, her eyes met his, and he grinned wickedly. He'd caught her staring. His voice was dark and deep. She'd drown in it if she weren't careful. "So, is that a yes, *ma princesse?*"

That broke whatever spell she was under. She tossed the brush aside, a familiar rush of anger forming inside her. "You don't want me. You want my kingdom."

One of his hands grabbed the beam again. His eyes and voice softened as he reached out with his free hand and traced the scar on her cheek. She almost turned into his gliding knuckles and kissed them. She physically had to stop herself. "I want peace," he whispered. "I want *you* to have peace. If we come together, it'll bring everyone else together as well. This is the way, Blanchette. The only way."

*I want you as well...* He didn't say the words, but she saw the naked desire in his gaze.

She felt it too. A fierce heat that began in her stomach, then spread through her body like wildfire.

She laid her hand on top of his and closed her eyes. Fissions of awareness shot through her palm. She curled her fingers between his much bigger ones, savoring the feel of him.

His strength.

The promises he'd made.

*Will trusting his promise compromise my own?*
*Where do I stand? And who do I fight for now?*

"Except you forget I'm no lamb, Rowan. I am a raven."

---

ROWAN GAZED down at the castle from the bailey's watchtower. The wood looked immense and never-ending—a sea of green soldiers spread out to forever. Rowan set his palms on the banister. It was likely constructed from a tree from that very forest. He imagined the watchtower with eyes carved into its body. What wars had it seen over the centuries? What weddings and celebrations? What tragedies and triumphs? How many couples had it watched steal a moment alone, perhaps there, just behind the stable or woodshop?

Rowan adjusted his posture, and the watchtower creaked beneath his weight. *It's talking to me,* he imagined. *Telling me its secrets... or maybe it's cursing me for trespassing.*

His thoughts dissipated as a haunting figure emerged in the bailey below. Draped in a scarlet riding cloak, Blanchette Winslowe moved gracefully through a swirling mist. Stopping beneath the watchtower, she revealed her golden curls as her pale hands pushed back the hood to puddle on her shoulders.

She gazed up at him, the cloak pooling around her body. Slowly, sensually, a smile spread across her lips. Lips as red as her cloak.

Lips the color of blood.

She wore her father's crown. It, too, drank in the moonlight.

He held his breath as she mounted the steps. He heard the watchtower groan and felt it sway. Soon, she stood before him... a vision in that sparkling golden crown and red cloak.

"Blanchette... come to me." Rowan's command hung in the air. She obeyed and closed the distance between them. A wicked smile crept across her lips. "I've been so cold," he confessed as he placed her hands on his leather-clad chest. His heart hammered against her small, pale palms.

"That's why I've come... to keep you warm. I'm cold too. So very, very cold. But we don't have to be any longer..." Her fair hands slid down the leather in a lazy perusal until they stopped at his waist, inches above his groin. He looked down at the large bulge in his trousers, then back up at her expression.

He found desire there. One that rivaled his own.

Only a hint of fear still lived in her eyes.

"Touch me, Blanchette. I want you to feel me. *All* of me."

She exhaled a long, sweet-smelling breath that heated his cheeks and mouth. He gasped as her palms slid over his trousers. Then her fingertips tracked over his arousal, outlining its jutting, rigid shape. He gasped again as her index finger traced the shaft from base to head. Then back up again. Her breath, warm and intoxicating, brushed against his face. She pinched her thumb and forefinger together and gently squeezed. She looked into eyes, reading him, seeing *into* him. The material of his trousers strained against his growing arousal. She teased him with another gentle but firm squeeze, and Rowan released a heavy moan.

She looked up at him with eyes so blue, so deep, that he felt himself sinking in them.

"How does it feel, Blanchette? Wearing your family's crown?"

She met his gaze. Held it. A fire came into her eyes that melted away the icy blue. Whatever fear he'd seen moments ago vanished. "Like power. I've dreamt about this, you know..."

"About wearing the crown?" he stupidly asked, his breaths coming short as she played with the front of his trousers. His arousal jerked against the material and her palms. He felt light-headed from desire. Weak in the knees. He grabbed an overhead beam to stabilize himself.

"This crown... and us. I've dreamt of touching you... tasting you." She knelt in front of him, her eyes never leaving his, her hands never leaving his painful arousal. She leaned forward and pushed her mouth against him, down there, sensually molding her lips around the fabric-covered shaft. Rowan gripped the beam and gritted his teeth as the stirrings of an intensely powerful climax built.

Her pink tongue pushed between her lips and circled the throbbing head. Once. Twice. Thrice. The fabric of his trousers clung to his skin as it grew damp from her mouth. Then he watched, mesmerized, as one of her hands slipped under her dress to touch herself between her legs. In this light, it was difficult to see where the crown ended and her golden curls began.

"Blanchette..."

"I often touch myself like this when I think of you. I imagine how good it would feel to take you inside my mouth, inside my body..."

"Oh God, Blanchette... please. I-I can't take much more. God—" His words choked off as her free hand tugged on the tie of his trousers to loosen the material. Then her fingers dipped inside and wrapped around his hard manhood. He gazed at the lofty trees. The watchtower was of a height with them, and Rowan felt like he was soaring.

He felt how she only circled three-fourths of him. He was so large, and she so small. His balls pulled tight as she squeezed and explored. She ran her fingers up and down the pulsating head, then traced the slit. Liquid seeped out, and that mounting feeling intensified. Her finger wiped it up, then she withdrew her hand. She sucked the liquid off the tip of her finger, the gold in her hair and on her crown glinting in the moonlight.

*God, if she touches me again... or looks at me like that again...*

He growled and yanked her to her feet. Before he knew what was happening, he'd pinned against the watchtower's wooden wall, his lips on her throat. She threw her head back and moaned. Panting, she whispered his name and dragged her hands down his back, her fingernails raking his skin through the jerkin. Then those hands tangled in his hair and pulled, increasing the pressure of his mouth and tongue as they slid over her bare skin. She tasted as sweet as he'd imagined. Like honey and sunshine. He hiked up her skirts and felt the wetness between her legs, dripping through her smallclothes.

"Rowan, yes... oh God, touch me, *teach me*... please... I want you inside me."

"I'm going to devour you, *ma princesse*. I'm going to fill every inch of you, slowly, so painfully slow, till you beg for it. I want to hear you scream my name. You are mine now."

His climax came powerfully. He moaned from the intense release and rode those waves of pleasure as they pulsed through him again and again...

... and caused him to wake inside his solar. As the tremors subsided, he leaped from the bed and cursed himself, feeling very much like a little boy who'd wet the bed.

Shame. Disgust. And a burning desire.

He felt that strongest of all.

Rowan stood at the window and stared at the outer bailey, where the watchtower jutted into the ink-black sky.

Waiting. Watching. As it had for centuries.

*What is it watching?* he mused. *And what secrets does it hold?*

---

ROWAN STOOD AT THE ANVIL, sweat pouring down his face as he pounded the hot metal with his hammer. His strikes echoed through the castle, bouncing off the stone walls like thunder. Sparks flew as he brought the hammer down again and again. Heat rose into his face, and his muscles began to shake from the force of his work.

He'd always shaped all his own armor. Woodworking. Smithing. Since he was a boy, he'd found peace working with his hands in this way.

He brought the hammer down hard as if he could strike away his desire like that. Images from that dream kept creeping back.

*I want her... and not just her body.*

*I crave so much more.*

The hiss of metal meeting the cool, damp air, the rhythmic thud of the hammer, and the steady beat of his heart melded into a chorus.

He recalled crafting his wolf helm years ago. It bore the essence of the night itself, its snarling fangs a tribute to the shadows that lurked in his soul.

Rowan shook away the memory and focused on the task at hand, shaping the metal with his hammer and forging it into something intense and resilient for *her*.

For Blanchette.

He paused in mid-strike as her face swam before his eyes. He stared forward into the rising steam from the forge. Her features took shape there. Her piercing blue eyes and hair as bright as the gold from Norland's mines.

On the edge of the anvil was a stack of arrowheads he'd finished hammering an hour ago.

He inhaled a long breath. His muscles strained as he swung his hammer down again, the hot metal glowing orange in the forge's light. Sparks flew from the anvil as he pounded the metal into shape, his face contorted with concentration.

He had been working on it since midday when the sun was still perched in the sky. Now darkness filled the world. He heard his men training in the yard, the clash of blades and the whirl of arrows cutting through the air.

It was a sword. He had to ensure it was perfect. Perfect weight. Perfect balance. Perfect length. Blanchette's life might well depend on it.

Rowan wondered what battles she might fight and what enemies she would face at the end of this blade.

Finally, it was done. Rowan held it up to the torchlight. The sword was sharp and well-balanced, and intricate designs adorned the hilt.

Ravens in flight.

*The power of life and death,* he thought.

# Fifteen

Blanchette and Governess Agnes idly sewed a pair of torn doublets. They'd just finished reviewing last season's ledgers and the plans for the next. Afterward, they fell into wistful chatter that helped Winslowe Castle feel a little more like home again. Despite herself, a smile spread across Blanchette's face, and a spark of sentimental joy ignited. The smile felt wrong and invasive. She tried to hold it back, but it sprang up, uninvited, at Governess Agnes's reminiscing.

"Do you remember when Isadora and I filled the steward's pillow with fish?"

"Oh, how shall I forget that?" Governess Agnes replied as she closed a hole in the doublet. "He was all in a rage. Didn't know where the stench was coming from for nearly a fortnight."

"He went to sleep with a clothespin on his nose." Blanchette giggled.

How strange it felt to laugh.

What right did she have to be happy when her brother and mother lay in the cold, dark crypts? *He's resting there now because of Rowan.*

"He did indeed. Blanchette? You look most troubled, my dear."

Blanchette lowered the doublet and ran her fingers over the rough fabric. The Black Wolf sigil adorned its chest. She traced the snarling wolf head and inhaled deeply. "I close my eyes at night. I close my eyes and try to see their faces. Mother's, my grandmother... Willem." Blanchette inhaled a shaky breath as she felt tears come to her eyes. Governess Agnes laid a hand on her wrist and gently squeezed. "But I can't. All I can see—all *who* I can see—is Rowan Dietrich. At first, I saw him, and I cursed him. He'd haunt my every nightmare. I'd see him standing there, in his crude armor and helm, his sword wet and dripping with the blood of my family's. There was a certain comfort in that, you know? A tangible feeling of hate and revenge I could hold on to. It was so clear to me... who he was and what my path should be. I was... anchored."

Governess Agnes gave a heartfelt sigh. "I felt the same way, my dear. But now..."

"But now," Blanchette agreed, her voice strained. "But now... I still see him when I close my eyes. But not his armor or twisted wolf helm. I see the man. The knight. I see Sir Rowan. I see the man who gave the children food, blankets, and clothes. I see and hear the man who speaks soft words to me, words of comfort and courage and admiration. I see the man who took my hand and led me to the crypts so my family might lie in peace with the rest of their kin. I see a man I'm starting to feel for, and I am lost. And the guilt I feel... God, what a betrayal!"

"It's not as simple as all that." Governess Agnes took the doublet from Blanchette's hands and set it aside. She squeezed her fingertips lovingly, reassuringly. Blanchette gripped her hands like they were lifelines. *Yes... I need to feel anchored.* "Listen to me, my dear. Listen closely. Your father committed horrible atrocities, but he did good too. People are not purely good or purely bad. There are light and shadows in all of us. And sometimes bad things must happen to bring about lasting good. Sometimes winter comes, and it's dark and painful, but it clears the earth for spring."

Blanchette broke off her gaze from her governess's and jerked toward the window. "Look! Riders."

From the clearing—the same clearing Rowan's army had once torn open—emerged a band of seven horsemen and an ornate wheelhouse.

And the Black Wolf was emblazoned on its door.

※

"Much better," Rowan said to Jonas as the squire wiped the sweat from his brow. Rowan took a sideways stance and maneuvered backward with graceful footing. "But you need to move more," he instructed in a low voice. "You need to stalk—"

"Like a wolf," the boy finished, raising his sparring sword and mimicking Rowan's stance.

"Aye, my lad. Like a wolf."

Three guardsmen burst into the training yard. "Riders just arrived, sir, asking for your audience. A Sir Jeremy was among them."

Rowan nodded, a nervous smile coming to his face. He sheathed his longsword. "Keep training, and we shall speak later," he said to the redheaded boy with a pat on his arm. "Raise the gate," he commanded his men as he crossed the bailey. He traveled past the watchtower and toward the imposing guardhouse.

The riders were mounted and armored in boiled leather and chain mail, and the two men flanking the wagon flew the Black Wolf's standard. Rowan watched with pride as it whipped and prowled in the crisp breeze.

"Sir Jeremy," he greeted as a knight dismounted with a broad smile and the Black Wolf sewn onto his tabard. "I wasn't sure I'd see you again, my friend." Jeremy's black beard had grown patches of white since their last meeting years ago. Yet he still wore the same lopsided smile that came easily to his weathered face.

"Aye," the man said. "You look worse for wear." They extended their arms in a forearm shake before Sir Jeremy yanked

Rowan into a hug. Rowan placed his hand on the knight's shoulder and said, "Thank you for coming and bringing her to me. I want you to stay and sit on my council. I need men I can trust. I need you."

"It'd be an honor, sir."

The carriage door burst open. Rowan's heart pounded as a lovely seven-year-old girl hopped out. She clasped a doll under her arm. A wary, tight-lipped smile was on her lips.

"Father?" she asked, and Rowan exhaled a breath he hadn't realized he'd been holding.

"Yes... it's me."

Shock stunned him into silence. In his daughter's place stood Blanchette when she was just a girl, her blond curls glittering in the afternoon sun, her blue eyes flashing.

The child tentatively glanced at him. Rowan closed the distance between them and came to one knee. "Mary... my, look how old you've gotten. You're a lady now. No longer a child."

She smiled at him hesitantly, and for a passing second, Rowan feared she didn't recognize him at all. She hadn't seen him for over five years. He'd barred that thought from his mind during his campaigns. And now it stared him straight in the face. "You're a proper little lady now. Your mother would be proud."

She smiled at that—a sweet, hesitant smile that set her blue eyes sparkling. Then a sadness surfaced in that gaze. One he knew all too well. One he saw often when he gazed into his looking glass. Rowan cleared his throat and came to unsteady feet.

Mary glanced up at the jutting towers, buttresses, and the commanding curtain wall that held everything in. Awe swept over her sweet features and brought a lively glint to her eyes.

He tracked her gaze with his own and pointed toward the highest keep. "She's a beautiful castle, to be certain. And as old as Norland herself. This shall be your home now, Mary."

EXCITED VOICES and overlapping commands drifted in from the window. Blanchette glanced out again, where the sight of that wheelhouse and several guardsmen she'd never seen before greeted her. She straightened out her skirt, then left her chamber, forgetting to bid Governess Agnes farewell.

She crossed the kitchens, where a little boy she'd known since he was born slipped her a lemon cake, then made her way into the great hall.

Rowan stood at the entryway surrounded by the guardsmen she'd spotted from her window. And before him was a charming little girl who appeared entirely lost.

*My God... she looks just like me.*

Rowan met her gaze from across the hall. Blanchette felt something in her heart tighten, and her breath audibly caught. Exhaling, she held her head up and crossed the chamber with quick strides. She stopped in front of the little girl and stood beside Rowan, a million questions flying through her mind with only a handful of words on her lips.

"Why, that's a lovely cloak, my lady," Blanchette said with a smile.

The little girl glanced up at Rowan before replying. "It's a wolf pelt," she finally said, and Blanchette thought she heard irony in her light voice.

Rowan gripped the child's shoulder. It was an awkward and strained movement, and that mere touch seemed to dwarf her. He turned back to the black-bearded knight. The man had kind eyes creased by smile lines and years under a beating sun. "Sir Jeremy, would you be so kind as to bring Mary's things into the castle?" After Sir Jeremy left, he said to Blanchette, "I'd like you to meet someone very special. This is my daughter, Mary Dietrich."

Blanchette's gaze shot up to Rowan's. She saw the beginnings of a story there. *What was it? How could he have had a daughter all this time?*

*Who is this man, really?*

Blanchette glanced at the little girl, who barely came to his waist. She'd removed her wimple, freeing a mane of blond curls that reminded Blanchette of her own. Without thinking, Blanchette smoothed down her own hair and gave the girl a smile that felt strained. The beat of her heart came a little faster, and when she knelt and enveloped the girl in her arms, she hoped Mary couldn't feel her shaking.

After a moment, Blanchette pulled out of the hug. She set a hand on each of Mary's delicate shoulders. "I'm so happy to meet you. I'm Blanchette Winslowe. You are most welcome here, Mary. And who is this?" she asked, running her fingers through the doll's streaming black hair.

"Her name is Lady Penelope."

The girl was all shy smiles and pink cheeks, no older than seven years. But there was also a sadness in those blue eyes... one that Blanchette knew well. *Eyes that are so much like my own.* "I'd love to show you and Lady Penelope to your room. Would you like to come with me, Mary?" She nodded shyly, her golden curls bouncing about her shoulders. Then she took her hand, and they left together, leaving the Black Wolf speechless behind them.

LATER THAT NIGHT, after Mary had settled into Willem's old chambers, Rowan Dietrich, the fabled Black Wolf of Norland, lounged before the hearth and read to his daughter. A wooden table sat beside him, overflowing with nuts, berries, crystal wine-glasses, and a bronze decanter.

She really was the sweetest-looking child Blanchette had ever seen. She was a vision in a vibrant brocade dress and a matching wimple. Wavy blond hair framed her slim shoulders. She looked impossibly small and bright beside Rowan—a sunbeam among shadows.

Rowan read to her softly, his voice barely audible over the popping hearth. Blanchette watched as Smoke's paws twitched while he slept. He laid his massive head on top of him, and his black fur camouflaged in the shadows.

Blanchette stepped to the side to better conceal *herself* in shadow, but her hip bumped against one of the long wooden benches that lined the walls. Smoke awoke, ever on guard, and lifted his head at the sound. Her breath caught as Rowan jerked his face toward her. He stood, and the room instantly vibrated with his presence. The fire silhouetted his tall, muscled body and legs that seemed to go on forever. Rowan had dressed in a simple tunic, the ties loose at the neck. Smooth, tanned skin peeked out there. Blanchette curled her fingers against the urge to caress that skin.

"Blanchette," he said, "come forward."

Blanchette felt her legs moving, yet it seemed like she was wading through a dream. The shadows were deep and dark as she wandered to the hearth. Only two braziers were lit. Their flames licked at the stone walls and murmured a cozy hum.

Rowan's eyes were riveted on her.

*Has he ever looked at me that way before?*

Rowan cleared his throat. Suddenly, he looked very uncomfortable. "Mary, the hour is late, and you've traveled far. Sir Jeremy will show you to your chambers."

Mary glanced up at Blanchette again, wary, the faintest smile playing on her lips. "Can... can Smoke come with me?"

"Aye... that shall be fine," Rowan tentatively said, giving his daughter an awkward pat on her shoulder.

Then she was off with the knight and the black wolf, her shimmering blond hair swallowed up by the shadows.

Several moments of silence passed. Finally, Rowan stepped near Blanchette, and she felt a rush of body heat envelop her. He looked at her in a way he never had before. It caused her breath to catch, sweat to form on her palms, and her heart to thunder. Blanchette eyed that patch of exposed skin at his neck and tightened her fingers against the temptation building inside her.

"I should have told you about Mary sooner."

"I understand," Blanchette finished because she *did* understand. "Really, I do. You were keeping her safe."

Rowan sighed, his beautiful eyes staring into the hearth. Then he sat in one of the wingback chairs and gestured to the adjacent one. Blanchette felt a little lightheaded from the turn of events. Gratefully, she took a seat. She would have fallen had she remained standing.

"I was keeping her safe, aye. But... well, it was more than that."

*Strange,* Blanchette thought. *And a bit eerie.* Watching Mary move through the darkness was like watching herself move through the castle as a child. She shivered from the queer thought. It was as if a ghost was in their midst, a ghost from her own past... a ghost of her former self.

But no, her mind objected while she gazed at Rowan's troubled features. This was Rowan's ghost—a phantom from his past who'd finally come home.

Rowan poured two glasses of wine from the bronze decanter, and Blanchette felt the warmth of his fingers as he handed her the glass. She inhaled the fragrant bouquet of the wine. The aroma of the fine red tantalized her senses. The sweet and inviting liquid filled her body with its fuzzy warmth. Beads of wine gathered on her bottom lip. She licked them away while Rowan's intense gaze never wavered from her.

His eyes were riveted on her again, and she saw blatant desire flashing in their depths. She took another sip and felt that lightheaded sensation grow.

*My God... I want him to kiss me... more than I've ever wanted anything before.*

"I'm sorry, Rowan," she managed to whisper. "Mary must have been very young... when it happened."

Rowan swirled his wineglass, then took a sip, and Blanchette caught the sweet scent of the wine on his breath.

*What would happen if he tossed the glass into the hearth, captured my face in his large hands, and kissed me senselessly?*

*How would he taste?*
*How would he feel in my arms?*

He held her gaze with unwavering intensity, drawing her deeper. She couldn't take her eyes off him—off the strong jut of his chin or how his raven-black hair fell just above his ears and curled slightly. She yearned to twirl that hair between her fingertips while his eyes gazed into her own.

"She was less than a year old," Rowan said, his voice heavy with pain. He swirled his glass, and the red wine soundlessly sloshed inside it. It reminded Blanchette of blood. "Not even ten feet away from the bed where her mother died."

Raw, visceral emotions emanated from Rowan. Never had he looked so vulnerable and defeated. That scared her a little. She laid her hand on his shoulder. His rigid muscles relaxed beneath her caressing palm. She kneaded the tight muscles and heard as his breathing slowed into a steady rhythm.

Then he shook his downcast head and stared at his blood-red wine. "It was my punishment for disobeying his orders. Sir Edrick had warned me. And I've suffered every day since. Mary has too..."

Panic coursed through Blanchette as she grasped the gravity of his words. She withdrew her hand, the weight of their reality crashing down once again.

"His orders? My father's, you mean," she stated firmly, leaving no room for ambiguity.

They both stared into the hearth as the silence rose around them. Firelight licked at the ravens engraved in the mantel and set them aglow.

Rowan emptied the contents of his glass with a single swallow before placing it on the table. It hit the wood with a jolting *bang*. Then he stood with a sudden nervous energy, pacing toward the hearth. His hands found purchase on the mantel, his palms cradling the Winslowe sigil. She watched the firelight swim in his dark hair and play off his handsome, drawn face.

*He looks lost. Like just another ghost haunting Winslowe Castle.*

His hazel eyes had transformed into two pits of miserable grief.

"Tell me, Rowan. Please. Help me understand."

With his inner turmoil lay bare, Rowan turned to Blanchette, that raw agony deepening in his eyes. "I don't understand it all myself."

And then he began.

# Sixteen

### Seven years earlier
### Dietrich Castle

Rowan knew things were amiss the moment he arrived. He stared up at his family's ancient holdfast, watching stoically as the two towers pierced a bruised dusk sky. A groomsman hustled to him within moments of his arrival. Rowan leaped down from Sunbeam while the groomsman took the reins and refused to meet his eyes. He had a nervous energy about him and an anxious air in his shifty gaze. That heightened Rowan's premonition.

*I'm too late.*

He glanced back at the way from which he came. The drawn portcullis resembled a mouth of rotten teeth, and the smoky, burned town lurked beyond it.

Rowan paced through his great hall, which was unusually barren.

With his hand wrapping his longsword's hilt, he took the stone steps by twos and raced down the darkening corridors. Only a handful of braziers were lit. They fought off the shadows, the flames licking at the stone walls.

He heard his boots pounding against the floor, echoing hollowly, his heartbeat banging in accord. He listened to his breaths coming fast and the blood rushing through his ears.

*God, please don't let me be too late.*

Two servants rushed by him, but Rowan gave them no more than a cursory glance. He was stalking his own halls, the heat of battle fever rising inside him. Stalking toward a reality he could already see take shape. Stalking, like the wolf that had guarded his family's sigil for so many years...

He'd crossed more battlefields than he could count, yet that walk through his halls had been harder than any of them.

Then he heard it—or thought he heard it—the long, mournful, drawn-out cry of a wolf somewhere beyond his castle's walls.

*An omen or a blessing?*

He reached his destination before he could ponder the answer. Three men stood outside her chamber, their swords drawn and coated with blood. They donned suits of chain mail armor. Rowan felt naked in his jerkin and leather trousers.

*Whose blood?* He thought of the baker's boy who stole sweets from the kitchens and of the kennel master's daughter, whom he'd taught to wield a sparring sword.

And, of course, he thought of his wife and child. He thought of them most of all.

Rowan's longsword was free of its sheath before he realized what he was doing. Close quarters made poor grounds for swordplay. The point of his blade shot through one of the guard's throats.

Then the other two were on him. Rowan ducked beneath a strike and countered with a fierce undercut, taking the second guard through his chain mail. The third guard seized his opening while Rowan's sword was down. Rowan felt the bite of steel skim his shoulder and neck. *Good God, the blade nearly took my head off.* Pain spiked through him as he raised his longsword with a wild groan and met the guard's blade in midair. A shrill scream echoed from inside the chamber.

Rowan's and the guard's blades locked. Rowan shoved forward, fully embraced by his fever now, and violently kicked the guard in the stomach.

He toppled back like the fool he was. An instant later, Rowan stood above him and drove his sword through the man's heart.

The fight was over.

Yet the battle had just begun.

He shoved open the heavy oak door, his longsword slick and dripping with blood, that panicked feeling rising inside him.

He saw the shape of Beatrice's body on the canopied bed, but before he could register any details, another man was on him. This one wielded a dagger, its metal shimmering with red.

*Whose blood? Beatrice's?*

*Or Mary's?*

Rowan moved fast despite the pain in his neck. It was over in an instant. They stood near each other, the man's impaled body closing the distance between them. Rowan released a guttural cry as he disengaged the sword and then dropped it. It *clanged* loudly within the quiet. Rowan raced over to the canopied bed, taking in the scene piece by piece—his wife's splayed body, the bloody sheets, Mary's wailing from inside the wardrobe—yet he perceived nothing.

Nothing and everything, all in the same breath.

Rowan collapsed beside the bed and carefully adjusted his wife's body.

*Let her live for Mary, if not for myself.*

He smoothed down the sodden material of her nightdress and found what he already knew to be there—several dagger wounds. All the while, Mary's piercing cries echoed shrilly. Across all the battlefields, he'd never heard a worse sound.

Rowan cupped his wife's cheek and felt tears coat his face. He ran his thumb over her parted lips. She was beautiful, dark-haired and dark-eyed, her skin as pale as fresh-fallen snow.

His gaze tracked down her body to the ruffled sheets and her bare legs. Her gown was bunched around her waist as if someone had urgently hiked it up. And the blood...

*Mercy, so much blood.*

Her thighs were bruised and stained with it.

Rowan followed the sound of Mary's cries and opened the wardrobe, his hands strangely steady. Beatrice had bundled her in a pile of skins and dresses on the floor. Mary's sweet face was flushed a bright pink, her chubby arms and legs flailing. Rowan picked her up and held her tight against his chest. He kissed her forehead and rocked her in his arms as her wailing dug at his soul.

And maybe—just maybe—the melancholy howl of a wolf joined in that song.

HE WAS in the great hall of Winslowe Castle again. The sweet feel of Blanchette's touch reeled him back into the moment. He turned to her, hardly believing he'd told her everything... and outright refusing to accept the yearnings the mere sensation of her touch elicited.

They stood a foot apart. He watched the firelight play off her curls and glitter in her beautiful blue gaze. Images from his dream surfaced... the way the crown had blended into her hair effortlessly like it'd be made to rest there... and how she'd teased and touched him until he'd exploded from his desire.

Her eyes held a sadness that went far beyond her years. He felt his insides clench, hating himself for the pain he'd brought into her life. So much of that sadness had come from his hands.

Rowan exhaled a tentative breath and searched her gaze. A wind picked up, and he heard the air whistling through the castle's crevices. He closed his eyes briefly—his wife's body waited for him in that darkness, like she always did.

"She hid Mary in our wardrobe," he said, seeing and feeling everything behind his eyes. The oak floorboards creaking below his boots. The sight of his wife's blood staining the bedsheets and his own hands.

*So much blood.*

He was drowning in it.

"She'd stayed silent."

"A blessing," Blanchette said, her voice thin. He didn't know what to make of it.

Bitter laughter spilled out of him, and he clenched his fingers several times as that mad anger ran anew. "I ran away and hid at Edrick's home after that. Sent Mary to live as a ward of Rochester Castle... my wife's uncle."

"It was right of you to summon Mary here now. She should be with you, Rowan... especially after all this lost time. God... I'm... I'm so sorry."

Blanchette shifted toward him, and Rowan felt some of the anger leave at the emotion he found in her eyes. Tears clouded her gaze, and when she spoke, her voice was a sweet whisper that reached every corner of his heart. "My father ordered her death?"

"As a punishment for refusing to stop another revolt. He commanded me to burn a village."

She shook her head. "We are not so different. We share a pain like two sides of the same coin... a dawn that breaks into dusk across the same landscape. I remember seeing you at the feasts. Your wife, too, so often sitting with my father... I can hardly believe he was capable of such cruelty. They seemed rather amicable."

*Indeed they were.* Rowan watched as she physically battled for the right words. "I can't undo any of the injustice that my father committed. I can't change our pasts. But I can be here for you now."

Rowan stepped closer to her until they were almost touching. The firelight turned her blond curls a molten gold. He tentatively reached out and ran his fingers through those tresses, his heart beating against his ribs. She smelled like the kingswood flowers she so often picked... like sunshine and summer.

"You bring me such warmth, Blanchette," he confessed, remembering his watchtower dream again. "One like I've never known." He desired her, desired her like mad, but he yearned for her simple friendship most of all.

She must have read the longing in his stare. "Yes... I am here for you. And I won't leave." She leaned into his touch until his open palm cupped her cheek. He felt the raised scar beneath his fingers and gently traced its path... from her ear all the way to the corner of her parted lips. How he wished he could undo her pain and help her forget.

Rowan heard her sharp intake of breath. Their gazes came together in a powerful union. "I thought I was strong," Rowan said, "but you showed me true strength. I could have never survived what you have. I'm so sorry for my role in your grief."

Blanchette held her hand over his, cupping her palm against his fingers. His hands were twice her size and battle-beaten.

Her red lips turned up in a small, sad smile. "It was my father who played that role. I'm learning that every day, I think."

---

HIS HAND REMAINED at her jaw, the smooth band of his thumb pad pressing against her scar. Her heart raced inside her chest until she could hardly hear through the blood rushing in her ears. She tipped her head back and glanced at Rowan. His eyes were above hers, and she found a smoldering desire there.

One her own body and soul echoed.

"I should hate you," she whispered, her voice barely audible over the crackling hearth. "And a part of me still does."

"Yes." His voice came at her like rolling thunder. "And I admire you." He bowed his head forward until his lips skimmed her hairline. "Although I shouldn't," he said, the heat of his words brushing against her skin. His lips ghosted across her forehead. She released a small sigh, and Rowan's throaty chuckle followed. He took her hand in his, his long, callused fingers sweeping across her knuckles in a soothing, fiery touch. The signet ring gleamed, and its golden band drank in the fire's light. Rowan held her hand and placed it over his chest. His heart raced beneath her palm, and Blanchette knew he was as nervous as she. It was remarkable, watching as the Black Wolf of Norland, this beast of a man, let his armor down and made himself vulnerable.

Low lights, cool and warm from moon and hearth, filtered through the shadows. His eyes found hers again. They studied her with a chilling focus. Her skin prickled as his gaze swept over her in a slow and lazy perusal. Then his head lowered again, and his lips were at her brow. Lower and lower, he shifted his lips, and Blanchette swore he could hear the frantic thumping of her heart.

"I hate you, Rowan Dietrich," she whispered. Blood rushed through her ears, and she felt her eyelids grow heavy at the erotic sensation of Rowan's arms encasing her, his lips mere inches from her own, the heat of his breath ghosting across her skin. The red wine scented his breath and deepened her desire. "I hate you." Her legs weakened beneath her, but Rowan's arms were there, solid and supportive, holding her body in place. He was her lifeline at that moment, and she couldn't imagine him letting go. *My anchor,* she mused ironically. "I hate you." She stepped nearer to him, closing the scant distance between their bodies. The shift caused her breasts to push against his lower chest. She inhaled his scent—sandalwood and wine—and felt herself let go. "I hate you."

She surrendered to the moment, the horrors she'd come to know, the grief and loss, and that corner of her heart that still held room for hope. She exhaled a breath and pressed her cheek against his. His hands found their way into her hair. Nimble fingers ran through her curls in soothing, intoxicating strokes. She stood on the tips of her toes until her ear was almost level with his chest. The beat of his heart thundered there—a beautiful accompaniment to the melody of her sensual breathing.

She drifted between fear and strange, delirious peace. It was a dangerous place to be. A place she could get lost in.

"I cannot hate you anymore, Rowan Dietrich."

*In fact, I think I'm starting to love you,* she thought as her body relaxed and heated all in the same breath. She was melting into him, and the lines she'd so carefully drawn in her mind blurred. She could no longer distinguish love from hate, sorrow from joy... and that notion scared her more than anything else.

*I could lose myself in you, Black Wolf.*

"My lord? My lady?" His captain's voice cut through the great hall. She moved away from Rowan, the blood rushing through her ears. Edrick stood in front of them, his feet shoulder-width apart, one hand wrapping the pommel of his sheathed sword.

"I... I must go," Blanchette said as she took her leave without another glance.

She rushed through the dark halls of her castle.

Up the winding stairwells and through the corridors where only a few braziers were lit. Moonlight streamed through the angled mullion windows in thin shafts.

*Oh God... what am I doing?*

Panic overcame her. She hastened her steps as if the devil were on her heels. Or a wolf that wanted to devour her. Sweat dripped from her hairline despite the night chill.

*What am I running from, really?*

After what might have been an hour or only minutes, Blanchette slammed her back against the corridor's wall as her legs weakened beneath her. Breathing hard, she leaned against that wall for support. She remembered the night of the siege. How she'd almost lost her sanity while leaning against these same walls.

*My promise... oh God, I am lost...*

As her eyes shut, Rowan's face surfaced in her mind. Her palms pushed against the coarse wall, seeking purchase, yet she felt his powerful arms encasing her, the heat of his breath rushing against her neck.

*I had promised...*

# Seventeen

"FOR EVERYTHING, there is a season, a time for every activity under heaven."

— ECCLESIASTES 3:1

Rowan cursed as Edrick stared at him, unblinking, with a frown of blatant disapproval.

"The port village is under attack? You're certain?" Rowan asked.

"I am certain. This wouldn't have come as a surprise if you hadn't been so preoccupied as of late."

Rowan said nothing. He paced past Edrick with Smoke at his heels. The three of them stormed through the entrance and into the inner bailey. Captains yelled orders as the night came alive to the clamor of weapons and armor.

"This is madness," Edrick said.

"My armor and my squire," Rowan shouted at a passing guard. "Find him! Now!"

Jonas brought Rowan Sunbeam minutes later, saddled and ready. He quickly donned his armor with his squire's help. The

Black Wolf swallowed Rowan Dietrich; where a man once stood stalked a plate-armored wolf.

"You mean to ride out now?" Edrick asked.

"Yes, but I won't be riding alone. I want you and twenty of our best men with us."

Rowan led a column of mounted soldiers down the dirt road and into the heart of the night. The wood rushed by in a swath of green and dark brown.

A full moon floated above him, halfway hidden behind a blanket of low-hanging clouds. The *clop-clop* of horse hooves sounded unsettlingly loud within the quiet. Rowan directed his men toward the smoky ruins of yet another village. As they encroached, they could hear the screams of the dying.

Moments later, they arrived at the mayhem. They observed the town from a hill overlooking the village. The town stretched almost a mile outside the lush outskirts of the woods, nestled against the sea.

*Thank God it isn't the central village.* He recalled visiting there with Blanchette, of the little children calling his name and the boisterous innkeeper.

*I am indeed distracted.*

*I'm making mistakes again.*

*This is my sin. More blood on my hands.*

He felt so very weary. And tired of fighting.

*A lifetime of fighting with no end in sight.*

As he drew closer, Rowan caught sight of his own banners. He glanced about, wildly confused, as the snarling black wolf of his sigil flew from lances and waved in the night.

Edrick cursed; his destrier whinnied and paced uneasily beneath him, sensing his building anger. "What is this madness?" Crudely armored soldiers hurried through the town on foot with torches in their hands. Rowan could make out the shapes of slain bodies littering the ground.

"Impostors," Rowan snapped. "Murderers." Indeed, they were flying his standard and killing the townsfolk in his name.

*But why?*

"Order our men to surround the village," he said, his voice heavy with anger and disbelief. Rowan pulled Sunbeam's reins and sank his boots into his haunches. "Enough!" he said as a bloodcurdling cry shivered through the night. "I won't stand idle. Not while people are still alive. I'm going down there now. Get the guard in a horseshoe. We want to take them by surprise. *Now.*"

Rowan kicked Sunbeam, and he was off. The destrier galloped down the steep hill and into the shadows. A column of men followed him, wrapping the side of the town in a half circle.

Two foot soldiers, who'd been busy looting corpses, jerked to their feet as the village center burst into bedlam.

"The Black Wolf! Look alive! It's the Black Wolf!" one man stupidly screamed in warning. Rowan's name was the last thing he ever said. His longsword cut in an upward arc, slashing through tendon and muscle and flesh. The man died on his sword before he even hit the ground. Sunbeam's pounding hooves killed the second soldier. Rowan galloped through the village as he and his men cut down the ill-equipped soldiers left and right who'd been busy terrorizing the town moments before.

Smoke appeared seemingly out of nowhere. He fought beside Rowan, an extension of himself, leaping through the shadows and tearing out throats and entrails.

He caught sight of Edrick, slicing down men with a calm efficiency that Rowan had always admired.

Rowan tugged on Sunbeam's reins in incredulity, causing the horse to rear onto his hind legs. The world was burning.

It was hell on earth.

Rowan glanced about helplessly, curses on his lips, smoke and ash in his eyes. He kicked Sunbeam's flank, and the horse obediently flew forward despite the sounds and scents of death.

Then the ground seemed to sail up at Rowan, knocking the wind from his lungs. He lay in the dusty darkness as Sunbeam stomped in agony and the homes and shops flamed around them.

Rowan cursed again, his longsword drawn, as he rose onto his feet. Being in full armor was no easy task. He rushed toward Sunbeam, who was panicking and tossing his great dark head.

An arrow jutted from his powerful rump, and the scent of death and smoke had unleashed something feral in the beast.

His hooves pounded against the dusty ground as he paced and tossed his head with pained sounds. Rowan could see the terror in Sunbeam's eyes, where the fire reflected.

A foot soldier ran at him—Smoke easily tackled the man and tore out his throat. Rowan grabbed Sunbeam's leather reins and soothingly ran his hands over the horse's side. He gazed from behind Sunbeam, where Smoke's glowing ember eyes stared back at him.

"Hush, boy, hush," he murmured to Sunbeam. "It will all be over soon. I—"

The *swish* of an arrow cut through the night. Rowan freed an anguished cry as the shaft went through one side of Sunbeam's head and out the other. The horse staggered on his feet for half a heartbeat before crashing to the ground, where he lay dead.

Rowan screamed again, a heart-wrenching sound that was torn from deep inside him. His sword drawn before him, he scanned the darkness and carefully edged away from Sunbeam. A dark pool of blood gathered beneath the horse's snout and stained the dirt.

Rowan crouched beside his fallen companion and gritted his teeth. He ran his palm over the horse's silky muzzle. Smoke tossed his head back, his muzzle dripping blood and strings of flesh, and howled.

The night vibrated with the sound.

Rowan's men buzzed around him, some tending to the wounded, others drawing water from the well and vainly trying to extinguish the burning buildings. The impostor soldiers either lay dead, dying, or had been scared off.

Rowan came to his feet and moved forward, quick as a lightning strike. He drew a lance from the earth. His standard fluttered at the top, the black wolf whipping against the black and starless sky. Rowan grabbed the reins of a panicked, riderless horse galloping through the smoky town. He mounted in a single, swift movement, his banner in hand, and then raced through the ruins. The inferno that raged around him crackled and hissed, casting eerie, dancing shadows upon the scorched earth.

The horse reared onto its hind legs as Rowan pulled hard on the reins. He halted before one of the shops. Flames traveled across the straw roof, and inside, screams resounded and made Rowan's blood curdle. A line of fire blocked the door. By God, someone was trapped inside and burning to death.

Rowan cursed, then leaped off the horse. An enemy came at him; Rowan plunged the lance through the man's chest, where he hung lifted off the ground. The lifeless body was suspended for a moment before Rowan withdrew the lance with a cry, sending the corpse crashing to the earth. He ran to the house without sparing another thought, those bloodcurdling screams calling out to him.

The wooden door creaked as he attempted to shove it open.

Nothing. Barred shut.

Rowan cursed, then stepped back and ran into it at full force. The splintering wood yielded to his strength with a deafening *crunch*.

He looped his forearm around his head and covered his mouth as he entered another sweltering ring of hell. He coughed into the mail armor, tracking after the panicked screams, blood and sweat running under his helm and visor.

"Help! Help us, please!" A part of the roof had fallen in. Straw and timber blazed in the middle of the house. The fire caused the air to blur and wave. Through the flames, Rowan saw two figures crouched against the farthest wall.

The structure creaked and moaned. He had only seconds until the whole thing would collapse. Rowan inhaled a sharp breath, then shot through the wall of flames. The heat was unbearable. Surely, the fire would cook him alive in his armor.

A half-conscious woman sat on the floor. Beside her, a small girl lay still with her head resting in her lap. The woman muttered incoherent prayers and pleas. There was no time to think. Rowan grabbed the child from the floor and cradled her against his chest.

Rowan lifted his visor and yelled over the roar of the flames. "Up, now! Or we all shall die!" He helped the sobbing woman from the ground. She rocked on her heels, ash covering her fair face. "We must get out!"

"God, no, please!"

"It's the only way out," he yelled again over the creaking house and roaring flames. It was about to implode. They had mere seconds to escape. "I shall go first. Follow right behind me."

"No, I can't! I can't!"

"You must! If you stay here, you'll leave your daughter alone in this world. You saw what happened tonight. Is that what you want? Now, are you ready?"

She nodded.

Rowan held the little girl close and plunged through the flames. Just as he and the woman burst out the door and fell onto the ground, the home collapsed.

The woman crawled across the dirt, her legs dragging behind her, her entire body wracked with sobs. Blood seeped from her forehead and trickled down the center of her face.

Rowan carefully laid the child down, panting hard, his heartbeat drumming in his ears. "Come on! Come on! Live. Live, damn you, live!"

An eternity seemed to pass before the small girl coughed, and her eyes blinked open. Rowan lay flat on the ground and stared at the ink-black sky, finally able to breathe.

---

BLANCHETTE STARED at the ledgers until the words blurred together. It was no good. She couldn't focus. Could barely breathe. She gave a nervous sigh, her insides a tangled mess, then re-read the sentence.

Then again.

It appeared their harvest would last through winter should there not be any unseen crisis.

*Like another attack,* she absently thought with a rush of sadness and anger. Rowan had left during the night, Smoke, Edrick, and a column of men in his wake.

She closed her eyes and remembered how he'd looked in the firelight and how his arms had felt wrapped around her body. How he'd smelled when she held him close.

Blanchette threw down her quill, unable to focus. She turned her gaze to her window, where a golden sun entered the sky. It was daybreak. Vibrant shades of red and orange streaked the horizon. She thought of Rowan, possibly injured or lying dead and forgotten among the burned ruins of a port town.

"You must relax, dear." She gave a yelp at the sound of Governess Agnes's voice. She was sitting by her hearth, knitting some tunic, her sharp features made sharper by the tension in her face. Blanchette had forgotten she was in the room.

"Mercy, you nearly stopped my heart."

"You are so tense, Blanchette. Please try to relax."

Blanchette turned to her and sighed. "I... I just fear for the villagers."

*And Rowan, most of all.*

*Come back to me,* she prayed.

---

ROWAN RETURNED on a horse Blanchette did not recognize. She barely recognized *Rowan.*

Dirt and blood covered his armor and wolf helm; he held the rein's in one hand, his standard in the other. Blanchette stood at the castle entrance, her red riding cloak fluttering behind her. She watched in a daze as the frayed banner whipped across the dawn sky, causing the black wolf to stretch and prowl. A column of soldiers followed Rowan under the raised portcullis.

They, too, looked worse for wear. Governess Agnes stood beside her, her features drawn into tight lines. She crossed herself and shook her downcast head. "Good God. Shall the blood never stop flowing?"

Blanchette locked eyes with her governess before turning back to Rowan.

Nay... it was not Rowan who'd returned, but the Black Wolf of Norland. The sunlight glinted off the crude, blood-speckled helm. He raised the visor and commanded the strange mount to a stop. Several stable hands cut across the inner bailey to tend to Rowan and his men.

Hardly thinking or breathing, she raced out to the bailey to meet him.

He removed his helm and handed it off to his squire Jonas. In that single movement, he became Rowan again—*her Rowan.*

His eyes found hers and held. Her breaths came quick and thin, and she realized how terrified she'd been of his absence.

She swung her arms around his neck and held him close. The gesture took him off guard. He hesitated and stiffened against her, then pressed his hand to her back after several weightless moments. Blanchette cleared her throat and stumbled out of his arms. She felt eyes burning into her. Edrick had a look of loathing stretched across his dirt-and-ash dappled face. She returned his stare, remembering what he'd done to poor Elise.

"You may go," Rowan said to him. "We shall speak later."

Blanchette waited until Edrick was out of earshot. "Good God. Rowan, what happened? What happened to the village? I was worried out of my mind."

"Were you?" Rowan gifted her with a small smile that brought a glow to his eyes. Then he sighed, looking utterly exhausted as if the weight of the kingdom lay on his shoulders. "Walk with me, Blanchette." He offered his arm, and Blanchette graciously took it. She paused before Governess Agnes and placed her hand on her shoulder.

Moments later, Rowan and Blanchette strolled past the guards of the castle. Spring had brought life and color to the world again. Months ago, the bushes and trellises had been naked and colorless. Now, roses and violets bloomed beautifully and bright.

Rowan seemed not to see anything before him—as if he was watching something unfold inside his mind. Finally, he gazed down at Blanchette, his eyes warm yet wary. "The port village was burned to the ground. They slaughtered the people like sheep. I'd hoped I'd get there in time... but it was too late." He hesitated, then ran an unsteady hand through his dark hair. Ash and smoke covered his cheeks, and his eyes appeared haunted. "The attackers were flying my banner. The Black Wolf."

"What? I don't understand?"

"Someone is against me. Someone is trying to turn Norland away from me, to drench my name in the people's blood. Someone is slandering me and killing innocents under my banner."

Blanchette shook her head as a creeping terror rose in her chest. "Did you see any other banners? Or sigils? Any... recognizable ornamentation?"

Rowan sighed, then absently glanced into the horizon. "No... but there was hardly time."

He stepped closer to her—a dark and regal shadow—and bowed his head. As his hands touched her waist, she closed the distance between them and rested her cheek on his chest. She heard the beat of his heart, as wild as the wolf on his sigil. Her own heartbeat leaped in response, and she allowed herself to sink into his comforting hold.

"Is Mary safe?" he asked.

"Yes, yes, she's fine," she replied. "She's with Sir Jeremy."

He nodded and released a drawn-out sigh. One large hand slipped up her spine and came to rest at the apex of her neck. His fingers wound in her curls, and the heat of his breaths fanned her forehead.

*What would they do now?* she wondered. *Shall the wolves never rest?*

*What shall we do?*

And then the answer came to her, an echo from not so long ago.

*Survive. We shall survive.*

---

THAT AFTERNOON dawned clear and bright. The heavy oak-and-iron door creaked in defiance as Blanchette raised the crossbar and pushed it open. The shutters were drawn inside the solar, allowing only the faintest light streams to trickle inside. Blanchette glanced behind her and into the empty corridor before slipping into her father's quarters.

*Rowan's quarters now,* her mind amended.

She hesitated, her back flat against the massive door, her thoughts exploding in a million different directions.

She smoothed her palms over her skirts, then eased inside to the center of the solar. Various documents covered the long table: half-written letters, maps, and sealed scrolls. Blanchette ran her hand over the wood surface as her gaze danced across the organized mess of ledgers and letters. Within her mind's eye, the room transformed, and she saw her father sitting before the table, a goblet of wine in hand. His thinning, golden hair gleamed in his candle's light, and his eyes resembled two empty vats. She looked closer—and for the first time, she *really* saw him. Beneath that void, something lurked... something cold and cruel. She stepped back and blinked until her father's ghostly image faded into memory, and only the empty high-back chair sat before her.

*I can see him now for what he was.*
*But who am I?*

Blanchette toyed with her signet ring. Then she crossed the

remainder of the solar and threw open the shutters. The window overlooked the training yard. She could see the watchtower and the formidable gatehouse and curtain wall.

The door creaking open nearly caused Blanchette to leap out of her skin. The smooth rumble of Rowan's voice followed.

"Blanchette. I'm glad you're here."

She turned to face him and leaned against the window seat. He was undoing the ties on his arm. She inhaled shakily, then crossed the solar to stand before him.

"Yes, well... I said I wasn't leaving you, didn't I?" she asked with a smile.

He paused his handiwork and stared down at her. His eyes looked exhausted, and a palpable sorrow was there.

She heard his sharp intake of air. Then he returned to the ties and wrestled with them. Blanchette shook her head and placed her small hands on his. They stilled at her touch, and for a moment, Blanchette allowed herself to savor the feel of his skin against hers. His fingers and knuckles were covered in ash. Tenderly, she brushed it away.

"Here, allow me," she whispered, her fingers finding the ties on his gauntlets. "You must be so weary."

He exhaled a sigh of agreement, then let his hand slip away from hers. She met his gaze and tentatively stepped closer so they were almost touching. The heat of his body radiated. Her head spinning, she cleared her throat and got to work on his armor.

How indecent it felt. She felt the color rising to her cheeks while her typically nimble fingers tripped over themselves. "Tell me more about the attack."

The sorrow returned to his eyes, and Blanchette fought to ignore the intense reaction she felt toward his pain. "It was madness, but I did what I could. I saved a mother and her daughter... so I suppose that's a small mercy. Even so, I should have stopped it before it started."

"You're the Black Wolf," she murmured, shaking her head,

"not a wizard. You can't always know such things. But I understand how this must pain you. How it must feel like a failure."

He nodded, then gave her a weary smile.

Two servants brought pots of hot water from the kitchens. They filled the wooden tub and scented the water with fresh-picked petals from the garden. Blanchette watched Rowan watch *her*; her heart raced as he pulled the shirt over his head. His chest was broad and well-muscled. It tapered off into a narrow waist and legs that seemed to go on forever. A light smattering of hair covered the contours and planes of his chest. As he bundled up the shirt, the peak of his biceps tightened and bulged. He was beautiful. Mesmerizing. She shouldn't have stared so ardently, but she couldn't tear her gaze away. She admired his quiet, confident power; the sleek lines of his body and how he moved with a grace and stillness that contrasted against his massive height and size.

She knew he was large and strong... but she didn't expect this. He stared at her from across the solar. Then he tossed the shirt aside, next to his armor, and brought his fingers to the laces on his pants. Blanchette cleared her throat as his fingers began to work, nimble and strong. She moved over to the window and stared dumbly at the shutters. From beyond the window came the rumble of voices, the thud of hooves, and the tread of boots on wooden stairs and walkways.

"You may also assist with these ties, *ma princesse*."

"You can manage fine without my help, I am sure," she said dryly. The rustling of clothes came next, puncturing the silence. She waited for the telling splash of water to subside as Rowan settled into the wooden tub.

A long breath escaped from her lips.

"I-I should go," she stammered.

She crossed the room, nearly falling over her own feet. His hand shot toward her and latched onto her wrist. She felt her breath hitch, and his fingers' warm, wet heat snaked around her skin. Her heart hammered loudly within the silent chamber, and she was sure Rowan could hear the godforsaken drumming. She glanced down at him. His eyes locked onto hers, pleading, reaching out to her. She inhaled a sharp breath at the longing she found there. "Please," he said, his voice a whisper. "Please, don't go."

Blanchette knew she couldn't leave him alone. She'd be leaving him at the mercy of something terrible. Something that perhaps only she could soothe.

"Yes, you're right. I... I shall stay." She moved behind him, and his fingers slowly eased from her wrist. She circled the tub, watching him watch her again. He'd kept his smallclothes on for decency's sake.

She wasn't sure if she was relieved or disappointed.

He hooked his arms over the wooden sides, and the candlelight bathed his muscles in an enticing glow. Her fingers ached to touch that smooth tan skin. He tensed slightly, and she saw the definition in his arms, the way muscle and sinew contracted and tightened. Beads of water rolled off the curve of his biceps.

How would it feel to have those muscles against her? To feel the hard planes of his body across her soft curves as his breaths whistled in her ear? To hear him speak French while sensually thrusting in and out of her body?

Blanchette fought back her blush too late. He tossed his head back and let loose a dark laugh. "Why, you're blushing like a maiden, *ma princesse*."

"I *am* a maiden," she murmured, shuffling around the tub until she stood directly behind him.

Fresh cuts and burn marks covered his back. Tentatively, shyly, she reached out and tracked her fingers over his left shoulder. The muscle grew taut beneath her delicate touch, then she felt the tension ebb away.

She brought her index finger to its point... slowly, ever so slowly, she tracked it over the firm ridge of his shoulder... across his upper back, at the apex of his neck. She heard his sharp intake of air as her finger lazily slid across his moist skin and traced the scar on his forearm. It'd healed well.

She felt his shoulders flex beneath her fingers. Blanchette swallowed deeply, hardly thinking, her body moving on its own accord. She knelt behind the tub and ran the band of her thumb across the nape of his neck and to his other shoulder, where another scar awaited.

"How did you get this one?" she asked, her voice a tender whisper. It followed the line of his shoulder and led almost to the base of his neck.

Rowan glanced over his shoulder. He met her eyes with his, and the emotion she found there shook her to her very core. "The night my Beatrice died. The night she was murdered..." He glanced away, seeming to watch something unfold inside his mind. "As I said, I found Mary inside the wardrobe. Wrapped her in a bedsheet and fought our way out of the castle. I took her on Sunbeam and nearly rode that horse until he fell into the dirt. I stayed at Edrick's castle with her for the better part of the year."

She ran her fingertip across his nape... the strong ridge of his shoulder... the peak of his biceps as either arm grasped the sides of the tub...

"You didn't return on him," she said. Her voice sounded airy, inflated with a note of desire. "Today, I mean. On Sunbeam. I... I didn't recognize the horse."

Rowan paused and seemed to weigh his words. Blanchette stepped out from behind him, one hand still on the curve of his bicep, to better gauge his state. His eyes gave little away.

"An arrow took him. Few things are worse than the sound of a horse in pain." Rowan shook his head. "Nay, he was more than a horse. He was my friend. One of my last friends, I suppose."

She recalled the first time she met Sunbeam and how he'd tried to nip her fingers off. She'd never seen more insolence or loyalty in a horse before.

Blanchette sighed and knelt beside the tub so their faces were the same height. She reached down and stirred the water with her fingertip. "I thought I am your friend now?"

His lip quirked at that. "I suppose you are, *ma chérie*. And there's Smoke, of course."

"Yes... I want to know more about you, Rowan," she said, placing her palm on his chest. Her hand was wet from the bathwater, and she felt the wild beat of his heart under her palm. "Tell me about *you*. About your life before you became a soldier. Tell me more about Mary."

"I've been a soldier for so long, it's hard to remember who I was before that. My father flew a gray wolf and commanded a small army."

"Yes... I've heard the stories," she said. "My father had quite admired him."

"They had a lot in common," Rowan murmured.

*They were both cruel, he meant to say.*

Blanchette bit her tongue.

She removed her hand from his heart and picked up a cloth beside the tub. "Go on," she pressed, dipping it in the water. Rowan watched as she swirled it around, distorting the water. Carefully, gently, she ran the cloth over the burns and cuts. He flinched slightly, but whether from pain or something else, she couldn't say.

She dipped the cloth in the water again, her movements slow and deliberate. The flickering candlelight cast shadows that danced across Rowan's sculpted chest.

She felt wicked... daring... and her most intimate part was aching and wet. Fighting off her blush, she lifted the cloth to Rowan's muscular shoulders. She watched in awe as his skin glistened from the bathwater. Then she looped her hand in front of his body, sliding the cloth over his abdomen. His stomach was as hard as a rock. She could see the outline of each muscle. She felt him suck in a breath as the cloth moved across that taut, glistening flesh.

As he spoke and his voice swelled the chamber, the area between her thighs grew hotter, more sensitive... tingled every time she shifted her weight. A pleasant sensation zapped through her, starting in her tummy and pouring down into that sensitive area between her legs.

"My father never allowed me to be a child. He put a sword in my hand shortly after I could walk. I always lived as a soldier —a mindless, sword-wielding... *beast*... who killed at a command and without rational thought. Never more so than the day I became a knight." He hesitated, causing her hand to still in midair.

"Tell me, Rowan."

"Keep doing that..." He sighed, signaling to her hand. "And I shall keep talking."

She resumed, her eyes riveted on him. She stared at his lips, their shape and movement.

*What would I do if he kissed me? If he wrapped his arms around me and dragged me into the tub's warm water? If he stripped away my dress and smallclothes and filled his hands with my breasts?*

Rowan groaned as she returned the cloth to his back and ran it over his shoulders. The confession seemed to pour out of him with little effort. "It was a small village. Two scores, but they had become a problem. Leaders had risen among them. Priests. They made their own weapons, forged in blood and tears. 'A plague, they are,' the king had told me. 'A disease in my kingdom, who've turned away from God and the law. We must cut it out, lest it spread and damn us all.'"

Blanchette paused and listened to the sounds of the castle. The *clanging* of swords and laughter wafted from the window.

*War, war, war... always at war...*

"I led the attack. But first, I came to the priests and offered gold and provisions for their surrender. They were starving, not killers. Not even fighters, truth be told. They handed over their weapons and swore they'd never lay a hand against the crown. When I returned with the news of a peaceful surrender, your father told me, 'I said to lead the attack, Rowan. Do as I command or suffer for it.' My men slaughtered them like sheep. I hanged the priests and whoever survived when we found them hiding."

Blanchette lowered the cloth, her hand frozen in midair. Rowan stared forward with an empty look in his eyes. "I still see them swinging, Blanchette. Every night. Your father knighted me for that. I served him for a year more, haunted and half alive. Shortly after Mary was born, he asked me to do it again. I gazed down at my daughter, then stared at myself in the looking glass... ashamed. I'd become worse than my father. I didn't want Mary to grow up in a world like that—a dark, cruel place full of shadows and monsters. I didn't want her to grow up near *me*. I went deep into the forest, searching for what? Answers? I can't even say. I think a part of me was looking for death. But it didn't find me. Instead, Smoke found me, and I turned my father's gray wolf banner into the black wolf. And, as they say, the rest is history." He leaned the back of his head against the tub. "I was visiting merchants by the port when it happened. As soon as I rode up to my castle's gates that night, I knew something was terribly, terribly wrong. He had my wife defiled and murdered in our bed. And poor Mary... well, he left her alive to keep me loyal. I secluded myself after that. Talked to hardly anyone but Edrick and Kath—" His voice faded in silence.

"And who?"

"Never mind," he murmured. "It doesn't matter anymore."

The silence grew again. Blanchette's heart pounded in her ears as a wind gusted through the castle. He'd committed atrocities... he was a dangerous man. She'd known this from the start, yet she found herself irresistibly drawn to him—like a moth to a flame.

"You were right to damn me, Blanchette," he whispered. "And you were right to fear me. I've done terrible and unforgivable things. I've tried... God, I've tried to reinvent myself. Whoever I was when I bore my father's gray wolf banner, when I followed the king's orders blindly—he's gone now. He's ash and bone. But when I think of all the horrors... all the death and blood and grief that came at my hand... none so haunts me more than the pain I brought to you." Suddenly, he took her hands in his own and gripped them with raw desperation. His palms and fingers were wet, and as he lightly pulled her forward, she felt the warmth from the bath water curling her hair. "You are good. You are the best of us. You are the change I was searching for in the woods that night. I believe that, Blanchette, more than I've ever believed in anything. The people of Norland need you... and so do I."

*Oh, God... what's happening to me?*

She excused herself and quit the solar before she could answer that.

---

THE FOLLOWING DAY, they came to a clearing at the edge of the woods, where the trees scraped the sky and came to a dead stop. Beyond them lay a dense wilderness and winding rivers. Blanchette slid off the horse, her boots touching the dirt road in a hushed whisper. She wound her arms about her body and gazed into the dark woods, past the gnarled and ancient trees she'd often pretended guarded her castle. An image of her mother's limp body tore into her thoughts.

Those trees were supposed to stand guard. Instead, they'd opened like the gates of hell, letting loose the Black Wolf's army of followers and rebels of the crown. *The people's army* she'd so often heard whispered in the halls of the castle and from the lips of wounded soldiers.

Her eyes opened, and he was beside her. Tall and dark, standing at that edge where the woods ended and her world began —and where her world had also ended last winter.

Rowan stared into the woods, too, gazing up at the trees with a numbing intensity.

*What does he see?* she wondered.

She was coming to know his ghosts well.

He shook his head as if dismissing a thought, then turned his gaze to her. His eyes softened, and the slightest smile lifted the corner of his lip.

"You look like you've seen a ghost," Rowan said huskily. She heard herself scoff, though deep inside, she was very scared. Terrified even.

"I could say the same about you, Rowan." She took a long breath and stepped back to better see those colossal and ancient trees. "I remember looking down at these trees from my window as a girl, believing with all my heart that they were silent watchers. My protectors. My own guard, protecting me and my family from whatever lay beyond them. Whatever horrors lay beyond my window were inconsequential. As long as the trees stood, we would as well." She smiled and felt the scar pull tight on her cheek.

Then she closed the distance between them and laid a hand on Rowan's shoulder. He adjusted his posture so his body aligned with her own. They stood side by side at the edge of the forest. Winslowe Castle towered behind them with the trees ahead of them.

"How... how is your forearm? The scar looked quite good," she added with a blush.

He grunted, then his face broke into a wolfish smile. The hard lines of his face softened when he smiled, though the darkness never faded from his brow. It was a shadow that followed him everywhere, just like the ghosts and shadows who followed her.

"Luckily for my enemies, I shall never block quite as fast or well again."

"Then you shall have to hit them harder."

"Aye," he agreed. "Though it's not as easy as you make it sound."

"No? Not even for Norland's Big Bad Black Wolf?"

"Especially not for him, Blanchette. After all, hunters enjoy a few things more than a wolf pelt at the foot of their beds."

It was her turn to smile, but it was sad... just as his words had been. She couldn't understand why, but they'd brought intense sorrow and hopelessness back into her heart. One she'd been trying so hard to banish yet always returned uninvited at the slightest provocation.

"Well, come, Black Wolf. It's my turn to show you something."

---

Rowan brought Shadow to a halt outside the yawning mouth of a cave. It was the auburn mare he'd tamed weeks ago in Harwin's stable. He'd broken horses more times than he could count, yet couldn't recall a more responsive creature. Wildness had bent down to loyalty within the last fortnight, and the mare seemed to regard him as an old friend.

Rowan thought of Sunbeam and how he'd never had to train him for battle. *Like he'd been born to it.*

Blanchette slid off Shadow's back. She'd led them to a waterfall nestled in the lush wood's heart. It cascaded over the mouth of the cave. Water flowed down from a rocky ledge, shining in the sunlight that peeked through the leaves. It fell in a curtain of liquid silver, and as it descended, it created an ethereal mist that clung to the air.

The sounds were a symphony of nature's harmony. The waterfall's gentle roar echoed through the woods, a melody that resonated with the very heartbeat of the earth.

Rowan tied the horse's lead to a branch and followed Blanchette.

They waded across the pond toward the waterfall. Its roar was so loud it drowned out the world around them. Rowan climbed out of the water and onto the rocks. He turned, dropped to a knee, and offered his hand to Blanchette. She took it, and as he pulled her up and into his arms, his blood rushed into his eardrums. They were both dripping wet—Rowan in his shirtsleeves and trousers, Blanchette in a simple linen dress and her red riding cloak. They stared into each other's eyes for what seemed a lifetime, the waterfall roaring behind them and echoing the beat of their hearts.

His gaze traveled down her wet, slender body, taking in the way the fabric of her cloak gripped her curves. Blond curls were plastered against her face and shapely breasts. Rowan felt an ache stir in his groin. How long had it been since he'd lain with a woman?

Blanchette smiled at him coyly, as if she could read his thoughts, a hint of mischief on her lips. Then she turned away and ventured onward.

Sunshine turned into a shadow as they entered the cave's mouth. Blanchette was just fine, but Rowan had to duck at the opening.

He heard the thunderous rush of the waterfall above his head. It sounded like they'd entered the belly of some ancient creature. Rowan moved farther inside the cave, where the light bowed to the darkness.

"How long have you known about this place?" he asked Blanchette. His voice echoed against the rocks, making it sound like there were seven of him.

Sunlight from the cave's opening cast Blanchette as an elegant silhouette. "Willem, Isadora, and I found it together. I was nine. I haven't been back here for years. Not since Isadora left for Demrov."

They trekked farther inside the cave, watching as the daylight grew fainter and the walls opened around them. Soon, they were in the middle of a vast and shadowy cavern.

"Why did you bring me here?" His voice echoed into the sonorous gloom, making him realize the cave was much larger than he'd first thought.

"Well, this is your home now too. I wanted to share its secrets with you. Share what makes Norland so beautiful and special to me."

Rowan placed his hand on her shoulder and absently fingered the damp material. It clung to her like a second skin. One he desperately burned to shed for her. "*You* are what makes Norland so special."

And she was. Firm yet delicate, wise beyond her years but still sheltered and unworldly. An enigma. A puzzle. He wanted nothing more than to take her apart gently, then put her back together again.

He'd piece her together, fitting himself within her so she'd be a part of him forever.

His eyes slipped over Blanchette, taking in the rapid rise and fall of her wet bosom and the way the fabric held tight to her pale skin.

"We used to run down here... Governess Agnes would chase us through the castle gates in a fury. We'd hide inside here," she said with a smile, gesturing to the dark space. "We'd hear Governess Agnes calling for us from behind the waterfall, as mad as an ox... 'Oh, you terrible, terrible children! Not fit to sit in a privy, let alone a royal seat. I shall whip all three of you for this.' Of course, she never laid a finger on us, let alone a switch. She loved us dearly, and we her. I think we were the children she never had. Her husband had died years before we were born, and Mother saved her from a life of destitute."

"I always admired Joanna. She was everything a queen should be."

"Yes. Yes, she was."

Blanchette tucked her hand into the cloak and withdrew a flint and torch. Then she walked to the wall, which was smothered by shadow. The aroma of earth and dampness filled the air, a subtle musk that tickled Rowan's nose.

He watched as her fingertips brushed the uneven surface of the cave wall. They danced lightly, like a lover's tender caress, until they found the perfect niche. There, she poised the flint against the stone. The friction was a tactile ballet, a rasp that sent sparks of excitement coursing through his veins.

But it was the moment of transformation that truly ignited his senses. The faintest glow began to take shape, an ember of warmth against the cold dark. The soft pop and crackle of the spark finding life was music to the ears. Rowan fixed his eyes on the nascent flame, captivated by the play of light and shadow it cast on the walls.

As the torch's fiery tongue licked the air, its warmth washed over him like an embrace, and the scent of burning pine mingled with the earthy aroma. The cave came alive with a newfound energy, a vibrant pulse that matched the rhythm of his racing heart.

Blanchette turned to him, her eyes now gleaming in the torchlight. At that moment, she was the keeper of light in this realm of shadows, a guardian of secrets in the heart of Norland's earth.

She returned to him, the torch in her hand, its wavering light throwing shadows along the cave. They stretched and crawled up and down the walls. *Beasts prowling in the night*. Her eyes shimmered in the fiery glow of the torch. A beautiful winter, kissed by the fire.

"My mother and sister... Willem... they were good," she finally said. Her voice was nearly inaudible beneath the torch's crackling hiss. "They would have died for their kingdom, and I suppose they did in the end."

Rowan shook his head. He took the torch from her and set it carefully on the cave's stone floor, where it flickered and licked at the walls. "And you, Blanchette... you are good. So very good. God, sometimes I look at you..." The words stuck to the roof of his mouth. He swallowed and exhaled a long, shaky breath, then pressed on. "Sometimes I look at you, and I can hardly believe you're real," he confessed. "Generations pass without a person like you coming into the world."

She smiled, then gazed down at the torch. The only sounds were the thundering waterfall, the hiss of the flame, and Rowan's uneven breaths.

He was making mistakes. Here, in this cave, and back at the castle. It wasn't like him. Rowan knew he was distracted... but that was okay. He'd been raised on war and bloodshed. For the first time in his life, he was no longer a soldier. He was simply a man, who craved a life free from bloodshed.

*A life with Blanchette Winslowe.*

"They weren't supposed to die." He held his breath again. Filled his lungs with the musky air, yearning for courage.

He felt her eyes on his skin like an actual touch. "Would you have spared them? Had they not escaped and drowned... had my brother not been mutilated by those monsters... would you have allowed my family to live?"

Something told him that everything balanced on his next words. Their weight could either crush them both or be a stepping stone to something better.

She wrapped his chin with her fingers when he looked away. "Please, Rowan... I must know."

His fingers enveloped her wrist, encircling it completely. "Yes, I would have spared them," he whispered and stepped closer. They were inches apart—a kiss away. "I would have had them exiled. I wouldn't have harmed your mother and Willem."

"And my father?"

Rowan sighed, then knelt on the stone ground. He picked up the torch, feeling the heat wash over his face.

---

SUDDENLY, it seemed very stupid to be alone with Rowan in this cave, in near darkness, where the waterfall would drown out any scream she might make.

He was impossibly tall. Dressed in only a simple tunic wet from the waterfall, he towered above her. She thought of his Black Wolf armor—the snarling helm, crude plate, and shining pommel. Then another image floated into her mind: Rowan Dietrich and his daughter by the fire, the soft lull of his voice filling the hall, Smoke slumbering beside them. She'd seen another side of Rowan—one she'd only glimpsed at in transient moments.

This was a man she could grow to love.

"My story is not a fairy tale," Rowan finally said, walking away from Blanchette and around the cave, holding up the torch so it chased away the shadows. "I'd loved your father once like a brother. I followed him into countless battles. My sword helped him keep his crown, and his faith in me kept my loyalty. But every summer cools and becomes winter. Everything has its season. Everything changes, for better or for worse."

Blanchette swallowed hard. The blood rushed in her ears, and she heard the erratic beat of her heart. It thundered as he spoke, a grim ambience to his words and the cave's hovering darkness.

Rowan gave a sad smile, the shadows accenting the hollow between his eyes. "A wise man once said, 'You go no place by accident.'"

"Which wise man was that?"

"Your father."

It didn't sound like something he'd have said. Not that man she'd known. And not the man he'd become.

"Does that surprise you?"

"It does," she admitted. He was holding the torch next to their faces; she felt the heat on her cheeks, and when he spoke, the wafts from his breath made the flame twitch. "The man I knew as my father was... cynical. I think he hated Norland. At times, I thought he hated me."

Blanchette moved past him, her heart beating like a rabbit's, and signaled him to follow her. They moved toward the very back of the cave, which, as she already knew, would have no wall. It narrowed into a space they had to navigate single file.

She felt the walls pressing close, felt the heat of the torch as it waved and flickered against the stone. The steady rush of the waterfall surrounded them. The wall curved and turned, and the shadows played a trick on her for a split second. She saw her sister, Isadora, slipping through the secret cavern just before her, her hair tumbling down to the small of her waist. She heard her laughter too—a rich, lively sound that brought light to the shadowed darkness.

Isadora had taken after their mother with an exotic beauty that was all her own. Demrovian descent, Blanchette thought. It was only fitting she'd sit on the throne there. She could imagine Isadora now getting into all kinds of trouble.

Blanchette frowned. She hardly knew her sister anymore. She was a stranger—a foreigner, the ruler of a country she'd never visited.

She remembered the letter she'd sent to Isadora. *I shall have to send another right away.* But what would she write now?

*What is the truth?*

Her nerves and the torch's heat brought sweat to the back of her neck. "Sorry, my thoughts got away with me," she murmured, then continued forward and through the winding walls. Soon, they opened up, and Blanchette finally took a breath.

They'd entered the very back of the cave—an ample space, as old as time itself, with walls that loomed forty feet high. A spring sat in the cavern's heart. The water looked like sleek glass.

"There," Blanchette said, pointing at a sconce on the cave's wall.

Rowan crossed the cave and hung the torch.

Blanchette stepped in front of the spring. Rowan followed her, then deftly worked the ties of her red riding cloak. Their eyes remained locked as he undid the ribbons, one after another. He peeled the fabric aside and let it pool at their feet. A blush seared her cheeks. Her damp, tousled curls clung to her back and the tops of her full breasts. Her hard nipples pushed at the fabric of her dress.

Coyly, she knotted her arms over her chest, but Rowan gently took her wrists and uncrossed them. "Let me see, Princess. You are so beautiful."

His fingers, which were usually so agile and capable, appeared clumsy as he unlaced the wet material of his shirt. Blanchette felt his hot, unwavering gaze on her as he worked the ties, then pulled the material apart. His muscular chest glistened in the torchlight. Blanchette exhaled a long breath and clenched her fingers to stop from touching him. The fire's light danced in his raven-black hair, bringing out bluish tones buried deep within.

His hands pulled away, and the white shirt fell to the floor in a puddle of fine silk.

"Time is a bit of a double-edged sword. Isn't it?" She hadn't meant to speak aloud, so her voice startled her. Rowan merely brought his fingers to the laces of his trousers, then shrugged off that material. A sly grin—*a wolfish smile*—spread across his full lips. He wore it well, and she felt her skin tighten in a way that wasn't unwelcome.

But his smile turned sad as he said, "Yes. I wish it weren't true. I wish time only healed wounds, but sometimes it festers them."

Blanchette's heart pounded like a war drum. And indeed, it felt like she was caught in an inward battle. She watched in trepidation as Rowan moved toward the edge of the spring, wearing only his smallclothes. He'd shed his boots as well.

He sank into the spring with a sharp groan. "Cold. Christ. But refreshing. Aren't you going to join me, darling? That's why you brought me here, is it not?"

Her fingers trembled as she pulled the dress's white fabric over her head. Now she stood only in her smallclothes; her breath hitched at the fire in Rowan's eyes. She watched with fascination as his gaze slid down her body, inch by painful inch, then came up again and settled on her eyes. Suddenly, the moment felt incredibly intimate—sharing this hidden secret with him, being with him all alone, nearly naked, the only light a torch that could wink out at any moment.

*Yes*, she admitted to herself, *this is why she brought him here.* Because he fascinated her. And frightened her. But the depths she'd glanced inside of him made her hunger to learn more.

To learn everything.

She stepped close to the spring, her nude feet whispering over the smooth stone floor.

She perched on the edge, a foot away from Rowan. He stretched out his massive arms on either side of his body so his fingers brushed her leg. She didn't move, allowing his touch to linger. It burned where he touched. It was a pleasant, deep burn that lit a fire from his finger to her very core. Between her legs, her womanhood throbbed and grew wet.

*The cold water shall be a welcomed respite.*

Her bottom squirmed against the stone ground as she plunged into the spring. She gasped from the rush of cold, then scowled at Rowan's booming laughter. It echoed, so it sounded like an army of his voice surrounded her.

She felt him watching her curiously. Then he shifted closer, making their bodies almost touch. With that small movement, everything seemed to go silent; even the waterfall hushed, and all she heard was the frantic beat of her heart. She tentatively traced her finger around his forearm, where the arrow had taken him months ago. He tensed, and his mesmerizing hazel eyes burned into her like wildfire.

"Does it still hurt?" she asked, her voice a small whisper that the walls amplified threefold. He visibly sucked in a breath, then let it out slowly. She moved her finger away, assuming she'd caused him pain. But he caught her wrist in midair and slowly brought her finger back to the ridge.

"No, it doesn't hurt anymore. In fact..." His deep voice dropped several octaves, almost like he was telling her a secret. She leaned toward him, drawn to the pull of his voice so as not to miss a wonder or nuance. Their shoulders brushed together, and a tingling sensation took root between her legs. "It feels quite... good. All of this does."

*Being here with you, in this hidden cave... only us and this moment, forgetting the past, the heartache, and especially the future.* That was what she heard. That was what her own inner voice echoed. She found herself nodding to that voice, and Rowan gave his wolfish grin as if he, too, could hear her thoughts and knew what she agreed to.

"Blanchette," he whispered, the grin leaving his mouth. "I am tired. Tired of fighting. I've been fighting all my life, one battle after another. I fought for my father for years. For the king. And then I fought for vengeance. But this... it feels *right*, simply resting here, with you beside me."

Something was building between them—an unspoken energy, a connection she felt in her bones.

*Is this what desire feels like?*

*God... is this what falling in love feels like?*

That thought scared her most of all. So long as that voice stayed silent, she was safe.

But this... it was positively dangerous.

*Aye, I am playing games with a wolf.*

# Eighteen

The hiss of arrows cut through the early morning haze. The sun began its lazy ascent, spilling a luminous glow across the castle. Its proud walls shimmered as they drank in the molten-gold sunrise. Although a chill still hung in the air, Rowan felt sweat bead from his hairline.

He lowered his longsword and stepped back, then gestured for Jonas to go to the center of the training yard. He obliged with a nervous look in his gaze. A man twice his age met him there, a veteran of the Siege of Winslowe Castle, with a dark mop of hair and a row of missing teeth. The teeth he still had were rotten stumps. He grinned at Jonas, flashing that smug and grisly smile.

Jonas made a poor contest, Rowan knew, but wars were a poor and nasty sport. And in this unforgiving world, every lesson in this training yard might mean the difference between life and death.

"Lift your sword, Jonas," Rowan commanded his squire, his voice as steady as a drum. "And remember all I taught you."

Rowan stepped back as the boy and the man crossed their sparring swords. The clash of blunted steel echoed and hung in the morning air. The acrid scent of sweat mingled with the earthiness of the soil. Rowan watched, his senses heightened, as Jonas struggled to parry the relentless strikes of his opponent.

He felt the tension in the very ground beneath him, the rumbling of footsteps and the thudding of blows. The training yard came alive with the rhythm of their sparring, the harsh impact of steel against steel. Rowan's eyes, sharp as a wolf's, took in every nuance of the duel, the sweat-drenched brows, the strained muscles, and the raw determination etched into his squire's young face.

Movement from across the yard caught Rowan's eye. At first, he took the slim hooded figure for Blanchette. "Well done," Rowan said to them. "Rest now. All of you return to the barracks." His eyes parted from Mary's petite form and scanned the sea of faces.

He crossed the yard swiftly, passing the anvil as a blacksmith pounded steel and bright red sparks flamed.

"Mary," he greeted. She lowered her hood, exposing her delicate pale features to the crisp morning air. Her nose shone bright red, and the apples of her cheek glowed. "What are you doing about the castle so early? The sun has barely taken to the sky."

She hesitated, then glanced down at Smoke and ran her gloved hand over his head. "I'm sorry, Father. I couldn't sleep."

Rowan nodded and gave her hesitant expression a once-over. "Don't be sorry. It can be difficult to sleep in a new place. Especially one as big and as formidable as this. Blanchette can bring you something to help you sleep until you become accustomed to Winslowe Castle."

Silently, she stared forward for several moments, and Rowan saw a debate in her eyes. Finally, she shook her head and sniffled, then rubbed the tip of her nose. "I can never really sleep."

Rowan felt something pull tight across his chest. He tentatively reached out to touch her curls, but his hand froze midair. His fingers clenched, closing in on themselves repeatedly.

*So close, yet so far away.*

"Come," he finally said, hesitantly setting his hand on her slim shoulder. "Let's break our fast inside."

※

SOLDIERS FILLED the long wooden trestle tables. Handfuls were in full armor, while others wore little more than beaten trousers and shirtsleeves. Rowan and Mary lounged relatively isolated as a pretty serving girl filled his tankard with ale and Mary's with water. Smoke lay beneath their table, his muzzle resting on his huge paws. The serving girl eyed the wolf warily.

Rowan nodded his thanks, his eyes shifting to the front of the hall. He examined the seats of high honor, and within his mind's eyes, the ghostly images of the king and queen took shape. It was suddenly ten years earlier, and merriment, drunk soldiers, and serving wenches filled the barren hall. King Bartholomew sat rowdy and drunk in his gilded seat beside his queen. The golden crown blended into his curls, the rubies and amethyst sparkling under the torchlights. Beside him sat Rowan's own wife. Beatrice's belly was swollen with child, and her cheeks were flushed— though not from the wine. He watched as she and King Bartholomew stole a glance from across the din.

Then they all vanished, and it was just him, Mary, and a handful of his soldiers again. "I noticed you've made friends with Smoke rather quickly," he said conversationally, drinking deep from his tankard. She nodded, her wide blue eyes scanning the great hall. "Have you always been so fond of animals? And they fond of you?"

*An answer I should already know.*

"I... I think so," she said. "They've always been my friends."

*They kept me company while I've been alone,* was what he heard. *When duty called, and you left me alone.*

Rowan forced a smile, but it didn't fit well. Then he reached across the wooden table and took her small hand in his. She gazed at him and blessed him with a beautiful smile. That feeling pulled tight again across his heart. A few moments later, the serving girl returned with two bowls of porridge seasoned with honey and cinnamon. "You are with me now, Mary. Where you should have been all along. You don't have to feel lonely anymore."

She nodded, her blue eyes sparkling. "All right. I'll... I'll try not to." Rowan returned her smile, and this time, it felt right.

Rowan read her eyes as she took in the great hall. "It's okay to be afraid sometimes."

"Are you ever afraid?"

"Every time I go to battle. But courage cannot exist without fear, Mary."

She nodded, visibly soaking in his words. He grabbed his tankard and drank a mouthful of ale. "I'm not *really* lonely anymore. Blanchette has been my friend," Mary said, her tiny voice nearly inaudible over the soldiers' chatter. They'd grown rowdier the past few minutes as the ale ran free and his men fell deeper in their cups. Mary dug her wooden spoon into her porridge. Steam rose into her face and curled her hair. "And Governess Agnes too."

"Blanchette has taken quite a liking to you," Rowan said over the mounting commotion. Then he reached forward and cuffed her ear. "And what's not to like?"

Mary giggled and slid back into another comfortable smile. Silence passed between them. "Do you think about her a lot?"

Rowan thought she meant Blanchette at first. But the sadness in her eyes told him differently. Rowan scanned the great hall, searching for the right words. He searched inwardly, too, but found nothing there to help. "Aye, I miss her. Not a night goes by that I don't think of her."

Another servant arranged plates of oatcakes, potatoes, and dry bread before them. Mary collected her fork and unenthusiastically picked at her breakfast. "I wish I could remember her."

"You were very young." He held up his hands a foot apart. "And very, very little when it happened."

"Oh." Mary paused. She speared an oatcake and nibbled on its dry corner.

Rowan watched her with interest. "Would you like to know about her? What she was like?"

Mary set down the oatcake, and a transient smile spread across her face. The gesture lit her eyes and brought a warmth to that icy blue.

Rowan folded his hands on the table as he lost himself in thought. In his mind's eye, he summoned Beatrice's features: a river of dark, pin-straight hair, emerald eyes, and full lips. He observed Mary's wistful, porcelain features and blond curls for several moments before the words came to him.

But before he could speak, Mary asked, "You said I was little when it happened. What happened? What happened to Mother?" Her voice held a mix of innocence and longing like she was trying to piece together a puzzle just out of reach.

Rowan scratched at his knuckles, feeling very much like a cornered beast. She was still young, only seven years old... but didn't she have the right to learn what had happened from his lips? To learn about that merciless place where the darkness lived and was coming for them all?

"I'd been gone, campaigning for the king. I'd heard that something was amiss—an attack on our castle. I raced home so quickly that I nearly broke poor Sunbeam's back. But I was too late. The king had betrayed me terribly... and the price was your mother's life. I'm so sorry. Sorry for everything I've stolen from you." He stared forward into the ashes of the great hall's fireplace, his memories and thoughts sinking inward. "Your mother was beautiful and spirited. I shall never forget her." He silently shook his head. His heart twisted and burned, and he forced himself to take a steadying breath. "Do I think of her often, you ask? I think of her every day."

*I think of Beatrice and all I might have done to protect her.*
*I think of how she looked at me with disdain those last few years.*

*I think of how you don't have a mother because of my mistakes and sins.*

Instead, he simply said, "You and your mother are the last things on my mind before I sleep."

*And Blanchette too.*

She smiled a little, then picked at her oatcake for a long silence.

"Would you like me to tell you about her? About your mother?"

Mary bit a corner of her oatcake and nodded enthusiastically.

Rowan drained his tankard, then signaled to a passing servant to fill it again. The girl looked afraid of him—like she was in the presence of some very dangerous beast.

*She thinks I burned that village.*

Rowan took a moment to fall deep into the long-buried memories again. It had been an arranged marriage, and he'd only met Beatrice once before they took their vows. She'd lived in Demrov most of her young life but quickly became one of the king's favorites once she appeared at court. King Bartholomew had arranged their marriage—just one more duty Rowan had performed on behalf of his king.

"She was spirited, beautiful, and more headstrong than she'd ever care to admit." *And she grew to hate me.*

Mary dropped some crumbs beneath the table. Rowan heard Smoke rustle to attention and gobble up the scraps. Mary's laughter filled the room, a bright sound amid the great hall's looming darkness.

Rowan managed an amused smile. "My... what mischief have you taught him?"

Mary whispered something to Smoke, and the wolf's intelligent eyes locked hers. She held her palm up, and to Rowan's awe, Smoke placed a paw gently in her hand. Mary's face lit up with delight as she scratched behind his ears.

Rowan's heart swelled with pride and unexpected love. He

nodded, his eyes shining with tears he had to fight back. He raised his tankard to her in a silent toast.

"I wish Mother was here now. What'd she look like? Like me?"

Rowan drank his ale and studied Mary over his goblet's rim. A long-denied fear came racing back.

Rowan set down the drink and smiled at his daughter.

Then he shook his head.

⁕

EDRICK STROLLED through the burned village. Hell had met earth; day blended with night. Aye, he couldn't tell whether it was night or day since the air was so choked with ash and smoke. One hand covered his mouth and nose; the other wrapped the pommel of his sword, where it always felt most at home.

Everywhere he looked, he found the dead or dying. Rowan's soldiers. Villagers. Men, women, and children. Soldiers dressed in Black Wolf tabards, bearing faces he'd never seen.

It was strange.

He got close to few and trusted even fewer. He made a point of knowing his men's faces as well as he knew his own. Knowledge was power, and he'd be damned if he didn't see into each man and what made him tick. What set fire to his sword? What thoughts kept him awake at night? He made it a point to walk every battlefield after a victory and defeat—to truly understand which tactics had trumped and which had caused his losses.

Rowan had taught him that firsthand... but this walk he made alone.

*He should be here, leading me.*

*Instead, he's amusing himself with that Winslowe whore.*

Somewhere in the distance, the forlorn cry of a wolf echoed the woods.

Edrick knelt beside a fallen soldier he didn't recognize. He'd taken a sword through his gut; dark blood stained the tabard, distorting the sigil of the Black Wolf. He recalled the countless battlefields where he and Rowan had fought side by side, proudly holding this very sigil.

Edrick shook his head and spat into the mud with disgust. The clever and ruthless knight he'd fought for and with all those years had vanished. It was that bitch princess, or queen, or whatever she was... that insipid Blanchette Winslowe. Rowan should have strung her from the castle's beams as soon as he'd conquered it. He wasn't made to sit and rule—and certainly not to fawn over a mere slip of a girl, the seed of his enemy. Rowan Dietrich was made for blood and battle and glory.

Yet he was becoming someone else entirely, Edrick knew. No longer the Black Wolf of Norland... but an impostor.

A mere shadow of himself.

Edrick continued his stroll through this village where only death now lay. A murder of crows already circled the deceased, and the bolder birds had stripped their flesh away.

A pair of fat birds *squawked* and angrily flapped their dark wings as they fought over the small body of a child. Edrick moved toward them and fanned them away with his hands. They gave a last defiant complaint before taking to the sky and moving on to easier prey.

Absently, he crossed his right arm over his body and wrapped his fingers over the pommel of his sword. He stood over the body and examined the bloody, dirt-speckled features. A bird had plucked one of the boy's eyes from its socket; only a vat of blood and gore remained. Mud and soot caked in his black hair, and burns and blisters covered his neck. It was difficult to make out his features beneath the ash and dirt and wounds—but not impossible.

Edrick ran his fingers over the stained tabard and tunic. An old man lay several feet away. A sword stuck out of his gut, his hand half-wrapping the pommel in death. Edrick sighed, then uncurled his bloody fingers. A sigil was engraved in the gold metal.

Edrick let out a sharp bark of laughter, then rubbed his eyes with his fingers. *And there it is.* He recognized the sigil and knew the house it belonged to, just as he knew almost every man who fought in Rowan's ranks and slept in the barracks.

---

Mary and Blanchette lounged beside the great hall's blazing hearth. Smoke lay between them, his massive paws twitching in sleep. Rowan leaned against a marble column as he felt every limb, every muscle, every sinew in his body slowly unwind and relax. He felt nearly a decade of sorrow recede into the shadows.

*This is what I've been missing all these years.*
*This is what I've been searching for...*
The realization nearly brought tears to his eyes.

Blanchette's gold skirts were spread about her and spilling across the floor. An enormous book lay in her lap as she silently read from the faded pages.

He saw the awareness awaken in her. Her reading stopped, and her beautiful, bright eyes left the pages. Thick blond curls slid about her shoulders as she lifted her head and scanned the great hall. She spotted him from his spot beside the column, and her eyes flickered with amusement. Mary lay beside her on her stomach, her chin propped onto the heels of her hands, also reading a book. She jolted into an upright position. Smoke shuffled beside her and bellowed a grumpy noise that sounded like a sigh and growl.

"Father," Mary called out to his surprise.

He stepped out from the shadows and placed his hand on the pommel of his sword. His fingers grazed the polished wolf's head as he crossed the hall swiftly.

He reached down and flipped the book open to read the cover. Blanchette tensed as his fingers brushed against her skirts.

He held his hand there, pressed against the covered flesh of her thighs.

Someone clearing their throat broke the silence. Rowan noticed for the first time since entering that Governess Agnes sat in one of the high-back chairs out of the range of the fire's glow.

Blanchette touched Mary's cheek. "It's quite late. Governess Agnes shall help you turn in for the night. Alright, sweetling?"

Rowan watched with a knot in his chest as Mary tossed her slim arms around Blanchette's neck and squeezed. They stayed that way for several moments in what could only be described as an affectionate embrace. Blanchette came to her feet, sliding out of the hug, and Mary stepped back with visible reluctance.

"Can we read together again tomorrow?" Mary asked. Her sweet voice sounded impossibly small in the vast great hall.

"Yes, my sweet girl. And even more the day after."

Rowan watched as Governess Agnes took his daughter by the shoulder and led her into the shadows. When his gaze returned to Blanchette, the question he'd been ignoring for weeks stared him straight in the face.

*Is Mary truly my child?*

⁂

BLANCHETTE LED Rowan up the steep staircase that lined the great walls of Winslowe Castle. Even at this late hour, the castle was a hive of activity. Clashing metal echoed from the training yard, where soldiers and squires sparred. The sharp, rhythmic *clinks* of swords meeting shields and the occasional triumphant shout added a vibrant urgency to the night.

Rowan's arrival at the castle had breathed a new life into it. During her father's reign, drunk merriment and feasts had often swelled the castle—but never this determination and tangible hope.

She glanced at Rowan, who walked behind her in silence. A black cloak, fastened by those snarling wolf heads, concealed him almost entirely. It whipped in the wind as they ascended the steep stone stairwell that led to the battlements.

He made a cutting image: a fierce, quiet darkness that deepened the shadows and gave the illusion of a ghost walking among the desolate walls of the castle.

Blanchette shivered. If a castle was ever entitled to some ghosts, Winslowe Castle was it.

Finally, they reached the roof and entered the battlements. Rowan and Blanchette drew close to the parapet wall and gazed down at the inner bailey from a crenel. The watchtower thrust into an ink-black sky. Torchlight glimmered from inside its mouth.

Blanchette felt Rowan's presence like a tangible force. Her skin tightened at the sight of him beside her, halfway hidden beneath his cloak, surveying the kingdom before them. *My domain,* her heart confirmed, wanting it with every fiber of her being. She swallowed and fidgeted with her signet ring for several moments. Then she reached up and hesitantly gripped either side of Rowan's hood. She removed it, sliding it off his head so the dark fabric pooled along the expanse of his shoulders. She expected to encounter that stony hardness in his eyes. But she found only gentleness... and a burning fire, which looked a lot like desire.

Rowan came forward until they stood inches apart. His large hands rested upon her shoulders; they were surprisingly light despite their size. She felt her muscles tighten and then relax. Deft fingers slid under her curls and up the length of her neck. Both thumbs came together at the base of her chin, where he traced gentle, invisible circles along her skin. Her eyes grew heavy and closed. Her head lolled forward as she lost herself to the magic of his caresses. How soothing they felt, his warm skin brushing against her own, the callused flesh of his thumbs sending fissions down her spine.

She released a long sigh... his hands slid up, up, up. His fingers traced the raised ridge of her scar from where it started next to her ear all the way to the corner of her lip. Then his thumb traced her mouth, first the bottom lip and then the top. Her mouth parted at the intimate touch. She heard Rowan's sharp intake of breath. Her tongue darted out and ran across his thumb pad. She could taste the wine on his skin.

"Rowan..." She whispered his name like a talisman. He came closer, if even possible, and her breath caught as his head dipped forward and his lips came to her forehead. His hands still cradled her chin. A choked sound emerged from her. A tear slid down her cheek, and Rowan brushed it away with his fingertip. His touch felt achingly sweet. *He* was achingly sweet. Her head spun, her mind a mad clash of thoughts. She leaned into the heat of his body, savoring the security he offered her. As he embraced her, the chaotic din of her thoughts hushed, and she savored a peaceful silence unlike she'd ever known.

The war, the siege, the tragedy she'd endured... they all faded into merciful silence.

When he spoke, his voice sounded tentative—not at all the characteristic and commanding tone he carried onto the battlefield and in the training yard. Yet his quiet confidence demanded her focus.

"Since I can remember, I've never believed in anything," Rowan whispered. She felt the brush of his breaths on her face. "I followed orders, and later I gave them... but faith? That was foreign to me. Something that had created a great divide between Beatrice and me. She told me to believe in God—to put my faith in Him. I would say the words, but they were always hollow. Spoken more for my wife's peace of mind than my own. For a while, I believed in vengeance. That's undeniable. I'd lay down to sleep, and my prayers wouldn't be of God but of the suffering I'd one day bring to your father. That was my faith for almost ten years. Even so, it was an empty belief. Unfulfilling. Cold. And I saw ghosts everywhere I walked. Everywhere I looked. A ghost can be almost anything, Blanchette. Anger. A memory. Pain. Grief, a daydream, a nightmare. Wherever I walked, I never walked alone. The ghosts stood beside me, whispering on the back of my neck."

He'd taken the words from her own heart. Never had she felt so connected to Rowan—or any other person.

Another tear slipped down her cheek. Hastily, she knuckled it away as his hands withdrew from his face. "You got your vengeance," she said. "Do you have faith now? Do you believe in anything?"

---

"I believe in you."

His words hung in the crisp darkness. He watched her take them in, her gaze weighed down with bittersweet emotion. Silvery moonlight painted a melancholic glow on the scene. He watched as Blanchette turned away and gazed at the castle's throng. Her blue eyes shimmered in the torchlight. Her gaze looked unfocused as if lost in the depths of her thoughts.

As the silence stretched between them, the night seemed to hold its breath, waiting for what might come next. At that moment, the castle's battlements were an island of solitude amid the sea of night.

*What would she do if I placed my hands on her cheeks, turned her lovely face toward mine, and kissed her? Would she pull away?*

God, Rowan craved warmth. He felt cold. So very cold for so very long.

The castle below, bathed in a pale lunar glow, revealed a different shade of the night. Torches lining the walls cast extended shadows, and the courtyard was a tapestry of darkness and light. Rowan's sentries and guardsmen patrolled, their armor clinking softly. The murmur of voices and laughter drifted from the great hall and barracks, carrying on the wind like the softest ballads.

Blanchette glided past Rowan and made her way toward the banister. She gazed down at the restless castle. Beyond the curtain wall, an angry mob of villagers lurked. They fought with the guards manning the gatehouse.

He faintly heard a tall, reed-thin woman in rags call out for Queen Blanchette. Or perhaps she said something else entirely, and his imagination was only at play.

*They believe I'm burning and pillaging the villages.*

However, Rowan saw Blanchette was not looking at the castle but at the scorched village in the distance.

He watched her curls flutter like a golden banner in the breeze. She looked regal—a true queen watching over her kingdom.

Blanchette momentarily left to summon a servant, whom she commanded to bring the looters baskets of meat, mead, and fresh fruit. When she returned, she smiled coyly at Rowan and surrendered to a small laugh.

"What is it?"

"I was just thinking. Ah, well, it's rather silly. Governess Agnes—she used to tell my sister and me a bedtime story when we were little girls. A story about a child who had lost her way in the woods. At least, she *thought* she was lost, but... well, she was merely distracted. Lured off her rightful path." Her small, pale hands came to the material of her cloak. "She wore a red riding cloak, just like this one." She smiled shyly again, her eyes softening, the memories visibly tumbling through her mind. "Sometimes... sometimes I suppose you must become lost to find yourself."

# Nineteen

Sunrays climbed through the slanted windows and illuminated the tapestries on the walls. Blanchette wandered into the throne room, the crowning jewel of her home, her fingers lightly grazing the fabric of a hanging. It depicted her family's royal coat of arms—a black raven against a sunrise in a field. Her house's words were there too. Rowan had never removed them. Not even after he'd taken the castle when his anger ran hot.

"Wither the trees of hate..." She whispered her house's motto into the empty room. Then she repeated them again, like a prayer or hushed plea. "Wither the trees of hate... wither the trees of hate..."

Her breath caught as she moved toward the three steps that elevated the throne for the rest of the room. The chair was a wonder to behold. It'd terrified her when she was a girl. And it scared her now.

She stood within a patch of light as the day ended and cloaked the castle in shadows. She saw her father sitting in that chair, the crown resting on his golden brow, his handsome, stern features drawn tight. His knuckles strained and turned white as he gripped the carved armrests.

She inched forward. Her breath caught. Beyond the walls, she could make out the din of the castle—Rowan's men at training. Always training. Her father's likeness faded into her memories as she crossed the marble floor. The heels of her kid-skin boots clicked melodically and echoed the beat of her heart, and her red riding cloak silently swept the ground.

When she finally reached the chair, her breaths came so fast that she could hardly think. Her hand shook in midair as she reached out. She watched the signet ring drink in the light, then tentatively rested her hand on the armrest. She ran her fingers up the smooth iron and intricate metalwork... circled the chair, her boots rapping loudly in the throne room's solemn quiet. Her pulse raced, her thoughts coming faster still.

Blanchette reached for her cross, finding again that it was no longer there.

She needed to pray.

THE COZY CHAPEL was a welcomed contrast to the coldness of the throne room. A candelabra burned gently in front of the altar. Mary sat beside it. Her hands were pressed together in prayer, and her white dress circled her body on the stone floor. She looked like an angel.

Blanchette stood in the archway, debating whether she should leave. It was a solemn, sad thing, watching a young child all alone in the gloom of a castle with only a candlestick for company.

Mary's head lifted, and she glanced over her shoulder, her eyes softening when they spotted Blanchette in the archway. Blanchette smiled, smoothed down her skirts, then entered the chapel.

"I didn't mean to interrupt. May I join you?" she asked.

Mary nodded, and Blanchette sat beside her on the ground. She smoothed her skirts around her and tucked her legs under them. "Beautiful, isn't it?" Mary nodded again. She was blushing, Blanchette noticed. "Did you have a chapel at Rochester Castle?"

"Yes. A small one," she answered, her blue gaze darting around the room.

"I'm glad to hear that," she said, meaning it. Blanchette playfully nudged her with her elbow. "So what did you pray for?"

"Pray?" Mary's brow tightened, and suddenly, she seemed much older than her seven years. "I... I don't really pray. Not anymore. I used to, every morning and night."

*What a sad child.*

Blanchette studied Mary's delicate features—her porcelain skin, upturned nose, and the light dusting of freckles that decorated it. Gently, she smoothed her palm over her long golden curls in soothing motions. "That makes me sad, Mary. What made you stop?"

Blanchette watched as she stared into the flame. It waved and danced, filling the small chapel with lively shadows. Blanchette glanced above the altar, where the Lord hung on his cross for all their sins.

*Even Rowan's.*

*Even my father's...*

A strange combination of horror and hope wrestled in her gut. Finally, Mary spoke, and the illusion was broken.

"Every morning, I'd pray at my bedside. I'd pray for Father to come home... for Mother to come back, too, although I knew she couldn't. She was with the angels. But Father *could* come back. And if God were good, he'd send him my message and bring him back to me."

"Didn't... didn't Rowan ever visit you?" Blanchette asked, already fearing the answer.

"I don't think so. I can't remember the last time I saw him."

Blanchette shook her head, her heart aching for the little girl. What could she even say? What could she do? "He regrets that. I know he does. But it's never too late, you know." Blanchette smiled at Mary, brushed the curls from her eyes, and tucked them behind her tiny ears. "You can know him now. Wouldn't you like that?"

Mary nodded, her pretty face breaking into a smile. Her front tooth was missing.

"God has given you both the gift of time. It's up to you how you spend it. I suggest you cherish it well, every day..." Blanchette felt Mary's eyes on her. She tried to harness the sudden rush of sadness. "You never know how much time you'll have left."

Mary gave a sulky look, then pulled her knees against her chest. "He's like a stranger."

"He's a good man. Truly."

Mary gazed up at her, her brows knitted in confusion. Blanchette observed as she stared into the flames with a strange intensity. Her blond curls seemed to catch fire. "Didn't Father do bad things to you? To your family?"

Blanchette shook her head and inhaled a fortifying breath. "It isn't as simple as all that, my love. It hasn't been easy, but I've come to see your father *is* a good man. Mine was not. You will come to see it, too, in time. I promise."

*I promise...*

Blanchette heard Governess Agnes's voice in her ear. *There is light, and there are shadows in all of us. And sometimes bad things must happen to bring about lasting good. Sometimes winter comes, and it is dark and painful, but it clears the earth for spring.*

Mary's eyes narrowed. She was looking inwardly, Blanchette knew. It was the same expression she often made before her looking glass when her thoughts shattered apart. "I don't know him at all," she whispered. Her breaths wafted close to the flame, making it waver. Blanchette watched as it cast long shadows on the stone walls. They shifted and seemed to change shape.

*What kind of shape? What are they transforming into?*

"He is doing everything he can to change that. He brought you here because he wants to know you, Mary. Because he loves you." Blanchette set her fingers on Mary's chin and tenderly lifted her face. "He deserves that chance. And so do you."

---

Rowan sat in the throne's massive chair, his fingers wrapping around the ends of the armrests. Prisms of light shot through the line of hexagonal windows and dappled the marble floor. Smoke sat in front of the chair like a loyal guardsman.

The royal crown rested on his lap, twinkling in the emerging dawn, its rubies and sapphires bright and furious. Rowan gripped the chair's gnarled armrests, his nails unconsciously digging into the wood. The massive oak door, studded with iron, pushed open. Edrick stared at him from the archway, his chain mail armor clinking as he sealed the door again with the crossbar.

"Sir Rowan," he said, his voice lacking any inflection. Rowan stared at the crown in his lap and gripped the armrests tighter.

"Come forward, Edrick."

He did as ordered. The sound of his boots rapped against the marble floor. He watched as Smoke's golden eyes narrowed on Edrick. The wolf lowered his head, and a deep, rumbling growl filled the room.

Edrick halted before the wolf, just at the edge of the stairs that elevated the throne from the rest of the great room. If he feared Smoke, he did a good job of hiding it. He folded his arms behind his back and raised his chin at a sharp angle.

*Defiant, and growing more so by the day.*

*Dangerous.*

*Especially with Blanchette and my daughter about.*

*When did our friendship come to this?*

Rowan met his steady gaze. "I have an assignment for you. One that shall take you from the capital."

The corner of Edrick's lip twitched. "With fighting all around us, what could be more important than having me here, in the city, by your side?"

Rowan took the crown into his hands. The metal felt cool against his fingertips as he traced its points. He set it on the armrest, then came to his feet. He recalled what Blanchette had said about her lady-in-waiting. And how Edrick had fervently denied any wrongdoing.

What was her name? Elise?

*Always remember their names and remember their faces.* He'd taught Edrick that. Nay... the Black Wolf had taught Edrick that.

*Who am I? Who am I becoming?* he asked himself for the hundredth time.

Rowan looked at him now, at the coldness in his friend's eyes. Edrick shifted his weight, his graying brows drawn together, his flat eyes hiding his emotions.

Rowan moved down from the top step. "As you may recall, Blanchette had a lady-in-waiting," he began.

"I am sure she had many," Edrick said in a voice as flat as his eyes.

"Aye," Rowan said, his tone sinking into a gravelly tenor. "And you had lied to me. She was quite fond of that lady-in-waiting." He took another step down the stairs. "I think you *did* meet her the night of the siege."

Edrick broke eye contact for half a second—the one telltale of his discomfort. "Perhaps. If I had, I don't recall. My thoughts were elsewhere that night."

Rowan took two more steps. Now he was close enough to where Edrick had to look up to meet his stare. "Maybe so. But it's not where your thoughts were that concern me."

"What do you mean to say, Rowan? Speak your mind."

Rowan came down the last step, and Edrick had no choice but to shuffle back. Smoke growled again, the ominous sound swelling the cavernous room. "You defiled her." It wasn't a question. He watched Edrick's face for any sign of regret or shame. It remained blank and unreadable, and Rowan knew he stood before a monster.

That decided him.

*God, this man was like a brother to me once.*

Edrick's lip twitched as his eyes shifted downward—just an inch. Then a stone-hard expression claimed his face. Smoke bristled beside Rowan and released another growl. It was menacing. A herald of death. The wolf lifted his paw and snapped at the empty air between them. "What about it? War is a ruthless and cruel business. Children starve, and men die crying for their mothers. And yes. Women are defiled. You have grown so soft, Rowan."

"That's where you're wrong. That's where you've always been wrong. My war wasn't merciless—it *was* a mercy. It is you and you alone who are cruel. I don't even know you anymore."

"That makes two of us."

Their gazes locked again. Whatever Edrick found in Rowan's eyes jarred him. He stepped back—just another inch—and his emotions were unearthed for once.

Fear was written plainly on his face. Edrick released an audible breath, then came forward, nearly to the first step. His eyes sharpened, and his voice was low and venomous when he spoke—steel biting through flesh. "I have been with you, Rowan, from the very beginning. Since you were a boy under your father's banner. I saw you after your wife's death, with your hands still wet with her blood. I saw the horror on your face. I wept with you. I took you into my home, into my daughter's home! I risked our lives to protect you!" Rowan heard the rage in his voice. Seeing Edrick show such emotion shocked him. "And then I followed you. I followed you across the battlefields and against the king's laws. I rode in your vanguard and held your banner. I believed in you as you had once believed in me..." Rowan felt his insides weaken as a dejected smile lifted the corner of Edrick's lip. For a moment— just a moment—he glimpsed the man he'd been before all this bloodshed. Before the madness had changed them both.

"And now you have failed me, Rowan. Your purpose, all of that... it's a lie." His eyes shifted away to the crown. It glinted in the light, basking in the rays like a longsword wallows in its victim's blood. "This conquest has become your greatest lie. You stand here and call me cruel when you have hidden behind your men's acts at every step. You killed those good soldiers for executing the prince, yet you knew it had to be done. You let them fall for it and pay for it before the country's eyes, yet in private, you were glad. They did what you couldn't do. Not while you called yourself the Black Wolf of Norland, the people's champion. You have become a coward."

Rowan swallowed against the scream in his throat. Then he balled his fingers into a fist, tightening and loosening, tightening and loosening. His nails dug into his palms, cutting through the callused skin. Suddenly, he felt like a stranger to himself.

*Does he speak the truth? Is everything I fought for—is my love, yes love, for Blanchette—nothing but a twisted manipulation?*

His destiny had always been so clear, the path carefully drawn and calculated. Like a map. Or a battle plan. And now it seemed he'd acted only in chaos... not like the Black Wolf, but with the rabid drive of a mad dog.

"Sir Edrick, as lord of this castle, I hereby banish you from the capital. Now get out of my city before I throw your head into the sea."

Edrick turned to leave. He stopped before the archway, his gaze fixed on the shining crown. "She'll never love you, Rowan. You know that. She will always see you as the monster... as the wolf... who savaged her home and family. But there was another lady who had loved you. And she's dead because of your neglect. Always remember that."

---

THE SUN WAS BLEEDING. It hung vivid and dark red over the horizon, soaking the forest and path in a cloak of molten gold. Everywhere the light touched seemed to bleed; it was a massacre by God's own hand.

Sir Edrick sank his heels into his mount and stormed across

the drawbridge and into that blistering world. Dust swarmed in the air as his horse tore the path apart. The sun blinded him. He blinked against the assaulting light, sweat beading from his brow and forming inside his kid gloves. He rode up a hill, an overlook that he and Rowan had used countless times to assess the village and country.

Heartache momentarily washed over him. In his mind's eyes, he saw his friend kneeling under his roof, his fingers wet from his wife's blood, tears dried on his cheeks. In her death, a demon had been born, and its name was Vengeance.

*I'd believed in him once. I'd loved him like a brother.*
*I would have died for him.*

But that had shattered... that and the promises Rowan had made to him.

*All lies.*

Lies he'd told to him and to *her.*

Edrick dug his hand inside his coat and withdrew the ornament he'd found in the village. It glittered in the sun's dying glow.

A goat's head.

He'd finished his business here, minutes ago, in the chapel.

Then in the rookery.

All the birds were dead.

And someone else too.

Now, he had business elsewhere. "You are cursed now, my friend," he said, his words carrying to the castle on a breeze.

---

THE DAY SHONE with a brilliance Rowan hadn't seen for years. Or maybe he was just looking through renewed eyes.

He surveyed the tranquility garden—a flowing patch of blossoms, hyacinths, roses, and climbing trellises. He inhaled the sea-laden air, allowing it to fill his lungs and heart. But his mind kept tracking back to his conversation with Edrick. He stopped and placed his fingers on the hilt of his sword, a dull pang spiking through his chest. Smoke clung near to his heel, his head low and eyes glowing.

Had Edrick been right? *Is everything I've stood for and fought for—is it all a lie?* He fancied himself as the people's champion, but after hearing Edrick's spiteful words, he wasn't sure what he was.

*I don't need to be the people's champion,* he thought. *Only Blanchette's.*

Except that wasn't true. If he wasn't fighting for the people, if all this bloodshed hadn't been for the greater good, then he was no better than King Bartholomew.

And therein where the danger lay. He exhaled a breath, then glanced at the towering castle, straight to Blanchette's room. The room looked dark... where was she? Rowan nervously rubbed his fingers on the wolf pommel before moving farther through the garden. He fought to anchor himself in the moment—but Edrick's words hung over him like a dark cloud. He still saw the young prince's mutilated body every time he closed his eyes... and every time he slept, his wife was there.

*There was another lady who had loved you.*
*And she's dead because of your neglect.*
*Always remember that.*
Like he could ever forget.
*When can I wake?* he thought.

Winslowe Castle seemed to glare down at him with a black judgment that he couldn't escape. He continued through the garden, listening to the clatter of blunted swords crashing, horses neighing, and the barking and whining of kennel dogs.

A stark-white figure came into view. Mary wore a white dress with long v-cut sleeves, her blond curls tucked into a hood. Smoke padded over to her. "Mary. There you are."

She bowed her head with respect, then came forward. The basket she clutched in her arms overflowed with herbs and blooms. The wolf followed her, as loyal as any foot soldier in Rowan's army.

"Those smell lovely," he said conversationally. Mary smiled, then plucked a thin, reedy-looking stem from the bunch.

"Blanchette's teaching me how to use them," she explained. Her blue eyes sparkled with interest in the early morning sun. "How to make medicine, I mean."

"Is she now?" Rowan asked, returning her tentative smile. "Walk with me, my child." *My child.* The word hung in his mouth, leaving behind a bitter taste.

Smoke followed them.

The path curved and led to one of the training grounds. Archer butts lined the wall, though the yard was otherwise empty. Rowan glanced down at Mary as a protective urge rushed through him.

He recalled the hatred in Edrick's eyes. The way he'd stared at him from under the archway before his exile.

He mussed Mary's hair with his hand—felt her tense under his touch—then moved toward the archery butts.

A longbow leaned against the wall. It was still too large for Mary, but he collected it from the ground and handed it to her regardless. She looked at him, perplexed; then a shy smile brightened her face and eyes.

"For me?"

Rowan nodded. Then he pulled a handful of arrows from a butt.

"Have you shot an arrow before?"

She shook her head. "Ladies aren't supposed to fight," she said, her voice a whisper.

Rowan got down to one knee, balancing his arm on the top of the bow. "The world is changing. Ladies aren't supposed to fight, aye... ladies *must* know how to fight. I want you to be safe. Always."

Then he rose to his feet and brought the longbow into place. "Watch me first." He slowly nocked the arrow, kept his shoulder low, drew back, and let it loose. It hit the butt dead center.

Blanchette watched them from her window.

*I wish Governess Agnes could see this.* Blanchette had looked for her that morning to no avail.

How regal yet gentle Rowan looked, guiding little Mary, clapping as her arrow loosed and hit nowhere near the archery butt. Blanchette crossed the gallery and made her way down the winding stairs. Something compelled her toward Rowan. She'd been drawn to him from the first, even when she cursed him with every breath. Even when she saw him as a monster. Something about him had always ruled her.

Rowan seemed to sense her as she entered the small training yard. She saw the awareness awaken in his body. He visibly tensed. His eyes jerked up from Mary and to Blanchette's. A current blazed between them. An unspoken heat. Blanchette stood silently for several moments.

She cleared her throat and ran her palms over her skirt. "Forgive me, I... I didn't mean to interrupt." Smoke raised his head at the sound of her voice. He padded over in a few graceful strides, moving as quiet as a ghost. Blanchette held out her knuckles for him to smell. He licked her fingers, and she rewarded the wolf with scratches behind his ears.

*We truly are friends now.*

"Not at all. I'm glad you've come," Rowan said, his rich voice filling her mind and body with its smooth timbre. "We're having a lesson, see," he said, gesturing to Mary and the crossbow, which was far too big for her. "About how ladies *must* know how to fight."

"Father is teaching me how to shoot arrows," Mary explained, a smile lighting her face.

"Ah, I can see that," Blanchette replied.

Mary smiled again, then loosed another arrow. This one hit the butt at its edge. They went on that way for the better part of the morning until Mary and Smoke left together so she could break her fast.

Rowan stepped intimately close to Blanchette, and suddenly, the training yard seemed to shrink. He stood over her, his eyes sparkling in the light, the sun's rays gleaming in his hair's deep black.

"Have you shot a longbow before?" he asked, his voice a sultry rumble that Blanchette felt move through her bones.

"No," she said, shuffling back just an inch. Dark memories came tumbling like water through a dam. "But I've used a dagger. An axe too," she added with a nervous, sad laugh, thinking of that night in the woods.

He closed the space she'd just gained. They were chest to chest, face-to-face. Nearly touching. Blanchette tried to take a deep breath, but her lungs felt tight. Her throat too. Her heart raced in her ears. She was sure he'd hear the sound. He looked down at her for several more moments of jittery silence. "The night of the attack. That was the first time you killed someone." It wasn't a question. But she nodded anyway.

"Here," he said, handing the longbow to her. It fit her much better than Mary. But why did her hand feel so damn clumsy as he wrapped it around the wood and carefully positioned her fingers?

"Keep your elbow up and your gaze on the target. Your eyes will send the arrow where it needs to go."

Blanchette felt heat emanating from Rowan's body as he stood behind her, guiding her posture. They fit together perfectly. His breath tickled her neck as he whispered, "That's it. Now, draw back the string and let it fly."

As she released the arrow, she couldn't believe how smooth the motion felt, almost like an extension of her own body. It sailed through the air, hitting the target with a satisfying *thump*. She turned to Rowan with a smile, and he grinned back at her.

He looked handsome... achingly wholesome, with a boyish look of triumph on his face.

"You're a natural," he said, his voice low and husky. "But we can always work on improving."

Blanchette's heart skipped a beat as Rowan's hand rested on her hip. He reached for another arrow. She could feel the heat of his body against her back, and the soft hairs on her arms stood up in anticipation. The hard ridge of his arousal strained against her bottom.

"This time, try to focus on your breathing," he said, his hot mouth against her ear. "In... and out..." *How in God's name?* she silently screamed. She felt close to fainting. Her skin tightened at the sound of his voice, the way he spoke those words against her neck as if they meant something else entirely.

She was acutely aware of every inch of her body, how her skin felt against the fabric of her dress, how her hair brushed against her cheeks in the cool breeze.

Blanchette felt the warmth of his body enveloping her. She could smell his scent—ale and sweat and leather and something indefinable that made her heart race. She was growing wet down there, between her hot thighs.

"You are very good with her. Mary, I mean."

He hesitated, then met her eyes. "When she was a babe, I was the only one who could put her to sleep. Not Beatrice or the wet nurse. I'd sing to her... I still remember how it felt, her little hand gripping my finger..." His confession faded into silence. Then he shook his head. "It doesn't matter now."

"But it does, Rowan. It matters more than anything. She yearns to be close to you. You—"

"Must keep your elbow up," he whispered close to her ear, his body brushing against hers, his arousal pushing against her hip. She grew wetter, hotter, and little currents sang in her veins. "Yes, right there, Your Grace."

Blanchette turned to face him. She was met with a gaze filled with a fiery intensity she'd never seen before. She could feel her cheeks flushing as she realized just how close they stood. They were practically one. His hand still rested on her hip, and she could feel the warmth of his fingers seeping through the fabric of her dress.

Rowan's eyes roamed over her face, taking in every feature, every curve, every nuance of expression. It was as if he was seeing her for the first time and couldn't look away. Their eyes locked for several weightless moments.

She parted her lips and expelled a long-drawn-out breath.

He studied her mouth.

*Kiss me...*

"Are you ready?"

She nodded.

*But ready for what?*

Blanchette closed her eyes, letting Rowan's words wash over her. She could feel her body relaxing under his gentle touch and guidance, and she took a deep breath in, holding it for a moment before letting it out slowly. He placed his large hand across her abdomen and applied gentle pressure.

"Good," Rowan murmured. "Now, draw back... and let go."

*Let go.*

*But if I let go, I shall fall...*

Blanchette's eyes sprang open. The arrow had hit the target dead center. She let out a small gasp of delight. Then she turned up to Rowan, excitement racing through her.

"I did it!"

Rowan smiled at her, his eyes darkening with a hunger she couldn't quite understand. "Yes, you did," he breathed. "And you'll do it again... and again... and again."

### Seven years earlier

"His orders were clear, Rowan. Are you mad? You cannot defy him. Not again."

Rowan unconsciously dug his heels into Sunbeam's sides as

he adjusted his body in the saddle. Edrick's mount stood beside him. Together, they looked down from the hill and across Norland's great expanse. Where farms and fields once grew in abundance, nothing lay but frozen earth. The winter had hit hard, and King Bartholomew had hit harder still.

"I promised them they'd walk free. So long as they laid down their swords and stopped this revolt, they could live under the king's peace again. I promised them their safety!"

"And what of yours? What of your family's?"

*Who am I without my honor?*
*What sort of knight harms the innocent?*
*What kind of monster am I becoming?*

"Nay, Edrick. I gave them my vow."

Edrick wheeled beside him and crossed his mail-covered hands over his horse's flowing mane. "At what price? Are you willing to pay with your life? That of your family's? I'd never put Kathryn at risk so recklessly. Please, Rowan, as your friend, I beg you to consider the consequences. I won't let you walk away. I care for you far too much. Ever since we were boys, you've been like a brother to me."

Rowan stared at his friend long and hard. Edrick's eyes pleaded with him. Rowan gripped the reins, a barely restrained heat pulsating through his veins. He could make out the townsfolk at work in the village below, not three miles south. Men, women, and children labored in the cold wasteland that had become their home, bundled under heavy skins and cloaks.

Those were the lucky ones. Many wore naught more than shirtsleeves—a mockery of warmth amid a relentless winter.

They stood there, mounts side by side, until the sun dropped from the sky and painted Norland in swashes of orange and red. It looked picturesque. Even peaceful. But inside of Rowan's heart... that was chaos.

He closed his eyes; the inside of his eyelids wept blood. He saw beautiful, exotic Beatrice, her hand on her belly, humming softly... a melody as sweet as Norland's summer wind.

*"Pray we to that child, and to his mother dear,
Grant them His blessing that now make cheer..."*

But that was when summer still sang, and the breeze blew warm. Now winter had come, and the chill in the air had frozen the blood in Norland's veins.

Rowan hanged them all by dawn. Priests and the villagers. He walked through the forest of gallows as the carrion crows and ravens circled the village. They *squawked* and screamed from naked tree branches, swooping down to pick at the hanging corpses when the opportunity presented itself. Rowan crossed his arm over his body and rested his hand on his sword's pommel. He traced the snarling wolf's head as he stood amid all that death and destruction—a massacre caused by his own hands.

*Who am I becoming...*

He wandered through that forest, feeling the agony of every soul. He stopped before a gallows, where a boy hanged in shirtsleeves far too thin for the weather. He'd picked up his father's sword for the first time a week ago. The promise of a rebellion that could bring warmth back into his life had seduced him.

And now here he hung, cold and alone. Rowan cursed, and his breath showed white against the frosty night air.

"They are supposed to be up all winter," Edrick cautioned. "I like it no more than you do."

"They've endured enough winter. Let them know some warmth in death, for mercy's sake."

He withdrew his longsword; it echoed shrilly, almost like a scream, as it left the scabbard. Then he cut into the rope just above the boy's head. It took three powerful slashes to get him down.

Rowan was out of breath from the exertion and surge of anger. His fingers loosened on the hilt, and the longsword made a dull, hollow sound as it hit the gallows' wood platform. Rowan fell beside his sword and the boy. Edrick gently placed a hand on his shoulder. "I'm so sorry. This pains me as well."

Rowan shoved his hand away and stared up at his friend with a look of pure loathing. "Leave me," he spat.

Rowan inhaled deeply, filling his lungs with Norland's ice-cold air. An hour later, he stood over a gaping hole in the earth. He stared off into the horizon, where the sun sank below a blanket of low-hanging clouds. Orange and red streaked the sky. He stood at the precipice of a cliff that overlooked the town. Edrick walked between the gallows and hanging bodies—the only sign of movement in that sea of death.

*Yea, though I walk through the valley of the shadow of death, I will fear no evil: for thou art with me; thy rod and thy staff they comfort me...*

But he was no shepherd. Rowan Dietrich was a wolf, he conceded, glancing at his waving banner in the distance.

*My father's gray wolf.*

He shrugged away his heavy cloak and wrapped the boy. He looked impossibly small, lost in the dark material, his flesh pale against the black of his cloak. Rowan inhaled, then slowly blew all the air out.

"I'm so sorry," he muttered, carefully scooping the limp body into his arms. Then he laid him down in the hole. Such an unfortunate place for so young a boy to dwell for eternity. That thought disturbed Rowan more than he could say. "Rest now."

He scooped a handful of earth, and just as he was about to sprinkle it over the body, the boy's face seemed to morph. His face's sharp, malnourished lines softened and shifted.

A nauseous feeling overcame Rowan as he looked down at his wife's features. He blinked, and her likeness faded away, leaving behind the poor boy's face again.

Rowan looked off into the horizon as if he'd find an answer there... or maybe forgiveness. He tried to bring a prayer to mind. None would come. Not while those priests hung.

Then he spotted Edrick again, and the words flowed like the Rockbluff River.

He covered the boy with earth, where his fragile, small bones would return to the dust.

"In sure and certain hope of the resurrection to eternal life, I commit this soul's body to the ground; earth to earth; ashes to ashes, dust to dust. The Lord bless him and keep him, the Lord make his face to shine upon him and be gracious unto him and give him peace. Amen."

Rowan bowed his head once more—not in prayer, but in shameful regret.

# Twenty

Someone had killed all the birds. Blanchette had made for the rookery after going over the coffers, meaning to send Isadora another letter.

Now, Blanchette walked through the halls, a candlestick in a silver dish clasped in her hand.

A dark premonition tightened around her gut.

The castle was quiet and still, much like a slumbering beast. Her grandmother's red cloak draped her shoulders and helped cut through the drafts that penetrated the walls. Spring had come, yet the chill never had melted away.

Blanchette pressed on the chapel's iron-studded door and entered the circular room. It was nearly black as pitch. Only her wavering candle and a stream of moonlight illuminated the space.

She stepped inside, and her heart jumped as the door cracked shut.

The tiny hairs on the back of her neck stood. Gooseflesh broke out across her bare arm.

She began her prayer in the softest of whispers. She could barely hear herself speak. She stepped in farther, toward the center altar. The ring of light from her candle skirted across the stone ground and crept into the far corner of the room.

There she saw it.

A figure against the far wall, its back resting against the stones so it appeared to sit.

Blanchette rushed over; she felt the cloak billow from her shoulders. She fell beside that figure, which the light showed as Governess Agnes.

The silver tray clattered like bones as she fought to hold her hand still.

"No…" Blanchette whispered into that darkness, her gaze drifting over her beloved governess's wrinkled, pale skin… the deep gash that ran across her throat and spilled her life's blood down the robe she'd worn and loved so well.

Her pale eyes were open… but what did they see?

Who would have committed such a vile act?

Blanchette's sobs came once the shock ebbed away. She squinted through her water-filled eyes and pressed her forehead against Governess Agnes's still chest. She was hard and cold. Death had chased away everything warm and soft about her.

No.

No.

*No.*

Her thoughts lapsed into memory, and she summoned an image of her and Isadora wading into the creek, Governess Agnes on their heels and lashing at them with her tongue…

That memory brought the tears again; tears for Governess Agnes, for her sister Isadora… whom she'd written to not so long ago… whom she might never see or laugh with again.

Instead, she had these icy walls—and a wolf who guarded them.

But he was not to blame. The Rowan she knew would tear apart the man who committed such an atrocity.

"You deserved better." Blanchette sniffled into her governess's motionless chest. She held her body tight and rocked her back and forth, her cries becoming torn sobs. "We all did. Oh, God… no… *no…*" With trembling hands, she unclasped the cross from her governess's neck and gripped the ornate metal in her palm.

Her memory lapsed again, this time to her grandmother.

She would keep her promise—and she had a wolf who'd help see it done.

---

Rowan had summoned a priest from a port village. Anger coiled in his belly like a snake as he stared down at the gaping hole in the earth, where four of his men lowered Governess Agnes's coffin.

Blanchette's features were drawn tight, etched with lines of heartbreak. Her gaze appeared to extend beyond the confines of the present moment. The vibrant blue of her eyes had dulled, replaced by an emptiness that mirrored the void left by Governess Agnes's departure.

*Her murder,* his mind amended.

Blanchette Winslowe looked beautiful. Lost. He longed to gather her into his arms, to kiss away the shadows that clung to her brow, but the chasm between them felt insurmountable. His hand, unconsciously seeking solace, found the hilt of his sword, its snarling wolf pommel a silent witness to the turmoil within him.

Mary stood beside him, at his left side, her tiny head bowed, curls falling about her shoulders like a golden shroud.

*Gold shall be their shrouds.*

*Everyone I've ever cared for...*

Guilt again. Rowan suspected he knew who was responsible for the governess's death. Once again, the Black Wolf had brought doom to Blanchette's door.

The priest's voice, gentle and consoling, washed over the gathering like a salve for wounded souls. But for Rowan, it only fueled the flames that raged within. A silent question echoed in the recesses of his mind—when would the cycle of pain and suffering finally come to an end?

As the earth swallowed the coffin and the priest's incantations faded into the quiet of mourning, Rowan couldn't escape that haunting question that lingered in the air.

How much pain and suffering must he cause the woman he'd grown to love?

※

BLANCHETTE WATCHED from her balcony as the setting sun cast streams of red and gold upon the world. Rowan directed his men in the training yard, his dark hair blowing.

Blanchette's eyes rose to the clearing just beyond the great walls of the castle; it was where Governess Agnes now slept and would sleep until the end of time. She saw herself as a girl, jetting into the canopy of trees, a young and wild heathen, poor Governess Agnes at her heels.

*Who would have harmed her?*

*God... what is happening?*

Her gaze tracked back to the training yard and stable. She saw herself again, walking through the crowds and past the clang of sparring swords, her curls drinking in the sunset.

As the figure approached, the delicate features became clearer —and Blanchette realized she wasn't looking at her ghost but at Mary Dietrich and Smoke.

※

"I REMEMBER SEEING Lady Beatrice on many occasions... at feasts and often in my father's company," Blanchette carefully said as she eased into what had once been the king's solar. Rowan turned from the window; he was dressed only in his shirtsleeves, which were untied at the neck, and the low-burning fire danced across his exposed skin. His face was stern yet sorrowful.

"Lady Beatrice had the look of her homeland, I recall. It was one of the things my father fancied about her. Dark eyes. Dark hair. She was exotic. Beautiful."

Rowan visibly tensed. She watched as he opened and closed his fingers several times. "Aye. A true dark-haired and dark-eyed beauty. No one could deny that. Especially not King Bartholomew."

Rowan lay his hands on either side of her face. She held in a breath, then released a drawn-out sigh as his thumbs traced the lines of her cheeks in soothing strokes. One finger tentatively traced the line of her scar—up the raised ridge, then down again, stopping right at the corner of her lip. Blanchette wetted her lips with her tongue. She heard and felt Rowan's shiver as her tongue kissed the edge of his finger. She smelled a fragrant ale on his breath—and in her mind's eye, it brought her back to the fields of Norland. She saw her and her sister running, the scents of wild fruit and earth around them.

Then her thoughts came full circle; she saw Mary, her curls as blond as her own, her porcelain skin glowing in the moonlight as she slid by the stable and through the training yard like a lost spirit.

Her eyes blinked open. She held Rowan's gaze, which was steady and probing. It seemed to echo the words she found so hard to speak—the truth that balanced on her tongue.

"I was watching Mary from my window. She looked so much like a ghost from my past... it was like I was watching myself. Watching her wander the castle alone, watching her observe the darkness around her but not really looking..." Blanchette bowed her head until her cheek lay across Rowan's beating heart. Several moments passed by before she finally met his eyes again.

The emotion, the intensity she found there, nearly stole her breath.

Rowan's lip lifted at the corner. He lowered his head until his lips grazed her forehead.

Blanchette realized then that this man—the Black Wolf of a

Norland, the knight who'd taken down her kingdom, the cause for such much unbearable pain and grief—was someone she could not lose. She'd lost so much so quickly, so the thought of never having his arms around her again, the feel of his warm breath on her face, unearthed her.

She swayed in his arms as emotion overcame her. He adjusted his grip and pulled her closer still.

No, she couldn't bear to lose him... it seemed he was the last thread tethering her to this world.

She met his eyes—beautiful and dark, commanding and gentle all at once. She thought of Mary's eyes, which were different from Rowan's and so like hers.

"Say what you must," he finally whispered, his gaze never breaking from her own. Shyly, she lifted her hands and reached for him. He dipped into her touch as her fingers wound in the thick black locks around his face.

*Mary isn't your daughter.* But she didn't need to say it. And she didn't have the heart to.

"How long have you known?" she asked instead.

He sighed. "A part of me has always known. That's why I sent her away as a ward. I kept that moat between us for these past seven years. I knew keeping her close would have dulled my hate for your family. After all, what sort of monster could tear apart a young girl's father? A mad dog, a hellhound. And if she was your father's child... well, what responsibility did I have to her? These are the mental games I've played with myself every night."

Blanchette glanced over Rowan's shoulder and out at the night. The sky was a lush, velvety black without a star in sight.

"Will you tell Mary the truth?"

"The truth? And what truth is that, Blanchette?" She released a tremulous sigh as his long fingers traced the curve of her cheeks. They skirted across her forehead as if drawing something there. "Your beauty was made for a crown resting upon your brow. Not all my intentions have been noble... that is another truth I cannot contest... but my vision's always been to heal this kingdom. Your goodness shall be the healing balm I could never provide." Blanchette could scarcely breathe and didn't trust herself to speak. He went on, his arms around her waist again, strong and sure and warm. "As for Mary... the truth is, she is my daughter. And I shall not let another day pass that she doesn't feel that truth."

---

*MEET me in the throne room at sundown.*

She'd found the letter that morning while she pored over the ledgers and tried to push her grief for Governess Agnes aside.

She stared at the stone throne chair—the source of so much pain and loss. The tears on her cheeks had dried, and her sorrow turned to anger. Her hands shook, and she exhaled a breath of agony.

"Good. I want you to use your anger, Blanchette."

Rowan whispered, yet it filled the grand, high-ceilinged throne room all the same. She turned to him and glanced at his hands. He held a bow, quiver, and a handsome-looking shortsword. An iron raven graced its pommel, its wings spread in flight. "These are yours."

"You made them?"

He nodded and held the dagger out for her. Its blade shone in the lantern. She hesitated—then wrapped her hand around the pommel. "It's beautiful."

"It's not for ornament," he said. "It's to kill with."

She returned his smile and held the blade up to the torchlight. "I gathered as much."

He took her hand, the one holding the pommel, and lifted it midair. His arm guided her own in a swift movement. He stood just behind her, his hard, muscled chest flush against her back. "Light, elegant, easy to wield, even for one with such short arms like yours."

She playfully scoffed and elbowed him. "Careful now, sir.

You're speaking to your queen." His chuckle rustled against her nape and sent chills racing down her spine.

"As you say, Your Grace." He adjusted his body. She felt him hardening down there, his manhood pressed against the curve of her bottom, as he guided her arm back and forth, up and down. "As I was saying, if the foe is lightly armored—leather, even chain mail—you want to go for the heart. The point is fine and will poke right through."

"The heart," she echoed, turning her head up to look at him. Silently, he nodded and adjusted himself again.

"Now, if they're farther away," he said, stepping back and handing her the bow. "This is what you'll use. Come with me."

---

HE BROUGHT her before the line of archery butts. The yard was nearly empty, with only a handful of young boys knocking and loosing arrows with silent determination. The soft *whooshing* echoed as they hit the straw more times than not.

Rowan gave her a grin, then took a moment to correct his squire.

"He quite idolizes you," she said when Rowan returned to her side.

"He's young. Young and far too brave for his own good. I'm afraid it shall get him killed."

Blanchette looked at the squire, then back at Rowan. His eyes seemed too distant, and there was a sadness in them that hit her hard. "Then we must protect him," she said, seeing Governess Agnes lying in the chapel all over again. "We must protect everyone who cannot protect themselves."

"That's why I've brought you here." He stared at her for a long stretch of silence, and Blanchette felt a rising flutter in her belly. A gentle breeze rustled his wavy black hair and swept the forelock across his thick, dark brows.

Her tummy did a flip as she felt his muscled body align with hers. His arms came around her shoulders, and he took her hands in his own. He lifted the bow, and his breath and voice were in her ears. "Now... let's resume our lessons, shall we? I made this bow to fit you perfectly. And I will teach you how to kill a man without him ever seeing you."

Her stomach flipped and turned again. She exhaled a long breath, then heard herself say, "I've killed too many men already."

She felt him stiffen behind her. His hands loosened, and the bow lowered several inches. He read her eyes and saw something there. "We all do what we must to survive. You were protecting your home and family. You were protecting yourself."

*And I failed,* she thought, a feeling of hopelessness rising inside her. Her parents. Her brother. Elise. Now Governess Agnes. Tears stung her eyes. She madly blinked them back, refusing to let them fall.

"Then teach me, Rowan," she finally said.

She felt him nod. One of his hands slid down her forearm. Long, deft fingers grasped her elbow and lifted it slightly. "Always keep your elbow up, Blanchette." The way her name sounded, leaving his tongue—like he savored its taste—made her light-headed. She blinked a few times and tried to remember not to let her elbow fall. She couldn't say why, but suddenly, it was vital that she impressed him.

*Because you're falling in love with him, you foolish girl. That's why. It's as clear as Norland's blue sky... and as treacherous as the winter snows and Rockbluff River.*

"Good," he said, the word sounding like an endearment. He nocked an arrow and guided her elbow back. "Now loose."

She did. Again and again and again until her arms and fingers ached and calluses began to form. Then she practiced some more, Rowan guiding her with soft instruction and touches as they watched the sun ascend over Norland.

HUNTLEY'S SHIP slid into Shadowmoor's harbor. It pushed through a haze that shrouded his family's sliver of the kingdom. Black towers thrust into the sky like an angry fist. The castle rimmed the edge of the bluffs and overlooked the ocean, where seven hundred longships sat in its shadow.

*I've, too, been lurking in its shadow.*

But now was his opportunity. His chance to carve a piece of the kingdom for him and his family… and God be damned if he wouldn't see that to the bitter end.

Huntley grasped the ship's railing as they passed through a low-hanging cloud. His free hand caressed the pommel of his dagger—he'd called it golden tooth, remembering his father's reaction to the name. That characteristic look of disdain had curled his thin lips. "Are you a boy or a lord?" he'd asked.

He'd been a boy of only nine years, but he'd answered as best as he could with a man's audacity. "I'll be the lord of Shadowmoor one day and a king."

*Which is more than anyone can say about you.* The boy in him stopped him from speaking that part aloud.

Huntley reached into his jerkin and withdrew a small, cast-iron thimble. He rotated it between his thumb and forefinger, his thoughts drifting to another time and place…

THE LONG HALL WAS COLD.

But the voice was colder.

"You're home," his father said, though it was far from welcoming. Huntley grasped the pommel of his sword and approached his father with long, fierce strides. He stood before the hearth, which was also black and cold.

"It was time. It's been too long."

His father made a noncommittal noise. Maybe a grunt. "The Black Wolf ravages Norland. Tongues have been wagging from every shadow of the castle and village. 'The Mad Dog,' many are calling him now."

Huntley's mouth ticked at the corner. "Then I'm doing my job well. And I much prefer 'The Hellhound.' I came up with it myself."

His father didn't offer a compliment. Only another noncommittal grunt. *Which is relatively high praise coming from this cold sack of bones.*

There was a sadness in Admiral James that Huntley could never empathize with. His eyes were small and stern, his lips resembling two thin worms, his nose like a beak. Fortunately, Huntley had been blessed with his mother's bright eyes and golden looks—something his father couldn't quite forgive.

"I've been sending raiding parties into Norland's villages," Huntley explained, searching his father's face. "Skeleton crews, really, attacking under the Black Wolf's banner."

"Not even man enough to your own dirty work?" Admiral James frowned. "No matter. It's time we bring the other houses into the fold." His eyes searched Huntley's expression in a way that unsettled him and caused his bowels to tighten. Huntley cursed himself for it, and their silence reached a feverish pitch.

*I've never grown up.*
*I'm still just a boy, playing at make-believe.*

"Most still stand by Rowan Dietrich, though I've been working hard to change that," Huntley said at length, more to hear the ring of his own voice than to engage in a back and forth with his lord father. Christ, he was tired. Tired and so very cold. There was a winter in his soul that never seemed to thaw.

"And what of the girl? How about your betrothed?" Admiral James asked, his lips pressing together. His pale eyes stared forward.

"I met her once, years ago. I doubt she'd recognize my face in a crowd. We've been out of the fold for so long, I don't think—"

"She is yours by right, and now so is Norland. You took a holy vow. You think too much like a child. Act like a man. It's time you grow up, Peter."

"I'm in the process, Father. And it's a vow I take quite seriously." That seemed to make his father happy. Or at least appeased. He nodded, the edges of his eyes crinkling under the pressure of hard thought. "I would see Norland burn to the ground before a traitor steals our legacy."

"By a hellhound."

"Aye. By a hellhound," his father echoed.

Then Admiral James stood. His small yet strong hand came to Huntley's shoulders, gripping hard. His pale eyes seemed to flash, and he saw a shred of pride there for the first time in years.

"That hellhound helped lead the attack on our family. Have you forgotten?" Admiral James asked. "Are we to allow him to keep stealing from us? This is your time to decide who you want to be. Your actions in the coming weeks will determine that... and the legacy of our house. I saw your strength when you were just a boy, and I see it now," he said, his fingers gripping Huntley's shoulders again. "That's why I chose you for this alliance and not your brother. Don't let me down, Huntley. There's power in being out of the fold. We have been undetected. And we can use that to our strategy."

"I understand."

"See that you do," he concluded, and Huntley blew out a breath he hadn't known he was holding until his father's hand withdrew. Huntley watched as his fingers tightened into a ball, pushing against some unseen pressure. "I need you to be strong. This is your hour, and time is moving fast. Make use of every minute."

Huntley sighed. A servant—some pretty wench—entered the hall, clutching firewood to her chest.

"Ah," Huntley greeted, "you read our mind."

"Yes, milord," she said, a light blush brightening her cheeks. She stepped between Huntley and Admiral James as if she were crossing between two rabid wolves having a go at each other.

She stoked a fire within minutes, but the chill still hung in the air. Huntley stared at the mantel, where the Greek god Pan embedded the wood.

Admiral James gestured to one of the high wingback chairs as the servant slipped past them again. Huntley watched as she left the room and was swallowed up by the castle. Then he sank into a chair and dragged it closer to the hearth. "Aren't you going to join me?" he asked his father, gesturing toward a parallel chair.

"I'd rather stand," he simply said. It held the ring of an insult—as if Huntley had failed some morbid test, and now his father basked in his victory.

Dark laughter bubbled inside Huntley, but he swallowed it back.

*I'd give my right hand for the luxury of rest,* he imagined his father saying.

Huntley withdrew the dagger from his scabbard. The blade shimmered in the fire's light. He ran his finger down the smooth, cold metal as he felt the pressure of his father's eyes on his every move. The warm fire seemed to kiss his hand; he flexed his fingers slowly, waiting for his father to speak.

He didn't. Only the ambient sound of the crackling hearth imbued the hall.

"Aye, most of the houses in Norland are still with him," Huntley finally said, twirling the dagger and watching the firelight dance off the metal. "Less by the day, but the majority still bows to their Black Wolf."

"Nine times out of ten, the side with the bigger numbers wins. We must steal them away, Huntley. *You* must steal them away."

Huntley twirled the dagger. Tossed it in the air and caught it by the handle. He leaned forward toward the hearth and felt the heat waft at his face. He stared at his family's sigil, unblinking, his heart racing. "Nay, you were right the first time. Our subtlety, being out of his notice—that's our strength. Most of the houses still side with him, true. But not all. Not the most important one."

Huntley came to his feet and slid the dagger back into its home in the scabbard. The scrape of metal was loud in the barren stone hall. "I've a letter to send," he said, placing his hand on his father's right shoulder in a mockery of the gesture he'd given not ten minutes ago.

"Be well," Admiral James said, his pale eyes showing no emotion. No fear. It was like looking into two muddy puddles.

"I intend to make war," he said.

Huntley patted his father's shoulder, then shuffled past him and across the hall. The din of his footsteps echoed dully. It was a hollow sound, and something about it put him on edge. His father's voice called him to a standstill as he reached the stairs.

"I loved this country once. Did you know that? I would have even died for it."

Huntley gave him a small, sad smile over his shoulder. "I know, Father. And I shall try to win that back for you."

And then he was gone, that stale promise already applying its force.

BLANCHETTE STOOD in front of the looking glass, where she beheld the past, present, and future all in one breath. She saw the naive and oblivious girl she'd been. She saw herself as she was now, with new wisdom in her gaze. Then she stared deeper into her eyes and found Mary—the girl who shared her blond hair and blue eyes—and Blanchette saw the woman she'd become.

Suddenly, the space behind her was filled. Rowan's massive body appeared in the looking glass, his dark form towering over her. She held her breath as his arms came around her body, and his hands gently touched her shoulders. He gave a firm yet gentle squeeze, which caused her insides to flip, then ran his hands down each of her arms in a tantalizingly slow movement.

Blanchette glanced at their reflections. Rowan loomed over her—dark, silent, and every bit the Black Wolf. Narrow hips gave way to a pair of broad, well-muscled shoulders. Her gaze crept down the length of his body with a mixture of fascination and tingling wariness.

His features were strong and decisively formed. He was far too masculine to be called beautiful. His very presence dominated every room in which he stood. He was impossibly tall, dwarfing her own body in comparison; she barely reached the middle of his chest. And despite his strength and large size, he possessed a sleek elegance she'd never witnessed in a man before.

*Like a wolf...*

Rowan turned into her hair and inhaled the scent. Callused hands massaged her throat. They delicately flittered across her neck as his fingers formed a steeple. Then he cupped her chin in the cradle of his palm and lifted her face. His thumbs brushed the scar on her cheek. Their eyes mingled in the reflection in an enticing swirl of blue and hazel. His fingers were surging with strength. Her neck fell limp in his grasp, and a sharp exhale fled her lips.

He stepped away for a heartbeat. She felt weightless without him there. When he returned behind her, he brought her father's crown to rest on her brow. The jewels drank in the firelight and sparkled like a thousand stars. She watched, transfixed, as Rowan's fingers slid away from the crown and moved through her curls. His hands came to her shoulders and slowly skated down her arms. Gooseflesh broke out across her skin, sending a delicious chill through her bones.

Then his fingers were at her neck, curling into her hair and pulling it aside. His lips came to her nape in a barely-there caress. His mouth grazed her skin, and her eyes shut in ecstasy. She felt the solid strength of his body behind her, the whisper of his lips on her skin, and the weight of her family's crown on her brow. She relaxed, falling back into his weight, the world around her fading.

She opened her eyes and took in their reflections again. The Black Wolf of Norland. How well he lived up to his name at that moment. His dark hair fell into piercing eyes—eyes that missed nothing. He wore a leather jerkin, which was open at the collar, exposing his hard upper chest. She spun in his arms, turning away from their reflection so they stood face-to-face.

His hands clasped her chin and tilted her head back. Before she knew what was happening, his lips came to her cheek. She exhaled a long sigh, and his mouth traced the line of her raised scar—from the edge of her hairline all the way to the corner of her lip.

She leaned her head against his chest, where his heart raced strong and sure.

"You are my queen," he whispered against her cheek.

"Rowan..." Her voice came out in a gasp. She started to speak again, but Rowan swallowed her words. Possessively, his mouth sealed over her own. His arms snaked around her body and grasped her tight. She felt his fingers digging into her hips and the curve of her bottom. She sank into him with a desperate moan, savoring the feel of his rock-hard body, his full lips moving against her own, massaging, urging her submission. He tasted of a sweet summer wine. She tilted her head and felt his tongue dart past the seam of her lips. He searched inside her mouth, his smooth tongue sliding against hers, his teeth gently nipping her lips and claiming her in a sweet, sensual possession.

She gave herself fully.

*My first kiss.*

How sweet it felt.

How right.

He tightened his grip on her as if she might slip away. Large palms ran up and down her back in firm strokes... then his hands came to her neck, and his strong fingers wound into her curls and urged her ever closer.

She pulled out of the kiss, breathless and aching. She watched as the first content smile came to his face and warmed those hazel eyes.

She smiled back at him.

*Yes, I am falling fast...*

---

SHE STOOD at the edge of a precipice that overlooked her kingdom. Below her, Norland spread out in vibrant patches of greens and yellows like a quilt. She observed the tiny ant-like figures moving through the village and down the roads. The people of her homeland. She closed her eyes and inhaled the salt-laden air, welcoming it into her lungs.

*You are my queen.*

When she opened her eyes again, she found herself in the middle of the woods. Massive trees stood around her, their gnarled arms reaching for a moonless sky. Blanchette's heart pounded. She held her hands out before her, but they were barely visible in the darkness.

It was cold... so cold.

Her breaths misted against the black, clashing against the frigid air. She pulled her cloak tightly about her body, then took a wary step forward. She felt the moist earth sink beneath her boots and heard the tree's skeletal branches quiver in the wind. She took another step. Then another, her fear and a sense of foreboding mounting with each one. The mournful cry of a wolf trembled through the wood.

Blanchette froze in mid-step as that wolf's howl shook through the wood again. She should have been frightened, yet that melancholy sound comforted her. She felt safe, knowing the woods belonged to *him*.

She held her breath and closed her eyes. The howl came again, a long, trembling cry.

The sound of snapping twigs. *Broken bones*, she absently thought.

A smooth, slick body brushed up against her skirts. Blanchette gasped aloud, her heart racing, then opened her eyes. Two hazel globes stared up at her, nestled in fur as black as night.

His head dropped low, his eyes remaining fixed on her. His lips curled back, flashing pearl-white teeth. A low growl reverberated in his throat and sent another shiver through her.

She leaned forward and ran her palm over his silky muzzle and dark fur. He bristled beneath her touch, and his muzzle broke out into a panting smile.

Then she heard a light creaking—the sound of a ship's broken mast moving in the wind... or the eerie creak and sigh of bones rattling. She looked up, up into the towering soldier pines. She saw the four of them above her.

Her brother's mutilated body, limp and hanging.

Her mother's dead eyes staring forward.

Her father, the spikes of his crown dripping blood, the crown itself hanging halfway off his brow... and Grandmother, too, her wrinkled white throat torn out and gushing red.

*As red as my red riding cloak.*

Without thinking, she tightened her hold on the wolf's dark fur. He tensed beneath her, and a low warning growl rolled through the forest.

Her mother's body creaked. Dead eyes moved in their sockets. She stared down at Blanchette, then wept tears of blood. They fell down her sunken cheeks and onto her red riding cloak, blending into the fabric. She couldn't tell where the blood began and the cloak ended.

"Mother... please..." she moaned. "Rowan, help me..."

The world twisted and flipped in a dizzying flurry. Blanchette was upside down, hanging from a pine, bloody tears falling from her eyes and wounded cheek. The Black Wolf lurked below her. His eyes shined like stars. Blanchette opened her mouth in a silent scream.

Only blood came out.

*Blood. So much blood.*

*I'm drowning in it.*

It pooled on the dark, muddy ground below her dangling head and body. She watched in horror as the Black Wolf lapped it up eagerly, slaver and blood dripping from his jaws...

# Twenty-One

The village they'd visited months ago now lay in near ruin. The scent of smoke and ashes and blood permeated the air. It was a stench not unlike most of the battlefields Rowan had walked.

*I shouldn't have brought her here,* he thought as he glanced at Blanchette. She rode a white mare with a banner of flowing silver mane. Smoke had remained behind with Mary, ever her guard dog.

Blanchette's blond hair was gathered under the hood of her cloak, and her beautiful blue eyes appeared to stare inward. Not at the destruction before her—but at some internal destruction. Something she couldn't look away from. She was strangely quiet, too, her lips pulled tight.

Although it was midday, the lingering smoke obscured everything and darkened the world. They both ordered their mounts to a halt. Rowan glanced at the few peasants who'd stayed in the town or survived the massacre.

Now, no children or mothers ran out to greet him. No one heralded his arrival with prayer-filled calls or waving wolf banners. Instead, they ran inside the shelter of the few remaining dilapidated houses. Mothers grabbed the hands of their sons and daughters and rushed them away as if a true wolf lay in their midst. Rowan tightened his hands on Shadow's reins and coiled his fingers.

*I should have listened to Edrick.*

*God, what have I done?*

He spotted a black flag staked into the soil. *A pirate raid.*

Blanchette dismounted.

Before he could stop her, she picked up the hem of her cloak and dashed over to a young woman. A whore or camp follower, by the look of her. She appeared as run-down as the village itself. Blanchette withdrew a handful of coppers from her cloak and gently placed them in the woman's thin hand. Her skin looked like hide stretched over a board.

The whore pulled her hand away, but Blanchette caught her small wrist in midair and held tight. "Please. Wait. I'm looking for someone," she said in a strained, husky voice. "His name is Jonathan. He... he has a child. They've lived here for years. With his wife, when she was still alive..." She trailed off as if she'd read something in the whore's glassy eyes. "Have you seen him? Did he... leave here in time?"

"He didn't leave, milady. But he's not here either."

Blanchette took in an audible breath. She gazed down at where her fingers wrapped around the whore's wrist almost completely. "I don't understand?"

The whore shook away Blanchette's fingers. Then she raised her hand and pointed toward a half-burnt home at the end of the road. Without another word, the woman turned away in a flourish of stained and torn rags and made off into one of the crumbling houses. They both had missed it at first glance; it was almost unrecognizable from the fire.

Rowan came to Blanchette's side and lightly touched her shoulder. He could feel her shaking under his palm. "Blanchette, I—"

"I must see," she said, her voice heavy with despair. "He was my friend. I need to know."

She whirled away from him and went after the home at the end of the road. Rowan watched as her red riding cloak fluttered behind her.

They entered the house together. She peeled back her red hood as she gazed at him, then tentatively crossed the threshold.

The first thing that hit them was the smell. It was one Rowan knew well. The scent of death. It hung heavy in the air with the musk and dirt and smoke.

He watched her expression shift as she took in what remained of the home. She ran her pale fingertips over the charred remains: the skeletal body of a table, blackened bricks of a hearth, a gaping cast-iron pot, and shreds of fabric. Blanchette shook her head, her eyes shimmering with unshed tears.

"He was good. He'd already lost so much. He risked his and his son's lives for mine—and this... this is how I've repaid him!"

"It's not your fault, Blanchette."

"I'm the queen!" Her eyes flashed, and he saw the anger visibly rising in her. "Murders and madmen roam my coast and countryside. If I can't stop them—if *we* can't stop them—no one will, and all is lost. All this death, all this heartache... it will have been for nothing. Nothing!"

Rowan stepped forward, watching as her eyes scanned the remains of the home. He gently took her hands in one of his own. "We shall set this right, Blanchette. All of it. For them," he said, motioning to the room, "for you, for us."

※

HER MIND REELED BACK to last winter. Gone were the brilliant tapestries and weavings; only ash and tattered fabrics remained. Gone was the slow-cooking stew and the aromatic scent it brought with it. The air felt thick, musty... dirty, much like her castle had smelled that night.

She felt her heartbeat high in her throat and Rowan's gentle hand on her shoulder. She wandered through, examining the remains of the tapestry below her feet. The Kingdom of Norland. Its glory had been reduced to burnt and frayed shreds. She passed under the doorway leading to the small chamber. The room she'd stayed in for nearly a fortnight after the siege.

*I survived because of Jonathan.*

The room was much as she remembered it—the bed and small wooden end table. The shuttered window looking out onto the village road. Silently, Rowan stood beside her, his head only a foot from the low ceiling.

Jonathan was in the far corner next to the bed, nestling Petyr in his lap. It looked and smelled like they'd been dead for hours. Their throats had been slit. The dagger lay directly next to Jonathan's right hand.

He'd ended their lives.

Blanchette choked back a sob. Then she collapsed to her knees, feet away from the entwined bodies. The pallor of death clung to Jonathan like a shroud. The passage of time had not been kind, and the effects of death had begun to manifest. His complexion had transformed into an ashen gray, draining away the warmth of life and replacing it with an eerie stillness.

Jonathan's lifeless eyes stared vacantly into the abyss. The sparkle that once lived within them had faded. His gaze seemed to pierce through Blanchette's as though he were peering into another world.

"He saved me. He did everything he could and risked his life to save me... yet he couldn't save his own child."

Rowan stopped beside her, carefully took her in his arms, and cradled her against him. He rocked her tenderly, side to side, like a mother might soothe a babe. Her throat tightened against a scream. In her mind's eyes, she saw her mother all over again, washed up and broken. Faintly, she recalled how it'd felt to teeter so close to madness...

She remembered rushing down the dark stairwell as the siege raged like a beast. She remembered losing herself to that terror.

She remembered almost ending her own life. And screaming until her throat seemed to rip open.

She'd forever be lost if she allowed herself to scream now.

She'd go mad. So she wept instead. She cried into Rowan's chest, cherishing the feel of his arms around her. Without him, she would have fallen to pieces.

"Oh God... Rowan... Rowan... *no...*"

"Shh," he whispered, the deep lull of his voice brushing against her temple. "I'm so sorry, Blanchette. I'm with you, darling. I'm here."

Blanchette pulled back from the warmth of his body, her cries melting away and anger rushing in their place. "Then why? Why did it happen? Who did this, Rowan? You were supposed to protect the people! What's happening to Norland? This... this cannot go on. No more."

"No more," he agreed. "This is what I fought to end all my life. It will stop, Blanchette. I'll make sure of it. *We'll* make sure of it."

*I just hope it isn't too late.* He didn't say those words, but she heard them all the same.

He bent down to the charred body and touched the bones. Closing his eyes, he said the words like a prayer, a promise, "No more."

---

## Days later

HUNTLEY ROSE from his chair as guards brought the guest inside, though his father didn't stir. The man was a warrior or knight, by the look of him.

"State your name and business," Huntley said, his voice carrying across the great hall.

"I am Sir Edrick Turner, first captain to Lord Dietrich."

"Are you, now?" Huntley turned to his father, who remained

mute and motionless, then slid forward. His hand found its way to his dagger's pommel—a golden goat head. "An envoy of Rowan Dietrich, I take it," he said with a laugh. "Looks like the wolf has sent a sheep to do his bidding."

"I am no envoy and no sheep." He tore at the wolf's head sigil clipped to his vest and tossed it to the stone ground. It echoed dully as it clattered at Huntley's feet. Huntley stepped over the ornament, his eyes fixed and unblinking on the intruder, his right hand wrapping the dagger's pommel again.

"I traveled far to speak with you. I think you'll find our goals are well aligned, my lords. Huntley, your conquests have also traveled far. I've heard much about you."

Huntley flashed a grin, then slid the dagger from its sheathe and idly spun it several times. "Sorry to say I've never heard of you."

Edrick exposed no emotion.

Huntley felt a cold sweep over him. He guessed that anger and joy would show on this man's face in equal shades. It was a terrifying prospect—not someone you'd want as an ally or enemy.

"And what do you know of me?" he asked, allowing a smile to slip across his face. He spun the dagger once, twice, three times, then shoved it back into its sheathe in a smooth movement. He placed his hands on his hips and studied the man's eyes.

*That's where the truth always dwells.*

*In the eyes.*

Edrick stood a little taller, and his lips tensed into a thin line. "I've heard you've kept the peace on our seas. That you've broken pirates before they could enter our kingdom or raid our villages. I've heard you were once one of the greatest houses. Once upon a time, you were royalty."

"We are still a great house," his lord father's voice cut in, his tone as cold as ice.

Edrick's mouth ticked at the corner. But again, no emotion showed. "Then why do you order your men to raid villages under the Wolf's banner? You slaughter those you've worked so hard to protect. That doesn't echo greatness—it screams of desperation."

Huntley felt his smile slip away. His father came beside him, his pale eyes sharp and penetrating. "You know nothing."

Edrick slid a hand into his coat and retrieved a shiny ornament —the sigil of Huntley's house.

Edrick ensnared his gaze with his own, then tossed the sigil to the ground, where it landed beside the snarling wolf's head.

"You should order your men to take greater care," Edrick said, his voice as flat as his lord father's eyes.

"Is this a threat?" Huntley replied, swiftly closing the distance between them, his hand unconsciously reaching for his dagger. "What do you want from us?"

Edrick did smile then. The very sight of it churned his stomach. He stepped forward, his eyes dropping to the dagger Huntley held in his hand. He froze in midair, and the blade came to a sudden stop.

Time seemed to stop with it.

When Edrick at last spoke, his voice was barely audible above the hearth's popping fire, yet the mettle behind his words was unmistakable.

"Lord Dietrich hides behind the walls of Winslowe Castle, his tail tucked between his legs, crushed by a victory he cannot fully appreciate. Broken beneath the burdensome weight of a crown he refuses to wear, and his head turned by a queen he can't help but love."

Huntley inhaled a breath. He turned to his father and met a gaze that betrayed itself and flashed with emotion.

*Indeed, the stone cracks.*

"I have tolerated many things during my time as Lord of Shadowmoor and the admiral of our fleet," his father finally said, his voice slow and calculated, sharp with distaste. "I've suffered a miserable castellan who thought he was a lord. I've suffered snows and famines, unruly peasants who overstepped themselves and swung by their necks for it. I've even suffered wolves. But this... I won't suffer it—this betrayal. That spineless whore took a vow before her kingdom and mine. And now she lies in bed with the wolf who tore down her house?"

Edrick said nothing for a long, anxious moment. Only the rattling wind made a sound. It whistled and moaned through the castle's cracks, fighting to break its way inside.

*There is no escaping the chill,* Huntley thought.

"I can't say that she's lain with him," Edrick answered at length. "Does that matter so much?"

"No," Huntley said quickly. "Rowan Dietrich is cunning... he's turned her head, I'm sure."

"This is true," Edrick said, "Rowan is quiet and calculated and underestimated nearly every time he makes a move. He's also making mistakes now. Dire mistakes. And I can help you," he added with a quietness Huntley didn't like.

"Why? Why are you betraying him, Sir Edrick? You've fought with him, feasted with him, traveled the country with him. Why turn your back on him now?"

"Because he turned his back on me," Edrick said, the faintest note of disdain entering his voice. "I've ridden with him, fought with him, bled for him, and helped him take Winslowe Castle. And for what? I've only received disregard and apathy. His heart has turned his mind from conquest, and now he sits on a throne without a crown, dining on the old king's larder and his daughter."

Huntley inhaled a breath. Then his fingers found their way to the hilt of his dagger, and a crooked smile came to his face. "I don't appreciate seconds," he said, that smile locked in place.

He was used to *being* second—second to his brother. Always. Now he'd be first.

They'd be kings again.

# Twenty-Two

### Days later

The Kingdom of Demrov was nestled on an island surrounded by pristine blue waters. Lush forests and gently sloping hills covered much of its inland. Many called it a close sister to France. Most natives spoke French, dressed in racy, sweeping dresses, and gluttoned themselves with lavish banquettes.

At midday, Huntley, Edrick, and a handful of guards from their respective houses landed at Demrov's port. The sun beat down and glimmered across the waters, and the air held that heady scent of saltwater that Huntley had grown to love so much.

It'd become an intricate part of himself, and for a moment, he wondered if he could ever sit on a throne without the sea air at his back, that salt-laden wind in his hair...

Anglers, merchants from all trades, and peasants gave them sideways glances as they broke through the afternoon hustle and mounted horses at the nearby inn Le Fleur.

Huntley preferred a deck beneath him rather than a temperamental mare. As he struggled with the beast, he eyed Edrick, who sharply dug his heels into his horse's side. The creature neighed in indignation. Another hard kick, and he settled down with a resigned whinny.

"Is that how you tame your women, sir?" he joked with the knight.

Edrick's face remained solemn and unchanging. "I ride them till they're broken."

Huntley waited for laughter that never came.

"Well, we best make haste if we want to arrive before dusk. Wouldn't want to be surprised by a wolf." Huntley laughed for the both of them.

※

THE SKY WAS moonless and black, slicker than ink. Huntley felt the trees pressing close as they tracked through Demrov's forest and made their way toward the castle.

Its face was Gothic, and countless buttresses and towers stabbed at the dark sky. Courtyards and corridors tied the buildings together. Collectively, the fortress was as large as a city.

The castle reminded Huntley of a crouching beast.

He pulled on his horse's reins as they approached the castle's curtain wall and grand facade. Guards walked the walls and stared down at them, their faces as hard as the stones that made up the castle. Gargoyles also perched there, far too many to count. They glared down from the buttresses as if to say *you're not welcome here*.

The wood-bolted drawbridge was down like a splintered tongue sticking out from a beast's yawning mouth. A command rang through the air, and Huntley's mount stomped her hooves as the portcullis noisily moaned and dragged open.

*This beast shall swallow us whole,* he thought, as his mare shied away. Huntley scratched her mane. Then they moved through the gate and into that beast's belly.

※

King Adam Delacroix II of Demrov received them in the throne room. It was a grand space—much more ornate than any castle he'd seen before. A dozen hearths lined the long room, each alive and flashing with fire. Ornate marble columns. Tapestries chronicling the Delacroix royal line for decades. The blazing salamander coat of arms. But most impressive was the man on the raised dais in front of it all. The imposing, barbed chair fit him like a glove. His eyes were blue ice, his hair black as the sky outside, his jaw hard and set, smooth-shaved and boasting that cleft all the ladies were so fond of.

Beside him sat a blond woman who reminded Huntley of his betrothed.

*The key to our alliance.*

Huntley bent into a bow. King Adam signaled him forward, a smile on his regal face. "Lord Peter Huntley. You may approach, *mon ami*. How were your travels?"

"Unadventurous," he said with a grin. "Uneventful. Usually, I'd complain, but my travels brought me safely to you and what I hope shall be a fruitful alliance."

"My sister, is she in danger?" the little queen exclaimed, her dark eyes sparkling with equal parts anger and what Huntley assumed was compassion.

"That I cannot speak to, Your Grace."

"I wasn't talking to you," she cut in. "I was talking to the man beside you. The man who aided this mad dog to kill my family and break my home!"

"Norland is your home?" Huntley said, leaving no room for Edrick to answer. "The crown wrapping your brow tells a different story."

The Queen of Demrov shot up from the chair. King Adam remained silent, a satisfied grin curling his full lips.

"Norland is in my blood. It shall always be my home after I've passed from this world and on to the next. Now, I command you, sir, how fares my sister? I'd received a letter from our governess," she pressed on, withdrawing said letter from her bodice.

Edrick stepped forward and held out his hand. She tentatively passed the letter over, her dark eyes hard. Huntley felt hatred there.

Edrick unrolled the parchment and flattened it across his palm. The seal was already broken.

"Aloud," King Adam commanded, his resonant voice filling the hall.

Edrick read from the parchment:

"*My dear Isadora,*

*Your sister is in grave danger. She's had everything taken from her—her family, home, integrity, and legacy. I fear if this goes on much longer, her life will be stolen as well, if not worse.*

*I helped raise you and Blanchette. It pains me to see your childhood home torn apart by a wolf—a monster—stone by stone. Send whatever help you can as soon as you can.*

*Pay no attention to any letters Blanchette sent you or shall send you in the coming days. She does so with a knife at her throat and a wolf in her bed.*

*Send help.*

*All my love, your Governess Agnes Belfort*"

The room fell silent. Only the crinkle of the parchment broke the quiet as Edrick rolled it shut.

"I'm afraid I bring more ill tidings, Your Grace," Edrick said. "Rowan Dietrich discovered your governess had sent this letter and murdered her for it."

They all saw the broken look on the queen's face. She would

have sobbed if she'd been alone. Yet her facade remained icy and resolute. She raised her chin in willful defiance. "Then let's not allow Agnes's death to be in vain." And without another word, she sat beside King Adam and nodded. Something about their silent interaction sent chills down Huntley's spine.

Huntley stepped forward. He saw the guards move toward him and ignored them. King Adam did nothing to stop him.

"I've accepted your meeting to hear from Huntley," the king said in an unmistakably kingly voice. "Not from the traitor Sir Edrick. Not from the Black Wolf's pup."

Huntley flashed his smile. It was a smile that'd landed him in more beds than he could count. "I'm glad to hear that, Your Grace. I believe our interests are closely aligned. This pup will prove invaluable to us, however. He knows Dietrich's mind inside and out and, more importantly, his heart."

*Did the Black Wolf really kill the governess?* Huntley didn't think so, but he held his tongue. Believing he was a monster was very much in his favor.

"How shall this alliance benefit Demrov?" the king asked plainly. But his face was far from plain.

"Aside from the safe recovery of the queen's sister? Lady Blanchette and I shall marry, as it's always been written—something she will be eager for once I pry her from the wolf's jaws and take back her castle. And when I sit on the throne, I mean to pay my debt back to you with generous interest. Ours will be an alliance they'll celebrate across the sea. I mean to hang your banner proudly from our masts."

"And you?" King Adam said, directing his glare past Huntley and straight at Edrick. "Why should you help us? Why sell yourself to benefit our alliance? Why trade your honor for… this? Whatever this farce is?"

Edrick bristled. Then he set his jaw and pinned the king with an unblinking stare.

"Because I don't mean to make the same mistake twice. I shan't sell myself short. I will teach you and your army how to break through the Black Wolf's defenses—and the castle's. If you agree to meet my price, that is."

He did.

---

The castle's woodshop had become a hidden sanctuary for Rowan. Surrounded by the earthy scent of aged timber, his hands deftly moved over the rough-hewn planks of oak, guiding the edge of his chisel with precision. The evening sun streamed through a high-set window, casting a warm glow over the bench, tools, and blocks of wood.

Rowan thought of Mary as he worked.

His focus remained unwavering as he carved a wooden block into a wolf. The toy was to be a symbol of strength, a reminder to Mary that she was as fierce and brave and very much *his* daughter. He envisioned her running through the halls and bailey, her golden hair flowing behind her, clutching the wolf with pride.

The scent of freshly cut wood enveloped him, mingling with the faint aroma of the linseed oil he used to polish the wood. He inhaled deeply, savoring the earthy fragrance that filled the air.

Time stood still as Rowan continued to carve, pouring his heart into every stroke. He felt an overwhelming sense of fulfillment—that he was doing something *right* and finally setting some wrongs.

As the last stroke of his chisel marked the final detail of the wolf, Rowan smiled to himself. He smoothed the edges with gentle hands and applied a final coat of linseed oil, enhancing the wood's natural grain and color.

The setting sun cast long shadows across the woodshop. Rowan carefully cradled the wooden wolf in his hands.

THAT NEXT MORNING, Blanchette dined with Mary and Rowan in the great hall. The three of them talked easily and comfortably as if they'd been brought together by something much sweeter than an almost decade-old tale of vengeance.

Blanchette quietly sipped at a rich summer wine and observed the Black Wolf. Only a few soldiers and servants filled the two dozen trestle tables. The hard lines of Rowan's face visibly eased and softened at the sound of Mary's laughter. For once, his dark, penetrating gaze seemed outward instead of within. Mary had opened like a rose to sunlight and chattered on about her years at Rochester Castle. And when Rowan and Blanchette's eyes met over the wineglasses, the air stirred and heated, and her head felt fuzzy.

And it wasn't from her drink.

"Governess Jane taught you your sums and letters, then?" Rowan asked Mary. She gave a smile that was very becoming of her, then nodded.

"Good. Then it's time you apply them here. One day, you may be the lady of Winslowe Castle."

The words caught Blanchette by surprise, but she didn't object. "Yes, Mary. It shall be great fun," she told her, "and I could use your help. Would you like that?"

"I would," she said shyly. "I'll be the lady one day?"

"When you're big," Rowan said. "Just like this." With a wolf-like growl, he swept her into his massive arms and, in a fluid movement, raised her onto his shoulders. Laughter burst from Mary, and the great hall suddenly seemed much brighter. Rowan's entire countenance changed. A luminosity came to his eyes, which Blanchette hadn't seen before.

"Run, Father! Faster! Faster!" Playfully, she kicked her little legs into his sides as if urging a pony.

He did as his daughter instructed, darting through the trestle tables and the archway, then into the bailey, where the morning sun beat down. Blanchette leaned against the castle wall, clasping her chest, as a group of Rowan's men stopped to watch the Black Wolf and the blond angel.

"Faster, faster, faster! Come on, horsey!"

Rowan lifted her in midair above his shoulders and spun her like a toy top. Mary's giggles and playful screams were music to Blanchette's ears.

Smoke found them out in the bailey and ran alongside Rowan and Mary. He gave a good-natured yelp and bounded onto his back legs. Blanchette watched from the shadows, her heart fairly pounding, as Rowan stopped, out of breath, his handsome cheeks flushed.

"This old man has to rest for a moment," he said, kneeling beside her with exaggerated gasps.

Then he withdrew a wooden wolf toy from inside his black coat. Mary beamed at the gift and hopped in place, her small arms flying around Rowan's neck and holding tight.

All the while, Blanchette clasped her heart again.

*What is happening to me?*

※

JONAS AND SIR ROYCE escorted Mary away an hour later, leaving Blanchette and Rowan alone. They returned to the king's solar with the plan to review the coffers. Instead, they found themselves contently seated and drinking wine, watching as the sun dipped into the woods beyond the window.

Blanchette sipped at her wine, willing her hand not to tremble as the candles emitted their soft murmur. It reminded Blanchette of a seductive whisper.

The grating sound of the chair scraped against the floorboards. Blanchette looked up from her wineglass as Rowan rose to his feet, the decanter and his glass in hand. She sucked in a breath as he walked down the line of empty chairs and seated himself directly beside her.

His mouth lifted into an intimate, knowing smile. Then his

fingers wrapped around her own, holding the glass, nudging it downward. He filled it with more wine, and she let out an audible sigh when he released her fingers.

A sigh of relief? Or of disappointment? Even she didn't know.

"How does it feel to hear Mary's laughter?" Blanchette asked conversationally.

Rowan smiled over his glass. "It feels like coming home."

"You told her she'd be the lady of this castle one day."

"She's your blood," he replied without hesitation.

Abruptly, he came to his feet and towered over her. She felt so small in his shadow, and a nervous flutter beat in her chest. He stepped behind the chair in a swift movement, and she felt his large hands come down on either side of her shoulders. His fingers worked their magic as they kneaded her skin with firm yet sensual caresses.

*He's so skilled with his hands.*

*What else could he do with them? How else could he help me relax and release my tension?* An image of herself lying naked in her privy on her wolfskin blanket invaded her mind. She saw his large hands kneading the flesh of her thighs, slipping higher and higher... right to that wet, achy spot between her legs.

He seemed to read her thoughts. "You're tense." His voice was in her ear, his hot breath on the back of her neck. "Do I make you nervous, Your Grace?"

She heard the challenge in the sultry tone of his voice. She breathed deeply, taking in a lungful of air for courage. "Nay, my lord. In fact... I think I make you nervous."

He released a low laugh that filled the solar and did funny things to her racing heart. His hands slid over the curves of her shoulders and gently came around her neck. She relaxed into his soothing touches, the air whistling between her parted lips.

*Kiss me again...*

"How about now, Your Grace? Are you nervous yet?"

She trembled, and she knew he felt it. His long fingers teased the back of her neck, sweeping away her hair and brushing over the sensitive skin. Just barely. Just enough to make her arch upward and into his touch. He released another husky laugh. His hands artfully moved across her nape. Down her neck, just to where her spine started.

That slight movement sent a fierce tremor through her bones. Her limbs grew heavy. She couldn't push away his touch, even if she wanted to. Her womanhood tingled as well... she could feel herself growing wet there. She pressed her thighs together, her hot legs sliding against each other from that growing wetness.

She closed her eyes and imagined him behind her—impossibly tall, his raven-black hair curling behind his ears, his broad shoulders tapering into his waist. His shirtsleeves would be partially unfastened, exposing his well-muscled chest and a sparse peppering of dark hair.

His fingers worked the flesh at the base of her neck in deep, soothing caresses. "I feel your tension, Your Grace," he mumbled in a sensual accent. *"Vous êtes nerveux, mais aussi très excité que je vous touche."* Hearing him speak French did funny things to her belly and that wet area. Her head rolled slightly to one side. His fingers took advantage of the access and kneaded the skin more persistently. She relaxed into his touches and felt the knots slowly becoming undone.

His hands made their way down her shoulders and the sides of her body. His fingers caressed the round peaks of her breasts, just barely...

She tightened against the chair as Rowan released a dark laugh that swelled the solar. "And now, Your Grace?" he asked in a teasing voice that invited her to spar. "Are you nervous yet?"

Blanchette swallowed deeply, then forced her body to relax. She began with the tips of her fingers, then her arms and shoulders and back. Her head rolled against the chair's high back. "Your Grace," she whispered, her lips smiling. "I am your queen, and you are mine to obey."

His hands stilled on the sides of her body. She stood from the chair on wobbly legs and stepped around it. His hands moved toward her body, but she stilled them in midair and gently pushed them down. "Sit, Sir Rowan," she said, her eyes never wavering from his gaze. "Your queen commands it."

The corner of his lip tilted into a smile. He gave a sharp nod, then stepped around the chair. She held her breath as he took his seat. "Now close your eyes," she said, and he did. She stepped in front of him, fascinated by how his immense body fit the chair perfectly. He filled it.

How would it feel to have him fill her? She blushed at the thought and grew wetter down there.

She imagined how her father's crown would look on his head. He'd look dangerous. Regal. Like a force to be reckoned with.

She tentatively reached out and placed her hand on his shoulder. Her fingers curled around the firm muscle, and he exhaled a long-suffering sigh.

"Does it still hurt?" she asked, alarmed and pulling her hand away. His own hand whipped out, quick as a lightning strike, and his fingers encircled her wrist. He held her like that, stilling her retreat. Then, with a sudden, delicious jerk, he brought her body forward and onto his lap.

"I'm going to kiss you again."

"*Yes...*"

Their lips crashed together in a movement neither one of them could control.

She lost herself in the feel of him, his taste, his scent. His manhood hardened against her, and she burned to relieve an ache. She moved against him urgently, feverishly, her bottom sliding across his lap. A moan ripped from her throat. She heard his breaths shorten, and he paused their kisses; his head slumped against her own. His large hands rested on her hips, and she felt as they helped guide her body. In circles. Up and down. Side to side. Right *there*, on the hard ridge of his arousal. He pushed down on her hips and lifted his own, increasing the sweet pressure between them. She ground against his hardness. Rubbing back and forth, he guided her movements with his massive hands and pressed down. Hard.

*My God...*

Something built inside her.

She was climbing a precipice... a steep pathway in which every step brought about a mounting anticipation, a tingling sensation that warmed her from the inside out.

She pressed more firmly against him until he hit the perfect spot. She tossed her head back, and Rowan's lips were on her exposed neck. She felt his teeth as he pulled his lips back into a hard moan. His hands moved from her waist and slid up her arching back slowly, sensually, *lovingly*.

He whispered her name, and his deep, rolling timbre sent her plummeting over an edge she hadn't known existed.

Waves crashed through her body. Her heart hammered against her ribs as that exquisite, tingling warmth shot through her. Her toes curled against the soles of her boots. She released an uncontrollable moan as those tremors blossomed inside her again and again.

She rode those delicious waves of pleasure as her heartbeat settled. Rowan's hands skirted up and down her back, up and down, caressing her with a sweetly comforting motion that brought tears to her eyes.

*Yes... I am lost.*

After a moment, she climbed off his lap and stood in front of him. His hazel eyes were hooded with desire, and sweat had formed in his dark hairline. Blanchette knelt before him, her legs unstable, hardly knowing what she was doing... only that she ached to return the pleasure he'd given her.

She set her palms on his knees and nudged his thighs open. Her hands trembled in time with her heart as she set her fingers on his trousers' ties. She undid them clumsily, watching as Rowan watched *her*. He'd braced his hands on either armrest, and she heard his quick intake of breath. Then she was pulling him free, moving as if in a dream. His flesh was silk and steel—

hard and massive in her small palm, encased in smooth, velvet-like skin.

"Blanchette," he breathed huskily. She recalled the wicked stories Isadora had told her years back. She lowered her lips to the tip of his manhood, then paused, her warm breaths brushing against his flesh.

"Can I kiss you here, Rowan? Would you like that?"

"You know I would," he said. His voice sounded choked like he was in pain. But when her wet mouth slid over the head, his pleasure-filled moan told her otherwise. She watched as he threw his head back and clenched his teeth. She took that as an invitation to go deeper and explore him further. And so she did. Her tongue swirled around the silky head, then down the long, throbbing shaft while her hands moved over any exposed skin.

She read his body language. The way he tensed and tightened and raised his hips, how his hands gripped the armrests, and his eyes squeezed shut. He murmured something in French; it sounded like liquid gold from his husky voice.

She went on like that for several minutes. Her hands and mouth and tongue worked in unison, drawing primitive sounds from her Black Wolf. Behind her, the sun was almost fully set, and a velvety sky hung over Norland.

Soon, her jaw ached as he seemed to grow and fill her mouth. His moans clamped off into shallow grunts, and she felt one of his large hands leave the armrest to lay on the back of her hair. He ran his fingers through her loose curls gently. Those sensual pulls on her scalp felt wonderful, commanding... she moaned lightly, and she knew he was reaching an edge. That same precipice she'd just discovered moments before.

"Please, God," he groaned. "Oh, Blanchette, darling..." She wasn't sure what he was imploring, but his bucking hips encouraged her to move faster, suck harder, grip tighter. She obeyed his command, encasing her mouth over the swollen head, her small hands working his shaft. Then she pressed her tongue along the slit and swirled it around. She felt him go taut everywhere, then expel a loud moan that she was sure the soldiers in the barracks could hear.

Hot liquid filled her mouth and throat. She felt him pulsing against her swirling tongue while his body gradually went limp.

After it was done, he swept her from the floor and into his arms. Laying her down on the bed, he kissed her forehead and held her tight, their hearts beating as one.

*Yes... we both are lost...*

---

Huntley felt very much at home, a deck below his feet, the salt-laden breeze in his hair, and an army behind him. Dozens of ships traveled in the *Nomad's* wake—carrying fighting men from the Kingdom of Demrov and into his command.

The Demrovian king and queen had been sympathetic to his cause. Almost surprisingly so. They'd sealed the alliance with minimal loss only after a fortnight of negotiations. Having Edrick at his side had colored the diplomatic visit, Huntley knew. Without the declarations of Rowan's cruel insanity, Huntley's plea would have fallen on deaf ears.

The story Edrick had told, the horror he'd described that his betrothed had undergone, had curled even Huntley's skin. And he didn't think that was possible anymore.

*She is mine,* he'd thought, the anger bubbling inside him—the parts of his father emerging as he heard more and more from Edrick.

*I shall protect her. I shall keep her safe.*

*And I shall earn my father's respect.* But Huntley didn't care about that. That was what he'd told himself each night and every morning as the sun fell and rose over the sea.

Edrick was suddenly beside him, shattering his thoughts. Damn, the man moved light on his feet, and he had an oily look about him. His eyes were hard as he stared out at the rolling waves.

Where Edrick was as still as stone, Huntley was flamboyant and restless. They were different but needed to become two sides of the same coin.

"You served with the Black Wolf for over seven years," Huntley said as he leaned on the ship's railing and ran his fingers over his dagger's hilt. "That's a long time, friend."

"I served *under* him," Edrick corrected, a bite in his voice.

"Tell me true, how deep does this change of heart go? He took a castle and fell for the princess. What is that to you? You were still his most trusted commander and adviser. You still got your glory and satiated your bloodlust."

Edrick gave a sharp bark of laughter. It sounded queer coming from him. "I've wetted my sword quite a few times, but serving Rowan quickly became a poor man's job."

"He took a castle. The capital seat. I'm sure there was more than enough plunder to go around."

"Aye, around the villages."

Huntley paused and took in a lungful of crisp air. He watched as a pair of dolphins broke through the wave's surface. They dove in and out of the water, following along the ship in an endearing and playful dance. Huntley felt a laugh escape. He turned back to Edrick, who gazed down at the dolphins, his features as hard as granite.

"Are you always so dour? God, how did Rowan stand it?" He shook his head and leaned against the railing. "What sort of monster am I up against, sir?"

"Not a monster," Edrick said. "A wolf. You shall be a plaything for him." Huntley bit back his retort. Instead, he focused on Edrick's unmoving eyes as he went on. "Sir Rowan is a proven commander—was a favorite of the king—and effortlessly won the people's hearts." A faraway look in Edrick's eyes gave Huntley a pause.

It was the first true flash of humanity he'd shown.

Where did it come from?

"A heart that's been broken, as of late," Huntley murmured,

thinking of the raids on the villages under the Black Wolf's banner.

"I promise you he's fully aware of your ruse by now. He took Winslowe Castle with the people, *for* the people. If you think they won't help him keep it, you're in for a rude awakening. You've bought time and discreetness. Nothing less and nothing more."

Huntley let go of his boisterous laughter like a loosed arrow. "Rowan Dietrich may be a wolf... but I'm a god."

"And humble too, it seems," Edrick finished with a sliver of a smile that showed a broken tooth.

"Aye, and humble," he echoed, deciding he could like this Sir Edrick.

The Greek god Pan, the shepherd of flocks, had a taste for mischief and despoiling maidens. Legend had it that Pan's very presence caused men to panic when crossing through dark woods.

*A worthy challenger of the Black Wolf, for certain.*

Yet Edrick had this look in his eyes... like he was dead behind his stare or quickly dying.

*What is this dangerous game I've joined?*

"Your pride shall be your downfall," Edrick said as if reading his thoughts.

Huntley laughed as a dolphin shot through the water and spun in midair. Edrick didn't share in his merriment. "Were you always this way, my friend?" he probed, his right hand fidgeting with his dagger's goat-head pommel.

Edrick looked at him and said nothing for a long spell. "And what way was that?"

"Were you always so somber? Always ready to turn on your lord at the nearest hint of a sweeter thing?"

Edrick remained in his sooty silence. Then, he did something altogether unexpected and broke out into laughter. It was a joyless sound totally at odds with the beautiful and bright day. "I was as loyal as a pup to its bitch. Then as loyal as a kicked dog to its master. I had risked my life for him."

"And now?"

"I stayed by Rowan Dietrich through the worst of it, when hope and glory were naught. I remained loyal to Rowan Dietrich for over seven years. Now, he is someone else. He's become a stranger. This war has turned him... and that girl, worst of all. It's not the first young girl he's turned."

Huntley studied the man's stony features. He watched as the rigid lines drew together, then visibly softened and showed something beneath. Not a full view, but just a peek.

Just enough.

*The stone cracks again.*

Huntley shook his head and turned to the sea, watching as a dolphin barreled through the waves. Absently, he reached inside his jerked and fumbled with the thimble he always kept near his heart.

"I imagine he was like a brother to you," he finally said, keeping his eyes on the ocean. He knew it'd bother Edrick if he turned his stare toward him. "Standing by his side all those years. Watching him grieve the death of his wife... following him across battlefields, through defeat and triumph, high on a promise of vengeance and a better world for all of us. I reckon he was your brother, your best friend, your confidant. It couldn't have been easy to watch him slip away, his entire purpose vanishing with him."

He heard Edrick's intake of breath. And then nothing else for several moments of quiet. "I trusted him. I helped raise him, fulfill his vengeance... but he couldn't do the same." Then, he added in a whispered afterthought, "Not for either of us."

"Either of you?" The solemn knight said nothing. The ship's deck creaked and moaned underfoot, sounding like a stirring beast. "I've never been the greatest fighter, the best at sums, healing, or even leading men into battle," Huntley said. "Hell, my father always made sure I knew that well enough. Beat it into me. My strength is in people. Knowing them, speaking to them, understanding them. Making them happy. You being here, hundreds of miles from the Black Wolf, your brother by choice... it's more than what you've said. It's personal. It reeks of it."

Edrick's eyes hardened. "What's it to you? You're getting his secrets. And with them, you'll buy back your little betrothed and her kingdom."

"Aye," he replied, unsheathing his dagger in a quick movement that sent Edrick back a step. "But at what price?"

*And can I afford it?*

"Personal, you say..." Edrick muttered as he stared out at the flat ocean that went on forever. "I never had a brother in Rowan, but I once had a son."

That perked Huntley's attention. He stilled his dagger mid-spin and turned to the weathered soldier. Edrick continued to stare into the horizon, which drank in the setting sun. Streams of red and orange spilled across the calm water, and a vibrant shaft of light divided the sky into two. They were alone on the deck. The soldiers were below and in the trailing fleet, probably eating or drinking or a little of both.

"You had a son, you say?" he asked.

"A smart lad, comely like his mother. But he ripped her open, coming into this world. The wet nurse handed me the boy as she lay dying. He started squalling, and before I could quiet him, Helene was gone. The last thing she heard was his bloody screams."

"Where is he now? Your son?"

Edrick seemed not to hear him. He placed one of his hands on the railing and gripped it tight. The shimmering sun enhanced the deep lines on his face instead of softening them. It struck Huntley as unnatural.

"I hated him. I cursed him. He took her away—clawed out of her like a demon from hell." Finally, he turned to him. Huntley felt a shiver at the black hatred he found in his eyes. "And that's where he is now if God is good. Back in hell."

They stood silently, watching the red sunlight spill across the water like blood. "Did you have any other children? Before she'd died. Or after?"

Edrick looked out to sea, his stone-hard features swathed in that red aura. "Like I'd said, Rowan could never do the same—for either of us."

Then he left.

Huntley sighed and rested his wrists on the ship's rail. Edrick had left him with more questions than answers. And the greatest one boomed inside his head, again and again. *What price must I ultimately pay for Norland? And truly... can I afford it?*

# Twenty-Three

Rowan didn't sleep that night. He was too swept up in emotion. Blanchette rested against the beat of his heart, which he found impossible to slow. He gazed down at her and watched as her lips parted. She exhaled dreamy breaths that stirred her golden hair.

Hours had passed, and he still couldn't quite believe what had transpired between them. She'd come to life in his hands. Watching and feeling her respond to him, hearing her intense climax, had brought him more pleasure than his own.

He'd never felt such a powerful release... one that extended far beyond the physical. Even his fantasies couldn't compare.

*A flesh-and-blood angel*, he thought with a smile, *and with a bit of sin in her*. A smattering of freckles peppered her turned-up nose; an endearing detail that made his heart ache a little more. The wound on her cheek had healed into a puckered ridge. It enhanced her beauty and reminded him of the warrior inside her —a soldier ready to fight and bleed for what she loved most. And it reminded him grimly of the horrors he'd brought down upon her. King Bartholomew, the queen, her brother... they were ghosts who'd never rest.

When he closed his eyes, he saw her brother's mutilated body hovering in that blackness. He saw his wife lying across the bed, soaked with blood, her beautiful dark eyes staring and seeing nothing.

He saw Edrick's disdain, and Rowan wondered if his friend had always been a monster. *I'd known him since we were boys. Had I just not seen it?*

*What else have I been blind to?*

Rowan sighed, then turned onto his side to admire Blanchette. She couldn't escape those ghosts and questions either, he knew...

Persistent knocking cut off his thoughts. He jumped from the bed and threw on his bedrobe, cursing at the banging. He didn't want Blanchette's sleep disturbed. And he certainly didn't want the castle to know she was with him.

He tossed open the door where Sir Jeremy and Sir Royce stood. They both looked restless and tired. Deep pockets hung under their eyes, and he could see the tension in their furrowed brows.

"What is it?" Rowan asked. He slipped out of the bedchamber and discreetly shut the door behind him.

"Sorry to bother you, sir, but we have urgent news," Sir Jeremy said. "News that can't wait till morning."

"Tell me."

They glanced at one another. "A Demrovian fleet was spotted off the sea, heading for our coast."

"They're coming for her," he muttered, speaking to himself.

"That's not all. Another flag was flying from the masts—a goat-head banner."

He knew the answer before he asked—but he had to hear it. "Have there been reports of Sir Edrick?"

They hesitated. Sir Royce spoke. "He was seen in Demrov, riding to the castle. We only have three days before they land."

"Then there's not a moment to stand idle. Call the council. Now."

The council came, and Rowan laid out his plans.

## Three days later

JONAS PROUDLY BARED the Black Wolf's banner as they rode out to the parley. Despite the grim circumstances, Blanchette noticed a smile on his face that he had trouble hiding. He even controlled his courser with impressive and quiet confidence.

Rowan had opposed her attendance at the meeting, but she'd insisted most passionately. After all, this was *her* home—and *her* betrothed was coming to claim *her*. She'd be damned if she simply sat by and waited helplessly in her chamber.

*Maybe I can stop the battle before it even begins.* Nausea reared inside her as they rode out under the Black Wolf banner. Only a handful of men cantered from the encampment to meet them, and the King of Demrov wasn't one of them.

Hope fled as quickly as it'd come. She knew little about her betrothed, Lord Peter Huntley—but she knew enough to understand he was a man of prickly pride and dangerous ambition. He wouldn't be easily swayed.

Reining up next to Huntley, sitting tall and straight as an arrow on his black destrier, was Sir Edrick.

That nausea resurfaced. She had to swallow it back lest she vomited all over her red riding cloak. She glanced at Rowan's expression. His face was as hard as stone. Unreadable. Determined.

She held her breath at the sight of him—the setting sunlight glinting off his armor, the way the breeze tousled his raven-black hair, and the gleam of his hazel eyes. Smoke also accompanied them. He padded alongside Shadow's hooves, his magnificent head angled low, those lantern-like eyes missing nothing.

The five of them cantered up a steep slope. Straight ahead loomed the wood, the ancient trees clustered tightly together like sentinels. To the right was the army encampment.

It was bustling. She could see soldiers sharpening their swords and weapons, mending their armor and clothes, and practicing their fighting techniques. They'd arranged makeshift tents to sleep in. Banners flapped in the breeze: gnarled elm trees, the salamanders of House Delacroix, and Huntley's eerie goat head.

Strong smells of sweat, dirt, and animal manure filled the camp. The scent of metal being worked on mixed with the aroma of cooking fires and food being prepared.

The noise level in the camp was high, with soldiers shouting and calling to each other as they prepared for battle. The clanging of swords and weapons being sharpened, the sound of horses whinnying and stomping their hooves, and the bustle of people moving about all added to the din. She heard musicians playing instruments and soldiers singing too.

Rowan, Sir Jeremy, Sir Royce, and Jonas came to a standstill. Four men met them where they stood moments later—two redheads with thinning hair who resembled twins, Sir Edrick, and a blond, handsome soldier who could only be her betrothed Huntley.

Huntley wore a crooked smile as if he was privy to a secret no one knew. He was also the first to speak.

"Ah, if it isn't the great Hellhound of Norland. So good of you to keep an eye on my fiancée." His smile grew, and he turned toward Blanchette in his destrier's saddle. "Though I've heard troubling reports," he added, now with a frown. "You massacred her family and kept her savagely as a prisoner. But what would one expect of a beast?"

"He's done no such thing." Blanchette cut in. "He—"

"No? He didn't storm your castle, bring down your family—a legacy that's endured for a thousand years?"

"*I* am my legacy. And I stand before you quite strong and well."

Huntley glanced at his men, then burst into mocking laughter. "Why, Sir Edrick, you have some explaining to do. Never the matter, that castle behind you is mine by rights, and you, my dear, are also mine."

Rowan thrust his heels into Shadow and closed the distance between them. Huntley's horse reared at the encroachment. Rowan's hand tightened and loosened into a fist. Tightened and loosened. "I've killed far bigger men than you without a scratch to show for it."

"Bigger men, but lesser." He eyed Smoke; a low, rumbling growl rustled in his throat. "What, the wolf on your banner wasn't enough?"

Blanchette took pleasure in the blatant fear in his eyes. "That wolf will happily rip your throat out," she said, sweetly returning his smile.

"Indeed? Which one?" He glared at Rowan with calm blue eyes.

"You'll find no easy conquest here. And I say *you are less* than a man," Blanchette spat. "What kind of craven slaughters a village while hiding under another's banner? I'm surprised you've shown your face at all today."

"I wouldn't have missed this for the world, love," he said to her.

Blanchette glanced at Rowan, shocked by the anger flashing in his eyes.

"What kind of man you ask? One with a mind for warcraft," Huntley said. "We've a third of our army to show for it because of your pillaging. They despise you. If you don't like the game of war, you shouldn't have played the first piece, Black Wolf."

Blanchette scanned the army encampment; her heart sank as she spotted boys dressed in rusted, mismatched armor made from flimsy leather. They laughed among themselves, oblivious to the lie and the horror that'd come at dawn. She felt the need to ride over to them, to tell them to go home, that Rowan would help them—that Huntley had deceived them terribly.

Those boys would likely die tomorrow.

"Where is the king?" she asked abruptly.

"Busy," Huntley answered with a slow smile he wore easily.

"But don't worry. I shall always make time for you, love. Should I bring your sweet sister back a message? Or, better yet, a kiss?"

"She's with you?" *My sister is here? My God, let it be true...* but he ignored her question. "You are a liar, sir. How dare you call Rowan a beast? You are worse than a beast. You're a monster and a coward. And if you think I'd ever marry you, you're also a fool."

"If I'm not mistaken, your father was fond of slaughtering villages. Your blood runs as black as mine," Huntley said with another secretive smile. "I believe we shall get along nicely. And you, Black Wolf, I believe you led many of those raids. Hung villagers for naught? Even priests? When you still flew your father's gray wolf banner? Or do I have my histories mixed up?" Blanchette saw the shame in Rowan's eyes. Huntley looked from Blanchette to Rowan, then back to Blanchette. His eyes burned into her, slipping over her like a touch. "You better come to my bed a maiden."

"Enough," Rowan cut in. His steel was borne and pointed at Huntley's throat a second later. "There's no reason innocents must die tomorrow. We can fight, you and me, right here, right now. We can end it. I already brought down one king from your house, and you're not even a king. Just a pretender."

Huntley laughed again—a dark and humorless sound. "I've heard you're one of the greatest swords around. Maybe that's true. Maybe it's not. No matter, I don't gamble, my friend. I play strategy. I play to win. I say the castle falls tomorrow. I say thousands will die. I plan on taking a couple of dozen myself." Blanchette watched as his eyes shifted between her and Rowan. His smile seemed to say *I know*. "How'd you like a wolf pelt for your wedding gift, my lady?"

"She's right. You are a coward." Rowan withdrew the sword with a grunt, his eyes seething. His words were directed at Huntley, but he fixed his eyes on Edrick.

He wheeled his horse to the side and came up in front of Edrick. His former captain neither budged nor blinked. He simply stared at Rowan.

Huntley lounged comfortably in his saddle, seeming to enjoy the tension.

*God, Rowan's stare.* It was like blades. Blanchette had never seen such naked hatred in a man's eyes. Even her mount grew uncomfortable and shifted below her.

"How is sweet Mary faring?" Edrick asked. "I'd hate for some tragedy to befall her."

"You," Rowan whispered to his old captain. "Tomorrow, I shall slay you myself. Sleep well, my friend."

And without a backward glance, Rowan broke into a gallop and rode back toward the looming castle. His cloak fluttered behind him like a pair of colossal wings, and Smoke raced at his heels—a shadow among the sunshine.

Suddenly, the fear was cold and hollow inside her.

*Oh God, I cannot endure another battle... I cannot endure losing more people I love...*

*I cannot...*

THE THRONE ROOM felt unnaturally still. Blanchette stood before the hulking chair on the third step, which separated it from the large audience chamber. The wind whipped at the walls, making the castle groan like a beast in agony.

And that wasn't so far from the truth. She'd woken disoriented and shaken, a dark premonition settling over her like a storm cloud.

Word had spread about Demrov's army; guards were whipping through the halls and endless rooms, battle gear in hand, as they readied themselves and their weapons for the coming assault.

Months ago, Blanchette would have flushed with relief at the news. But now only dread filled her.

She made her way up the next few steps until she stood on the seventh and final one. Beyond the castle walls, the wind moaned, whistling through the cracks. She glanced down at her red riding cloak. She closed her eyes and saw her grandmother knitting in bed, her privy's hearth alive and flashing. Blanchette felt the tears sting her eyes, but she stayed them. Grandmother Sybil wouldn't want her to cry anymore. Not for her. Maybe for her country, but not for her memory.

Blanchette released a shaky breath. Then she grazed her fingertips over the carved arms of the throne.

*My throne.*

She saw her father sitting there, looking every bit like a king. Proud. Arrogant. Dangerous. Highborn ladies and men would have filled the room. She craned her head back to look into the gallery, where lutes and ladies in their fanciest frocks lounged. Laughter and flowing ale had swelled the hall, while in the village nearby, the peasants had starved themselves into their graves.

She felt Rowan's presence before she heard him. Her skin prickled, and the very air shifted. She turned away from her family's throne and gazed at him. He was at the bottom of the stairs, his longsword at his side, dressed in chain mail and boiled leather. His eyes held a haunted and faraway look.

"I wrote to Isadora months ago," she said, her voice flat despite her rattled nerves. "I begged for her help. I told her I was a prisoner in our home, held by a monster who'd stolen everything we'd held dear." She smiled softly. Rowan sighed and made his way up the steps, his heavy boots echoing in the colossal room.

"It's okay. Blanchette..."

"Shh," she whispered. "I know." She reached out her hand and laid it on his stubbly cheek. He dipped into her touch, a long breath escaping his lips and brushing her skin. He wrapped his hand around hers, then kissed the center of her palm.

"Months ago, such news would have come as a breath of relief... but everything has changed. I can't bear the thought of losing you, Rowan. I cannot."

He climbed the last few steps and closed the distance between them. "You shall never lose me."

"Do... do you mean to surrender? Perhaps there can be peace. A negotiation. Something. Anything. So many innocent lives..."

She heard the desperation in her own voice and winced. A vengeful army was here for them, carried by Norland's sea. The chance for peace was slim, the likelihood of bloodshed a grave certainty.

*How much of this is my fault? Because of the letter I wrote to Isadora...*

Rowan's gaze flitted past her and planted on the throne. She watched the tension tighten his brow, and his lips sulked at the corners. "If I surrender," he said, his voice slow and deep, swelling the room with its dark and resonant brilliance. She felt it move through her too. "If I surrender, I surrender *you*. Everything I've fought for. Everything I've fought *against*." He stepped closer and dropped his head so his hot breaths moved against her cheeks. She caught the scent of ale. "You've seen what Huntley's done. I must stop him."

"Huntley," she said, a wave of sudden nausea overcoming her. "My betrothed... I should have seen this."

"Him, yes—and Edrick. *I* should have seen it. I'm a fool, and I've failed you. And I'll be damned if I allow either of them to take you from me."

Blanchette swallowed. She felt lightheaded. "Will it ever end? My father brought so much bloodshed... the siege... and now this. Isn't there a better way?"

※

SHE LOOKED small and fragile inside the immense throne room. *She could get lost here,* Rowan thought, his heart beating heavily in his chest. He drew toward her, like a moth to a flame, watching as her red lips parted at his approach. Her golden curls were loose and full, tumbling down her slender shoulders. He gazed down at her, and his hands came to the side of her face. She dipped into his left palm, rubbing the scar against his skin, the soft wisp of her breaths coming shallow and fast.

He swallowed hard, all his armor shedding off him. A harsh wind slapped against the castle's stones and sent a loud bellow through the hall. And beyond that, he heard the din of a castle readying itself for the assault.

"Would you have me, Blanchette? This is all yours. It shall always be *yours*. Could I sit beside you? Would you fight with me for Norland—for your people?"

Her eyes fluttered open and lifted to his gaze. His insides heated at the fire in her stare. It was forward. Sensual. *Loving*. Her face lifted from his palm, and a smile claimed her lips. "When this is all over, I will marry you in front of the kingdom. I—"

He covered his mouth with hers. She opened for him, and her slim arms snaked around his waist. He felt as she shifted on her heels and nearly lost her balance. He wrapped his right arm tightly around her and held her toward the refuge of his chest. He felt her breasts straining against him, her mouth moving with his, the feel of her fingers raking at his back... digging, searching, looking for something with a raw desperation he easily matched. Her hand smoothed up and down his spine, up and down, and she moaned into his mouth.

SHE TASTED THE ALE, tasted Rowan, the fabled Black Wolf of Norland. The area between her thighs grew hot and wet as she remembered the pleasure he'd brought her and the taste of him in her mouth.

How would it feel to give herself to him completely?

She felt as his firm hands rode up the sides of her body and brushed the edges of her breasts. She shivered in his arms and heard a breath of wind sighing through the castle's crevices. His hands entwined in her curls and tugged gently. She moaned as her head bowed back. His mouth moved away from her lips and down her throat. He kissed her sensitive skin, his tongue drawing invisible circles, his hot, sweet breath moving against her like a summer breeze.

She jerked back, breaking away from his mouth and touch. He breathed hard, and his hazel eyes seemed to hold a fire all their own.

"What if something happens to you? Or Mary?" she whispered. She could barely hear herself over the wind and the castle's drafts. "I couldn't bear it, Rowan... I couldn't."

Rowan gazed at her, his eyes softening. "That shall never happen. I am yours, and you are mine."

*Aye, but for how much longer?*

### The next day

HER HOME WAS ALIVE, and a battle fever pumped through its veins.

Every corner stirred with the sounds of men readying themselves for battle. She couldn't recall when the halls and wards had looked so alive. She raced across the bridge connecting one tower to another, the din of the castle flooding the bailey like a restless ocean. Hollers and barking hounds and the sound of clanging steel were everywhere.

She stopped in the middle of the bridge as she caught sight of Rowan in the training yard. He stood as still as a statue, a mailed fist planted on either hip, his eyes fixed on the line of soldiers nocking and loosing their arrows at the target butts.

*The calm in the eye of a storm.*

The arrow shafts cut through the sky with soft hisses. The bridge rocked beneath her, jolting her from an inward trance as three soldiers bounded across. They discussed where they thought the army would first attack—at which gate, with how many men, and what sort of weapons.

But it sounded all wrong.

She turned toward them in a flurry of skirts and her red cloak. "They won't attack the West Gate," she said, causing the men to stop in mid-stride. "It's much too strong, and right below is a row of murder holes. They'll attack the East Postern Gate if they know anything about the castle. It's the weakest by far and away from the core defenses."

The men shared glances, then ducked into shallow bows. "Aye, Your Grace, we'll inform Sir Dietrich."

"See that you do." She moved past them in a swish of red fabric, her heart thrumming. A nervous excitement—an exhilaration—inflated her. This was her chance to defend her home and people, to protect all she cared about and put her life on the line for them if needed.

Her father had called it battle fever.

Blanchette called it keeping a promise. She reached inside her cloak and gripped Governess Agnes's cross, which hung over her heart.

"I shall inform him myself," she finished in a clipped tone, though they were out of earshot now. *Mother and Grandmother would be proud.* That brought a sad smile to her face. She felt it pull at her scar, and her exhilaration turned into steely determination.

This was her moment.

---

BLANCHETTE LOOKED OUT HER WINDOW, watching the trees in the silent dusk. Movement stirred them... or was it just her imagination? She held her breath as a dark figure slipped into the clearing. She stepped closer to the window until her nose brushed against the glass.

A wolf...

*Smoke returning from his hunt.*

Suddenly, she stood in Rowan's shadow. His large hands came

to rest upon her shoulders. She exhaled a small breath and watched as it steamed the glass. The world outside the castle was clouded and hidden for a moment, and only Blanchette and Rowan Dietrich existed.

He gently rotated her body so she spun in his arms and her chest aligned with his. She tilted her head back and met his beautiful eyes.

"Blanchette..." His head dipped forward until his chin pressed against his muscular chest. He enveloped her in the circle of his arms.

"Blanchette," he said again. She felt the heat of her own name gliding across her skin. One hand grasped her wrist. He lowered her hand away from her cheek and kissed her knuckles. She shuddered against him, her heart beating against her ribs like a battering ram.

Then Smoke was there with them, his muzzle and snout bright red from his hunt. He sat silently beside his master, his sleek fur glistening in the torchlight. His golden eyes shone brightly, seeming to reflect the very light. He held his head high, his ears perked and alert to the bustling castle, taking in its surroundings with a keen gaze. He was truly a magnificent creature, fierce and majestic.

*Just like Rowan.*

She'd never get used to that wolf. Not if he stalked these corridors for a thousand years.

Rowan wore his wolf armor, the snarling helm clasped tightly in his left hand. His other hand lay on the pommel of his sword.

"Listen to me. Should anything happen—should the castle fall... I want you to flee through the tunnels. I shall have guards there waiting. Do you understand me, Blanchette?" he asked with a rough shake of her wrist that jarred her from her trance. "You will vacate this place and flee with Mary. My men will take you somewhere safe. You will live and grow old. You will survive all of this. Promise me."

"I... I promise."

She watched as Rowan shifted uncomfortably, his hand planted on the pommel of his sword. He traced the snarling wolf head with long, nimble fingers.

"When you told me about your lady-in-waiting... about what Edrick did to her... I didn't believe you. I didn't believe he was capable of such horror." He reached out and wrapped his large fingers around her chin. He grazed her skin tenderly, his hazel eyes alive with a torrent of emotion. "I'm sorry, Blanchette. About everything you've endured."

She let the silence settle all around them. Her gaze tracked across her dimly lit chamber as if looking into her past. She crossed the room, her steps as quick and frantic as her beating heart. She came to her bureau, where an engraved glass hung above it. Her finger shook as she traced her family's crest.

"My queen—"

"Queen... I was never born to be a queen. I wasn't born to sit on a throne. I was born to be the lady of some noble lord, in some castle, in some faraway land. Willem—he was born to be the king of Norland. He was bred for it. He learned to ride when he could barely walk. Learned to shoot arrows. He played with swords and shields, and I hunted the countryside for herbs and flowers. I hunted the countryside for myself," she confessed with a frown. "I learned as much as I could. I armed myself with letters and numbers and as much knowledge as possible while Willem took up sword and shield." She turned to Rowan.

"As I got older, I'd lain awake... God." Her words choked off into a sob. She placed her fist to her mouth. Rowan came beside her, his hand curled about her shoulder in a gentle and reassuring touch. "I would lay awake so many nights, Rowan... wishing it were *me*. And when I dreamt, it was me. I sat on the throne, and Willem lay under me in the crypt." She felt tears slide down her cheeks. "And you know what? In my dream, I was glad. I was glad he was dead and out of my way. I hadn't dreamt of that for years. Not until months ago. But it's different now. Now when I dream, I sit in the throne room—alone and in the dark. And down below me, I feel something stirring. Not Willem tossing in his grave... but a beast stalking the crypt. Then I hear its howl and realize—" She took Rowan's hands tightly and squeezed his fingers. "I realize it's not just howling—it's crying. And I am too. *I am crying!*" She brought his hand to her tearstained cheek. "Oh God..."

"Listen, Blanchette. For countless years, I sought vengeance. Every move, every march, and every battle plan were all extensions of my anger. But what was right? I thought I knew, but I was blind. Stupid, even. It's you. *You* are right. You are everything right with this kingdom... with this world. I've been fighting to set things right, but I was looking the wrong way. I'd fought for what I'd lost—what had been stolen. But now... now, Blanchette, none of that matters."

He brought her hands to his lips and sweetly kissed her knuckles. His eyes fell shut, and he exhaled a long breath. Beyond the walls of her castle, she heard the blacksmith's hammer striking the anvil and the hollering of men.

The hour was fast approaching.

"I am yours, Rowan," she said, her voice as thin as the hope she felt, "as you are mine."

*"Je suis à vous. Pour toujours et à jamais,"* he repeated, his voice heavy with palpable emotion. "Blanchette... I love you and wish to tell you that with every waking breath I have left. I will defend Norland tonight with everything in me. And you... you will rule as you were meant to rule. I shall stand by your side, now and always."

Their gazes came together in a powerful hold. Rowan took Blanchette's hand in his. He pressed his lips gently against hers, and she responded with passion.

Their lips moved together in perfect synchronization as if they had been made for each other. Rowan wrapped his arms around Blanchette, pulling her close and deepening the kiss.

Blanchette could feel her heart racing as she kissed Rowan again and again. She ran her fingers through his jet-black hair, feeling the soft, curling strands between her fingers. His hazel eyes glittered in the candlelight and drew her in. His lips came to her neck passionately, tenderly, kissing a line down her throat. A sigh fled her lungs, and as the sound of battle blossomed beyond the walls, she felt the tears slip from her eyes again.

Minutes later, they stood together and gazed out the window, where a brilliant red-and-gold sunset blossomed. She smiled as he embraced her from behind. "Isadora often said a sunset is like the brushstrokes of God. You'll never again see the same painting again, even if you stared at the same sky, night after night, for the rest of your life. That sunset is there for just moments, and then it's gone forever."

She felt Rowan hold her tighter as if that movement would prevent them from ever losing each other. "That cave…" She rotated in his arms and whispered against his lips. "Let's go back there."

He gazed into her eyes and seemed to bury himself there. "That's my dream, Blanchette. That's what I've been chasing these ten years."

"But we found the cave too late. Didn't we, Rowan?"

The din of the coming battle filled the silence. It spoke for both of them.

THE CASTLE TREMBLED as yelling and stampeding men echoed through the stone walls. Rowan stood at the wooden door to Mary's chamber. The candlelight flickered, casting dancing shadows across the room. The soft, golden curls of his daughter's hair framed her innocent face as she looked up at him from the bed, her big blue eyes filled with fear.

"Are you going to fight those bad men?" Mary asked, her voice quivering.

Rowan knelt before her, his rugged, battle-hardened hands

gently cupping her cheeks. "Yes, Mary," he whispered, his voice heavy with emotion. "I must. I must protect you and our home."

Tears welled in her eyes as she threw her tiny arms around her father's neck, hugging him tightly. Rowan held her close, inhaling the scent of her golden hair. He savored the warmth of her embrace, which contrasted with the icy fear gripping his heart.

Two guards, clad in armor and bearing swords, stood nearby and at the ready, their faces grim but determined. Rowan nodded to them, trusting them with his most precious treasure. "You will keep her safe?"

The guards exchanged a solemn glance. "We swear by our honor."

Rowan kissed Mary's forehead, his lips lingering there as he murmured, "You're my brave girl, Mary. Remember: courage cannot exist without fear. You're a wolf, like me. Never forget that."

"I won't. I love you, Father."

Rowan crossed the chamber, where he found the wooden wolf toy. He pressed it between her palms and held them together tightly. He watched as she clasped the wood and smiled up at him. "Keep him with you, near to your heart," he whispered. "He'll watch over you while I cannot."

As he joined the fray beyond the castle walls with Smoke at his side, Rowan carried the image of his daughter with him.

*Aye... she's a wolf. Just like me.*

# Twenty-Four

Blanchette watched the crush of activity from her father's solar window.

A solitary candle burned on the large oak desk, casting a ring of shivering light. Blanchette nearly jumped out of her skin when she heard the door creak open. She whirled around in the high-back chair and saw a massive outline in the doorframe.

A steel wolf.

The meager light transformed Rowan into a plate-covered silhouette. The sight chilled her to the bone. She felt like she stood in the presence of a stranger... or some dangerous, wild beast.

As if reading her thoughts, she watched with bated breath as he lifted the helm from his head and placed it on her father's table. The sound of the crude metal hitting the wood blasted through her. Behind him stood his squire, Jonas, the red-haired lad she'd often spotted training in the yard with him.

Rowan came before her, slow and steady, the candlelight shining off his chest plate.

"Leave us, Jonas," Rowan murmured. As Jonas quit the solar, Blanchette made out two orbs in the doorway: Smoke's eyes. The wolf silently padded inside the room, his head low, moving as quiet as a shadow.

The look in Rowan's eyes commanded her to stand. She dared not disobey. Blanchette came to her feet and steadied herself with her palm on the desk's surface. She anchored herself, focusing on the feel of the grains below her skin and the slight swerves in the wood. Here there was an indentation. There a nick. She closed her eyes and imagined her father placing the dagger in the wood, allowing it to stand upright in the morning sun as he mused over a heap of ledgers.

She felt the exquisite slide of Rowan's fingers grazing her cheek. Keeping her eyes shut, she dipped into his touch and sighed. He stepped closer, and his hard plate metal brushed against her. Then his large hands were on her hips, and he rotated her away from him so she faced the window.

He swept her curls aside and pressed his lips to her nape. A shiver rushed through her, and she grew hot and wet between her legs. His lips snaked a damp line across her neck. Her knees turned weak, and she felt herself falling back into Rowan. He steadied her with a low, rolling laugh that reverberated against her spine.

Emotion welled up inside her. "Loving you is not easy, Rowan Dietrich. It's not simple. But I do love you in my own way... so very much."

Rowan rotated her in his arms so they stood face-to-face. He kissed her scarred cheek ever so gently. His lips caressed her skin. Just below her ear. Her chin. She savored his closeness and the way he felt against her. "My darling Blanchette," he whispered against her skin, his hands running down her sides and to her hips. "I wouldn't have it any other way. I want your love, and I want it in your way."

As Rowan held her, she glanced toward the doorway, where Smoke stood like a silent sentinel.

ROWAN SPRINTED the length of the eastern battlements. Dejectedly, he yelled orders to a soldier, his voice booming inside his helm.

Lightning split the night. It had snuck up on the castle, seemingly from nowhere. Seven heartbeats later, the sound of thunder rolled while fat drops of rain fell on the helm.

An ill omen, one that sent an unexpected shiver down his spine.

Another flash lit up the bailey.

*One, two, three, four, five, six, seven,* he counted, welcoming the thunder again.

Where was Blanchette? His mind raced, and he lost his focus. *This will be the end of everything if I don't get ahold of myself,* he inwardly commanded. He was slipping away fast, falling between a hairline crack he'd never escape.

Indeed, he'd barely seen it coming. Now that crack was opening up to swallow him whole.

He continued to yell orders and adjust his men methodically, but he wasn't really there.

*This isn't who I am anymore.*

His mind raced back to all those months ago. The ghostly sound of the portcullis lifted like a beast's yawning mouth. He saw himself and his men whipping through the line of trees and into the castle.

Rowan patrolled the battlements until the sun sank below the horizon and darkness fell upon Norland. Scouts rushed to him and reported the movement of the Demorvian army. He kept walking until the night grew cold and quiet, and his men sleepily manned their posts. Calluses and blisters formed on his feet, and his legs felt like lead. He continued to walk the battlements as that quiet ruptured. The melodic sound of drums awakened the world, and his own men sounded a war horn to get every fighter to their feet.

*Awoooooo,* the horn rudely blared, blasting the castle awake.

He stood at the balustrade and watched. The forest stirred as if a gigantic monster were moving through its trees. And that wasn't far from the truth. They were coming. And they were bringing catapults and scorpions in tow.

They were upon them.

The giant trees swayed, ghostlike, as the army pounded through them and broke into the clearing. He saw himself at the head of the army for half a heartbeat, dressed as he was now... the Black Wolf of Norland at the head of his pack. A pack of purebreds and mongrels alike. He remembered what Blanchette had said about those trees standing guard. How her mother had spun a pretty tale about them being silent sentries, and so long as they stood tall, no harm could breach the castle.

But it was all a lie. King Bartholomew had built his kingdom out of lies and upon the backs of corpses. So many corpses. They could have filled that entire forest with all the nooses they'd hung from.

His men were behind the gates, ready to defend the castle. Rowan walked the battlements to get a clear view of the bridge and portcullis. Both were secure. *But for how much longer?* It'd be a bittersweet revenge, no doubt. When it came to vengeance, he considered himself somewhat of an expert.

The sky was restless, with clouds racing in from east to west in a mad flurry. They looked heavy and ominous—out of place on a brisk spring evening. Rowan wasn't a superstitious man, yet he felt a mounting dread.

It was an omen. Every governess, every priest, every holy man would have said so. He might have crossed himself if he'd been a sacred man. Instead, he turned away from the sky in a flurry of well-oiled chain mail and plate, then stalked across the bridge toward the rookery tower. Idly, he thought of all the pigeons Edrick had killed... how no birds would fly on the morrow, carrying words of his victory or defeat.

Dozens of men gathered inside the inner bailey and looked up at him expectantly. Sir Jeremy. Sir Royce. And Jonas, he felt his gaze most of all. Rowan sighed against his visor, the beat of his heart thundering in his ears. He removed his wolf's helm and shook out his hair, his eyes searching the sea of faces below. If he thought too hard about them—about Jonas or the servants he'd drunk with—he'd drown in his fear.

※

THE ARMY BROKE APART like a horseshoe and raced toward the East Postern Gate. Just like Blanchette said they would. Rowan rushed across the battlements, his helm under his arm, and yelled to the line of men in his most commanding voice, "Rain fire on them!" Archers dipped their arrows in flaming braziers and set the spearheads aglow.

His order echoed down the line. "Nock. Draw. Loose!" The soft hiss of arrows cut through the air. Rowan watched as they bowed through the darkness like shooting stars. The din of screams swelled the walls, and he watched as men collapsed to their knees and lay dead or dying.

"Knock. Draw. Loose. Knock. Draw. Loose. Knock, draw, loose." Screams. So many screams. And so it went on like that, and time seemed to stand still. "Knock. Draw. Loose." Screams. They were the only three words that existed during that time. "Knock. Draw. Loose." Screams. His life became measured in knocks and draws and looses and screams.

The familiar rush of battle fever livened in his veins. Defenders poured hot oil through the murder holes and rained fire from the arrow slits. The screams were palpably close now—he could smell the burning flesh of men dying. The air was rancid with it. His pulse jetted, his veins on fire, and his flesh tingled. Smoke remained at his side, a comfort, a part of him, his comrade.

Thirty minutes later, as he continued yelling commands down the line and setting the night aglow, he watched as a dozen men rushed toward the East Postern Gate under the cover of a wooden turtle. They clasped a large battering ram between them.

Rowan pressed against the balustrade and struggled to make out the faces.

*I mean to make out a single face,* his mind corrected. That of Edrick's. But most of the soldiers were well-armored and visored, and the darkness concealed any bare features like a cloak.

*I can hide, too,* he thought with a wolfish grin that a nearby comrade visibly shrank away from. *I have my own escape... my own mask.*

Rowan Dietrich slipped into his wolf helm—into his wolf's skin—and snapped the visor shut.

He was no longer Rowan Dietrich. In that single movement, he'd become the Black Wolf of Norland.

---

THE FIRST LADDER went up about an hour after the siege began. "Rain hell on them!"

Soldiers flanked the ladder and heaved rocks down the wall. He watched as it hit one of the climbing soldiers and smashed his head in like a melon. The next soldier took the rock in his chest. He tumbled to the ground and broke into pieces on the stones below.

Second and third ladders shot up from the darkness as they scaled the walls. Rowan raced to the third one as men swarmed up the rungs. An unlucky bastard reached the top, only to find Rowan's sword through his chest and out his back. Rowan pulled the blade free, then slammed his fist into the man's bleeding chest, sending him reeling into the night. He, too, splattered on the ground below.

Heavily armored soldiers marched toward the castle gates, their faces set with determination. The clanking of their armor and the pounding of their boots echoed off the castle walls, and the smell of sweat and fear hung heavy in the air. At the front of the group was a massive wooden structure shaped like a giant tree trunk with iron bands around it—a battering ram. The soldiers behind the ram hefted it back, then swung it forward with all their power, slamming it into the gates with a thunderous crash.

The gates shuddered but held firm.

Lightning illuminated the battlements and momentarily set the world ablaze. *One, two, three, four, five.* Rolling thunder filled the world and echoed inside Rowan's helm. He walked the battlements, his sword hanging at his side, blood dripping from its tip, his fingers tight and white-knuckled around the pommel.

"Oil! Rain the oil on them!" The defenders on the castle walls poured boiling oil and hot sand down onto the attackers. A few soldiers wielding the ram were hit and cried out in agony, but others took their place and continued the assault. The smell of burned flesh filled the air, mixing with the acrid smell of smoke from the oil. The ram swung back and forth, crashing into the gates again and again. Each impact sent a shock wave through the castle walls, and small cracks appeared in the wood.

"Repair! Repair, now!"

Defenders frantically tried to repair the gates, using boards and nails to patch the damage. The repetitive clanging of the battering ram echoed in the night. Rowan scaled the battlements, signaling to a handful of men as he did so. Sir Jeremy and Jonas stuck close to his side.

"They're going to get through," Rowan said under his breath, speaking to himself. "Come with me. It's time."

*For Blanchette Winslowe.*

They crossed the bailey, moving across one of the connecting bridges like shadows. Smoke padded along at Rowan's heels. The wolf's eyes were as bright as stars, and his breath misted the air. He curled his fingers in the scruff of his collar.

Another lightning strike, followed by a deafening thunderclap.

*Stay with me, my loyal friend,* he thought as the battle screamed through the night. Rowan, Smoke, and his comrades marched down the spiral staircase single file. The stairs never seemed to end, and the walls shook with the force of the battle.

They crossed the bailey and halted before the postern gate. It hid in the wall and was wide enough for only three men to ride through abreast. Rowan withdrew his sword and held it up to the wavering torchlight that glittered from the walls. The repetitive crash of the battering ram shook the castle like thunder. Fat raindrops fell from the sky and pattered loudly against his helm.

"They're going to bust through," Jonas said in a choked voice.

"Then let's push them back. Do you hear me?" More men gathered around him. He looked down at their eager faces, the fear plain in their eyes. He gazed beyond the castle walls to the edge of the woods. The din of the battle and the battering ram's crash seemed to fade away. Rowan removed his helm so he could look his men in their faces, person to person. He raised his voice, letting it ring off the stone walls. Faces he knew well popped out to him in the crowd. Beside him, Jonas stood silent and straight as an arrow, his hand braced on his pommel. "Listen, my friends, listen. You've fought with me. You came with me to Winslowe Castle to tear down a tyrant who cared nothing for any of us. Now, the enemy lies before us, a threat to all our freedoms. But it shall not deter us, for we are the defenders of justice and righteousness. We are the protectors of our homes and families. We are the ones who will stand tall and fight.

"So let us march forth with all our strength and courage. Let our swords and shields ring out with determination.

"Let us emerge victorious, knowing we have done all we can to defend what we hold dear. Our wives and children. Everything. This is our purpose and calling. And we shall not falter but will rise and triumph over all that stands in our way!"

A unified chant rose around him. *Black Wolf! Black Wolf! Black Wolf!*

"With me, men!" he yelled, replacing his helm, his longsword lifted overhead and glinting. He saw Blanchette standing in the battlements, scaling the walls in her little red riding hood. But he knew he dominated the scene. The Black Wolf of Norland, stalking through the inner ward—not running, never running, always taking his sweet time.

His longsword was not a sword at all but just an extension of his arm and hand. Smoke was an extension of him, too, slamming bodily into his enemies and taking out their throats with a painstaking bloodlust. Rowan lifted his visor. Anger brewed inside him, a madness and thirst for *red* as he came full circle, exacting a vengeance he'd been after for over seven years...

*When the blood has been drawn, when all is said and done, what is left?*

He looked up and straight into a murder hole. A rope—a noose—shot through the hole and swayed in midair. That noose was wound around a neck, whose body swayed eerily in the castle's dusky gloom.

Torchlight cast eerie shadows on the face. It was a woman. Her features contorted. Now, he saw a young peasant, his vacant eyes seeing nothing. He saw his wife, blood spilling from her open neck. He saw Mary Dietrich, still alive and squirming at the end of the rope.

He saw Blanchette, her mouth agape in a silent scream, the scar on her cheek pulling tight.

He blinked, and then they all vanished into the shadows. He stepped away from the murder hole just in time—just as hot oil rained through and turned a man's face to wax.

Rowan straggled back, momentarily shaken, and inhaled a deep breath.

*Get yourself together. Get yourself together, or die and lose everything.*

He looked around again and found that Smoke had vanished from his side. A shudder coursed through him, a dark premonition woken by his sudden absence.

He found his bearings in time to stop a chain mace from taking off his head. The ugly flail swung inches from his face; he'd have felt the air against his cheeks if he hadn't had his helm. He dodged backward almost a second too late. The well-armored soldier advanced, but Rowan skirted to the sky and ducked, allowing the flail to swing. Rowan unsheathed his dagger, fast as a lightning strike, and plunged the fine point through the soldier's chain mail and into his gut. He died at the end of the blade. Rowan withdrew the dagger with a war cry and sheathed it again, the battle fever setting fire to his veins.

The dance began. Uppercut, undercut, jab, parry, slash, sidestep. Soldiers broke beneath his blade left and right.

Rain and the sounds of battle clogged the air. The clashing of swords and the cries of men fighting for their lives. Screams of the dying. Vain prayers and curses. The din crashed together in a dizzying crescendo. Lightning flashed, and the thunder growled like a beast.

An axe came swinging at Rowan, seemingly out of nowhere. Smoke hurdled through and tackled the man with a fierce yelp. He ripped out his throat, flesh and blood filling his mouth. "To me, Smoke," Rowan yelled, and the Black Wolf battled on.

# Twenty-Five

She watched the mayhem from the battlements. Her breath held tight in her throat as the battering ram rocked the castle. Except it wasn't a ram at all. It was a twisted goat's head.

*Huntley's sigil.*

The beam was mounted on a frame and suspended by ropes. A dozen men swung the battering ram back and forth, delivering powerful blows to the Eastern Gate.

Terror cut through her like a knife. She grasped at the material of her red riding cloak and watched the mist of her breath in the air.

Suddenly, she knew where she was meant to be... what she was meant to do.

---

She ventured into the cold of her family's crypt. There, she made out a glow pulsing within the dark. Her steps slowed, and she descended the stairwell, where the air volleyed toward her. She felt like she'd crossed into a dream... as if she were sleepwalking and would soon awake in bed. Except she'd been ten years old again, her family would be alive, her father the king, her brother still next in line for the crown.

Her breath caught. Her steps sent vibrations through the very foundations of the crypt.

"Hello?" Her voice echoed within the darkness. In the distance, the sounds of screaming men and clanging steel filled the world. "Hello," she asked of the darkness again, this time just to break it. She took a few more steps, pacing toward that light. She felt the hairs on her neck stand on end.

"Blanchette." At first, she thought she was seeing a ghost. The figure held a candle and was robed in a plush, samite coat. Its fabric was a pure white embroidered with the salamanders and gold flames of House Delacroix. The hood was pulled over her face, and Blanchette watched as the light illuminated her sister's porcelain features and the pink tip of her nose.

"I... I don't believe it."

"Believe it, Sister," she replied, tossing back her furry hood in an elegant movement that she remembered so well. Her dark eyes shone within the candle's light.

Blanchette reeled forward with a cry of disbelief and thrust her arms around her sister's shoulders.

"Careful, Your Grace, careful," she whispered, angling the candle away from the two of them.

Blanchette felt something inside her snap; something she hadn't known was on the verge of breaking. She buried her face in her sister's warm coat and sobbed. Her entire body shook with her cries, and she felt something tight slowly unwind inside her heart. She felt like she could breathe again.

"Oh, my sweet sister, shhh," she murmured, ever the tender heart. "Your cheek." Isadora dabbed at the raised scar.

"It's nothing. Really." Isadora wriggled free of Blanchette, set the candle down on a nearby altar, and held her at arm's length. Blanchette glanced at the statues beside them: Willem, Father, Mother. "That's where my real pain lies. They were taken from us far too soon, Isadora."

Isadora shook her head, her tears shimmering. "I haven't seen them for years. What I would give to speak with Mother once more."

Blanchette softly smiled. "Down here, they can hear us, you know. Mother and Governess Agnes always said that. You can still speak to her. Willem too."

Isadora's eyes turned to cold ice. "He shall pay for this. You *are* the queen now, Blanchette. Adam's army shall slay the Black Wolf. I promise you."

Blanchette felt her skin flush. "No, you don't understand. It's not what it looks like. He's... not the monster I thought he was."

"But your letter? And Governess Agnes's letter?"

"I sent that before I learned many hard truths. What do you mean? Governess Agnes wrote to you?"

Her hands slid away from Blanchette's shoulders. She dug inside her cloak and withdrew a piece of parchment.

She handed it to Blanchette while the din of battle and thunder bellowed above them. Blanchette carefully unrolled the parchment, her hands quaking as she felt her sister's eyes on her.

She shook her head, feeling the wet slide of a tear tracking her cheek. Hastily, she wiped it away with her wrist. "It's her hand, but not her words. She must have been threatened and forced to write this. She knew. She saw, and she learned what Rowan was really like. And she was murdered for it."

Her sister smiled softly, her eyes glittering in the candlelight. "Yes? And what is he like?"

Blanchette exhaled a long breath and rolled the parchment with clumsy fingers. After a moment of silence, gazing into the dark hollows of the crypt, she met her sister's eyes again. "He is good. He is good to me, good to the people of Norland. He is everything our father was not."

Isadora remained as silent as the crypt in which they stood. Finally, she shook her head, her sweet features drawn together in a mask of horror. "How can you say that? He's bewitched you,

Blanchette! That monster massacred our family. Burned our villages. He—"

"No, you don't understand. That wasn't him. It was Peter Huntley, my betrothed. And I know it... it sounds all wrong. I know it so well. I loved Willem and Mother and our Governess Agnes... God, part of me died that night. But it's more complicated than all that. You must trust me."

Her sister scoffed, looking at her as if she'd gone mad.

*And maybe I have.* She recalled that night—how she'd screamed until her throat seemed to rip itself open, how she cried until her eyes were raw wounds.

She'd thought she'd lost her sanity then.

It had come back to her, though, like the senses do when waking from a horrific dream.

"Why are you here? You've put yourself in grave danger," she finally asked, her voice a tentative whisper that filled the crypt.

"I was quite safe. I had a wheelhouse and was well protected... I knew I could find you as no one else would—and I thought I could get you away safely, secretly—but maybe I was wrong to come here." She shrugged her pretty shoulders. "And I suppose I wanted to see home again."

"I'm not a captive. But I'm glad you're here. So very glad. It was right of you to come." She wrapped her arms around her and pulled her into a hug. "I've missed you more than I can say, Isadora. God, I'm so happy you're home with me."

The sound of screaming men echoed beyond the crypt. She watched her sister shudder.

"You really trust this man? After everything that's happened? After everything he's done?"

"After everything that's happened," she confirmed, "and after everything he's done. I trust this man. I love him." She stepped closer to her sister and grasped her hand with raw desperation. "You think I'm mad, I know. But it's the world that was mad... and our father. I just didn't see it before. You came this far for me. Now I need your help."

EDRICK PULLED off his armor inside the refuge of the crypt. It was dark, near pitch black, except for the flaming torch he'd brought with him.

The battle raged above him, echoing the bailey and courtyard like a roaring beast. He heard the metallic clash of steel against steel, the screams of dying men, the tune of war drums, and the hiss of arrows slicing through the night. The walls would likely hold, even against the battering ram... and that was fine. It'd be a distraction. The true key to Rowan Dietrich lay within the walls of the castle.

He tore off his tunic and jerkin and replaced them with the dingy, mismatched armor he'd removed from a dead man. Whoever owned it sewed the Black Wolf sigil crookedly on the left breast. He took a moment to count the slanted, frayed stitches. It'd been sewn on in a hurry, he knew. Good. That meant the attack had come as a surprise to Rowan's men.

Well, the surprises were only starting.

Edrick donned a rusted helm, then fetched his torch from the ground. He scaled the wall for that secret passageway...

Indeed. The veritable treasure lay within the castle, and the governess had been the key. Foolish old hag. She'd told him everything.

He laughed aloud, and the hollow sound echoed through the crypt like a ghost mocking him from its grave.

*She better not have been lying. I'll raise her from the dead and kill her all over again.*

He ventured on, his mind scraping for the last words that prune-faced governess had given him.

It would be at least a mile into the earth and covered by a broken statue. The torchlight glittered off the dusty, stone faces of kings past. Did Rowan think he'd immortalize himself down here? Nay, he'd never coveted a crown. He'd wanted vengeance.

But what had he taken?

As Edrick made his way through the dim corridors, he felt a sense of dread creep up. The stone statues of the dead kings loomed over him, their cold stone eyes following his every move. They stood like silent sentinels, guarding the secrets of the castle and the ghosts that haunted it.

*You don't belong here,* they sneered. *You are not welcome to our secrets or in our home.*

The statues radiated ominous energy as if warning him to turn back. A shiver raced down his spine as he met the cold, unfeeling eyes of King Bartholomew. Was his corpse fished from the Rockbluff River and buried there? Or had he returned to Norland's soil?

*Go away,* the dead king whispered. *You are trespassing on something sacred.*

"Shut up, old man."

Grunting, he moved a heavy statue out of the way. He threw it onto the ground, watching as the stone shattered into trivial pieces.

*See how easily kings fall?* He thought of Rowan. How he'd ignored his counsel at almost every turn. How he'd refuse to bend, no matter the consequences.

*See what happens to those who don't bend? They break into a thousand pieces.*

Then there it was. The broken statue Governess Agnes had spoken of. It was an old king of Norland whose eternal face had crumbled away. He shoved at the slab of stone, and it rumbled aside, echoing the underground.

He set down his torch and continued onward, squeezing through the secret passageway and into the heart of Winslowe Castle. As Edrick made his way through the tunnel, he could feel the chill of the underground crypts receding and the air growing warmer. The narrow passageway had rough, damp walls that seemed to go on forever. The light was almost nonexistent. One hand slid along the wet wall, feeling his way through.

After what felt like an eternity, he emerged from the tunnel and found himself in the great hall. Women tended to wounded soldiers from wall to wall. Edrick walked through the injured and dying, scanning the faces of the women, sure he'd find Blanchette Winslowe among them.

He scowled in dismay. He didn't see her pale, pert features—only nurses and nuns from some village who'd come to pray upon the dead and dying.

*She's a tyrant and a liar like her father. She never cared a hair for healing. She'd only used it as a ruse to escape...*

He scowled again, remembering the day she'd led good Sir Royce into the woods, fooling them all.

He crossed the hall with quickened steps and entered the gallery. Moments later, he disappeared into the darkness of the corridors with no one the wiser.

---

ROWAN'S SWORD burst through the chain mail like a knife through butter. He pulled his steel out of the dead man's chest, absently thinking how grateful he was that the arrow hadn't injured his sword-yielding shoulder instead of his forearm. His mind sank back to that night... to chasing Blanchette through the woods... how his heart had nearly stopped when he found her pinned against that tree.

*Keep your focus.*

Jonas fought beside him, taking down their enemies with grace. He watched with a wistful pride as he dodged a soldier's axe, deflected a blow from another, and put an end to them both with a thrust and spinning slash.

Rowan and his men stormed the battering ram; the assault interrupted the heave beautifully as Rowan's sword found its way into the separation of the man's greaves. In nearly the same breath, the dagger he'd pounded out not long ago thrust into the slit in a second man's visor and through his eye.

Rain pattered against his helm.

Lightning illuminated the chaos.

Thunder boomed. It was so loud he could feel it in his bones.

Yet the clash of swords dominated the world. Rowan ducked and tumbled, evading a burst of arrows from a line of archers. He wondered how many of those arrows were from his own men perched on the battlements. He and Jonas fought side by side; it was like a dance as they covered for each other and swung around in a tight, unified circle.

A stream ran along the side of the castle like a winding snake. A knight in full plate armor charged at Rowan. He shoved him back into the water and watched him sink.

An attack came from his left. Rowan was ready for it, expertly parrying the blow and counterattacking with a riposte. The soldier staggered backward. Seeing the opening, Rowan pressed his advantage, unleashing a series of feints and cuts.

Rowan delivered the decisive blow with one last swing—his sword slicing through the air and striking off his opponent's head.

Two well-armored soldiers advanced on him. Rowan stumbled back again, still recovering from the previous assault, eyeing the Demrovian sigil on their plate breastplates of entwined twin salamanders set on fire. Each man yielded swords and shields. They moved like liquid gold—sleek and skilled. Determined and, above all, patient.

They were true warriors.

The taller of the two advanced, his sword front-facing. Rowan blocked his hacking blow and spun around. The clash of steel rang out, the prospect of death balanced on every stroke. The smaller knight blocked Rowan's strike with his shield while the other flew forward, his sword clanging against Rowan's helm.

Rowan seized the opening to jab his sword forward and through the knight's neck. The second it took for him to regroup was all it took. The other fighter raised his sword, aiming for the opening in his visor. But before he dealt the killing blow, a point of a longsword burst out of his neck.

Jonas nodded at Rowan, a grin spread across his unhelmed, boyish face.

Then a sword took him in the head. The attacker withdrew the weapon, leaving a bubbling hole where the steel just was. "Rowan," Jonas murmured. Blood streamed from his squire's lips. Rowan heard an unearthly cry emerge from somewhere deep inside himself. He watched Jonas fall to the ground, his glazed eyes staring up at him.

Where Jonas was a moment ago stood Huntley. And he wore a smile.

Blood speckled his face and wavy blond hair. He held a dagger in one hand and a shortsword in the other. Mockingly, he bowed to Rowan before raising his blades and settling into a side stance. Jonas's brains and blood dripped from the shortsword's point. Rain struck them both and blurred the world around them.

Rowan exhaled a steadying breath. Suddenly, his longsword felt twenty pounds heavier, and the plate and chain he was so used to wearing was crushing.

"Well met, Rowan Dietrich," Huntley said lightly. One hand was on his hip holding his dagger. "A friend of yours, I take it?"

The battle seemed to hush, leaving only them two in the world. Absently, Rowan cut down a soldier who advanced from his left. His eyes never parted from Huntley's. As Rowan stalked forward, Huntley moved with surprising grace and lightness. Mail or plate didn't burden him. Instead, moss-green, boiled leather covered him from head to toe.

The dance began.

Huntley dodged and weaved, struggling to find an opening in Rowan's plate. The clash of metal on metal rang out as they exchanged fierce blows. Rowan jumped back, parrying a flurry of attacks, sending their swords singing. Huntley flew at him and continued to press the attack. High, low, backslash, overhand, hacking and slashing as fast as his armor would allow.

*My God*, Rowan thought, *he fights well.* Rowan slipped on a wet stone. Righted himself just as Huntley's shortsword jetted down. His boisterous laughter cut through the night.

Huntley's lightning-fast style made a powerful match for his heavy sword and armor. Their swords met and sprang apart and then met again. Rowan's blood heated and sang as he pushed the advance and nearly cut Huntley's blond head from his shoulders.

*A good-looking lad. But he won't be so handsome when I'm through with him.*

"You are quite legendary," his opponent said with a dry smile. "Not half bad for a maiden. Might I have this dance?" he asked mockingly, sending Rowan into a spinning cut.

*The banter shall defeat him,* Rowan thought, continuing to press the pace with calculated strokes.

He found a sweet opening.

Rowan raised his longsword high and went in for a sweeping slash. Huntley met his blade in midair with his shortsword and stayed Rowan's arm with surprising strength. They stood locked like that, weapons and arms in midair for what felt like a season. Rowan winced as his arm began to ache. His injury. The one Blanchette had so tenderly attended to...

*Loving you isn't easy.*

Huntley swiped a dagger in an upward arc and between where his spaulder met the breastplate. Rowan groaned and stumbled back, intense pain riffling through him. Huntley came forward, not missing a beat.

Huntley poised his dagger and shortsword for the death blow. Rain struck at his face and washed away some of the blood.

Rowan tried to lift his wounded sword arm, but the pain shackled it in place. He groaned and stared at Huntley, who wore his customary smile on his handsome face. His eyes shone with amusement.

"I rather admire you, you know," Huntley said, his hair shimmering in the moon and torchlights. "Killing you was never my ambition. And neither was killing your squire or so many good men. Perhaps I should have accepted your offer for a one-on-one duel. All these tales of the Black Wolf being unbeatable..." He scoffed and shook his head. "I see now you're nothing but a lie. Sir Edrick was right. I'm disappointed, Black Wolf."

Mary's cries rang in his mind.

He scanned the battle as it raged around him and Huntley.

*Who am I, really?*

*What is this all for?*

*For Blanchette.*

Rowan raised his longsword again as a second wind carried him. As he lifted his arm, Huntley's dagger was there...

But an arrow came first and embedded in Huntley's right shoulder, plunging through leather, flesh, and muscle. He staggered backward with a grunt of pain. Clasping his bleeding arm, queasy from his own pain, Rowan glanced up at the battlements. Blanchette stood there looking down, her longbow still poised.

She lowered it slowly and nodded.

*I've taught her well,* he thought.

Then the world melted into dazed chaos.

Thundering hooves shook the ground. Rowan's gaze shot to the far side of the battle, where the grass and dirt roads lost themselves to the trees. A light cavalry had burst from the coverage and stormed toward the castle guardhouse. Maybe fifteen, twenty mounted soldiers. Leading the charge was King Adam II of Demrov. He wore no crown and didn't need to. His gilded armor spoke for itself. Even from a distance, he cut a resplendent, kingly figure.

A majestic cloak sewn from layers of cloth of gold hung heavily. It barely stirred amid his charges. Two salamander clasps held it in place, poised to strike, while a third salamander entwined his great helm. Ruby eyes inlaid all three salamanders. His steel-plate armor gleamed with dark crimson enamel and ornate scrollwork. His rondels were sunbursts, and the steel shone like flames in the torchlights.

King Adam brandished an ornate sword above his head and waved it in midair. Rowan could make out the intertwined salamanders that decorated its pommel. "Pull back! Cease the attack! Pull back at once, by order of your king! Pull back!" His lieutenants rode in front and back of him, echoing the command.

Rowan watched with a detached sense of reality as two soldiers grabbed Huntley and pulled him away from Rowan. Huntley continued waving his shortsword and blood-soaked dagger, cursing at Rowan, his eyes burning, gore speckling his face. The din of the retreat and thundering horse's hooves muffled his words.

"It's done, Huntley! You hear me?" His men yelled to him over the clamor and Huntley's curses. "The battle's over. King's command!"

Rowan scanned the mounted lieutenants and captains amid the confusion and retreating soldiers, searching for one face and one alone.

His hand tightened on the hilt of his sword. He glanced down at the blade, watching as moon and torchlight set its bloodstained face aglow.

*Where is he, dammit? Where?*
*And where is Smoke?*
*Where is my black wolf?*
Disoriented.
Walking the line between another time and place.
*I am lost.*
And then it came to him.
*Aye. I know where he is.*
*Good God... I only hope I'm not too late this time.*

# Twenty-Six

It was seven years ago all over again. He was stalking the halls of Dietrich Castle, the heat of battle fever rising inside him. Stalking toward a reality he could already see take shape. Stalking, like the wolf that had protected his family's sigil for so many years...

Three guards had stood outside the door, he remembered.

And all three of them were dead.

Rowan snapped back into the moment, staring down at those strewn bodies. Holes punctured their chests. Some fine-pointed weapon had found its way through their chain mail.

*Good men*, Rowan thought, *just like on that night seven years ago.* He carefully stepped over them. He was just outside Mary's chamber. *I suppose I need to acquire better guards*, he thought with hysterical mirth.

*Or truer friends.*

He swallowed back a heave of laughter, biting his tongue until it bled. The metallic flavor pooled in his mouth.

What would he find when he opened the door? His wife, sprawled across their bed, her throat open from ear to ear?

*Or my beloved Blanchette?*

Rowan gripped the hilt of his sword a little tighter. He felt himself teetering along that razor-sharp edge of sanity.

The door swung open with just a nudge. Within, the hearth was burning, filling the space with its soothing crackle.

And in front of the carved, four-poster bed, waiting for him to come inside, with madness in his pale eyes and a dagger at his daughter's throat, was a man who'd been an ally, a comrade, a best friend.

*Somehow, I knew.*

*Somehow, I've always known it would come back to this. Another mistake from my past.*

Because ghosts don't die. They only change shape.

The better to haunt you.

The better to hear your prayers and deepest secrets.

The better to see your fears and desires.

The better to defeat you.

*A ghost can be almost anything, Blanchette. Anger. A memory. Pain. Grief, a daydream, a nightmare. Wherever I walked, I never walked alone...*

"Father!" Mary cried out, tears tumbling down her cheeks. Edrick twisted dirty fingers in her curls, pulling her neck back to expose her throat to his dagger.

"Why?" Rowan heard himself asking, though he feared he already knew the answer.

Edrick tightened his grip on Mary's hair until he was sure it'd tear from her scalp. She was sobbing now. Lightning and thunder cracked outside the window.

"Shut up, stupid girl, or I'll open your throat." Rowan had never heard Edrick speak with such ferocity. Usually, he kept his voice a little above a mumble.

"Why?" he asked again. He tried to keep the panic and desperation from his tone.

Edrick gave no reply.

"Kathryn," Rowan finished for him, icy dread snaking down his spine. He adjusted his grip on his longsword. In close quarters, it wouldn't serve him well. He needed to keep Edrick talking, to distract him until he could advance into the proper position.

"Aye, Kathryn. So you haven't forgotten her."

"Of course I haven't forgotten her," he said cautiously. "She was a good woman."

"She was my child!" Edrick screamed with a thundering agony. "The only thing I've ever cared for, ever loved. And you—you stole her from me!"

"Nay," he said, more carefully still, taking another step forward. "I would have never harmed Kathryn. You know this. I—"

"No. Don't you dare say it. Don't you dare say you loved her. Utter those words, and I'll cut her throat. I swear to you, Black Wolf."

Rowan inched forward again, just barely, hoping Edrick was too consumed by grief to notice the movement. Another flash of lightning. It lit the chamber, and Rowan felt the thunder as it bellowed through the castle.

"Lower the dagger," he said. "I'll do whatever you want. Please. Just lower your dagger."

"First, I want you to hear what happened to her. To my Kathryn. I want you to live with what you did before you watch your own daughter die."

*She's not my daughter,* he absently mused. *Not truly my blood. Yet I love her all the same.*

*And Blanchette too... God, how I love her.*

He fixed Edrick with his stare, his voice steady. "Tell me, then. Tell me everything and be at peace."

Edrick glared at him over Mary's head with a crazed look.

*He doesn't know whether I'm mocking him.*

"After your wife was murdered and you came to me... I know what you did with my Kathryn."

"What we both did."

"Aye, what the two of you did. You took her maidenhead. She

loved you, the stupid girl, did you know that? When you left, she mourned for you like a sick pup."

"I knew. Edrick. I knew. Now stop it. Stop this madness. Can't you see you're hurting her? Edrick?"

He didn't respond to the sound of his name. Instead, he brought the dagger under Mary's chin and drew a faint line of blood. She sobbed, her blue gaze pleading with Rowan. "Eye for an eye. That's the game we're playing tonight."

"The battle is done," Rowan said. "My men will come to look for me soon."

"Oh, this will all be over by that time. Don't worry about that. And I don't plan on surviving this night. I'll die, most certainly, but not without taking your precious daughter with me."

Rowan ignored all that. He fought to keep his voice steady. "What happened to Kathryn? You never told me, never spoke of her in all these years." She'd died, he knew, but Edrick had never revealed the details, and Rowan hadn't prodded that wound.

Three more steps.

"She killed herself," he snapped. Rowan paused in mid-step. The room seemed to sway. He unclenched and clenched his fingers around the hilt of his longsword.

"How?"

"I found her hanging from the rafters." He tightened his grip on Mary's hair and gave a cruel twist that made her scream. "Do you know what that's like, cutting your daughter's corpse down? No. I don't suppose you would."

Edrick sank a hand into his coat and pulled out a piece of parchment. "This is all she left for me. And your name was all over it." He tossed it at Rowan, the hatred in his eyes burning like fire.

Cautiously, Rowan glanced down at the parchment. What did he want? For him to read it? Hopelessness rose inside him. He pressed his palms together and gave Edrick a pleading look.

"Please... she is an innocent child, Edrick." He took a cautious step toward them.

"So was Kathryn's unborn babe."

Rowan's face paled. He waited, feeling the seconds tick off like a man waiting for the headsman.

"You didn't know." *Of course I didn't know. I would have never left her had I known.* "She was heavy with child. *Your* child. You... you killed them both. And now I'm here."

*Yes, we are here... but where is that?*

Rowan's eyes moved from Mary to Edrick, and horror wrapped around his heart like an iron manacle. He saw the determination and grief in his comrade's gaze—and he knew, sure as the sunrise, he meant to kill Mary as a twisted sort of vengeance.

*One I am no stranger to.*

"Why then? Why did you follow me, Edrick? Why drink with me, fight with me, share my table and hearth? You kept this a secret for years. Why?"

Rowan saw some of the resolve vanish from Edrick's eyes. Some of the madness too. For a moment, he lowered the blade, and his voice softened. "I had believed in you still. Faith can be a strong thing... a blinding thing. But you ignored my counsel at every turn. You forgot me entirely, and when I saw the way you fell into her hands—the daughter of a tyrant and a whore—while my Kathryn lay cold in the dirt..."

*Yes*, he thought. *Faith is a strong thing. I put far too much faith in you... I underestimated a friend.*

Rowan glanced over his shoulder, finding Blanchette standing soundlessly in the open door. Tears and blood and ash stained her cheeks. She looked at Rowan frantically, her heart in her blue eyes.

"Edrick," he said, turning back to his comrade. "Please. This is not her fault."

"It doesn't matter now. It's over." His eyes hardened again. He pulled on Mary's hair, forcing her closer. He poised the blade at her cheek and brought it down, shallowly cutting her flesh as he whispered, "Any last words, girl?"

Then Smoke was leaping past Blanchette, quicker than a lightning strike. He came full bodily at Edrick, his massive paws slamming into his chest and shoving the air out of him. A sick snarling filled the room as Smoke went for Edrick's throat. He fought him off with his hands, blaring an inhuman sound—then plunged his dagger deep into Smoke's face. The wolf crawled off him, yelping, the blood already soaking his dark fur. Then he padded over to Rowan, fell halfway across the chamber, and died, his eyes never parting from his master's.

"Go," Rowan yelled to Mary, "go to Blanchette. Now!"

Blanchette wrapped Mary in her arms and gave him a pleading glance as they vanished into the corridor.

An ominous quiet engulfed the castle as Edrick straggled onto his feet, paced to Smoke, and withdrew the bloody dagger from the wolf's face.

Edrick laughed. Frantically. Madly.

Rowan withdrew his longsword and advanced.

"Now it's over," he said as he jammed the length of his longsword through Edrick's throat, finishing what Smoke had started.

What Smoke had started eight long years ago.

The Black Wolf was no more.

THE BLADE WENT through him the same way it went through all those men he'd killed. Rowan had found the sweet spot, surpassing all his armor like a knife through butter. The longsword jutted through the front of his neck and out the back.

The pain was blinding, and in that suspended moment, he wondered if this was how Rowan's wife felt when her throat was slit. He gazed into the dark corridor beyond the bedchamber. Sconce torches flickered there, casting long shadows along the stone floors. And in the doorway, he saw his Kathryn one last time.

Silently, his daughter stood there, her long, chocolate-colored hair falling across her body. She held her fair hands out to him, palms up. Edrick reached out, trying to close the space between them... but she was too far away.

He'd strayed too far.

And now he was lost.

Absently, he realized he'd lost control of his bowels then... and he gazed into Rowan's eyes before the world went black. He found pity there. A cold, hard, black pity. Then he fell into that blackness.

And the abyss stared back at him.

⁂

Rowan pushed open the door, which communicated between Mary's chamber and his solar. She'd fallen asleep within minutes of being moved there. Now, as the world outside the window hung black and cold, he stood before her bed and watched her sleep.

His heart ached and tightened at the sight of her small body curled up, the cut on her neck slick with a salve. The wooden wolf toy was clasped in her hand and nestled against her heart.

He saw so much of Blanchette in her. For a moment, it frightened him.

*She's not my blood, but she's my daughter all the same.*

He sat beside her for what felt like an eternity. He couldn't bring himself to leave her side.

Finally, the pain in his arm was too much to bear. He'd received prompt help to stop the bleeding, but the cut throbbed. Holding his arm, he came to his feet and leaned over Mary. Warmth filled him, and he released a long breath of true contentment.

He swept away her curls and gently kissed her forehead. His heart ached with the love he felt for her.

"I'm so sorry, Mary," he whispered next to her ear. "No one shall ever hurt you again. I promise..."

*I promise...*

Rowan came to Blanchette's chamber as the sun climbed over the castle. A blood-red tinted the horizon. She stood on the balcony, watching as the dead were looted and carried away in carts. Pyres for the fallen men burned just outside the curtain wall. Absently, she fiddled with her signet ring, watching as the burst of light set it aglow. Her other hand gripped Governess Agnes's cross.

"Rowan! Oh, thank God," she exclaimed, crossing herself in a clumsy motion. "I've been waiting for you, watching for you. *God is Good...*" She raced to him and threw her arms around his waist. He winced at the pressure on his wound. "Oh, my love. Is it bad?"

He gazed deeply into her eyes. "No, not so bad. Not any longer. But you were supposed to escape, Blanchette. Damn you," he said, grasping her hands.

"I shall never leave you. I am yours, Rowan. Remember?" She smiled and felt tears tumble down her cheeks. Knuckling them away, she led him to the writing desk, where she'd prepared bandages, ointments, and a needle and thread. A chair stood before it. He sank down into it, his gaze never parting from her.

His fingers went to the laces on his shirt. Deftly, Blanchette moved them out of the way. "Here, let me care for you. Just relax now."

She dunked a cloth in the warm water and herbs basin, wrung it out, and lightly slid it over the wound. He grimaced and audibly ground his teeth together.

Once she finished cleaning and sewing the wound, Blanchette wrapped it with a cloth.

"So much death," she whispered. He stood, and she felt his

muscular arms envelop her waist. She leaned against him and released a long-suffering sigh, feeling the knots loosen in her chest.

"Thanks to you, not nearly as much as there might have been. You saved the city and thousands of lives."

She smiled wearily. Pushed her head against his chest so she could look up at him. "My sister did, really... We shall sup with her and King Adam tomorrow, before they return to Demrov." He nodded, then kissed the crown of her forehead. "Is Mary well?"

"Well enough. I fear the questions she'll ask when she wakes." He sounded exhausted.

"I'm so sorry. About Smoke and Jonas. I—"

His mouth crashed against hers and swallowed her words. Her small hands came up between them, fisting in the loose material of his linen shirt. His hair was damp, and he smelled freshly bathed—the scents of lemon and sandalwood aroused her senses. His lips worked against hers, and she felt the pressure of his strong hands spanning her back. She moaned into his mouth as one palm formed around the shape of her behind. The other wedged between their bodies. Long fingers grazed her cheek, her neck, and finally, the top of her breasts, where they strained against her soft cotton dress. Their mouths moved with raw desperation. Her thrashing heart knocked in her ears.

She longed to lose herself in him... to feel him on her, *inside her*, until the rest of the world faded, and there was only them.

Rowan scooped her off her feet, cradling her in his arms like a doll. She stared up at his handsome features and hazel eyes... into the face she'd grown to know and understand and *love*. He crossed the chamber with quick steps, his gaze never parting from hers. Plush wolfskin pressed against her back. He laid her on the four-poster bed and stared down at her, his eyes heavy with affection and desire. Brittle shafts of sunlight came in from the balcony and shone in the black of his hair as he visibly took her in.

She squirmed under the heat of his stare and rubbed her hot thighs together. "Please, I need you, Rowan. All of you."

Carefully, he crawled on top of her. She gazed up at him, his face filled with an agonized need. She drew him into a heated kiss. His lips parted beneath the pressure of her own. Their heads tilted to opposite sides, and he feasted on her mouth with the fervor of a starved man. Slow and deep. She gasped as his masterful hands ran over the rise of her breasts and kneaded the flesh. Her nipples sprang to life while his thumb rubbed against the peaks, teasing the buds into firm points. He tenderly massaged her flesh, and she arched into his hands, wriggling underneath him. Resting on his elbow, he cradled her head in both hands and covered her face in tender kisses. Each eyelid. Her brows. Her cheeks.

Then he moaned softly and took her mouth in a hard possession. Slowly, sensually, he drove his body against hers.

Her heart raced as he kissed her breasts through her dress. One then the other. The wet material clung to her skin. His breath felt hot through the fabric, his hair like fine silk.

She felt his muscular arms, the peaks of his biceps, and wondered at his sinewy power. A thrill of fear mixed with admiration ran through her. She would never really tame this black wolf.

And she much preferred it that way.

"Blanchette... you drive me out of my mind. You have from the first," he whispered. Her spine tingled from the pressure of his voice. She loved the guttural, sultry rumble of his timbre... a voice so strong, so commanding, it could send her to pleasure without any assistance from his hands or mouth.

Favoring his uninjured arm and propping up on an elbow, he claimed her lips again in an all-consuming kiss. Desperately, she arched upward—her body struggling to be one with his—their mouths molded together. Rowan dipped into her body and wrapped his other hand around her back. He urged her torso upward to meet his; she moaned at the rock-hard feel of him pressing against her most intimate places. Her fingers went to the ties on his white shirt. They tripped over each other in the urgency to feel his skin on hers.

She splayed the soft material aside. His muscles rippled under her tentative touches, and a husky moan escaped him.

"Blanchette..." Her name leaving his lips was like music.

He swept her curls aside and exposed her neck. His mouth tracked over her skin in a ghostlike touch that sent shivers through her. He undid the ties on her dress, and Blanchette shrugged the fabric over and down her shoulders.

Weathered hands skimmed over the valley of her curves as Rowan traced each bend over her body. He pressed a wet line of kisses down her neck... her torso... and drew invisible shapes with the point of his tongue...

Hot wetness circled her nipple. Then he sucked it between his lips and pulled. Softly. Deftly. She moaned and fisted handfuls of his black hair. His hands rode between her thighs and grazed her hot heat.

"God, darling, you're so wet..."

Thumb and forefinger rolled over her nipple and then gently pinched. She moaned as the sensitive bud tightened into a knot of pleasure. His lips detached from her other nipple and sought the center of her throat. Her pulse quickened, hurdling to life as his lips traced the architecture of her collarbone.

Every nerve caught fire. She twisted her fingertips in the thick waves of his hair and pulled him from her neck. Their lips crashed together and worked in harmony as if attempting to consume the other's spirit.

His hot, wet kisses snaked down her throat, between her breasts, over her tight stomach... and lower still...

She squirmed beneath the weight of his body, her fingertips tousled in his raven-black hair.

Then Rowan parted her intimate curls and circled the sweet bud in repetitive strokes, stabbing in and out of her moist heat. He angled his lips and drew the tip into the hot cavern of his mouth. Long, teasing sweeps fell across the hardened bud. He applied delicate pressure... a little more... more... *just enough*...

A long, thick finger slipped inside her body. It formed a

hooked shape as his lips sucked at the tender bud. Beard stubble tickled her sensitive flesh... then his mouth encased her mound completely, and she felt the firm, slow strokes of his tongue lapping, swirling, around and inside the tight hole. The point of his tongue traced that bundle of nerves, circling it and sweeping up and down...

Violent moans ripped out of Blanchette's body. He steadied her hips as he suckled and swirled his tongue and finger in unison, drinking her in deep. She cried out in a burst of pleasure, swept with euphoria, every inch of her tingling and on fire. Intense spasms quaked through her body. Every bit of her shook with the force of her release. She rode those waves and cried out. Rowan chuckled darkly against her wet thighs, then tenderly kissed each one.

"Oh God..." she moaned to herself as her inner walls rhythmically clenched and continued to spread a warm, shooting pleasure through her body. That rippling, bone-deep pleasure seemed to go on and on, crashing in waves that she rode with heavy breaths. Just when she thought they'd end, another trill burst through her. "Oh, my..."

"It's my pleasure to serve you, my queen," Rowan sensually whispered against her dripping-wet thighs. Finally, her breathing returned to normal, and those powerful convulsions slowed. She tingled everywhere, all at once, feeling hypersensitive between her legs.

Rowan slid up her body and claimed her lips in a powerful kiss. She tasted herself on his mouth.

"Sweet Blanchette..."

He grasped onto her pale hand and guided it down the front of his trousers. She massaged him through the material, wrenching a tangle of moans from his throat. He felt harder than steel and impossibly large. Slender fingertips molded around the hidden length... massaging, moving up and down... down and up...

His hot breaths fanned against her flushed neck and breasts as she worked him. He panted brokenly, then tucked his face into the crook of her neck. His unique scent filled her—sandalwood and lemon and Norland's woods. His hips bucked against her hand, and she felt him growing harder and longer through his breeches. Damp hair fell in front of his hazel eyes, and as he leaned forward, it clung to his cheeks.

Her fingers went to the laces on his breeches, unlacing them with clumsy hands that tripped over each other. Rowan chuckled darkly in her ear. The rich, arousing sound traveled straight to her wet groin.

She reached inside his breeches and gripped him. The thick shaft filled her small hand and felt like hot steel against her palm. She wrapped her fingers around his length and slowly moved them up and down, savoring the sound of his quick breaths in her ear, the feel of them wafting against her, the smell of him surrounding her. His head fell forward as she enveloped him with her fingers, sliding firmly up and down his rock-hard shaft, stopping only to cup the soft flesh below...

"Blanchette, darling..." His breathing grew shorter as she increased her speed and pressure. He groaned into her neck. Her fingers curled under the waist of his breeches and pulled them down legs that seemed to go on forever. He kicked them off, letting them join the ever-growing pile of clothing on the floor.

She remembered how he'd felt and tasted in her mouth. She adjusted her legs beneath him, savoring the wet slide of her thighs. His hot, silky flesh slid against her opening in a maddening tease. She felt his swollen head push between her folds, just slightly, and rub against the tender bud. Rain pattered against the castle—a soothing accompaniment to his breaths in her ear.

"Take me, Rowan," she moaned as he arched over her. His muscles shimmered in the candlelight as he shifted his weight. He aligned his manhood at her wet opening and gently pushed, sliding the head inside. Just that seemed to fill her. She squirmed beneath him and arched upward, causing his shaft to glide halfway inside her.

She gave a little scream of delight mixed with pain.

Then he was inside her all the way.

They were one—their legs entwined, heartbeats pressed together. Another moment more of discomfort, then a feeling of completeness washed over her as she felt him fill her most intimate part completely.

He remained inside her, perfectly still, as her body gradually accepted him.

While he waited, he raised her hand to his lips, kissing her palm and fingers until her pain became her pleasure.

After several moments, she watched him close his eyes in ecstasy, and she raised her hips, inviting him deeper. She slid her arms around him and kissed him soundly, spreading her legs wider, hooking her calves over his strong hips. He moved, grinding and twisting his muscular body, pushing his flesh in and out of her.

His groans clamped down into hard, primal grunts that came faster and faster with his motions. Sweat rolled down his sides. Her nails dug into his skin, forcing him deeper still. She squirmed against him and cried out.

They remained joined, and he kissed the scar on her cheek and hastened his rhythm, moving in and out with urgent, sensual thrusts. She made a soft moaning sound, but she was hardly aware of doing so. She was wrapped up in Rowan, and nothing outside their unity seemed to exist or matter. Her heavy breasts shook with his rhythm. Her hands gripped his back, and her moans wound with his, each one louder than the next.

Time seemed to stand still as he picked up speed and took her with a passion that equaled her own. Their breaths shortened, and Blanchette felt that ticklish warmth spreading below again. It flowed through her body like fine summer wine until it spilled over and broke with the force of a wave crashing against Norland's beaches. Her pulsing inner walls gripped Rowan while that warm tidal wave of pleasure rocked through her again and again. A little scream ripped out of her. She trembled from head to toe, her entire being wracked up in the exquisite release of her pleasure.

"Oh my God, Blanchette," he gasped, sweat dripping from his brow, his eyes closing in ecstasy. "I can feel you gripping me."

He picked up his pace and fell into a smooth, rocking cadence. Deep. Sensual. As if he meant to claim every corner, every crevice, of her body. She felt him tense, then shudder and slow his pace until he hardly moved. A husky half groan, half growl burst from his lips. The strong muscles of his back shuddered under her palms.

He kissed her deeply as the tears fell from her eyes. After a moment, she realized he was crying too.

They held each other like that, their tears mingling, bodies and hearts connected, as a new dawn came upon Norland.

# Twenty-Seven

Smoke's limp body was no easy burden to carry. Rowan and Blanchette silently passed through the castle's raised portcullis. She held two shovels, and an intense emotion swarmed her gaze.

The outer bailey was alive with servants and squires cleaning up the disarray from the battle the night before. As Rowan and Blanchette passed through, they bowed their heads and whispered words of gratitude and condolences.

Rowan glanced at Blanchette. She had a strange look on her face... sorrow and joy, all mixed together.

Moments later, the ancient, gnarled trees towered around and above them, blotting out the spring sky. They came to a small clearing close enough to the river so they could hear its rhythmic murmur. Rowan knelt and laid Smoke's body on the forest floor. The air was crisp and carried a hint of dampness. An earthy aroma emanated from the moss-covered ground, mixing with the sweet scent of pine needles and the musty odor of fallen logs.

Rowan tenderly ran his hand over Smoke's smooth black fur, then whispered, "Thank you, my old friend, my most loyal comrade," before returning to his feet. Blanchette had stuck the shovels into the dirt, so they stood upright beside Smoke's still body. The angelic sight of her—the way the sunlight set her beautiful face aglow—unlocked something inside him.

She must have read the emotion in his eyes. Blanchette murmured a soft sound and came to him. She wrapped him in a loving embrace and tucked her head under his chin. He sagged against her hold and felt her slim arms tighten around his waist. "He was a true friend," she said about Smoke, her hands flattening up and down his back in reassurance. "I'm so sorry, Rowan."

Rowan inhaled a steadying breath as he stared at Smoke over the curve of her shoulder. "I wonder if that's how darkness wins," he whispered, "by convincing us to trap ourselves inside rather than release it. I don't want it to ever win again, Blanchette."

She stepped away. Smiled knowingly and gazed into his eyes. Love poured from her stare. The intensity stole his breath. Then she gathered his hands and ran her thumbs across the rough skin. She brought his knuckles to her lips, kissing each finger. "You've escaped that fate, Rowan. And I forgive you... for everything. All I ask now is that you stand by me. As my king, my best friend, and my love."

Rowan kissed her—madly, truly, deeply. Breathless, he knelt before her and withdrew his longsword from its scabbard. The blade seemed to whistle as it came free and he held it before her. Tears of joy fell from his eyes. He tasted them as they tracked down his cheeks and crept between his lips.

They tasted sweet.

They tasted like victory.

His head bowed, his voice bursting with love and promise, he promised, "My queen... my sword is yours. My heart is yours. I am yours."

They kissed again, sealing a legacy.

# Epilogue

Queen Blanchette watched Rowan from the doorway. One hand lay protectively over her swollen belly.

*King Rowan Winslowe,* she corrected herself. The day of Rowan's coronation—the day he'd taken her name—had been the biggest testament to the peace he'd found. It'd concluded a ten-year-old vengeance while summoning a dynasty that might last a thousand years.

*The Black Wolf and the Raven.*

He sat on the edge of Mary's bed, vibrantly telling her a story. One he'd told her many times over the past year. And one that Mary never tired of.

"Once upon a time, a fair maiden named Little Red Riding Hood lived in a quaint village. She was known for her blond hair and striking appearance and went about donning a scarlet hooded cloak her beloved grandmother had sewn one winter…"

Blanchette glimpsed at the far wall, where her red riding cloak hung. She smiled as Rowan fell deeper into the story and changed his voice to sound like a wolf's. Mary's eyes widened, and she shrank under the cover. A muffled squeal rang out as she pulled it over her head and buried inside. "Oh no, no, no!"

"You're not scared of a wolf, are you?" he asked in a growly voice that inspired another burst of giggles from Mary. "Hmm, my Little Red Riding Hood?"

"No wolf! Please, Father, not the wolf!"

Blanchette tiptoed inside the room, a wavering candle in hand, fighting hard not to disturb them. She watched as her signet ring sparkled in the dim chamber.

A black wolf pup lay at the foot of the canopied bed. Its ears were floppy and far too large for its small head. It tilted its face at Blanchette's approach and gave a defiant *yelp*.

Mary pushed down the cover, an enormous smile on her face.

Blanchette sighed and lay her hand over her belly, where little Joanna or Willem kicked.

She smiled at the trio as warmth spread through her. *We're soon to be a foursome.*

Rowan returned her smile with a grin that looked downright *wolfish*.

Beyond the window, a light snow glided from a bespectacled, star-filled sky and blanketed Norland—a kingdom fully at peace.

And somewhere, hidden among the wood's sentinel trees, a wolf howled.

## THE END.

**I live in California with my dashing husband, who inspires my romance books every day!**

Writing has always been an integral part of my identity.

I graduated from Chapman's film school, where I often received the feedback on my scripts, "Your stories and characters are great, but this reads like a novel!" That's when I realized my true calling.

In my free time, I frequent reptile expos, lift double my body's weight, and indulge in dinosaur trivia.

I'm passionate about writing stories that explore what it means to be human and to be loved. My books focus on hope, courage, and redemption in the face of adversity.

**Enjoyed this book?**
Read Beauty of the Beast
Fairy Tale Retellings, Book One

*I love connecting with my readers!*
RachelDemeter.com

Made in the USA
Columbia, SC
28 October 2024

f7e4637d-ce8f-4335-bd92-68f164dc2fc0R01